AUG 2 2 2002

S0-ALJ-970

MURDER MOST POSTAL

AUG 2 2 2013

MURDER MOST POSTAL

Homicidal Tales That Deliver a Message

Edited by
Martin H. Greenberg

Fort Morgan Public Library
414 Main Street
Fort Morgan, CO
(970) 867-9456

CUMBERLAND HOUSE
NASHVILLE, TENNESSEE

Copyright © 2001 by Tekno Books

All rights reserved. Written permission must be secured from the publisher to use or reproduce any part of this work, except for brief quotations in critical reviews or articles.

Published by Cumberland House Publishing, Inc., 431 Harding Industrial Drive, Nashville, TN 37211

Cover design by Gore Studio, Inc.
Text design by Mike Towle

Library of Congress Cataloging-in-Publication Data

Murder most postal : homicidal tales that deliver a message / edited by Martin H. Greenberg.
    p. cm.
    ISBN: 1-58182-162-X (pbk. : alk. paper)
    1. Detective and mystery stories, American. 2. Written communication—Fiction. 3. Letter writing—Fiction. 4. Postal service—Fiction. I. Greenberg, Martin Harry.
    PS648.D4 M8755 2001
    813'.087208355—dc21   2001017244

Printed in the United States of America
1 2 3 4 5 6 7 8 9—06 05 04 03 02 01

Contents

Introduction   vii
John Helfers

Like a Bone in the Throat   1
Lawrence Block

The Purloined Letter   27
Edgar Allan Poe

An Act of Violence   45
William F. Nolan

The Corbett Correspondence   53
"Agent No. 5 and Agent No. 6"

Agony Column   67
Barry N. Malzberg

Graduation   77
Richard Christian Matheson

Someone Who Understands Me   93
Matthew Costello

Letter to the Editor   101
Morris Hershman

The Coveted Correspondence   107
Ralph McInerny

A Nice Cup of Tea   131
Kate Kingsbury

Letter to His Son   143
Simon Brett

The Poisoned Pen   161
Arthur B. Reeve

A Literary Death   181
Martin H. Greenberg

The Adventure of the Penny Magenta   185
August Derleth

Letter from a Very Worried Man   199
Henry Slesar

Pure Rotten   203
John Lutz

Computers Don't Argue   209
Gordon R. Dickson

A Letter to Amy   225
Joyce Harrington

The Adventure of the One-Penny Black   243
Ellery Queen

Make Yourselves at Home   263
Joan Hess

Deadlier than the Mail   279
Evan Hunter

Contributors   297

Copyrights and Permissions   305

Introduction

"All letters, methinks, should be as free and easy as one's discourse, not studied as an oration, nor made up of hard words like a charm."
—Dorothy Osbourne (Lady Temple)

"An odd thought strikes me—we shall receive no letters in the grave."
—Samuel Johnson

Although cultural anthropologists have come up with several reasons to account for the advancement of mankind, including our use of tools and trial-and-error problem solving, the development of our ability to communicate might be the ultimate key to our dominance of this planet.

It is man's ability to relate thoughts, abstract concepts, and ideas clearly and distinctly to another human being that fosters growth and learning in human society. Ever since the first caveman sketched out the bison hunts in the Lascaux caves more than sixteen thousand years ago, mankind has constantly been trying to improve our methods of communication, particularly the speed at which we send messages. From smoke signals to drumbeats to the Pony Express and on to the telegraph, telephones, and e-mail, we have always wanted faster, better, more reliable modes of communication.

This is not to say that some methods of discourse have fallen by the wayside. Consider the mailed letter. Until well into the twentieth century, the letter for centuries had been the most popular form of individual communication across any distance. Kings, popes, lords, heads of state, scholars, and authors all used the simple device of pen and paper to plot against one another, gossipmonger, woo and win each other's hearts, and play the intricate games of court and social intrigue still popular in this day and age. In fact, in London, communication by letter was so popular that the mail was often delivered two or three times a day. Of course, this was at a time when literacy was primarily enjoyed by the nobility, thereby limiting the number of letters sent. It was also before the age of advertising, so every letter also actually had a point to it. Nowadays, the U.S. Postal Service would be hard-pressed to try and deliver the mail more than once a day. (Indeed, sometimes they cannot even manage this.)

In today's fast-paced society of fax machines, cellular phones, and lightning-fast e-mail, the emphasis has shifted from content to the incredible speed at which a message can be sent. Accompanying this shift of priorities from literary merit to haste has been an alarming rise in the instances of bad manners being used in composing and sending e-messages, something that a letter writer would never have done in years gone by.

No matter which new ways of communications are discovered in the future, the mail for now is still a fairly effective way to deliver messages, as anyone who has sorted through a voluminous pile of junk mail can tell you. Even the letter itself can send a clear message before it is opened. A letter from a friend can make a recipient smile with the anticipated pleasure of reading it. A letter from a law firm, of course, usually engenders an entirely different response.

In the following twenty-one stories, all by masters of the mystery genre, the mail itself takes center stage, as we reveal tales of purloined postage, larcenous letters, and contemptuous correspondence. The first master of the short mystery story, Edgar Allan Poe, is here with his classic detective tale of a missive gone astray and the cunning way in which it is retrieved. Mystery Writers of America grandmaster Lawrence Block tells of the correspondence between a death-row inmate and the brother of the woman he killed, and of the deadly consequences for both. A series of letters from "Agent No. 5 and Agent No. 6" (Issues of national security prevent us from revealing their real names here) takes us on a cloak-and-dagger chase in search of an unpublished manuscript that is so terrible, everyone wants to possess it. The inestimable Ellery Queen makes an appearance to investigate a puzzling philately theft. We've even taken a step into the twenty-first century with Matt Costello's story of letters in cyberspace, as one man pours out his heart to a chat-room stranger in the last messages he will ever write.

From stolen stamps to murder-by-mail, the stories in this volume are all prime examples of just how dangerous delivering a message can be. So, after you've sorted the pile in your mailbox, thrown out the junk ads, paid your bills, and caught up on your correspondence (and don't forget the stamp!), sit back for a well-deserved break and enjoy these stories of *Murder Most Postal.*

MURDER MOST POSTAL

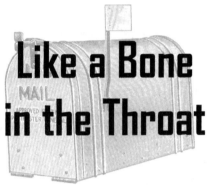

Like a Bone in the Throat

Lawrence Block

THROUGHOUT THE TRIAL PAUL DANDRIDGE did the same thing every day. He wore a suit and tie, and he occupied a seat toward the front of the courtroom, and his eyes, time and time again, returned to the man who had killed his sister.

He was never called upon to testify. The facts were virtually undisputed, the evidence overwhelming. The defendant, William Charles Croydon, had abducted Dandridge's sister at knifepoint as she walked from the college library to her off-campus apartment. He had taken her to an isolated and rather primitive cabin in the woods, where he had subjected her to repeated sexual assaults over a period of three days, at the conclusion of which he had caused her death— by manual strangulation.

Croydon took the stand in his own defense. He was a handsome young man who'd spent his thirtieth birthday in a jail cell awaiting trial, and his preppy good looks had already brought him letters and

1

photographs and even a few marriage proposals from women of all ages. (Paul Dandridge was twenty-seven at the time. His sister, Karen, had been twenty when she died. The trial ended just weeks before her twenty-first birthday.)

On the stand, William Croydon claimed that he had no recollection of choking the life out of Karen Dandridge, but allowed as how he had no choice but to believe he'd done it. According to his testimony, the young woman had willingly accompanied him to the remote cabin and had been an enthusiastic sexual partner with a penchant for rough sex. She had also supplied some particularly strong marijuana with hallucinogenic properties and had insisted that he smoke it with her. At one point, after indulging heavily in the unfamiliar drug, he had lost consciousness and awakened later to find his partner beside him, dead.

His first thought, he'd told the court, was that someone had broken into the cabin while he was sleeping, had killed Karen, and might return to kill him. Accordingly, he'd panicked and rushed out of there, abandoning Karen's corpse. Now, faced with all the evidence arrayed against him, he was compelled to believe he had somehow committed this awful crime, although he had no recollection of it whatsoever, and although it was utterly foreign to his nature.

The district attorney, prosecuting this case himself, tore Croydon apart on cross-examination. He cited the bite marks on the victim's breasts, the rope burns indicating prolonged restraint, the steps Croydon had taken in an attempt to conceal his presence in the cabin. "You must be right," Croydon would admit, with a shrug and a sad smile. "All I can say is that I don't remember any of it."

The jury was eleven to one for conviction right from the jump, but it took six hours to make it unanimous. *Mr. Foreman, have you reached a verdict? We have, Your Honor. On the sole count of the indictment, murder in the first degree, how do you find? We find the defendant, William Charles Croydon, guilty.*

One woman cried out. A couple of others sobbed. The DA accepted congratulations. The defense attorney put an arm around his client. Paul Dandridge, his jaw set, looked at Croydon.

Their eyes met, and Paul Dandridge tried to read the expression in the killer's eyes. But he couldn't make it out.

TWO WEEKS LATER, at the sentencing hearing, Paul Dandridge got to testify.

He talked about his sister, and what a wonderful person she had been. He spoke of the brilliance of her intellect, the gentleness of her spirit, the promise of her young life. He spoke of the effect of her death upon him. They had lost both parents, he told the court, and Karen was all the family he'd had in the world. And now she was gone. In order for his sister to rest in peace, and in order for him to get on with his own life, he urged that her murderer be sentenced to death.

Croydon's attorney argued that the case did not meet the criteria for the death penalty, that while his client possessed a criminal record he had never been charged with a crime remotely of this nature, and that the rough-sex-and-drugs defense carried a strong implication of mitigating circumstances. Even if the jury had rejected the defense, surely the defendant ought to be spared the ultimate penalty, and justice would be best served if he were sentenced to life in prison.

The DA pushed hard for the death penalty, contending that the rough-sex defense was the cynical last-ditch stand of a remorseless killer, and that the jury had rightly seen that it was wholly without merit. Although her killer might well have taken drugs, there was no forensic evidence to indicate that Karen Dandridge herself had been under the influence of anything other than a powerful and ruthless murderer. Karen Dandridge needed to be avenged, he maintained, and society needed to be assured that her killer would never, ever, be able to do it again.

Paul Dandridge was looking at Croydon when the judge pronounced the sentence, hoping to see something in those cold blue eyes. But as the words were spoken—*death by lethal injection*—there was nothing for Paul to see. Croydon closed his eyes.

When he opened them a moment later, there was no expression to be seen in them.

THEY MADE YOU fairly comfortable on Death Row. Which was just as well, because in this state you could sit there for a long time. A guy serving a life sentence could make parole and be out on the street in a lot less time than a guy on Death Row could run out of appeals. In that joint alone, there were four men with more than ten years apiece on Death Row, and one who was closing in on twenty.

One of the things they'd let Billy Croydon have was a typewriter. He'd never learned to type properly, the way they taught you in typing class, but he was writing enough these days so that he was getting pretty good at it, just using two fingers on each hand. He wrote letters to his lawyer, and he wrote letters to the women who wrote to him. It wasn't too hard to keep them writing, but the trick lay in getting them to do what he wanted. They wrote plenty of letters, but he wanted them to write really hot letters, describing in detail what they'd done with other guys in the past, and what they'd do if by some miracle they could be in his cell with him now.

They sent pictures, too, and some of them were good-looking and some of them were not. "That's a great picture," he would write back, "but I wish I had one that showed more of your physical beauty." It turned out to be surprisingly easy to get most of them to send increasingly revealing pictures. Before long he had them buying Polaroid cameras with timers and posing in obedience to his elaborate instructions. They'd do anything, the bitches, and he was sure they got off on it, too.

Today, though, he didn't feel like writing to any of them. He rolled a sheet of paper into the typewriter and looked at it, and the image that came to him was the grim face of that hard-ass brother of Karen Dandridge's. What was his name, anyway? Paul, wasn't it?

"Dear Paul," he typed, and frowned for a moment in concentration. Then he started typing again.

> Sitting here in this cell waiting for the day to come when they put a needle in my arm and flush me down God's own toilet, I found myself thinking about your testimony in court. I remember how you said your sister was a goodhearted girl who

spent her short life bringing pleasure to everyone who knew her. According to your testimony, knowing this helped you rejoice in her life at the same time that it made her death so hard to take.

Well, Paul, in the interest of helping you rejoice some more, I thought I'd tell you just how much pleasure your little sister brought to me. I've got to tell you that in all my life I never got more pleasure from anybody. My first look at Karen brought me pleasure, just watching her walk across campus, just looking at those jiggling tits and that tight little ass and imagining the fun I was going to have with them.

Then when I had her tied up in the backseat of the car with her mouth taped shut, I have to say she went on being a real source of pleasure. Just looking at her in the rearview mirror was enjoyable, and from time to time I would stop the car and lean into the back to run my hands over her body. I don't think she liked it much, but I enjoyed it enough for the both of us.

Tell me something, Paul. Did you ever fool around with Karen yourself? I bet you did. I can picture her when she was maybe eleven, twelve years old, with her little titties just beginning to bud out, and you'd have been seventeen or eighteen yourself, so how could you stay away from her? She's sleeping and you walk into her room and sit on the edge of her bed . . .

He went on, describing the scene he imagined, and it excited him more than the pictures or letters from the women. He stopped and thought about relieving his excitement but decided to wait. He finished the scene as he imagined it and went on:

Paul, old buddy, if you didn't get any of that, you were missing a good thing. I can't tell you the pleasure I got out of your sweet little sister. Maybe I can give you some idea by describing our first time together.

And he did, recalling it all to mind, savoring it in his memory, reliving it as he typed it out on the page.

I suppose you know she was no virgin, but she was pretty new at it all the same. And then when I turned her facedown, well, I can tell you she'd never done *that* before. She didn't like it much either. I had the tape off her mouth and I swear I thought she'd wake the neighbors, even though there weren't any. I guess it hurt her some, Paul, but that was just an example of your darling sister sacrificing everything to give pleasure to others, just like you said. And it worked, because I had a hell of a good time.

God, this was great. It really brought it all back.

Here's the thing; the more we did it, the better it got. You'd think I would have grown tired of her, but I didn't. I wanted to keep on having her over and over again forever, but at the same time I felt this urgent need to finish it, because I knew that would be the best part.

And I wasn't disappointed, Paul, because the most pleasure your sister ever gave anybody was right at the very end. I was on top of her, buried in her to the hilt, and I had my hands wrapped around her neck. And the ultimate pleasure came with me squeezing and looking into her eyes and squeezing harder and harder and going on looking into those eyes all the while and watching the life go right out of them.

He was too excited now. He had to stop and relieve himself. Afterward he read the letter and got excited all over again. A great letter, better than anything he could get any of his bitches to write to him, but he couldn't send it, not in a million years.

Not that it wouldn't be a pleasure to rub the brother's nose in it. Without the bastard's testimony, he might have stood a good chance to beat the death sentence. With it, he was sunk.

Still, you never knew. Appeals would take a long time. Maybe he could do himself a little good here.

He rolled a fresh sheet of paper in the typewriter.

Dear Mr. Dandridge, I'm well aware that the last thing on earth you want to read is a letter from me. I know that in your place

I would feel no different myself. But I cannot seem to stop myself from reaching out to you. Soon I'll be strapped down onto a gurney and given a lethal injection. That frightens me horribly, but I'd gladly die a thousand times over if only it would bring your sister back to life. I may not remember killing her, but I know I must have done it, and I would give anything to undo it. With all my heart, I wish she were alive today.

Well, that last part was true, he thought. He wished to God she were alive, and right there in that cell with him, so that he could do her all over again, start to finish.

He went on and finished the letter, making it nothing but an apology, accepting responsibility, expressing remorse. It wasn't a letter that sought anything, not even forgiveness, and it struck him as a good opening shot. Probably nothing would ever come of it, but you never knew.

After he'd sent it off, he took out the first letter he'd written and read it through, relishing the feelings that coursed through him and strengthened him. He'd keep this, maybe even add to it from time to time. It was really great the way it brought it all back.

PAUL DESTROYED THE first letter.

He opened it, unaware of its source, and was a sentence or two into it before he realized what he was reading. It was, incredibly, a letter from the man who had killed his sister.

He felt a chill. He wanted to stop reading but he couldn't stop reading. He forced himself to stay with it all the way to the end.

The nerve of the man. The unadulterated gall.

Expressing remorse. Saying how sorry he was. Not asking for anything, not trying to justify himself, not attempting to disavow responsibility.

But there had been no remorse in the blue eyes, and Paul didn't believe there was a particle of genuine remorse in the letter either. And what difference did it make if there was?

Karen was dead. Remorse wouldn't bring her back.

HIS LAWYER HAD told him they had nothing to worry about, they were sure to get a stay of execution. The appeal process, always drawn out in capital cases, was in its early days. They'd get the stay in plenty of time, and the clock would start ticking all over again.

And it wasn't as though it got to the point where they were asking him what he wanted for a last meal. That happened sometimes; there was a guy three cells down who'd had his last meal twice already, but it didn't get that close for Billy Croydon. Two and a half weeks to go and the stay came through.

That was a relief, but at the same time he almost wished it had run out a little closer to the wire. Not for his benefit, but just to keep a couple of his correspondents on the edges of their chairs.

Two of them, actually. One was a fat girl who lived at home with her mother in Burns, Oregon, the other a sharp-jawed old maid employed as a corporate librarian in Philadelphia. Both had displayed a remarkable willingness to pose as he specified for their Polaroid cameras, doing interesting things and showing themselves in interesting ways. And, as the countdown had continued toward his date with death, both had proclaimed their willingness to join him in heaven.

No joy in that. In order for them to follow him to the grave, he'd have to be in it himself, wouldn't he? They could cop out and he'd never even know it.

Still, there was great power in knowing they'd even made the promise. And maybe there was something here he could work with.

He went to the typewriter.

My darling, the only thing that makes these last days bearable is the love we have for each other. Your pictures and letters sustain me, and the knowledge that we will be together in the next world draws much of the fear out of the abyss that yawns before me.

Soon they will strap me down and fill my veins with poison, and I will awaken in the void. If only I could make that final journey knowing you would be waiting there for me! My angel, do you have the courage to make the trip ahead of me? Do you love me that much? I can't ask so great a sacrifice of you, and yet I am driven to ask it, because how dare I withhold from you something that is so important to me?

He read it over, crossed out *sacrifice*, and penciled in *proof of love.* It wasn't quite right, and he'd have to work on it some more. Could either of the bitches possibly go for it? Could he possibly get them to do themselves for love?

And, even if they did, how would he know about it? Some hatchet-faced dame in Philly slashes her wrists in the bathtub, some fat girl hangs herself in Oregon, who's going to know to tell him so he can get off on it? *Darling, do it in front of a video cam, and have them send me the tape.* Be a kick, but it'd never happen.

Didn't Manson get his girls to cut X's on their foreheads? Maybe he could get his to cut themselves a little, where it wouldn't show except in the Polaroids. Would they do it? Maybe, if he worded it right.

Meanwhile, he had other fish to fry.

Dear Paul, I've never called you anything but "Mr. Dandridge," but I've written you so many letters, some of them just in the privacy of my mind, that I'll permit myself this liberty. And for all I know you throw my letters away unread. If so, well, I'm still not sorry I've spent the time writing them. It's a great help to me to get my thoughts on paper in this manner.

I suppose you already know that I got another stay of execution. I can imagine your exasperation at the news. Would it surprise you to know that my own reaction was much the same? I don't want to die, Paul, but I don't want to live like this, either, while lawyers scurry around just trying to postpone the inevitable. Better for both of us if they'd just killed me right away.

Though I suppose I should be grateful for this chance to make my peace, with you and with myself. I can't bring myself to ask for your forgiveness, and I certainly can't summon up whatever is required for me to forgive myself, but perhaps that will come with time. They seem to be giving me plenty of time, even if they do persist in doling it out to me bit by bit . . .

WHEN HE FOUND the letter, Paul Dandridge followed what had become standard practice for him. He set it aside while he opened and tended to the rest of his mail. Then he went into the kitchen and brewed himself a pot of coffee. He poured a cup and sat down with it and opened the letter from Croydon.

When the second letter came he'd read it through to the end, then crumpled it in his fist. He hadn't known whether to throw it in the garbage or burn it in the fireplace, and in the end he'd done neither. Instead he'd carefully unfolded it and smoothed out its creases and read it again before putting it away.

Since then he'd saved all the letters. It had been almost three years since sentence was pronounced on William Croydon, and longer than that since Karen had died at his hands. (Literally at his hands, he thought; the hands that typed the letter and folded it into its enve-lope had encircled Karen's neck and strangled her. The very hands.)

Now Croydon was thirty-three and Paul was thirty himself, and he had been receiving letters at the approximate rate of one every two months. This was the fifteenth, and it seemed to mark a new stage in their one-sided correspondence. Croydon had addressed him by his first name.

"Better for both of us if they'd just killed me right away." Ah, but they hadn't, had they? And they wouldn't either. It would drag on and on and on. A lawyer he'd consulted had told him it would not be unrealistic to expect another ten years of delay. For God's sake, he'd be forty years old by the time the state got around to doing the job.

It occurred to him, not for the first time, that he and Croydon were fellow prisoners. He was not confined to a cell and not under a sentence of death, but it struck him that his life held only the illusion of freedom. He wouldn't really be free until Croydon's ordeal was over. Until then he was confined in a prison without walls, unable to get on with his life, unable to have a life, just marking time.

He went over to his desk, took out a sheet of letterhead, uncapped a pen. For a long moment he hesitated. Then he sighed gently and touched pen to paper.

"Dear Croydon," he wrote. "I don't know what to call you. I can't bear to address you by your first name or to call you 'Mr. Croydon.' Not that I ever expected to call you anything at all. I guess I thought you'd be dead by now. God knows I wished it . . ."

Once he got started, it was surprisingly easy to find the words.

AN ANSWER FROM Dandridge.

Unbelievable.

If he had a shot, Paul Dandridge was it. The stays and the appeals would only carry you so far. The chance that any court along the way would grant him a reversal and a new trial was remote at best. His only real hope was a commutation of his death sentence to life imprisonment.

Not that he wanted to spend the rest of his life in prison. In a sense, you lived better on Death Row than if you were doing life in general prison population. But in another sense the difference between a life sentence and a death sentence was, well, the difference between life and death. If he got his sentence commuted to life, that meant the day would come when he made parole and hit the street. They might not come right out and say that, but that was what it would amount to, especially if he worked the system right.

And Paul Dandridge was the key to getting his sentence commuted.

He remembered how the prick had testified at the presentencing hearing. If any single thing had ensured the death sentence, it was Dandridge's testimony. And, if anything could swing a commutation of sentence for him, it was a change of heart on the part of Karen Dandridge's brother.

Worth a shot.

"Dear Paul," he typed. "I can't possibly tell you the sense of peace that came over me when I realized the letter I was holding was from you . . ."

PAUL DANDRIDGE, SEATED at his desk, uncapped his pen and wrote the day's date at the top of a sheet of letterhead. He paused and looked at what he had written. It was, he realized, the fifth anniversary of his sister's death, and he hadn't been aware of that fact until he'd inscribed the date at the top of a letter to the man who'd killed her.

Another irony, he thought. They seemed to be infinite.

"Dear Billy," he wrote. "You'll appreciate this. It wasn't until I'd written the date on this letter that I realized its significance. It's been exactly five years since the day that changed both our lives forever."

He took a breath, considered his words. He wrote, "And I guess it's time to acknowledge formally something I've acknowledged in my heart some time ago. While I may never get over Karen's death, the bitter hatred that has burned in me for so long has finally cooled. And so I'd like to say that you have my forgiveness in full measure. And now I think it's time for you to forgive yourself . . ."

IT WAS HARD to sit still.

That was something he'd had no real trouble doing since the first day the cell door closed with him inside. You had to be able to sit still to do time, and it was never hard for him. Even during the several occasions when he'd been a few weeks away from an execution date, he'd never been one to pace the floor or climb the walls.

But today was the hearing. Today the board was hearing testimony from three individuals. One was a psychiatrist who would supply some professional arguments for commuting his sentence from death to life. Another was his fourth-grade teacher, who would tell the board how rough he'd had it in childhood and what a good little boy he was underneath it all. He wondered where they'd dug her up, and how she could possibly remember him. He didn't remember her at all.

The third witness, and the only really important one, was Paul Dandridge. Not only was he supplying the only testimony likely to carry much weight, but it was he who had spent money to locate Croydon's fourth-grade teacher, he who had enlisted the services of the shrink.

His buddy, Paul. A crusader, moving heaven and earth to save Billy Croydon's life.

Just the way he'd planned it.

He paced, back and forth, back and forth, and then he stopped and retrieved from his locker the letter that had started it all. The first letter to Paul Dandridge, the one he'd had the sense not to send. How many times had he reread it over the years, bringing the whole thing back into focus?

"When I turned her facedown, well, I can tell you she'd never done *that* before." Jesus, no, she hadn't liked it at all. He read and remembered, warmed by the memory.

What did he have these days but his memories? The women who'd been writing him had long since given it up. Even the ones who'd sworn to follow him to death had lost interest during the endless round of stays and appeals. He still had the letters and pictures they'd sent, but the pictures were unappealing, only serving to remind him what a bunch of pigs they all were, and the letters were sheer fantasy with no underpinning of reality. They described, and none too vividly, events that had never happened and events that would never happen. The sense of power to compel them to write those letters and pose for their pictures had faded over time. Now they only bored him and left him faintly disgusted.

Of his own memories, only that of Karen Dandridge held any real flavor. The other two girls, the ones he'd done before Karen, were almost impossible to recall. They were brief encounters, impulsive, unplanned, and over almost before they'd begun. He'd surprised one in a lonely part of the park, just pulled her skirt up and her panties down and went at her, hauling off and smacking her with a rock a couple of times when she wouldn't keep quiet. That shut her up, and when he finished he found out why. She was dead. He'd evidently cracked her skull and killed her, and he'd been thrusting away at dead meat.

Hardly a memory to stir the blood ten years later. The second one wasn't much better either. He'd been about half drunk, and that had the effect of blurring the memory. He'd snapped her neck afterward, the little bitch, and he remembered that part, but he couldn't remember what it had felt like.

One good thing. Nobody ever found out about either of those two. If they had, he wouldn't have a prayer at today's hearing.

After the hearing, Paul managed to slip out before the press could catch up with him. Two days later, however, when the governor acted on the board's recommendation and commuted William Croydon's sentence to life imprisonment, one persistent reporter managed to get Paul in front of a video camera.

"For a long time I wanted vengeance," he admitted. "I honestly believed that I could only come to terms with the loss of my sister by seeing her killer put to death."

What changed that? the reporter wanted to know.

He stopped to consider his answer. "The dawning realization," he said, "that I could really only recover from Karen's death not by seeing Billy Croydon punished but by letting go of the need to punish. In the simplest terms, I had to forgive him."

And could he do that? Could he forgive the man who had brutally murdered his sister?

"Not overnight," he said. "It took time. I can't even swear I've forgiven him completely. But I've come far enough in the process to realize capital punishment is not only inhumane but pointless. Karen's death was wrong, but Billy Croydon's death would be another wrong, and two wrongs don't make a right. Now that his sentence has been lifted, I can get on with the process of complete forgiveness."

The reporter commented that it sounded as though Paul Dandridge had gone through some sort of religious conversion experience.

"I don't know about religion," Paul said, looking right at the camera. "I don't really consider myself a religious person. But something's happened, something transformational in nature, and I suppose you could call it spiritual."

WITH HIS SENTENCE commuted, Billy Croydon drew a transfer to another penitentiary, where he was assigned a cell in general population. After years of waiting to die he was being given a chance to create a life for himself within the prison's walls. He had a job in the prison laundry, he had access to the library and exercise yard. He didn't have his freedom, but he had life.

On the sixteenth day of his new life, three hard-eyed lifers cornered him in the room where they stored the bed linen. He'd noticed one of the men earlier, had caught him staring at him a few times, looking at Croydon the way you'd look at a woman. He hadn't spotted the other two before, but they had the same look in their eyes as the one he recognized.

There wasn't a thing he could do.

They raped him, all three of them, and they weren't gentle about it either. He fought at first but their response to that was savage and prompt, and he gasped at the pain and quit his struggling. He tried to disassociate himself from what was being done to him, tried to take his mind away to some private place. That was a way old cons had of doing time, getting through the hours on end of vacant boredom. This time it didn't really work.

They left him doubled up on the floor, warned him against saying anything to the hacks, and drove the point home with a boot to the ribs.

He managed to get back to his cell, and the following day he put in a request for a transfer to B Block, where you were locked down twenty-three hours a day. He was used to that on Death Row, so he knew he could live with it.

So much for making a life inside the walls. What he had to do was get out.

He still had his typewriter. He sat down, flexed his fingers. One of the rapists had bent his little finger back the day before, and it still hurt, but it wasn't one that he used for typing. He took a breath and started in.

"Dear Paul . . ."

> Dear Billy,
> As always, it was good to hear from you. I write not with news
> but just in the hope that I can lighten your spirits and build
> your resolve for the long road ahead. Winning your freedom

won't be an easy task, but it's my conviction that working together we can make it happen. . . .
Yours, Paul.

Dear Paul,
Thanks for the books. I missed a lot all those years when I never opened a book. It's funny—my life seems so much more spacious now, even though I'm spending all but one hour a day in a dreary little cell. But it's like that poem that starts, "Stone walls do not a prison make / Nor iron bars a cage." (I'd have to say, though, that the stone walls and iron bars around this place make a pretty solid prison.)

I don't expect much from the parole board next month, but it's a start. . . .

Dear Billy,
I was deeply saddened by the parole board's decision, although everything I'd heard had led me to expect nothing else. Even though you've been locked up more than enough time to be eligible, the thinking evidently holds that Death Row time somehow counts less than regular prison time, and that the board wants to see how you do as a prisoner serving a life sentence before letting you return to the outside world. I'm not sure I understand the logic there . . .

I'm glad you're taking it so well.
Your friend, Paul.

Dear Paul,
Once again, thanks for the books. They're a healthy cut above what's available here. This joint prides itself in its library, but when you say "Kierkegaard" to the prison librarian he looks at you funny, and you don't dare try him on Martin Buber.

I shouldn't talk, because I'm having troubles of my own with both of those guys. I haven't got anybody else to bounce this off, so do you mind if I press you into service? Here's my take on Kierkegaard . . .

Well, that's the latest from the Jailhouse Philosopher, who is pleased to be
Your friend, Billy.

Dear Billy,
Well, once again it's time for the annual appearance before parole board—or the annual circus, as you call it with plenty of justification. Last year we thought maybe the third time was the charm, and it turned out we were wrong, but maybe it'll be different this year. . . .

Dear Paul,
"Maybe it'll be different this time." Isn't that what Charlie Brown tells himself before he tries to kick the football? And Lucy always snatches it away.

Still, some of the deep thinkers I've been reading stress that hope is important even when it's unwarranted. And, although I'm a little scared to admit it, I have a good feeling this time.

And if they never let me out, well, I've reached a point where I honestly don't mind. I've found an inner life here that's far superior to anything I had in my years as a free man. Between my books, my solitude, and my correspondence with you, I have a life I can live with. Of course I'm hoping for parole, but if they snatch the football away again, it ain't gonna kill me.

Dear Billy,
. . . Just a thought, but maybe that's the line you should take with them. That you'd welcome parole, but you've made a life for yourself within the walls and you can stay there indefinitely if you have to.

I don't know, maybe that's the wrong strategy altogether, but I think it might impress them.

Dear Paul,
Who knows what's likely to impress them? On the other hand, what have I got to lose?

BILLY CROYDON SAT at the end of the long conference table, speaking when spoken to, uttering his replies in a low voice, giving pro forma responses to the same questions they asked him every year. At the end they asked him, as usual, if there was anything he wanted to say.

Well, what the hell, he thought. What did he have to lose?

"I'm sure it won't surprise you," he began, "to hear that I've come before you in the hope of being granted early release. I've had hearings before, and when I was turned down it was devastating. Well, I may not be doing myself any good by saying this, but this time around it won't destroy me if you decide to deny me parole. Almost in spite of myself, I've made a life for myself within prison walls. I've found an inner life, a life of the spirit, that's superior to anything I had as a free man . . ."

Were they buying it? Hard to tell. On the other hand, since it happened to be the truth, it didn't really matter whether they bought it or not.

He pushed on to the end. The chairman scanned the room, then looked at him and nodded shortly.

"Thank you, Mr. Croydon," he said. "I think that will be all for now."

"I THINK I speak for all of us," the chairman said, "when I say how much weight we attach to your appearance before this board. We're used to hearing the pleas of victims and their survivors, but almost invariably they come here to beseech us to deny parole. You're virtually unique, Mr. Dandridge, in appearing as the champion of the very man who . . ."

"Killed my sister," Paul said levelly.

"Yes. You've appeared before us on prior occasions, Mr. Dandridge, and while we were greatly impressed by your ability to forgive William Croydon and by the relationship you've forged with him, it seems to me that there's been a change in your own sentiments. Last year, I recall, while you pleaded on Mr. Croydon's behalf, we sensed that you did not wholeheartedly believe he was ready to be returned to society."

"Perhaps I had some hesitation."

"But this year . . ."

"Billy Croydon's a changed man. The process of change has been completed. I know that he's ready to get on with his life."

"There's no denying the power of your testimony, especially in light of its source." The chairman cleared his throat. "Thank you, Mr. Dandridge. I think that will be all for now."

"WELL?" PAUL SAID. "How do you feel?"

Billy considered the question. "Hard to say," he said. "Everything's a little unreal. Even being in a car. Last time I was in a moving vehicle was when I got my commutation and they transferred me from the other prison. It's not like Rip Van Winkle. I know what everything looks like from television, cars included. Tell the truth, I feel a little shaky."

"I guess that's to be expected."

"I suppose." He tugged his seat belt to tighten it. "You want to know how I feel, I feel vulnerable. All those years I was locked down twenty-three hours out of twenty-four. I knew what to expect, I knew I was safe. Now I'm a free man, and it scares the crap out of me."

"Look in the glove compartment," Paul said.

"Jesus, Johnnie Walker Black."

"I figured you might be feeling a little anxious. That ought to take the edge off."

"Yeah, Dutch courage," Billy said. "Why Dutch, do you happen to know? I've always wondered."

"No idea."

He weighed the bottle in his hand. "Been a long time," he said. "Haven't had a taste of anything since they locked me up."

"There was nothing available in prison?"

"Oh, there was stuff. The jungle juice cons made out of potatoes and raisins, and some good stuff that got smuggled in. But I wasn't in population, so I didn't have access. And anyway it seemed like more trouble than it was worth."

"Well, you're a free man now. Why don't you drink to it? I'm driving or I'd join you."

"Well . . ."

"Go ahead."

"Why not?" he said, and uncapped the bottle and held it to the light. "Pretty color, huh? Well, here's to freedom, huh?" He took a long drink, shuddered at the burn of the whiskey. "Kicks like a mule," he said.

"You're not used to it."

"I'm not." He put the cap on the bottle and had a little trouble screwing it back on. "Hitting me hard," he reported. "Like I was a little kid getting his first taste of it. Whew."

"You'll be all right."

"Spinning," Billy said, and slumped in his seat.

Paul glanced over at him, looked at him again a minute later. Then, after checking the mirror, he pulled the car off the road and braked to a stop.

BILLY WAS CONSCIOUS for a little while before he opened his eyes. He tried to get his bearings first. The last thing he remembered was a

wave of dizziness after the slug of Scotch hit bottom. He was still sitting upright, but it didn't feel like a car seat, and he didn't sense any
movement. No, he was in some sort of chair, and he seemed to be tied
to it.

That didn't make any sense. A dream? He'd had lucid dreams
before and knew how real they were, how you could be in them and
wonder if you were dreaming and convince yourself you weren't. The
way you broke the surface and got out of it was by opening your eyes.
You had to force yourself, had to open your real eyes and not just your
eyes in the dream, but it could be done. . . . There!

He was in a chair, in a room he'd never seen before, looking out
a window at a view he'd never seen before. An open field, woods
behind it.

He turned his head to the left and saw a wall paneled in knotty
cedar. He turned to the right and saw Paul Dandridge, wearing boots
and jeans and a plaid flannel shirt and sitting in an easy chair with a
book. He said, "Hey!" and Paul lowered the book and looked at him.

"Ah," Paul said. "You're awake."

"What's going on?"

"What do you think?"

"There was something in the whiskey."

"There was indeed," Paul agreed. "You started to stir just as we
made the turn off the state road. I gave you a booster shot with a hypo-
dermic needle."

"I don't remember."

"You never felt it. I was afraid for a minute there that I'd given you
too much. That would have been ironic, wouldn't you say? 'Death by
lethal injection.' The sentence carried out finally after all these years,
and you wouldn't have even known it happened."

He couldn't take it in. "Paul," he said, "for God's sake, what's it all
about?"

"What's it about?" Paul considered his response. "It's about time."

"Time?"

"It's the last act of the drama."

"Where are we?"

"A cabin in the woods. Not *the* cabin. That would be ironic,
wouldn't it?"

"What do you mean?"

"If I killed you in the same cabin where you killed Karen. Ironic, but not really feasible. So this is a different cabin in different woods, but it will have to do."

"You're going to kill me?"

"Of course."

"For God's sake, why?"

"Because that's how it ends, Billy. That's the point of the whole game. That's how I planned it from the beginning."

"I can't believe this."

"Why is it so hard to believe? We conned each other, Billy. You pretended to repent, and I pretended to believe you. You pretended to reform, and I pretended to be on your side. Now we can both stop pretending."

Billy was silent for a moment. Then he said, "I was trying to con you at the beginning."

"No kidding."

"There was a point where it turned into something else, but it started out as a scam. It was the only way I could think of to stay alive. You saw through it?"

"Of course."

"But you pretended to go along with it. Why?"

"Is it that hard to figure out?"

"It doesn't make any sense. What do you gain by it? My death? If you wanted me dead all you had to do was tear up my letter. The state was all set to kill me."

"They'd have taken forever," Paul said bitterly. "Delay after delay, and always the possibility of a reversal and a retrial, always the possibility of a commutation of sentence."

"There wouldn't have been a reversal, and it took you working for me to get my sentence commuted. There would have been delays, but there'd already been a few of them before I got around to writing to you. It couldn't have lasted too many years longer, and it would have added up to a lot less than it has now, with all the time I spent serving life and waiting for the parole board to open the doors. If you'd just let it go, I'd be dead and buried by now."

"You'll be dead soon," Paul told him. "And buried. It won't be much longer. Your grave's already dug. I took care of that before I drove to the prison to pick you up."

"They'll come after you, Paul. When I don't show up for my initial appointment with my parole officer—"

"They'll get in touch, and I'll tell them we had a drink and shook hands and you went off on your own. It's not my fault if you decided to skip town and violate the terms of your parole."

He took a breath. He said, "Paul, don't do this."

"Why not?"

"Because I'm begging you. I don't want to die."

"Ah," Paul said. "*That's* why."

"What do you mean?"

"If I left it to the state," he said, "they'd have been killing a dead man. By the time the last appeal was denied and the last request for a stay of execution turned down, you'd have been resigned to the inevitable. They'd strap you to a gurney and give you a shot, and it would be just like going to sleep."

"That's what they say."

"But now you want to live. You adjusted to prison, you made a life for yourself in there, and then you finally made parole, icing on the cake, and now you genuinely want to live. You've really got a life now, Billy, and I'm going to take it away from you."

"You're serious about this."

"I've never been more serious about anything."

"You must have been planning this for years."

"From the very beginning."

"Jesus, it's the most thoroughly premeditated crime in the history of the world, isn't it? Nothing I can do about it either. You've got me tied tight and the chair won't tip over. Is there anything I can say that'll make you change your mind?"

"Of course not."

"That's what I thought." He sighed. "Get it over with."

"I don't think so."

"Huh?"

"This won't be what the state hands out," Paul Dandridge said. "A minute ago you were begging me to let you live. Before it's over you'll be begging me to kill you."

"You're going to torture me."

"That's the idea."

"In fact you've already started, haven't you? This is the mental part."

"Very perceptive of you, Billy."

"For all the good it does me. This is all because of what I did to your sister, isn't it?"

"Obviously."

"I didn't do it, you know. It was another Billy Croydon that killed her, and I can barely remember what he was like."

"That doesn't matter."

"Not to you, evidently, and you're the one calling the shots. I'm sure Kierkegaard had something useful to say about this sort of situation, but I'm damned if I can call it to mind. You knew I was conning you, huh? Right from the jump?"

"Of course."

"I thought it was a pretty good letter I wrote you."

"It was a masterpiece, Billy. But that didn't mean it wasn't easy to see through."

"So now you dish it out and I take it," Billy Croydon said, "until you get bored and end it, and I wind up in the grave you've already dug for me. And that's the end of it. I wonder if there's a way to turn it around."

"Not a chance."

"Oh, I know I'm not getting out of here alive, Paul, but there's more than one way of turning something around. Let's see now. You know, the letter you got wasn't the first one I wrote to you."

"So?"

"The past is always with you, isn't it? I'm not the same man as the guy who killed your sister, but he's still there inside somewhere. Just a question of calling him up."

"What's that supposed to mean?"

"Just talking to myself, I guess. I was starting to tell you about that first letter. I never sent it, you know, but I kept it. For the longest time I held on to it and read it whenever I wanted to relive the experience. Then it stopped working, or maybe I stopped wanting to call up the past, but whatever it was I quit reading it. I still held on to it, and then one day I realized I didn't want to own it anymore. So I tore it up and got rid of it."

"That's fascinating."

"But I read it so many times I bet I can bring it back word for word." His eyes locked with Paul Dandridge's, and his lips turned up in the slightest suggestion of a smile. He said, "'Dear Paul, Sitting here in this cell waiting for the day to come when they put a needle in my arm and flush me down God's own toilet, I found myself thinking about your testimony in court. I remember how you said your sister was a goodhearted girl who spent her short life bringing pleasure to everyone who knew her. According to your testimony, knowing this helped you rejoice in her life at the same time that it made her death so hard to take.

"'Well, Paul, in the interest of helping you rejoice some more, I thought I'd tell you just how much pleasure your little sister brought to me. I've got to tell you that in all my life I never got more pleasure from anybody. My first look at Karen brought me pleasure, just watching her walk across campus, just looking at those jiggling tits and that tight little ass and imagining the fun I was going to have with them.'"

"Stop it, Croydon!"

"You don't want to miss this, Paulie. 'Then when I had her tied up in the backseat of the car with her mouth taped shut, I have to say she went on being a real source of pleasure. Just looking at her in the rearview mirror was enjoyable, and from time to time I would stop the car and lean into the back to run my hands over her body. I don't think she liked it much, but I enjoyed it enough for the both of us.'"

"You're a son of a bitch."

"And you're an asshole. You should have let the state put me out of everybody's misery. Failing that, you should have let go of the hate and sent the new William Croydon off to rejoin society. There's a lot more to the letter, and I remember it perfectly." He tilted his head, resumed quoting from memory. "'Tell me something, Paul. Did you ever fool around with Karen yourself? I bet you did. I can picture her when she was maybe eleven, twelve years old, with her little titties just beginning to bud out, and you'd have been seventeen or eighteen yourself, so how could you stay away from her? She's sleeping and you walk into her room and sit on the edge of her bed.'" He grinned. "I always liked that part. And there's lots more. You enjoying your revenge, Paulie? Is it as sweet as they say it is?"

The Purloined Letter

Edgar Allan Poe

Nil sapientiae odiosius acumine nimio.

—Seneca*

A T PARIS, JUST AFTER dark one gusty evening in the autumn of
18——, I was enjoying the twofold luxury of meditation and a
meerschaum, in company with my friend, C. Auguste Dupin, in his little back library, or book-closet, *au troisième*, No. 33 *Rue Dunôt*,
Faubourg St. Germain. For one hour at least we had maintained a profound silence; while each, to any casual observer, might have seemed
intently and exclusively occupied with the curling eddies of smoke that
oppressed the atmosphere of the chamber. For myself, however, I was
mentally discussing certain topics which had formed matter for conversation between us at an earlier period of the evening; I mean the
affair of the Rue Morgue, and the mystery attending the murder of
Marie Rogêt. I looked upon it, therefore, as something of a coincidence, when the door of our apartment was thrown open and admitted
our old acquaintance, Monsieur G——, the Prefect of the Parisian
police.

*"Nothing is more hateful to wisdom than too little keenness of insight." (Latin)

27

We gave him a hearty welcome; for there was nearly half as much of the entertaining as of the contemptible about the man, and we had not seen him for several years. We had been sitting in the dark, and Dupin now arose for the purpose of lighting a lamp, but sat down again, without doing so, upon G.'s saying that he had called to consult us, or rather to ask the opinion of my friend, about some official business which had occasioned a great deal of trouble.

"If it is any point requiring reflection," observed Dupin, as he forbore to enkindle the wick, "we shall examine it to better purpose in the dark."

"That is another of your odd notions," said the Prefect, who had the fashion of calling everything "odd" that was beyond his comprehension, and thus lived amid an absolute legion of "oddities."

"Very true," said Dupin, as he supplied his visitor with a pipe, and rolled toward him a comfortable chair.

"And what is the difficulty now?" I asked. "Nothing more in the assassination way I hope?"

"Oh, no; nothing of that nature. The fact is, the business is *very* simple indeed, and I make no doubt that we can manage it sufficiently well ourselves; but then I thought Dupin would like to hear the details of it, because it is so excessively *odd*."

"Simple and odd," said Dupin.

"Why, yes; and not exactly that either. The fact is, we have all been a good deal puzzled because the affair is so simple, and yet baffles us altogether."

"Perhaps it is the very simplicity of the thing which puts you at fault," said my friend.

"What nonsense you *do* talk!" replied the Prefect, laughing heartily.

"Perhaps the mystery is a little *too* plain," said Dupin.

"Oh, good heavens! Who ever heard of such an idea?"

"A little *too* self-evident."

"Ha! ha! ha!—ha! ha! ha!—ho! ho! ho!" roared our visitor, profoundly amused, "oh, Dupin, you will be the death of me yet!"

"And what, after all, *is* the matter on hand?" I asked.

"Why, I will tell you," replied the Prefect, as he gave a long, steady, and contemplative puff, and settled himself in his chair. "I will tell you in a few words; but, before I begin, let me caution you that this is an affair demanding the greatest secrecy, and that I should most probably lose the position I now hold, were it known that I confided it to any one."

"Proceed," said I.

"Or not," said Dupin.

"Well, then; I have received personal information, from a very high quarter, that a certain document of the last importance has been purloined from the royal apartments. The individual who purloined it is known; this beyond a doubt; he was seen to take it. It is known, also, that it still remains in his possession."

"How is this known?" asked Dupin.

"It is clearly inferred," replied the Prefect, "from the nature of the document, and from the non-appearance of certain results which would at once arise from its passing *out* of the robber's possession— that is to say, from his employing it as he must design in the end to employ it."

"Be a little more explicit," I said.

"Well, I may venture so far as to say that the paper gives its holder a certain power in a certain quarter where such power is immensely valuable." The Prefect was fond of the cant of diplomacy.

"Still I do not quite understand," said Dupin.

"No? Well; the disclosure of the document to a third person, who shall be nameless, would bring in question the honor of a personage of most exalted station; and this fact gives the holder of the document an ascendancy over the illustrious personage whose honor and peace are so jeopardized."

"But this ascendancy," I interposed, "would depend upon the robber's knowledge of the loser's knowledge of the robber. Who would dare—"

"The thief," said G., "is the Minister D———, who dares all things, those unbecoming as well as those becoming a man. The method of the theft was not less ingenious than bold. The document in question—a letter, to be frank—had been received by the personage robbed while alone in the royal *boudoir*. During its perusal she was suddenly interrupted by the entrance of the other exalted personage from whom especially it was her wish to conceal it. After a hurried and vain endeavor to thrust it in a drawer, she was forced to place it, open it was, upon a table. The address, however, was uppermost, and, the contents thus unexposed, the letter escaped notice. At this juncture enters the

Minister D———. His lynx eye immediately perceives the paper, rec-
ognizes the handwriting of the address, observes the confusion of the
personage addressed, and fathoms her secret. After some business
transactions, hurried through in his ordinary manner, he produces a
letter somewhat similar to the one in question, opens it, pretends to
read it, and then places it in close juxtaposition to the other. Again he
converses, for some fifteen minutes, upon the public affairs. At length,
in taking leave, he takes also from the table the letter to which he had
no claim. Its rightful owner saw, but, of course, dared not call attention
to the act, in the presence of the third personage who stood at her
elbow. The minister decamped; leaving his own letter—one of no
importance—upon the table."

"Here, then," said Dupin to me, "you have precisely what you
demand to make the ascendancy complete—the robber's knowledge
of the loser's knowledge of the robber."

"Yes," replied the Prefect; "and the power thus attained has, for
some months past, been wielded, for political purposes, to a very dangerous extent. The personage robbed is more thoroughly convinced,
every day, of the necessity of reclaiming her letter. But this, of course,
cannot be done openly. In fine, driven to despair, she has committed
the matter to me."

"Than whom," said Dupin, amid a perfect whirlwind of smoke, "no
more sagacious agent could, I suppose, be desired, or even imagined."

"You flatter me," replied the Prefect; "but it is possible that some
such opinion may have been entertained."

"It is clear," said I, "as you observe, that the letter is still in the
possession of the minister; since it is this possession, and not any
employment of the letter, which bestows the power. With the employment the power departs."

"True," said G.; "and upon this conviction I proceeded. My first
care was to make thorough search of the minister's hotel; and here my
chief embarrassment lay in the necessity of searching without his
knowledge. Beyond all things, I have been warned of the danger
which would result from giving him reason to suspect our design."

"But," said I, "you are quite *au fait* in these investigations. The
Parisian police have done this thing often before."

"Oh, yes; and for this reason I did not despair. The habits of the
minister gave me, too, a great advantage. He is frequently absent from

home all night. His servants are by no means numerous. They sleep at a distance from their master's apartment, and, being chiefly Neapolitans, are readily made drunk. I have keys, as you know, with which I can open any chamber or cabinet in Paris. For three months a night has not passed, during the greater part of which I have not been engaged, personally, in ransacking the D——— Hotel. My honor is interested, and, to mention a great secret, the reward is enormous. So I did not abandon the search until I had become fully satisfied that the thief is a more astute man than myself. I fancy that I have investigated every nook and corner of the premises in which it is possible that the paper can be concealed."

"But is it not possible," I suggested, "that although the letter may be in possession of the minister, as it unquestionably is, he may have concealed it elsewhere than upon his own premises?"

"This is barely possible," said Dupin. "The present peculiar condition of affairs at court, and especially of those intrigues in which D——— is known to be involved, would render the instant availability of the document—its susceptibility of being produced at a moment's notice—a point of nearly equal importance with its possession."

"Its susceptibility of being produced?" said I.

"That is to say, of being *destroyed*," said Dupin.

"True," I observed; "the paper is clearly then upon the premises. As for its being upon the person of the minister, we may consider that as out of the question."

"Entirely," said the Prefect. "He has been twice waylaid, as if by footpads, and his person rigidly searched under my own inspection."

"You might have spared yourself this trouble," said Dupin. "D———, I presume, is not altogether a fool, and, if not, must have anticipated these waylayings, as a matter of course."

"Not *altogether* a fool," said G., "but then he is a poet, which I take to be only one remove from a fool."

"True," said Dupin, after a long and thoughtful whiff from his meerschaum, "although I have been guilty of certain doggerel myself."

"Suppose you detail," said I, "the particulars of your search."

"Why, the fact is, we took our time, and we searched *everywhere*. I have had long experience in these affairs. I took the entire building, room by room; devoting the nights of a whole week to each. We examined, first, the furniture of each apartment. We opened every

possible drawer; and I presume you know that, to a properly trained
police-agent, such a thing as a 'secret' drawer is impossible. Any man
is a dolt who permits a 'secret' drawer to escape him in a search of this
kind. The thing is so plain. There is a certain amount of bulk—of
space—to be accounted for in every cabinet. Then we have accurate
rules. The fiftieth part of a line could not escape us. After the cabinets
we took the chairs. The cushions we probed with the fine long needles you have seen me employ. From the tables we removed the tops."

"Why so?"

"Sometimes the top of a table, or other similarly arranged piece
of furniture, is removed by the person wishing to conceal an article,
then the leg is excavated, the article deposited within the cavity,
and the top replaced. The bottoms and tops of bedposts are
employed in the same way."

"But could not the cavity be detected by sounding?" I asked.

"By no means, if, when the article is deposited, a sufficient
wadding of cotton be placed around it. Besides, in our case, we were
obliged to proceed without noise."

"But you could not have removed—you could not have taken to
pieces *all* articles of furniture in which it would have been possible to
make a deposit in the manner you mention. A letter may be com-
pressed into a thin spiral roll, not differing much in shape or bulk from
a large knitting-needle, and in this form it might be inserted into the
rung of a chair, for example. You did not take to pieces all the chairs?"

"Certainly not; but we did better—we examined the rungs of
every chair in the hotel, and, indeed, the jointings of every description of furniture, by the aid of a most powerful microscope. Had
there been any traces of recent disturbance we should not have
failed to detect it instantly. A single grain of gimlet-dust, for example, would have been as obvious as an apple. Any disorder in the
gluing—any unusual gaping in the joints—would have sufficed to
insure detection."

"I presume you looked to the mirrors, between the boards and the
plates, and you probed the beds and the bedclothes, as well as the curtains and carpets."

"That of course; and when we had absolutely completed every particle of the furniture in this way, then we examined the house itself.
We divided its entire surface into compartments, which we numbered,

so that none might be missed; then we scrutinized each individual square inch throughout the premises, including the two houses immediately adjoining, with the microscope, as before."

"The two houses adjoining!" I exclaimed; "you must have had a great deal of trouble."

"We had; but the reward offered is prodigious."

"You include the *grounds* about the houses?"

"All the grounds are paved with brick. They gave us comparatively little trouble. We examined the moss between the bricks, and found it undisturbed."

"You looked among D———'s papers, of course, and into the books of the library?"

"Certainly; we opened every package and parcel; we not only opened every book, but we turned over every leaf in each volume, not contenting ourselves with a mere shake, according to the fashion of some of our police officers. We also measured the thickness of every book-*cover*, with the most accurate admeasurement, and applied to each the most jealous scrutiny of the microscope. Had any of the bindings been recently meddled with, it would have been utterly impossible that the fact should have escaped observation. Some five or six volumes, just from the hands of the binder, we carefully probed, longitudinally, with the needles."

"You explored the floors beneath the carpets?"

"Beyond doubt. We removed every carpet, and examined the boards with the microscope."

"And the paper on the walls?"

"Yes."

"You looked into the cellars?"

"We did."

"Then," I said, "you have been making a miscalculation, and the letter is *not* upon the premises, as you suppose."

"I fear you are right there," said the Prefect. "And now, Dupin, what would you advise me to do?"

"To make a thorough research of the premises."

"That is absolutely needless," replied G———. "I am not more sure that I breathe than I am that the letter is not at the hotel."

"I have no better advice to give you," said Dupin. "You have, of course, an accurate description of the letter?"

"Oh, yes!"—And here the Prefect, producing a memorandum-book, proceeded to read aloud a minute account of the internal, and especially of the external, appearance of the missing document. Soon after finishing the perusal of this description, he took his departure, more entirely depressed in spirits than I had ever known the good gentleman before.

In about a month afterward he paid us another visit, and found us occupied very nearly as before. He took a pipe and a chair and entered into some ordinary conversation. At length I said:

"Well, but G., what of the purloined letter? I presume you have at last made up your mind that there is no such thing as overreaching the minister?"

"Confound him, say I—yes; I made the re-examination, however, as Dupin suggested—but it was all labor lost, as I knew it would be."

"How much was the reward offered, did you say?" asked Dupin.

"Why, a very great deal—a *very* liberal reward—I don't like to say how much, precisely, but one thing I *will* say, that I wouldn't mind giving my individual check for fifty thousand francs to any one who could obtain me that letter. The fact is, it is becoming of more and more importance every day; and the reward has been lately doubled. If it were trebled, however, I could do no more than I have done."

"Why, yes," said Dupin, drawlingly, between the whiffs of his meerschaum, "I really—think, G., you have not exerted yourself—to the utmost in this matter. You might—do a little more, I think, eh?"

"How?—in what way?"

"Why—puff, puff—you might—puff, puff—employ counsel in the matter, eh?—puff, puff. Do you remember the story they tell of Abernethy?"

"No; hang Abernethy!"

"To be sure! Hang him and welcome. But, once upon a time, a certain rich miser conceived the design of sponging upon this Abernethy for a medical opinion. Getting up, for this purpose, an ordinary conversation in a private company, he insinuated his case to the physician, as that of an imaginary individual."

"'We will suppose,' said the miser, 'that his symptoms are such and such; now, doctor, what would *you* have directed him to take?'"

"'Take!' said Abernethy, 'why, take *advice*, to be sure.'"

"But," said the Prefect, a little discomposed, "*I* am *perfectly* willing to take advice, and to pay for it. I would *really* give fifty thousand francs to any one who would aid me in the matter."

"In that case," replied Dupin, opening a drawer, and producing a checkbook, "you may as well fill me up a check for the amount mentioned. When you have signed it, I will hand you the letter."

I was astounded. The Prefect appeared absolutely thunderstricken. For some minutes he remained speechless and motionless, looking incredulously at my friend with open mouth, and eyes that seemed starting from their sockets; then apparently recovering himself in some measure, he seized a pen, and after several pauses and vacant stares, finally filled up and signed a check for fifty thousand francs, and handed it across the table to Dupin. The latter examined it carefully and deposited it in his pocket-book; then, unlocking an *escritoire*, took thence a letter and gave it to the Prefect. This functionary grasped it in a perfect agony of joy, opened it with a trembling hand, cast a rapid glance at its contents, and then, scrambling and struggling to the door, rushed at length unceremoniously from the room and from the house, without having uttered a syllable since Dupin had requested him to fill up the check.

When he had gone, my friend entered into some explanations.

"The Parisian police," he said, "are exceedingly able in their way. They are persevering, ingenious, cunning, and thoroughly versed in the knowledge which their duties seem chiefly to demand. Thus, when G—— detailed to us his mode of searching the premises at the Hotel D——, I felt entire confidence in his having made a satisfactory investigation—so far as his labors extended."

"So far as his labors extended?" said I.

"Yes," said Dupin. "The measures adopted were not only the best of their kind, but carried out to absolute perfection. Had the letter been deposited within the range of their search, these fellows would, beyond a question, have found it."

I merely laughed—but he seemed quite serious in all that he said.

"The measures, then," he continued, "were good in their kind, and well executed; their defect lay in their being inapplicable to the case and to the man. A certain set of highly ingenious resources are, with the Prefect, a sort of Procrustean bed, to which he forcibly adapts his designs. But he perpetually errs by being too deep or too shallow for the

matter in hand; and many a school-boy is a better reasoner than he. I
knew one about eight years of age, whose success at guessing in the
game of 'even and odd' attracted universal admiration. This game is
simple, and is played with marbles. One player holds in his hand a
number of these toys, and demands of another whether that number is
even or odd. If the guess is right, the guesser wins one; if wrong, he loses
one. The boy to whom I allude won all the marbles of the school. Of
course he had some principle of guessing; and this lay in mere observation and admeasurement of the astuteness of his opponents. For example, an arrant simpleton is his opponent, and, holding up his closed
hand, asks, 'Are they even or odd?' Our school-boy replies, 'Odd,' and
loses; but upon the second trial he wins, for he then says to himself:
'The simpleton had them even upon the first trial, and his amount of
cunning is just sufficient to make him have them odd upon the second;
I will therefore guess odd';—he guesses odd, and wins. Now, with a simpleton a degree above the first, he would have reasoned thus: 'This fellow finds that in the first instance I guessed odd, and, in the second, he
will propose to himself, upon the first impulse, a simple variation from
even to odd, as did the first simpleton; but then a second thought will
suggest that this is too simple a variation, and finally he will decide
upon putting it even as before. I will therefore guess even'—he guesses
even, and wins. Now this mode of reasoning in the school-boy, whom
his fellows termed 'lucky,'—what, in its last analysis, is it?"

"It is merely," I said, "an identification of the reasoner's intellect
with that of his opponent."

"It is," said Dupin; "and, upon inquiring of the boy by what means
he effected the *thorough* identification in which his success consisted, I
received answer as follows: 'When I wish to find out how wise, or how
stupid, or how good, or how wicked is any one, or what are his thoughts
at the moment, I fashion the expression of my face, as accurately as possible, in accordance with the expression of his, and then wait to see
what thoughts or sentiments arise in my mind or heart, as if to match
or correspond with the expression.' This response of the school-boy lies
at the bottom of all the spurious profundity which has been attributed
to a Rochefoucault, to La Bougive, to Machiavelli, and to Campanella."

"And the identification," I said, "of the reasoner's intellect with
that of his opponent, depends, if I understand you aright, upon the
accuracy with which the opponent's intellect is admeasured."

"For its practical value it depends upon this," replied Dupin; "and the Prefect and his cohort fail so frequently, first, by default of this identification, and, secondly, by ill-admeasurement, or rather through non-admeasurement, of the intellect with which they are engaged. They consider only their *own* ideas of ingenuity; and, in searching for any thing hidden, advert only to the modes in which *they* would have hidden it. They are right in this much—that their own ingenuity is a faithful representative of that of *the mass*; but when the cunning of the individual felon is diverse in character from their own, the felon foils them, of course. This always happens when it is above their own, and very usually when it is below. They have no variation of principle in their investigations; at best, when urged by some unusual emergency—by some extraordinary reward—they extend or exaggerate their old modes of *practice*, without touching their principles. What, for example, in this case of D————, has been done to vary the principle of action? What is all this boring, and probing, and sounding, and scrutinizing with the microscope, and dividing the surface of the building into registered square inches—what is it all but an exaggeration *of the application* of the one principle or set of principles of search, which are based upon the one set of notions regarding human ingenuity, to which the Prefect, in the long routine of his duty, has been accustomed? Do you not see he has taken it for granted that *all* men proceed to conceal a letter, not exactly in a gimlet-hole bored in a chair-leg, but, at least, in *some* out-of-the-way hole or corner suggested by the same tenor of thought which would urge a man to secrete a letter in a gimlet-hole bored in a chair-leg? And do you not see also, that such *recherchés* nooks for concealment are adapted only for ordinary occasions, and would be adopted only by ordinary intellects; for, in all cases of concealment, a disposal of the article concealed—a disposal of it in this *recherché* manner—is, in the very first instance, presumable and presumed; and thus its discovery depends, not at all upon the acumen, but altogether upon the mere care, patience, and determination of the seekers; and where the case is of importance—or, what amounts to the same thing in the political eyes, when the reward is of magnitude—the qualities in question have *never* been known to fail. You will now understand what I meant in suggesting that, had the purloined letter been hidden anywhere within the limits of the Prefect's examination—in other words, had the principle of its concealment been comprehended within the principles of the Prefect—its discovery would have been a matter altogether beyond question. This functionary, however, has been thoroughly mystified; and the remote source of his defeat lies in the supposition that the Minister is a fool, because he has acquired renown as a poet. All fools are poets; this the Prefect *feels*; and he is merely guilty of a *non distributio medii* in thence inferring that all poets are fools."

"But is this really the poet?" I asked. "There are two brothers, I know; and both have attained reputation in letters. The Minister I believe has written learnedly on the Differential Calculus. He is a mathematician, and no poet."

"You are mistaken; I know him well; he is both. As poet *and* mathematician, he would reason well; as mere mathematician, he could not have reasoned at all, and thus would have been at the mercy of the Prefect."

"You surprise me," I said, "by these opinions, which have been contradicted by the voice of the world. You do not mean to set at naught the well-digested idea of centuries. The mathematical reason has long been regarded as the reason *par excellence*."

"'*Il y a à parier*,'" replied Dupin, quoting from Chamfort, "'*que toute idée publique, toute convention reçue, est une sottise, car elle a convenue au plus grand nombre*.' The mathematicians, I grant you, have done their best to promulgate the popular error to which you allude, and which is none the less an error for its promulgation as truth. With an art worthy a better cause, for example, they have insinuated the term 'analysis' into application to algebra. The French are the originators of this particular deception; but if a term is of any importance—if words derive any value from applicability—then 'analysis' conveys 'algebra' about as much as, in Latin, '*ambitus*' implies 'ambition,' '*religio*' 'religion,' or '*homines honesti*' a set of 'honorable men.'"

"You have a quarrel on hand, I see," said I, "with some of the algebraists of Paris; but proceed."

"I dispute the availability, and thus the value, of that reason which is cultivated in any especial form other than the abstractly logical. I dispute, in particular, the reason educed by mathematical study. The mathematics are the science of form and quantity; mathematical reasoning is merely logic applied to observation upon form and quantity.

The great error lies in supposing that even the truths of what is called *pure* algebra are abstract or general truths. And this error is so egregious that I am confounded at the universality with which it has been received. Mathematical axioms are not axioms of general truth. What is true of *relation*—of form and quantity—is often grossly false in regard to morals, for example. In this latter science it is very usually *untrue* that the aggregated parts are equal to the whole. In chemistry also the axiom fails. In the consideration of motive it fails; for two motives, each of a given value, have not, necessarily, a value when united, equal to the sum of their values apart. There are numerous other mathematical truths which are only truths within the limits of *relation*. But the mathematician argues from his *finite truths*, through habit, as if they were of an absolutely general applicability—as the world indeed imagines them to be. Bryant, in his very learned 'Mythology,' mentions an analogous source of error, when he says that 'although the pagan fables are not believed, yet we forget ourselves continually, and make inferences from them as existing realities.' With the algebraists, however, who are pagans themselves, the 'pagan fables' *are* believed, and the inferences are made, not so much through lapse of memory as through an unaccountable addling of the brains. In short, I never yet encountered the mere mathematician who would be trusted out of equal roots, or one who did not clandestinely hold it as a point of his faith that $x^2 + px$ was absolutely and unconditionally equal to q. Say to one of these gentlemen, by way of experiment, if you please, that you believe occasions may occur where $x^2 + px$ is not altogether equal to q, and, having made him understand what you mean, get out of his reach as speedily as convenient, for, beyond doubt, he will endeavor to knock you down.

"I mean to say," continued Dupin, while I merely laughed at his last observations, "that if the Minister had been no more than a mathematician, the Prefect would have been under no necessity of giving me this check. I knew him, however, as both mathematician and poet, and my measures were adapted to his capacity, with reference to the circumstances by which he was surrounded. I knew him as a courtier, too, and as a bold *intrigant*. Such a man, I considered, could not fail to be aware of the ordinary policial modes of action. He could not have failed to anticipate—and events have proved that he did not fail to anticipate—the waylayings to which he was subjected. He must have foreseen, I reflected, the secret investigations of his premises. His frequent absences from home at night, which were hailed by the Prefect as certain aids to his success, I regarded only as *ruses*, to afford opportunity for thorough search to the police, and thus the sooner to impress them with the conviction to which G———, in fact, did finally arrive—the conviction that the letter was not upon the premises. I felt, also, that the whole train of thoughts, which I was at some pains in detailing to you just now, concerning the invariable principle of policial action in searches for articles concealed—I felt that this whole train of thought would necessarily pass through the mind of the Minister. It would imperatively lead him to despise all the ordinary *nooks* of concealment. *He* could not, I reflected, be so weak, as not to see that the most intricate and remote recess of his hotel would be as open as his commonest closets to the eyes, to the probes, to the gimlets, and to the microscopes of the Prefect. I saw, in fine, that he would be driven, as a matter of course, to *simplicity*, if not deliberately induced to it as a matter of choice. You will remember, perhaps, how desperately the Prefect laughed when I suggested, upon our first interview, that it was just possible this mystery troubled him so much on account of its being so *very* self-evident."

"Yes," said I, "I remember his merriment well. I really thought he would have fallen into convulsions."

"The material world," continued Dupin, "abounds with very strict analogies to the immaterial; and thus some color of truth has been given to the rhetorical dogma, that metaphor, or simile, may be made to strengthen an argument as well as to embellish a description. The principle of the *vis inertiae*, for example, seems to be identical in physics and metaphysics. It is not more true in the former, that a large body is with more difficulty set in motion than a smaller one, and that its subsequent *momentum* is commensurate with this difficulty, than it is, in the latter, that intellects of the vaster capacity, while more forcible, more constant, and more eventful in their movements than those of inferior grade, are yet the less readily moved, and more embarrassed, and full of hesitation in the first few steps of their progress. Again: have you ever noticed which of the street signs, over the shop doors, are the most attractive of attention?"

"I have never given the matter a thought," I said.

"There is a game of puzzles," he resumed, "which is played upon a map. One party playing requires another to find a given word—the name of town, river, state, or empire—any word, in short, upon the motley and perplexed surface of the chart. A novice in the game generally seeks to embarrass his opponents by giving them the most minutely lettered names; but the adept selects such words as stretch, in large characters, from one end of the chart to the other. These, like the over-largely lettered signs and placards of the street, escape observation by dint of being excessively obvious; and here the physical oversight is precisely analogous with the moral inapprehension by which the intellect suffers to pass unnoticed those considerations which are too obtrusively and too palpably self-evident. But this is a point, it appears, somewhat above or beneath the understanding of the Prefect. He never once thought it probable, or possible, that the Minister had deposited the letter immediately beneath the nose of the whole world, by way of best preventing any portion of that world from perceiving it.

"But the more I reflected upon the daring, dashing, and discriminating ingenuity of D———; upon the fact that the document must always have been *at hand*, if he intended to use it to good purpose; and upon the decisive evidence, obtained by the Prefect, that it was not hidden within the limits of that dignitary's ordinary search—the more satisfied I became that, to conceal this letter, the minister had resorted to the comprehensive and sagacious expedient of not attempting to conceal it at all.

"Full of these ideas, I prepared myself with a pair of green spectacles, and called one fine morning, quite by accident, at the Ministerial hotel. I found D——— at home, yawning, lounging, and dawdling, as usual, and pretending to be in the last extremity of *ennui*. He is, perhaps, the most really energetic human being now alive—but that is only when nobody sees him.

"To be even with him, I complained of my weak eyes, and lamented the necessity of the spectacles, under cover of which I cautiously and thoroughly surveyed the whole apartment, while seemingly intent only upon the conversation of my host.

"I paid especial attention to a large writing-table near which he sat, and upon which lay confusedly, some miscellaneous letters and other papers, with one or two musical instruments and a few books.

Here, however, after a long and very deliberate scrutiny, I saw nothing to excite particular suspicion. At length my eyes, in going the circuit of the room, fell upon a trumpery filigree card-rack of pasteboard,
that hung dangling by a dirty blue ribbon, from a little brass knob just
beneath the middle of the mantelpiece. In this rack, which had three
or four compartments, were five or six visiting cards and a solitary letter. This last was much soiled and crumpled. It was torn nearly in two,
across the middle—as if a design, in the first instance, to tear it entirely up as worthless, had been altered, or stayed, in the second. It had a
large black seal, bearing the D———— cipher very conspicuously, and
was addressed, in a diminutive female hand, to D————, the Minister,
himself. It was thrust carelessly, and even, as it seemed, contemptu-
ously, into one of the uppermost divisions of the rack.

"No sooner had I glanced at this letter than I concluded it to be
that of which I was in search. To be sure, it was, to all appearance,
radically different from the one of which the Prefect had read us so
minute a description. Here the seal was large and black, with the
D———— cipher; there it was small and red, with the ducal arms of
the S———— family. Here, the address, to the Minister, was diminutive and feminine, there the superscription, to a certain royal personage, was markedly bold and decided; the size alone formed a
point of correspondence. But, then, the *radicalness* of these differ-
ences, which was excessive; the dirt; the soiled and torn condition
of the paper, so inconsistent with the *true* methodical habits of
D————, and so suggestive of a design to delude the beholder into
an idea of the worthlessness of the document;—these things, together with the hyperobtrusive situation of this document, full in the
view of every visitor, and thus exactly in accordance with the con-
clusions to which I had previously arrived; these things, I say, were
strongly corroborative of suspicion, in one who came with the intention to suspect.

"I protracted my visit as long as possible, and, while I maintained
a most animated discussion with the Minister, upon a topic which I
knew well had never failed to interest and excite him, I kept my attention really riveted upon the letter. In this examination, I committed
to memory its external appearance and arrangement in the rack; and
also fell, at length, upon a discovery which set at rest whatever trivial
doubt I might have entertained. In scrutinizing the edges of the paper,

I observed them to be more *chafed* than seemed necessary. They presented the *broken* appearance which is manifested when a stiff paper, having been once folded and pressed with a folder, is refolded in a reversed direction, in the same creases or edges which had formed the original fold. This discovery was sufficient. It was clear to me that the letter had been turned, as a glove, inside out, re-directed and re-sealed. I bade the Minister good-morning, and took my departure at once, leaving a gold snuff-box upon the table.

"The next morning I called for the snuff-box, when we resumed, quite eagerly, the conversation of the preceding day. While thus engaged, however, a loud report, as if of a pistol, was heard immediately beneath the windows of the hotel, and was succeeded by a series of fearful screams, and the shoutings of a terrified mob. D——— rushed to a casement, threw it open, and looked out. In the meantime I stepped to the card-rack, took the letter, put it in my pocket, and replaced it by a *facsimile* (so far as regards externals) which I had carefully prepared at my lodgings—imitating the D——— cipher, very readily, by means of a seal formed of bread.

"The disturbance in the street had been occasioned by the frantic behavior of a man with a musket. He had fired it among a crowd of women and children. It proved, however, to have been without ball, and the fellow was suffered to go his way as a lunatic or a drunkard. When he had gone, D——— came from the window, whither I had followed him immediately upon securing the object in view. Soon afterward I bade him farewell. The pretended lunatic was a man in my own pay."

"But what purpose had you," I asked, "in replacing the letter by a *facsimile*? Would it not have been better, at the first visit, to have seized it openly, and departed?"

"D———," replied Dupin, "is a desperate man, and a man of nerve. His hotel, too, is not without attendants devoted to his interests. Had I made the wild attempt you suggest, I might never have left the Ministerial presence alive. The good people of Paris might have heard of me no more. But I had an object apart from these considerations. You know my political prepossessions. In this matter, I act as a partisan of the lady concerned. For eighteen months the Minister has had her in his power. She has now him in hers—since, being unaware that the letter is not in his possession, he will proceed with his exactions as if it was. Thus will he inevitably commit himself, at once, to his political destruction. His downfall, too, will not be more precipitate than awkward. It is all very well to talk about the *facilis descensus Averni*, but in all kinds of climbing, as Catalani said of singing, it is far more easy to get up than to come down. In the present instance I have no sympathy—at least no pity—for him who descends. He is that *monstrum horrendum*, an unprincipled man of genius. I confess, however, that I should like very well to know the precise character of his thoughts, when, being defied by her whom the Prefect terms 'a certain personage,' he is reduced to opening the letter which I left for him in the card-rack."

"How? Did you put any thing particular in it?"

"Why—it did not seem altogether right to leave the interior blank—that would have been insulting. D———, at Vienna once, did me an evil turn, which I told him, quite good-humoredly, that I should remember. So, as I knew he would feel some curiosity in regard to the identity of the person who had outwitted him, I thought it a pity not to give him a clew. He is well acquainted with my MS., and I just copied into the middle of the blank sheet the words—

"——— ———*Un dessein si funeste,*
S'il n'est digne d'Atrée, est digne de Thyeste."

"They are to be found in Crébillon's 'Atrée.'"

An Act of Violence

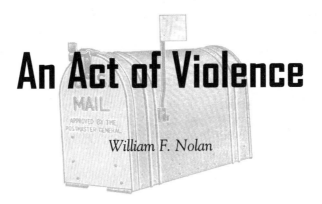

William F. Nolan

June 20, 1994

To Janice Coral Olinger,
Having read every word you've written, I feel I know you well enough to address you as "Dearest Janice," but of course this would not be socially appropriate. I'm a fellow writer who stands in your very tall shadow—but (to my honor and delight) we have shared many an anthology contents page together. Thus far, nine of my humble tales have been selected for anthologies in which your fine work has appeared. But I doubt that you read my contributions or even know I exist, since you probably have no time for the work of obscure writers such as myself. (I know how busy you are: *Conversations with Janice Coral Olinger* lists ninety-eight books in a thirty-year career span, and at least twenty-five of these are major novels. Amazing output!) But, hey, you don't have to know me because this letter will serve to introduce me to you.

My reason for writing at this time is to extend my sincere and heartfelt condolences on the very recent death of your husband, Theodore N. Olinger. I know that you and "Ted" were both very devoted to one another and that his sad passing (isn't cancer a bitch!) was a severe blow to you emotionally. Ted (if I may so refer to him) was a wonderful poet and an astute critic, and I realize that you both shared an intellectual and creative seedground as well as an abiding physical attraction. Your sex life with Ted is naturally none of my business, but a strong sexual bond was evident from your mutual behavior in public. The way you held hands and *touched* each other at that P.E.N. awards dinner made this very clear to me. (Yeah, I was there.)

Anyhow, please accept my deepest sympathy at this immense and tragic loss in your life. I trust that once you have weathered your period of mourning you will again return to the role you were born for: that of a supreme artist of the written word.

With profound respect and good wishes,
Alex Edward
P.S. My address is on the envelope in case you wish to reply—and I *do* hope you will wish to do so.

July 30, 1994

Dear Janice Coral Olinger,
Well, the Great Wheel of Time grinds ever onward and I see that more than a full month has gone by without a reply from you to my missive of 20 June. That's fine, really it is. I had, of course, hoped for a reply, but I am certainly not surprised that I failed to receive one. In view of your personal family loss, this is quite understandable, and I bear you no malice. I'm sure your mail has been piling up from many other devoted readers and that you simply have not been up to answering it. (Bet you get a *ton* of letters!)

However, now that you have been granted suitable time to pull yourself together, I *would* ask that you be kind enough to honor me with a personal reply.

I'm excited about your latest novel, *Whose Blood Is It, Anyhow?* (what a bold and splendid title!) which I have had the pleasure of reading as they say "cover to cover." (In fact, I was up most of last night lost in those final, dynamic chapters!) May I say that I am truly awestruck at the passion and artistry evident on every page of this epic work. Your short stories are marvelous watercolors, but your novels are many-layered oil paintings. (At least, that's how I think of them.) And your dialogue . . . wow! No one in America today handles dialogue with your deft, incisive touch. Just one example (of oh, so many!): when your dying politician, Arthur (invoking shades of Camelot, right?) bids his final farewell to Morgana (a clever reversal of character names in terms of darkness and light), their exchange left me literally breathless. The entire scene was illuminated by your brilliant dialogue. *Viva! Bravissimo!*

I could go on for pages about *Blood*, but I'll let the critics rave for me—as they most certainly will. Let me just say how much your work has inspired my own, how your fire and passion have transformed my life. I am a better man, a better human being, because of Janice Coral Olinger. *Salud!*

By the way, to prove whereof I speak, I have every one of your books in mint first editions, with each dust jacket carefully protected by a clear plastic cover.

As a writer, you are numero uno. No one else has your heart, your spirit, your expansive imagination. I stand in humble awe of your powers.

Enough. Write to me soon and let me know your reaction to this letter. I eagerly await your response.

> With sincere admiration,
> Alex Edward

August 25, 1994

Dear Janice Coral Olinger,
I'm frankly perplexed. All these weeks have gone by and I
haven't heard a peep out of you. I know you received my letters since my return address was plain on each and I never
got them back from the post office. Have you been ill? On a
trip? Away on a lecture tour? What's the problem? All I have
asked is that you take a few minutes to reply to someone who
has shown his deep and sincere respect for your boundless
creative gifts. Truly, I don't see why you can't write me a letter (however brief) acknowledging my existence. Why do
you continue to ignore me in this disturbing fashion when it
is obvious I so greatly admire you? (It seems that common
courtesy alone would dictate a reply.) I repeat, what's the
problem?

Last night I reread your short story, "The River Incident"—
which rightfully earned the O. Henry prize in '82 (go,
Janice!). And once again I was struck with your employment
of raw violence within the context of a higher sense of
morality. Your characters *transcend* death, even though they
may themselves die or cause others to die. In "The River
Incident," when Cara shoots her father on the riverbank, her
act is not an act of violence, but of release. (Obviously, this
is what the O. Henry judges realized.) Knowing there is no
hope for the old man's future, knowing that life has become
a terrible burden on him, Cara sends a .45 slug into his brain,
allowing him ultimate freedom and a release from the crip-
pling cage of his body. (Which is exactly what the great lady
poet Sylvia Plath accomplished with her suicide; I *know* you
agree.) "Go, my father, go," she says, pressing the barrel
against his temple and pulling the trigger. She is sending him
on a wondrous journey. Thus, her act is one of great compassion.

I am curious. What was your motivation for this story? Did it
come out of your own life—or did you hear about an incident
like this when you were growing up in that house by the river
in Maryland? (The story has a ring of stark truth which cannot

be denied.) Or did it all flow from your incredible imagination? Please, write and let me know.

Devotedly yours,
Alex Edward

September 2, 1994

Dear (silent) Janice Coral Olinger,
Here we are into September and I've had *no* word of any kind from you. I am baffled (and, I must confess, somewhat hurt) by your continued silence and lack of human response. Why are you treating me in this manner? Why are my letters to you being ignored? Why am *I* being ignored? It is obvious from what I've written how much I admire you and your works. I have made this abundantly clear. Why, then, have you chosen to bypass me utterly, as if I don't exist? I simply do not understand why you cannot spare a few random minutes for me (no matter *how* busy you may be).

This is not like you, not in character with your work. Your books, for all their overt violence, are extremely humanistic at their core, and I know you to be a gentle, caring person, a creature of warm compassion. (What was it Ted said of you in that *Newsweek* piece? . . . that you were "a vessel of tenderness.") One look into those round dark luminous eyes of yours clearly reveals your compassionate soul. Well, what about sending some of that compassion in my direction? I could *use* a little. All I'm asking of you is a simple note, after all. A few kind words, letting me know you appreciate my devotion as a dedicated reader. Is this too much to ask? I think not. Right now, with my letter before you, write and let me know you *care*.

Vaya con Dios!
Alex Edward

October 15, 1994

Janice Coral Olinger,

I find that I can no longer address you as "Dear." Your cold,
unresponsive silence has rendered such a salutation impossible. I checked my files today and find that I first wrote you a
letter (and a fine, warm one it was!) on 20 June—almost *four
full months ago*! I followed up this initial missive with those of
30 July, 25 August, and 2 September, all without a *single word*
back from you. There is no excuse for this kind of rudeness.
You insult me with your stubborn refusal to respond to my letters. It is no longer possible for me to maintain positive feelings toward you. Your cruelty has also tainted your work, and
this is most unfortunate. I now look at your shelved books and
mourn the past. You have wounded me deeply. Additionally,
you have made me look like a fool. I wrote to praise you and
got nothing back. I'm becoming very angry at you, Ms.
Olinger—or however the hell you like to be addressed. Just
who do you think you are, some goddess living up in the
clouds? You live right here on good ole Mother Earth, just like
I do. We both breathe, eat, and shit, like everybody else on
this lousy planet. You're no goddess, lady. You may know how
to write novels and stories, but you sure don't know much
about common courtesy.

And what do you say to this?

In frustration,
Alex Edward

December 10, 1994

Olinger bitch . . .

Again, you have chosen to callously ignore my letter of 15
October. You obviously don't give a flying fuck about me, or my
opinions, or my words, or anything else having to do with Alex
Edward. Normally, I'm a real easygoing guy, patient, reasonable, quick to forgive and forget—but you've gone over the
line. Your snotty silence is just too fucking much. I will *not* be
treated this way. Not by you or by anybody. Let me state my
position loud and clear: either I get a letter of apology from you
within the next ten days or I'll be over to your house in
Baltimore to give you a Christmas present you *won't* like.
Remember what the witch said to Dorothy in that Oz film . . .
"and your little dog, too!" Well, I'll also have a present for that
witless little pansy poodle you lug around in your arms for all
those dust jacket photos. I think you should know that what
you are doing is directly promoting an act of violence. You are
really one rude bitch and if I don't hear from you this time, I'm
sure as hell going to pay you a personal visit.

Think I'm bluffing? Just blowing off steam? Think I won't act?
Then think again, sister, because you are dealing with a guy
who has your number. The way you mistreat people means you
don't *deserve* to go on living.

It's like in that *Harper's* story of yours, "Dark Angel." Take my
word, unless your apology is in my mailbox by 20 December
,I'm *your* Dark Angel come Christmas.

This is one letter you better not ignore.

Alex E.

PRESS ANNOUNCEMENT—FOR IMMEDIATE RELEASE

On the morning of December 26, 1994, in the den of a private home at 6000 Roland Avenue, Baltimore, Maryland, the body of noted writer Janice Coral Olinger was discovered by neighbors. She had been shot once in the left temple and had died instantly. Her white poodle, "Snowball," was found lying beside her. The dog had also been shot to death.

Local police were called to the scene. Lieutenant Angus Campbell of Baltimore Homicide has issued this public statement:

Several handwritten letters, dated from June into December of this year, were found on the desk of the deceased. They were all signed "Alex Edward."

Ms. Olinger's father, A. E. Coral, was for many years a prominent Baltimore banker, and was known to have a violent temper. Police records show that he had frequently been cited for physically abusive incidents involving his wife, Barbara, as well as Janice Coral (later Janice Coral Olinger), their daughter. Records indicate that Janice Coral left the family home as a teenager and apparently never saw her father again. His initials, A. E., stand for Alexander Edward, which correlate with the signatures on the letters.

In the opinion of Dr. Thomas F. O'Rourke, a respected Baltimore psychiatrist, the emotionally shattering death of her husband, noted poet Theodore Olinger, caused a fracture in Janice Coral Olinger's personality. She took on a second, wholly separate identity based on the male persona of her violent father and, as "Alex Edward," wrote the series of deranged letters leading to the tragedy.

Her death, by gunshot, was apparently self-inflicted. The police department theorizes that she first shot her pet, then put the weapon to her own head. Dr. O'Rourke explained it as an "acting out of what her father might have done to her had she remained in the family home." (The banker was later jailed for attempting to murder his wife, Barbara Coral, and is now serving a term in the Maryland state prison.)

The death of Janice Coral Olinger is tragic and senseless, the product of what Dr. O'Rourke describes as "a lingering and ultimately fatal childhood trauma." Funeral arrangements are pending.

The Corbett Correspondence

"Agent No. 5 & Agent No. 6"

Merrivale Hall
Dunseaton
Reading, Berks.

NOVEMBER 1ST, 1995

Dear Agent No. 6,

How refreshing to have a female operative in the Secret Service!
You are an example to us all. That clapped-out Volkswagen is
the perfect camouflage for you, though a trifle Third Reich for
my own taste. However, it is the ideal complement to the Luger
pistol you keep strapped to your right thigh.

Calamity! Delightful as it was to have you as my guest at
Merrivale Hall last night, there has been an unforeseen consequence. A few hours after you left, Balzac, my butler, happened

to try the door of the bedroom where you slept. It was locked from the inside! Balzac alerted me at once and I produced the master key, which I keep hidden in my wardrobe beneath a pile of discarded false mustaches. We gained entry to the bedroom to be met by a hideous sight.

Lying in the middle of the floor was a dead body. He (for the corpse was patently male) was an Oriental gentleman with a sinister cast of feature. His shoes were of such contrasting sizes—four and ten, respectively—that we can only assume he walked with a pronounced limp. There were no marks of violence upon him, but a steady trickle of blood was coming from his mouth, staining my Turkish carpet, a treasured gift from a grateful government in Ankara.

There was, alas, nothing in the man's pockets to suggest his identity. Grasped tightly in his left hand was the manuscript of an unpublished novel by someone called James Corbett. My butler and I agreed that we were gazing at a murder victim.

To preserve the good name of the Department, I wish to solve this crime rather than hand it over to those baffled buffoons at Scotland Yard. I am in urgent need of your help. Did anything strange happen in your bedroom last night? Is the murder connected in some way with Halloween? Was the room unoccupied when you departed this morning? And who is James Corbett?

Needless to say, I questioned my staff closely. They are four in number. Balzac is above suspicion, having been with me for twenty years, presented by a French administration indebted to me for services rendered. I would likewise exonerate Deeck, my valet, who, though American and thus subject to fits of grandiosity, is utterly trustworthy. About my cook, Dante, I am less sure. He can be temperamental.

Garbo, the maid, is another unknown quantity, having been recently bestowed upon me by a thankful Swedish parliament for my success in exposing the Stockholm Scandal.

I ask two special favors. Can you throw light on this mystery? And do you know a technique for removing bloodstains from a Turkish carpet?

Yours in desperation,
Agent No. 5

A safe house,
a secret place,
somewhere in England

November 2nd, 1995

Dear Five (let's be informal),

You don't surprise me one bit. Without disrespect to your hospitality, I had one hell of a night (or what was left of the night after you abandoned me in such haste after chancing upon my Luger). You call it the bedroom where I slept, but I had no sleep at all. Shortly I'll explain why.

First, I must tell you about James Corbett, the writer of the manuscript you found in the dead man's grasp. Corbett was a prolific author of mystery novels—he claimed seventy-three—written between 1929 and 1951. In those more trusting times many of his books were bought by the unwary, but by the 1950s he was ready for oblivion, his work turgid and unreadable to a public weaned on Fleming's James Bond. I tried reading Corbett myself, and I'm at a loss to understand how such drivel was ever published. How could anyone seriously devise a plot revealing the villain as an unknown twin? Corbett tops that: in *The Monster of Dagenham Hall*, twins are present from the beginning and he produces an unknown triplet. In another work, which I skimmed, a character produces a "single-chambered revolver." Elsewhere, someone is "galvanized into immobility." I could go on; Corbett did, for twenty-two years.

Here is the crunch. For some arcane reason, over the last couple of years dealers in used books have been deluged by requests for Corbett novels. Prices have gone crazy. I heard of one woman in California who said she would kill for a copy of *Death Comes to Fanshawe*. Another, in Bethesda, Maryland, is said to have her Corbett collection insured for a million dollars; it is kept, unread, in a bank vault. Madness on this scale is dangerous. It has thrown the book market into turmoil and is even threatening the stability of the money markets. Instead of hoarding Impressionist paintings or uncut diamonds, people are putting their fortunes into Corbetts. Inevitably, all this activity attracted the attention of the security services. Recently the CIA and MI5 called a secret meeting. I was given a mission to investigate.

I won't go into the tortuous trail that led me last weekend to your ancestral seat, except to state that I was acting on alarming information from an impeccable source. London had been advised that an unpublished manuscript by Corbett had been discovered in a Tibetan monastery. This script is said to be so unspeakably dire that in 1938 it was rejected by every publisher in London. Imagine the excitement! What mutilations of the language, what contortions of plotting, could sink below anything Corbett ever had in print? A novel worse than *Devil-Man from Mars*? The script will be coveted by all who are infected with this Corbett-mania. In auction it will fetch an unimaginable sum, maybe as large, I was told, as the entire British budget. It will destabilize the international money markets and make the Wall Street crash look like a blip.

My mission is to seek and destroy. The Corbett manuscript *must* be shredded or incinerated. My name has been circulated as an expert capable of validating a genuine Corbett. The CIA calculated that this might persuade the possessors of the manuscript to make contact. Obviously they did.

My petal, I urge you, for the sake of us all, for the future prosperity of our children and our grandchildren—if that script is still in your possession—DO NOT READ ANY PART OF IT. DO NOT ALLOW YOUR SERVANTS TO READ IT. Destroy it at once.

For the record, here is what happened in the bedroom. Soon after you limply quit the room, I heard a tapping on the door. Thinking your vigor might have been restored, I blithely unlocked and discovered Balzac, your butler, who handed me a sealed message. I assumed it was from you, perhaps apologizing for what had happened (or failed to) between us. But the message was apparently in secret code. I devoted the rest of the night to trying to crack it, without success.

The rest is a blur. Sweetie, did you know that the bedroom you gave me has a secret passage behind the erotic tapestry? As dawn was breaking, I heard a sound from the general area of the Roman orgy and the whole thing moved. A secret door! Instinctively, I used my training in the martial arts and swung a stiletto heel toward the intruder's marriage gear. He fell at my feet. I didn't stop to examine the size of his shoes or the contents of his left hand. I rushed through the secret passage and came out at the railway station, where I boarded the first train. My Volkswagen must be still on your drive. Only today, with the aid of a Tibetan/English dictionary, have I translated the message. Roughly it runs:

Honored Lady,
We shall shortly give you an opportunity to examine the first female private eye novel ever written, Farewell, My Handsome, *by James Corbett. Your expert valuation is awaited with interest by the owners.*

Honeybunch, I am sorry about the inconvenience. What is one dead man between agents? But PLEASE heed my warning and destroy the Corbett. You can save the world from financial ruin. And the best I can suggest for your carpet is to stain it red.

I eagerly await your reassuring reply.

Devotedly,
Agent No. 6

Merrivale Hall
Dunseaton
Reading, Berks.

November 3rd, 1995

Dear Sexy Six,

Let me first put your mind at rest on one score. It was not lack
of desire that made me leap out of your bed so unceremoniously. I despised myself for having to leave you at the very second when your Luger was about to go off with a bang. This was
such uncharacteristic behavior on my part that I consulted a
doctor next day.

Blood tests revealed the presence of a drug that inhibits per-
formance and causes loss of nerve at the critical moment. It
must have been administered to me in my soup. The drug is
made from a poppylike flower that only grows in the vicinity
of Florence, where it is used by the local maidenry to control
the bambino rate. My temperamental cook, Dante, is a native
of Florence. He made the soup.

On the other hand, it was Garbo, the maid, who served it to
us, under the supervision of Balzac, the butler. All three had
the opportunity to spike the master's soup. I incline toward
Dante as the culprit. He has been surly toward me ever since
I caught him standing outside the maid's window, serenading
her with a mandolin. I happened to be with Garbo at the time,
tucking her into bed with a concern for the bodily comfort of
my female staff that has always made me a model employer.
Dante was understandably vexed when I leaned naked over
the balcony and asked him to play "O Sole Mio!"

Your warning about James Corbett came too late. A curiosity
born of my Secret Service training made me read *Farewell, My
Handsome*. It was excruciating. An Albanian telephone directory has more narrative drive. The novel features a female private eye called Miss Marbles who has the attributes of Sherlock
Holmes, Dick Tracy, and Boadicea rolled into one. A woman
of advanced age, she keeps a derringer in her ear trumpet and

a stiletto beneath her wig. Her walking stick is also a blowpipe and she fires poison darts—having first removed her dentures—with alarming accuracy. Needless to say, she is a mistress of disguise.

There is worse to come. Since the dead courier was of Oriental origin, I decided to read the book backward and made AN AMAZING DISCOVERY. *Farewell, My Handsome* conceals a second novel called *Devil-Woman from Venus*. Instead of using twin characters, Corbett has outdone himself this time by writing twin novels, back to back! I thought at first I'd made the greatest literary discovery since the Rosetta Stone. Then I read *Devil-Woman* through. It beggars belief. Its protagonist is yet another female private eye, Dame Agatha Tea Cozy, who learns the state secrets of enemy powers by seducing their agents while wearing a rare perfume that makes her irresistible. The perfume can only be obtained from a demented, one-eyed French apothecary in Tours. A bizarre coincidence. Balzac, my butler, is a native of Tours.

I need your help more than ever, my Lugerbelle. Self-defense is not murder. You were right to kill the bearer of bad Corbett. Big questions remain. Your nocturnal visitor would have needed a key to open the subterranean door to the secret passage. Who gave it to him? Balzac has a key (and unfulfilled ambitions of being a novelist). Deeck, my valet, has one as well, though it has mysteriously gone astray. Dante's key turned up in my soup last night. And Garbo's key, alas, is in her bedroom door—she wants to be alone.

We found your Volkswagen on the drive, but we also found a bomb attached to its exhaust pipe. It was defused with great skill by Deeck, who, it transpires, was taught Bomb Disposal as part of his routine work as a civil servant in Washington, D.C. Do you see what this means? They wanted you to authenticate the Corbett manuscript and then blow you up for your pains! I couldn't bear to lose you, my angel. Thank God we frustrated their dastardly scheme.

Who is behind all this? If one Corbett novel could cause a financial earthquake, would not two bring an end to civilization as we know it? How can I tell if this double-barreled drivel really is authentic Corbett? When can you come to view it? I ask for two reasons. First, the fate of humanity may hang on your word. Second, I miss you dreadfully. (My doctor was highly complimentary about the love-bites you left upon my anatomy. He had never seen such fearful symmetry outside a tiger cage.)

The bloodstained carpet is no longer a problem. It and the dead body have both vanished, and there have been unconfirmed sightings of them heading across the channel in the direction of Tibet.

By the way, I hid the Corbett manuscript in a lead container and buried it fifty feet under ground. When I dug down this morning, to make sure that it was still there, I met Deeck digging his way up. Am I wrong to trust my valet?

Come soon, my darling!

Excitedly,
Five

Still a safe house, I think,
a secret place,
somewhere in England

November 4th, 1995

My Poor Demented Five,

Didn't I implore you in the name of everything you hold dear NOT to read the Corbett manuscript? Your latest letter plunges me into despair, because it is obvious that Corbett has driven you out of your mind. You underestimated the power of his prose. I know of others who ended up as gibbering idiots after reading just a paragraph from one of his books, and I had hoped to preserve you, my genial host, my pajamaed playmate, from a similar fate.

Too late.

How can you expect me to believe this nonsense about reading the book backward and discovering a second book? You say *Devil-Woman from Venus* beggars belief. I say that your story does. This is clearly the product of a demented mind. Dame Agatha Tea Cozy, indeed!

Can I believe any of the rest of your letter? Is it really worth my while agitating my gray cells to probe the mysteries of the master's soup, the key to the secret passage, the bomb beneath the Volkswagen, and the valet with the burrowing instinct? Are you trying to tell me in coded language that you fear Deeck is a mole? I am desperately concerned for more reasons than I can reveal at this stage. I will only state that a theory about your domestic staff is beginning to form in my brain.

Dear Five, for the sake of those few unfulfilled minutes we spent together, I am willing to give the benefit of the smidgen of doubt I still entertain as to your sanity. If you will dig up the Corbett manuscript and send it to me at once, then I shall see for myself if *Devil-Woman from Venus* is a figment of Corbett's imagination, or yours.

I remain your impatient, ever-loving,
Six
P.S. I rather care for Lugerbelle as a name.

Merrivale Hall
Dunseaton
Reading, Berks.

November 5th, 1995

My dear Lugerbelle,

How can you question my veracity? Have you forgotten that moment of truth we had in the blue bedroom at Merrivale Hall? Why do you doubt my sanity? I have been trained by the

British Secret Service—the envy of lesser nations—and am therefore impervious to brain rot and to corruption by the written word. For the sake of what (almost) happened between us, you must believe me, my divine darling. You are the only woman who has seen me in my Union Jack pajamas without laughing. For that reason alone, I will never lie to you.

There is Malice Domestic in my household, and I need you to plumb its ugly depths. To convince you that I speak in earnest, I am enclosing a number of items.

(1) An article from the *Tibetan Astronomy Journal* about a UFO (Unidentified Flying Oriental) seen crossing the Himalayas on a bloodstained carpet.

(2) A report from an independent geologist proving that a fifty-foot hole was dug in my garden on the third day of this month. Soil samples attached.

(3) An infrared photograph of Deeck, my valet, burrowing into the main lawn last night. When questioned about his nocturnal recreation, he put it down to the fact that he was born prematurely when his mother became overagitated while watching the film of *Journey to the Center of the Earth*. "I can't help it," said Deeck. "I have to dig. It's in my blood."

(4) Fragments of the bomb found beneath your Volkswagen. Since it is November 5th, we detonated it as part of our Guy Fawkes Day bonfire celebrations.

(5) One of the poppylike flowers used to make a drug that can render a man impotent. The flower was found hidden beneath the chef's hat of Dante, my cook, but—and this was a shock to me—Balzac, the butler, was wearing it at the time. A French-Italian conspiracy?

(6) Garbo's membership card from an organization called Corbettaholics Anonymous. When people get the urge to read Corbett, they rush off to a therapy session and talk themselves out of it before committing suicide instead. Corbett in Swedish! Ye gods!

Every member of my staff is a prime suspect, and only you can pick out the real culprit or culprits. The future of the English language hangs in the balance. Save it, my dove. I am sending you the manuscript of *Farewell, My Handsome* along with its Siamese twin, *Devil-Woman from Venus*. I am sure that they are genuine—they even bear Corbett's signature.

To ensure safe passage, the manuscript will come inside a reinforced steel strongbox, inside a picnic hamper, inside a coffin, inside a bulletproof hearse. The vehicle will be driven by Deeck, the Maryland Mole. The four suspects will deliver it to you in person, so that you can authenticate the document and nab the villain in one fell swoop.

If it is bona fide James Corbett, you must destroy it at once in the name of justice, freedom, linguistic integrity, and the spirit of international harmony. Unless, of course, its value is so immense that we can afford to retire from the Secret Service on the proceeds. In that event, my pumpkin, I would like to offer you my hand in marriage and my heart in perpetuity. Pronounce it a best-seller and I am your agent.

Yours with drooling passion,
Five
P.S. Where shall we spend our honeymoon?

A safer house,
more secret,
somewhere in England

November 9th, 1995

My Incorruptible One,

Before you read any of this, pour yourself a large scotch. Now knock it back. All of it. And pour yourself another. Ready?

You are going to be gob-smacked by what you read, but bear with me, dear heart.

The hearse arrived the day before yesterday with its precious contents intact and your four untrusty servants aboard. Believe it or not, they had an uneventful journey. I questioned them all in depth, and your sanity and integrity are not in doubt. Each of those bizarre incidents happened, no question. Now I shall explain.

First, has it ever occurred to you why you were appointed Agent Number Five? Think about it. For me, there is no difficulty. I am Agent Number Six because I was recruited shortly after they gave you your box of false mustaches and sent you back to Cambridge University to learn the spy trade. I was the next in line. Simple.

But have you ever speculated about Agents One, Two, Three, and Four? Have you never wondered why you were not introduced to them? Probably, being the upright fellow you are, you decided that, as this was the Secret Service, you had better not ask. I can now reveal that, until four days ago, they were all employed in your household. To you they are known as Balzac, Dante, Garbo and Deeck. Number One, "Balzac," is the kind of spy known in the jargon of our trade as a sleeper, which is why he has been in your service as butler for twenty years. Number Two, "Dante," the temperamental cook, is in fact the world's foremost authority on passion-reducing drugs. His presence was necessary because Number Three, "Garbo," your maid, is the Mata Hari of the Service, the beautiful woman who extracts secrets by seduction; she has to be subdued at times. Number Four, your American valet "Deeck" with the burrowing tendency, is a CIA mole who recently defected to our side in order to devote himself to the study of the subversive writer James Corbett.

You must be asking why this formidable quartet infiltrated your domestic staff. It was on the instruction of "M," our spymaster. Their quest—and mine—was to probe your integrity and discover beyond all doubt whether you were reliable. The British Secret Service has had too many unfortunate episodes in the past with Cambridge men. Yes, my fearless Five, you were set up, put in the frame, and tested to the limit. I, too, joined in the deception, as did Harry Kirry, the well-known corpse impersonator. The Oriental gentleman in my bedroom was only Harry performing his turn. A pale face, a little stage blood, and the ability to stop breathing can produce wonderfully deathlike effects.

The bomb attached to my car was genuine, as you discovered, but it was put there to add credibility to the operation. I was hoping to get rid of that old beetle once and for all.

The Corbett manuscript was also a "plant." It was genuinely written by James Corbett, as "Deeck" will attest, but the claims I made as to its value were much exaggerated, simply to see if you could be tempted by the lure of money. You were not. You behaved impeccably, passing every test we set you. Even Garbo has sworn to me that nothing happened between you and her, naked as you were when Dante spotted you on the lady's balcony. In fact, Garbo erroneously believes you must be undersexed, for you are the first not to have succumbed to her charms. I didn't disillusion her. She has her professional pride.

All of this has been reported to "M."

What none of us anticipated is your discovery that the Corbett novel, read backward, is *Devil-Woman from Venus*. Using the manuscript in the deception was my idea, and now I must tell you something in the strictest confidence. That manuscript has been lying in an attic in my house for years.

You see, in civilian life I am Constance Corbett, the granddaughter of the author. In Grandpa's lifetime the script was rejected by every publishing house in Britain, but none of them had the wit to read it backward, as you did. What we have, my brilliant confederate, is a property that must be worth an enormous sum, notwithstanding its literary limitations. It is unique. It will be a sensation. That is why I shall not be destroying it. The final part of your penultimate paragraph said it all (though I liked the ultimate paragraph, too):

Its value is so immense that we can afford to retire from the Service. Grandpa's book is a surefire best-seller. You, brave-heart, can remain an agent, but not of the secret kind. You are to be my LITERARY AGENT. You will find that the skills required are not dissimilar.

I accept your proposal of marriage, on one condition: that you do not ever call me "Con." So pack your Union Jack pajamas at once, and jump into the Volkswagen and hit the gas. I can hardly wait for our joint debriefing.

What a happy ending!

Your devoted Lugerbelle

Between 1929 and 1951, James Corbett published more than forty novels, including the immortal Devil-Man from Mars, Death Is My Shadow, Her Private Murder, The Monster of Dagenham Hall, Agent No. 5, Murder While You Wait, *and* Vampire of the Skies. *The study of this British mystery "legend" became a Malice Domestic tradition when William F. Deeck, the world's leading Corbettologist, began writing a regular "Corbett Corner" feature in Malice's newsletter,* The Usual Suspects, *and in other mystery periodicals that illuminated Corbett's* bon mots. *It also led to such Malice panels as " 'He Sat Up Like a Full-Blown Geranium': The Genius of James Corbett." In this story, two renowned Corbettologists pay a skewed tribute to this mystery author, "a master," says Deeck, "of the language. Unfortunately, no one knows which language it was."*

Agent No. 5 and Agent No. 6 are, respectively, Edward Marston and Peter Lovesey. Now retired from the Secret Service, they have published nearly forty books between them and are living happily ever after at the Corbett Institute for Demented Authors.

Agony Column

Barry N. Malzberg

GENTLEMEN:
I ENCLOSE MY short story, "Three for the Universe," and know you will find it right for your magazine, *Astounding Spirits*.
Yours very truly,
Martin Miller

~

Dear Contributor:
Thank you for your recent submission. Unfortunately, although we have read it with great interest, we are unable to use it in *Astounding Spirits*. Due to the great volume of submissions we receive, we cannot grant all contributors a personal letter, but you may be sure that the manuscript has

been reviewed carefully and its rejection is no comment upon its literary merit but may be dependent upon one of many factors.

Faithfully,
The Editors

Dear Editors:

The Vietnam disgrace must be brought to an end! We have lost on that stained soil not only our national honor but our very future. The troops must be brought home and we must remember that there is more honor in dissent than in unquestioningly silent agreement.

Sincerely,
Martin Miller

Dear Sir:

Thank you for your recent letter to the editors. Due to the great volume of worthy submissions we are unable to print every good letter we receive and therefore regretfully inform you that while we will not be publishing it, this is no comment upon the value of your opinion.

Very truly yours,
The Editors

Dear Congressman Forthwaite:

I wish to bring your attention to a serious situation which is developing on the West Side. A resident of this neighborhood for five years now, I have recently observed that a large number of streetwalkers, dope addicts, and criminal types are loitering at the intersection of Columbus Avenue and Twenty-fourth Street at almost all hours of the day, offending passersby with their appearance and creating a severe blight on the area. In addition, passersby are often threateningly asked for "handouts" and even "solicited." I know that you share with me a concern for a Better West Side and look forward to your comments on this situation as well as some kind of concrete action.

Sincerely,
Martin Miller

Dear Mr. Millow:
Thank you for your letter. Your concern for our West Side is appreciated and it is only through the efforts and diligence of constituents such as yourself that a better New York can be conceived. I have forwarded your letter to the appropriate precinct office in Manhattan and you may expect to hear from them soon.

Gratefully yours,
Alwyn D. Forthwaite

Dear Gentlemen:
In May of this year I wrote Congressman Alwyn D. Forthwaite a letter of complaint, concerning conditions of the Columbus Avenue–West Twenty-fourth Street intersection in Manhattan and was informed by him that this letter was passed on to your precinct office. Since four months have now elapsed, and since I have neither heard from you nor observed any change in the conditions pointed out in my letter, I now write to ask whether or not that letter was forwarded to you and what you have to say about it.

Sincerely,
Martin Miller

Dear Mr. Milner:
Our files hold no record of your letter.

N. B. Karsh
Captain, # 33462

Dear Sirs:

I have read Sheldon Novack's article in the current issue of *Cry* with great interest but feel that I must take issue with his basic point, which is that sex is the consuming biological drive from which all other activities stem and which said other activities become only metaphorical for. This strikes me as a bit more of a projection of Mr. Novack's own functioning than that reality which he so shrewdly contends he apperceives.

Sincerely,

Martin Miller

Dear Mr. Milton:

Due to the great number of responses to Sheldon A. Novack's "Sex and Sexuality: Are We Missing Anything?" in the August issue of *Cry*, we will be unable to publish your own contribution in our "Cry from the City" Column, but we do thank you for your interest.

Yours,

The Editors

Dear Mr. President:

I was shocked by the remarks apparently attributed to you in today's newspapers on the public assistance situation. Surely, you must be aware of the fact that social welfare legislation emerged from the compassionate attempt of 1930 politics to deal with human torment in a systematized fashion, and although many of the cruelties you note are inherent to the very system, they do not cast doubt upon its very legitimacy. Our whole national history has been one of coming to terms with collective consciousness as opposed to the law of the jungle, and I cannot understand how you could have such a position as yours.

Sincerely,

Martin Miller

Dear Mr. Meller:
Thank you very much for your letter of October eighteenth to the president. We appreciate your interest and assure you that without the concern of citizens like yourself the country would not be what it has become. Thank you very much and we do look forward to hearing from you in the future on matters of national interest.

Mary L. McGinnity
Presidential Assistant

Gentlemen:
I enclose herewith my article, "Welfare: Are We Missing Anything?" which I hope you may find suitable for publication in *Insight Magazine*.

Very truly yours,
Martin Miller

Dear Contributor:
The enclosed has been carefully reviewed and our reluctant decision is that it does not quite meet our needs at the present time. Thank you for your interest in *Insight*.

The Editors

Dear Senator Partch:
Your vote on the Armament Legislation was shameful.

Sincerely,
Martin Miller

Dear Dr. Mallow:
Thank you for your recent letter to Senator O. Stuart Partch and for your approval of the senator's vote.

L. T. Walters
Congressional Aide

Dear Susan Saltis:
I think your recent decision to pose nude in that "art-pho-
tography" series in Men's Companion was disgraceful, filled
once again with those timeless, empty rationalizations of the
licentious which have so little intrinsic capacity for damage
except when they are subsumed, as they are in your case, with
abstract and vague "connections" to platitudes so enormous
as to risk the very demolition of the collective personality.

> Yours very truly,
> Martin Miller

Dear Sir:
With pleasure and in answer to your request, we are enclosing
a photograph of Miss Susan Saltis as she appears in her new
movie, Chariots to the Holy Roman Empire.

> Very truly yours,
> Henry T. Wyatt
> Publicity Director

Gentlemen:
I wonder if Cry would be interested in the enclosed article
which is not so much an article as a true documentary of the
results which have been obtained from my efforts over recent
months to correspond with various public figures, entertain-
ment stars, etc., etc. It is frightening to contemplate the
obliteration of self which the very devices of the twentieth
century compel, and perhaps your readers might share my
(not so retrospective) horror.

> Sincerely,
> Martin Miller

Dear Sir:
As a potential contributor to Cry, I am happy to offer you our
"Writer's Subscription Discount," meaning that for only five
dollars and fifty cents you will receive not only a full year's

subscription (28 percent below newsstand rates, 14 percent below customary subscriptions) but in addition our year-end special issue, *Cry in the Void*, at no extra charge.

Subscription Dept.

⌒‿

Dear Contributor:
Thank you very much for your article, "Agony Column." It has been considered here with great interest and it is the consensus of the Editorial Board that while it has unusual merit it is not quite right for us. We thank you for your interest in *Cry* and look forward to seeing more of your work in the future.

Sincerely,
The Editors

⌒‿

Dear Congressman Forthwaite:
Nothing has been done about the conditions I mentioned in my letter of about a year ago. Not one single thing!

Bitterly,
Martin Miller

⌒‿

Dear Mr. Mills:
Please accept our apologies for the delay in answering your good letter. Congressman Forthwaite has been involved, as you know, through the winter in the Food Panel and has of necessity allowed some of his important correspondence to await close attention.

Now that he has the time he thanks you for your kind words of support.

Yours truly,
Ann Ananauris

⌒‿

Dear Sir:

The Adams multiple murders are indeed interesting not only for their violence but because of the confession of the accused that he "did it so that someone would finally notice me." Any citizen can understand this—the desperate need to be recognized as an individual, to break past bureaucracy into some clear apprehension of one's self-worth, is one of the most basic of human drives, but it is becoming increasingly frustrated today by a technocracy which allows less and less latitude for the individual to articulate his own identity and vision and be heard. Murder is easy: It is easy in the sense that the murderer does not need to embark upon an arduous course of training in order to accomplish his feat; his excess can come from the simple extension of sheer human drives . . . aided by basic weaponry. The murderer does not have to cultivate "contacts" or "fame" but can simply, by being *there*, vault past nihilism and into some clear, cold connection with the self. More and more the capacity for murder lurks within us; we are narrow, and driven, we are almost obliterated from any sense of existence, we need to make that singing leap past accomplishment and into acknowledgment and *recognition*. Perhaps you would print this letter?

Hopefully,
Martin Miller

Dear Sir:

Thank you for your recent letter. We regret being unable to use it due to many letters of similar nature being received, but we look forward to your expression of interest.

Sincerely,
John Smith for the Editors

Dear Mr. President:
I intend to assassinate you. I swear that you will not live out the year. It will come by rifle or knife, horn or fire, dread or terror, but it will come, and there is no way that you can AVOID THAT JUDGMENT TO BE RENDERED UPON YOU.

Fuck You,
Martin Miller

Dear Reverend Mellbow:
As you know, the president is abroad at the time of this writing, but you may rest assured that upon his return your letter, along with thousands of other and similar expressions of hope, will be turned over to him and I am sure that he will appreciate your having written.

Very truly yours,
Mary L. McGinnity
Presidential Assistant

Graduation

Richard Christian Matheson

J ANUARY 15

DEAR MOM AND DAD:
It has been an expectedly hectic first week; unpacking, organizing, getting scheduled in classes, and of course fraternizing with the locals to secure promise of later aid should I need it. I don't think I will. My room is nice though it has a view which Robert Frost would scoff at; perhaps a transfer to a better location later this semester is possible. We'll see.

I had a little run-in with the administration when I arrived; a trivial technicality, something about too much luggage. At least more than the other dormitory students brought with them. I cleared it up with a little glib know-how. As always. Some of the guys on my floor look as if they might be enjoyable and if I'm lucky maybe one or two will be interesting to talk to as well. But I can't chase after "impossible rainbows." That should sound familiar, Dad, it's from your private collection and has been gone over a "few" times. A few. But maybe this time, it's true. Anyway, the dormitory looks as if it's going to work out well. Pass the word to you-know-who. I'm sure it will interest him.

The dinner tonight was an absolute abomination. It could easily have been some medieval mélange concocted by the college gardener utilizing lawn improver, machinist's oil, and ground-up old men. And I question even the quality of those ingredients. I may die tonight of poisoning. Maybe if I'm lucky it will strike quickly and leave no marks. Don't want Dad's old school to lose its accreditation after all. However, I'm a little concerned that the townspeople will be kept awake tonight by the sound of 247 "well-fed" freshmen looking at their reflections in the toilet bowl. Today while I was buying books an upper-classman called me green for not getting used ones. If he was in any way referring to the way my face looks right now, he should be hired by some psychic foundation. He can tell the future.

Anyway, Mom, I certainly do miss your cooking. Almost as much as I miss my stomach's equilibrium. Ugh.

The room gets cold early with the snow and all. But I have plenty of blankets (remember the excessive luggage? . . . guessed it) so that poses no difficulty. I'll probably pick up a small heater next week, first free day I get. For now I'll manage with hot tea, the collected works of Charles Dickens, and warm memories of all of you back home. Until I write again, I send my love and an abundance of sneezes.

Here's looking achoo . . .

> Yours regurgitatively,

February 2
Dear Mom and Dad:
Greetings from Antarctica. It is unbelievably cold up here. If you can imagine your son as a hybrid between a Popsicle and

a slab of marble, you've got the right idea, just make it a little colder. In a word, freezing. In another word, numbing. In two other words, liquid oxygen. I may be picking up that heater sooner than I thought. I see no future in becoming a glacier.

I met my professors today, all of whom seem interested and dedicated. My calculus class might be a trifle dreary, but, then, numbers put a damper on things any way you look at it. The other courses look promising so far. Tell you-know-who that he-knows-who is genuinely excited about something. I'm sure he'll be cheered by that forecast of future involvements.

Burping is very popular in my wing of the dormitory and some of the guys have been explaining its physical principles to me, complete with sonic demonstrations to validate their theories. One guy, Jim, who looks a little like a bull dog with slightly bigger eyes (and a much bigger stomach), apparently holds the record in two prestigious areas: he drinks the most and belches the loudest. For your own personal information files, he also seems to know the fewest words a person can possess and still communicate with. I estimate that the exact number of words is a high one-digit counting number, but I could still be going too easily on him. His belches, however, are enormously awesome. He is able (he whispered to me when I bumped into his drunken body in the hallway last night) to make time stand still temporarily with one of his burps.

Furthermore (he said), that would be one of his lesser efforts. Were he to launch a truly prize-winning belch (he said), civilization as we know it would be obliterated and the earth's atmosphere rendered noxious for two thousand years. Personally, I feel he exaggerates a bit. Maybe fifteen hundred years.

Jim doesn't stop burping until one or two in the morning, which makes studying a degree harder. It's like having a baby in the dorm, with Jim erupting and gurgling into the A.M. hours. Except that he weighs three hundred pounds. But I'm learning to live with it. Occasionally, he gets to be more than a petty annoyance and I get upset, but it's really nothing to worry about. So tell you-know-who to not put himself into a state. I'm fine.

If we could harness the secret of Jim's aberration and regulate it at timed intervals, perhaps Yellowstone Park would be interested. Oh well, he'll probably quiet down soon. I miss you all a lot and send my fondest love. Until I thaw out again, bye for now.

Bundlingly yours . . .

P.S. Avoid telling you-know-who I'm "cold" up here. He has this thing about that word.

February 22
Dear Mom and Dad:
An enlivening new roommate has entered my monastic quarters. He is slight in frame and says very little; a simple kind of person with a dearth of affinities, except for cheese, which he loves. I call him Hannibal owing to his fearlessly exploratory nature. You see, Hannibal, while not easy to detect, is very much present. He comes out to mingle only during the evening. The late evening. More precisely, that part of the evening when I like to try and catch some sleep. Hannibal is evidently on a different schedule than I.

In short, I have mouse trouble.

Hannibal, in all fairness, is but one of the offenders. He is joined each evening by a host of other raucous marauders who squeal and scratch until dawn, determined to disturb my rest. They're actually quite cute, but are, regardless of angelic appearances, a steadily unappreciated annoyance.

I mentioned my visitors to some of the other students in the dormitory and they said I wasn't the only victim of the whiskered nocturnal regime. They advised setting traps and, failing that, to use a poison which can be purchased from the student store. It is rumored to yield foolproof results. I know it sounds altogether like a cross borrowing from Walt Disney and an Edgar Allan Poe story, but, regrettably, I must do something.

As an alternate plan, I thought of possibly speaking with a brainy flutist I know from orchestra class, who is quite talented. Whether or not he would care to revivify a Gothic tale simply for the benefit of my slumberous tranquility is something we will have to discuss. Also the question of playing and walking at the same time may come up. But I'll try to circumvent that aspect. It's a slightly off-beat gig but it seems an improvement on the other method. I'll speak with him.

My classes are going fairly well, with no serious laggings in any subject despite the effects of Jim and Hannibal's henchmen upon my alertness. Thanks for the letter and a very special thanks for those fantastic cookies, Mom. They were delicious. You really made my day. And the traveling scent of your generosity made me quite sought after for a "little sample" of what food can really taste like. Jim went ape over them and said he wouldn't mind taking the whole next box off my hands. Which is something like a man with no legs admitting that he, occasionally, limps. Good old Jim. He'll probably eat himself to death one day. Although it would take him at least two days to do it right.

In light of the popularity of your largess, I have determined that everybody else must have the same immense regard for the school cook I do. He is acquiring a definite reputation, the likes of which has been shared by a handful of historical figures. Lizzie Borden, Jack the Ripper. The man has no regard for the human taste bud. All in all, I'm convinced that our chef will most assuredly go to hell.

Anyway, Mom, thanks again for the cookies. They were eaten with rapturous abandon. And you may have saved several students from ulcers. What better compliment? All my love to everyone back home. Including you-know-who.

> Thwarted by burps, squeaks,
> and bad food . . .

P.S. I think Jim (our resident sulphur spring) finally knows what it's like being kept up at night. He too has mouse trouble. (At least someone will visit him.)

March 9

Dear Mom and Dad:

Got in a small amount of trouble today as a result of being late to class and complicating matters by arguing with my professor over a dumb thing he said about me.

You see, in Philosophy I, as it is taught by Marshall B. Francis, you are not allowed an impregnable viewpoint. It must always be open to comment. And he says he likes to analyze. I told him he likes to shred and butcher. Whereupon he requested a "formal presentation of my personal philosophy of life's purpose."

Since, as you know, my philosophy responds unfavorably to direct assault, I refused. Mistake number one.

He told me if I didn't cooperate he'd have me leave the class and withdraw all credit from my participation thus far. I thought this unfair, so we started yelling at one another and in the clouded ferocity of our exchanges I accidentally slashed him on the cheek with my pen. It wasn't deep, but it scared him a lot. It wasn't at all like it may seem; I say that only because I know what you're probably thinking. Believe me, it was just a freak accident with one lost temper responding to another.

We talked in the infirmary later and he said he understood and would allow me a second chance. After that kindness, I volunteered my philosophy without hesitation (rather sheepishly), and he smiled at my completion of the apologies. He said that sometimes you have to be willing to fight for your beliefs and that he respected my actions in class, saving the accident, of course. I think we'll be great friends by the end of the year (if he doesn't get infected and die); however, philosophers consider life to be a danger so I guess it wouldn't surprise him too much.

It is still very cold with no trace of warmth. Jim continues to noisily burn (or is it burp) the midnight oil much to the chagrin of everyone in the dorm. If a sonic boom occurred during the evening, it would be completely overlooked. Buried.

Once again, my love to all of you back home, and I sure would like to hear from you, so please write. Better not tell you-know-who what happened to me today. He'll get the wrong impression. He has enough people to worry about as it is.

With new-found philosophy,

P.S. Hannibal is no longer with me. He and his men are squeaking across those great Alps in the sky. That poison really was foolproof.

March 18
Dear Mom and Dad:
My social horizons are expanding here in Isolation City. In one day, I met the remainder of my floormates (truly a rogues' gallery) at a party and also a very nice girl who works as my lab partner.

I met my across-the-hall neighbor quite by chance over a game of poker. I beat him over and over and he had to write me a few IOUs. When I asked him what room he was in (so I might stop by and "collect"), it turned out to be the room directly across from mine. It's weird how you can overlook someone who is right under your nose. Anyway, he's a nice guy, but is badly in need of tutoring in the finer points of the gentlemanly wager. He is absolutely the worst gambler I have ever encountered. I suspect that his brain has decomposed from excessive exposure to Jim, who is his favorite card player. They play to one another's caliber it seems. Two drunks leading each other home.

My neighbor's name is Marcum Standile Jr. As a rather unusual point of insight into his personal life, we figured out tonight (in my room after the party) that Marcum owes roughly $40,000 to various other dormitory inhabitants with whom he has played poker. This sum is exceeded only by Jim's, whose debts accrued in two short months amount to a figure which is something akin to the annual budget for Red China. Perhaps my training in calculus is coming in handy for once.

I'll write more about Susie later. Everything is pretty good academically speaking and the sun is even occasionally making a token appearance. Miss you very much and send all my love.

With endless computation,

P.S. Got a letter from you-know-who. Guess he took the accident a little too seriously. Tell him to relax.

April 4
Dear Mom and Dad:
I'm rich! Marcum got his monthly allotment from his financially overstuffed folks and came through with over $400 for yours truly. So far, this much money has me in quite an influential position since word of my monetary windfall has spread like an epidemic. I am popular beyond belief. I've considered opening up a loan service (with determined interest) so as to make the entire endeavor worth my expended energy, as well as expended funds. An idea which I took from a movie with George Segal, *King Rat*. The entire prison camp where he was being held captive by the enemy, had less money than George so he became the nucleus of all existing finance. The concept appeals to me. I'll probably just buy a heater and an electric blanket, though. Fancy dies so quickly in a young man's heart. Sniff.

I am referred to alternately as "Rockefeller" or "pal," depending on the plight of who I'm speaking with. I never dreamed any one person could have so many "pals." Last night, someone pinned a sign to my door that says "Fort Knox North." It's only right. Being rich is such toil. Tell you-know-who I will use it wisely.

My lab partner and I have become even better friends in the past few weeks. I think I mentioned in the last letter that her name is Susie, actually Susan Johnson. What I failed to include in that brief description is that she is kind of like my girlfriend, stunningly beautiful, intelligent, and popular, and maybe the first girl, since Beth's death, that I really care about. Without pouring forth excessives about Susie, I'll simply say that I know you'd love her. She is quite a unique person and around here that's a godsend, the prevailing ambiance being composed of uptight females. I only hope that she feels the same about me. But that will come in time. I think it would crush me if she were just experiencing feelings of friendship. But I suspect that her eyes are the best spokesman for her affections and they tell me everything is going perfect. Tell you-know-who not to hold his breath. She isn't at all like Beth, so don't let him even attempt to connect things. Beth was just something that happened. I'm sorry about it, but it was, after all, an accident and I think I would resent you-know-who making more of this than there is. Or maybe making less of it. It feels right to me. Not like with Beth. So please keep you-know-who off the subject completely; it's not fair.

By the way, I think I might make the dean's list, so cross your fingers. Philosophy I is going very well and Marshall B. Francis and I are becoming friends of the close variety. As I predicted.

I miss you all very much and send my love. Please write.

With Krupp-like fortune,

P.S. Thanks for the latest batch of cookies, Mom. I'm not sure I can eat all of them myself. Plenty of willing mouths around here, though.

April 17
Dear Mom and Dad:
Terrible news. Remember Jim, the guy who belched and kept everybody up? He was found this morning, in his room, dead. The school won't issue any kind of statement, but everyone thinks it might have been suicide. I don't think there was a note or anything, and it could have just been an accident.

If it was suicide, it would have made a lot of sense, speaking strictly in terms of motivation. He wasn't a very happy person, his weight and all making him almost completely socially ostracized. He was only eighteen years old. It's a shame things like this have to happen.

It certainly is going to be quiet around here without his belching and carryings-on; which is kind of a relief even if the circumstances are so tragic. Nobody has mentioned the funeral, but I hear his parents are going to have him buried locally. That's the nicest thing they could do for him. He really liked the college and the town and everything, and although unhappy, was happier here than he would have been anywhere else. It's going to be abnormally quiet around here. Maybe with the improved conditions we'll get some new scholars out of this dorm. I know I'll sleep better. Still, I feel as if every death has a meaning; a reason for happening. I may bring that up in Philosophy I. Anyway, it's a damn shame about Jim. Marcum lost a great card partner.

On a slightly cheerier note, Susie and I are still seeing each other, but I have a difficult time figuring her out. Maybe she isn't the demonstrative type. If that is the case, I can understand her reticence, but if not, I can't help wondering what's wrong. We talk all the time, but she doesn't seem to be able to let me know she cares. It's odd because Beth was similar in that way.

I'm sure time will make its own decision. Sound familiar, Dad? It's another one of your polished "classics." What would life be without my father's inimitable cracker-barreling? A bit more relaxing perhaps . . . Incidentally, the loan business is beginning to take shape. I'll write more about it later. For now, it's looking quite hopeful. Monte Carlo, here I come.

Pass the word to you-know-who, about my business. It's what he likes to hear. Former client makes good and all that stuff.

Miss you all very much and send my deepest love.

Destined to be wealthy
(but in semi-mourning),

P.S. My room is starting to bother me. Maybe a change!

April 25

Dear Mom and Dad:

You-know-who wrote me a letter I received today. He wants me to come home. The onslaught of Jim's death along with the isolating geography up here has him surprisingly alarmed. He feels that the milieu is just too strenuous for me to manage. I disagree with him completely and feel that I'm taking Jim's death very well. I'm not overreacting beyond what is reasonable. After all, Jim and I were almost complete strangers. Maybe the ease of detachment comes because of that.

I wrote you-know-who tonight after dinner, but I think a word from you might help to quell his skepticism. I know you told him about the death out of good conscience, but, as I recommended, it may have been a bad idea. All in all, I couldn't be happier and the thought of leaving depresses me very much. I think my letter will stand on its own merit, but a word from you would assist the cause enormously.

Business is in full swing here at Fort Knox North. I've made over fifteen dollars in interest this week. Once again, I'm baffled as to how to spend the newly mounting sums. Perhaps a place where liquor and painted women are available to book-weary students? However, I'll probably squander my gain away on decent food. The indigenous delicacies are becoming as palatable as boiled sheet metal. Really disgusting. I look forward to a meal by the greatest cook in the known world. I hope you're listening, Mom.

I talked to the dean of housing today about changing rooms and he told me (morbidly enough) that the only available room is Jim's. It seemed grisly at first, but I gave it serious thought and am going to move in tomorrow. It's been cleaned up (all but boiled out) so there is no trace of anything that indicated someone lived in it. Or died in it. For obvious reasons, I think you would agree, telling you-know-who would just fuel the flame. He can't expect everyone to react to death the same way. It doesn't spook me to be in Jim's room.

I wonder, though, if his spirit will inhabit my lungs and create zombie burps. All, no doubt, from your cookies, Mom. He was really hooked. Phantom gases are an interesting concept, but don't exactly arrest me esthetically. Quiet, I think I hear a cookie crumbling.

My studies are going exceptionally well. Something interesting happened in Philosophy I today. Remember I told you I was going to mention the point about Jim's death maybe being the happiest salvation he could have chosen? Well, I made the point and nobody would talk about it. They all seemed disturbed about the personalized nature of the question since it wasn't just a hypothetical inquiry. Some people even made peculiar comments. People are unpredictable when it comes to death.

Things are "OK" with Susie. We're supposed to go to a concert tonight. Will tell you about that in next letter. Miss you all hugely and send my fondest love.

Sleeping better,

P.S. Susie may get my class ring tonight. Lucky girl.

April 26
Dear Mom and Dad:
Something ghastly has happened. It's hard to even write this letter as I am extremely upset.

Susie and I returned from the school auditorium sometime after midnight, following the concert, and sneaked into my dormitory room to listen to some music. I had planned to ask Susie how she felt about me after we settled down. The concert had been very stimulating and we were both being quite verbal, competing for each other's audience as many thoughts were occurring to both of us. We talked for several hours and were almost exhausted from the conversation before quieting down.

As we sat listening to the music, on my bed together, I bent over to her cheek and, kissing her gently, asked her how she felt about our relationship and where it was going. She was silent for what must have been minutes. Then she spoke. In almost a pale whisper she said that we would always be good friends and that her regard for me was quite sincere but that she couldn't feel romantically about me ever. She didn't explain why, even though I asked her over and over.

Maybe the fact that I was tired had something to do with it, but I began to cry and couldn't stop. Her admission had taken me entirely by surprise. I had thought things were just beginning to take shape.

I guess Susie sensed that my hurt was larger than even the tears revealed and she got up from the bed to walk to the other side of the room. Working things out in her mind, I guess. She walked to the window to let in some air. As she raised it I could feel the cold wind rush in, and I looked up to see Susie's hair blowing as she kneeled near the window, looking out over the fields. It was so quiet that the whole thing seemed like a dream; the cold air plunging in on us, the music playing with muted beauty for us alone, the near darkness making shadowy nothings of our separateness.

Susie leaned out the window, and I watched her, transfixed, thinking that what she had said was a story, that she was only playing. She only continued in her silence, staring into the night's blackness.

I guess she wanted more air or something because she raised the window, and as I rose to help her with it, a screaming cut the air.

She kept screaming until she hit the walkway below. Then there was silence again. She was taken to the hospital and operated on for a fractured skull, broken shoulder, and internal injuries.

She was pronounced dead at 6:30 this morning.

The police questioned me today about the accident but seemed satisfied that it was a tragic accident. They could, I'm sure, see my grief was genuine.

I am left with almost nothing now. Susie was everything I worked for other than school, and without her here, that means nothing. I am thinking of coming home. You-know-who needn't say anything to you or me about what he thinks. He's wrong. And, at this point, I don't need advice. My treatment will be mine alone from now on. I don't want interference from him anymore.

I am very seriously depressed. I keep thinking that had Susie told me long ago that she cared we wouldn't have spent so long, last night, in my room. If only she had cared, everything might have been different. I think these thoughts must occur to anyone who loses someone cherished. I didn't think something like this could happen to me. I find it hard to go on without someone caring. If you don't care about someone who cares about you, why should you even exist? Without that there is no reason.

In deepest hopelessness,

P.S. Maybe no letters from me until I feel better.

~

April 28
Dear Mom and Dad:
Things are no better with me than my last letter reported. Since Susie's death I am unable to concentrate on studies and am falling seriously behind in my classes. I sit alone most of the time in my room, watching the fields as the winds create giant patterns. Before today, I had thought it the most beautiful view in the dorm.

Speaking of the dorm, I now find myself unable to associate with any of the other residents. They all remind me of Susie. I almost hate this building because it remembers everything that happened in it. It will not forget anything and each time I get inside it I feel subsumed by its creaking examinations of me. I am now easily given to imaginings about many things and question all things. I trust only myself now.

My loan business is being attended to assiduously with the scrutiny of a watchmaker fearing he has left out a part from a shipment of hundreds of timepieces. I am losing money now. The clientele is not paying me back punctually or with owed amounts adequately covered. Everybody on my floor and many people scattered throughout the building have taken out loans. Almost none have returned them. I am almost at my wit's end trying to get the money. But you can't torture people to get it. I'm really getting desperate. I have such contempt for those who borrow things and either refuse to return them or consciously allow themselves to let their obligation slide through negligence. Negligence should beget negligence. It's only fair that way.

I have been going to concerts the past two nights. They seem to help me relax. I despise returning to the dormitory more and more. Every time I get inside I feel suffocated. I realize that I must try to adjust and get back into the swing of things, but it is not easy. I am trying. Tell you-know-who.

That's all I can tell you. I can't foresee much of anything now. My dearest love to both of you. Please write.

Confused with sickness,

April 30
Dear Mom and Dad:
Last night, almost as if the dormitory knew my hate for it (like a dog who senses its master's loathings), it took its own life along with the lives of many inside its cradling horror.

As I walked back from a 10:30 concert (Chopin) at the campus center, I came upon the dormitory burning bright orange in the night. Firemen say it was caused by an electrical short circuit or something. Nineteen students were eaten by flames, unable to escape the building. The remains were charred beyond recognition and teeth and dental records are being matched to discern who the students were.

It doesn't seem to matter who someone is once he is dead.
Only what he did while he lived. An honorable life will not
tolerate an impure death. But the life that deceives and
cloaks its meaning with artifice and insensitivity cannot die
reasonably. Perhaps Marshall B. Francis would have something to say about that. All death seems to need is an
attached philosophy to resolve its meaning. Otherwise it is
just an end. I may talk to him.

There is nothing left for me now of course. I am numbed by
the death which surrounds me here. My room and belongings
were destroyed in the fire, and the purpose of my schooling
has become inconsequential to both myself and what I want.

I will try another school, in another place. Things must be different elsewhere. Somewhere there must be a safe place. A
place where things such as what I have seen haven't happened. If there is, I will find it.

I'm catching a plane tomorrow at noon and should arrive at
about 5:30. My love to you until then.

Forward looking,

P.S. I got an A in philosophy. Hooray!

Someone Who Understands Me

Matthew Costello

Welcome to Chat Room 13!
Attending: 2
>> Nightmover
>> Paladin

WHO WOULDN'T HAVE BEEN curious?

I mean, there was so much talk about virtual sex and virtual relationships in cyberspace, you'd have to be a mole to be uninterested.

And I am not a mole.

I also had the number-one prerequisite of someone seeking adventure on the net: time . . . and lots of it.

It wasn't always that way.

But these days, I had—

>> **What changed, Paladin? How come *you* had so much time?**

Oh . . . sorry. Didn't think you'd be interested.

You see, my company sold paper goods, real paper made from real trees. Imagine giant forests ripped down to make a zillion telephone books, and that was our business.

But paper was an endangered species. Now we had the paperless office . . . and everybody acted as if that were a good goddamn thing. Hey, the World Wide Web is filled with pages and pages that— ta-da!—don't use paper.

The paper business started to collapse. It was only a matter of time until my boss waddled into my cramped little office and said, "Jack, I'm afraid I have *pre-tty* bad news."

Only a matter of time . . . and I had plenty of time.

>> **So you went on the Net?**

Yes. I surfed, I skipped, I zapped from page to page, with my office door locked and not a hell of a lot of work to do. That's what I did . . . until I found ChatWorld . . . and I met Cynarra.

>> **Cynarra? Nice screen name.**

Yes. Though I immediately wondered whether it was real. Cynarra . . . it sounded like something out of a novel. We started chatting. And when I came back the next day, she was there, waiting for me. It became something . . . to look forward to.

>> **And you're married . . . I presume?**

Yes. Married. *Imprisoned* is more like it. I guess I could have divorced my wife—but what would my life have been like? All the money we had was Bev's money, old money from her old family. And I was about to be unemployed. If I left Bev, would I end up on the street? The idea of living in an old refrigerator box wasn't too appealing.

>> **No kids?**

Our two kids were all grown. Out of the house and glad of it. It was just Beverly and me. Bev and Jack, sitting in their co-op, quietly seething.

>> **Sounds like you were ready for some fantasy.**

Oh, yes. Fantasy, reality. I was ready for *something*. At first, Cynarra and I simply talked. She seemed cloaked in mystery. She described herself as a "dark-haired, dark-eyed beauty." I thought about that *a lot*. Later she said she had full lips and a sexy smile. We just talked at first, but then—

>> **You developed a cyber relationship? Cool!**

Yeah, cool. A cyber relationship. I was at work, talking to Cynarra. Always waiting for her to come on-line.

>> **Did you use your real name?**

No way. I used my "screen name"—Paladin. Remember that old show, Paladin? *Have Gun, Will Travel?*

>> **Nope. Paladin? Before my time. Sorry.**

No problem. So . . . I was Paladin and she was Cynarra. And I described myself to her, embellishing it a bit. I said I was tall . . . even though I'm only 5' 7". 1 didn't think that she'd ever see me. I said I was slender and muscular, with deep-set blue eyes. Ha—well at least I do have blue eyes.

>> **And then?**

>> **You still there?**

>> **Paladin . . . ?**

Sorry. I felt this pain . . . in my stomach. Sharp pain. But—where was I?

>> **She was Cynarra and *you* were Paladin.**

Yes. So we started talking about intimate things.

>> **Sex?**

Well, I don't want to make it sound like we just talked about sex, that we only tried to get each other hot and bothered. It was more than that. She opened herself to me, she told me about the slob she was married to, how badly he treated her . . . how she couldn't stand him.

I started feeling bad. for her. No, worse than bad. I felt as though, in all my copious free time, I wanted to protect her.

She told me that her husband came home and smacked her.

Once she told me that she had an ugly bruise on her cheek where he slapped her. And she told me that the only thing—the only thing!—that made her feel better was knowing that I was out there, waiting for her.

>> **And how were things at your home?**

Oh great, terrific. I'd come home . . . and Bev and I wouldn't have two words to say to each other. Then, when she went to sleep, going to bed so early as though she actually had something to do the next morning, I'd creep in the den and use our home computer to check for any messages from Cynarra. I knew that she couldn't log on—but there might be a message.

I soon discovered that the only thing I lived for were words from Cynarra.

>> **So . . . you arranged to see her?**

No. That's the funny thing.

What happened started out as a joke. We were just kidding. And I wrote: "Wouldn't it be great if we could get rid of our respective spouses. If somehow they were *dead*, and we could be together. Wouldn't that be great?"

>> **And you were kidding?**

Right. I mean, we—

>> **Hello?**

>> **Still there? Paladin? Are you—**

Sorry. Started coughing. Couldn't stop. Anyway, it was a joke. I mean, I had never seen this person, my dark-eyed Cynarra. Most likely she didn't resemble her description at all. But that didn't matter. No, not when she fired me with this incredible fantasy. Then she typed something interesting.

She wrote, **<<There are poisons, you know. Undetectable poisons.>>**

The first thing I wondered was whether ChatWorld was secure. I mean, could anyone eavesdrop and listen to our private tête-à-tête? But that was a big selling point of ChatWorld. . . their motto . . . "Let yourself go . . . it's your own private world . . ."

>> **Like now?**

Exactly. Like now. No one can "hear" us. So, Cynarra told me about a Web site, a place called Dead.com. She told me to check it out.

>> **Dead.com. Sounds cheery.**

That Web site was creepy, lots of pages dealing with death and mutilation. And sure enough, there was a page on poison. And on that page I found something called a fungoid colloidal suspension.

>> **Sounds yummy.**

Toxic mushrooms, fermented and turned into a slightly sweet mixture. It causes intense gastral pain, contractions, hemorrhaging, and— it was rumored—a death that was virtually unrecognizable from—

>> **Yes . . . ? Unrecognizable from—Paladin?**

Sorry again. The person who died from that poison was most likely to be diagnosed as having a spontaneous hemorrhage.

>> **Neat.**

Now, Cynarra and I talked about almost nothing else. There were still those tender moments when we imagined touching each other, caressing . . . but now we had a new shared enthusiasm. We imagined being *free*.

>> **So you went down to your local mushroom store.**

No. No, I had to search the city to find out where you'd get these stupid mushrooms. But it turned out that they are a vital food source for the Munghip Lizard, a small green lizard from the Central Amazon. If you had a Munghip as a pet, you absolutely *had* to have these mushrooms. I told Cynarra.

>> **She went there too, eh? Quite a run on toxic mushrooms.**

She didn't tell me that she did that. I thought: maybe for her this was all a fantasy, and I was helping her create this fantasy. I didn't know if she was serious.

But I told her what I was going to do. I told her that she had me entranced, that I didn't care what she really looked like . . . if she was bald and toothless. She was my *Cynarra*, and she gave me the dream to be free.

>> *And* **financially secure.**

Yes. If this worked, I'd have the money I needed to live. That wouldn't be a problem. When the ax fell, when the business collapsed, I'd be okay.

>> **So when did you do the deed? Was it a dark and stormy night?**

It was morning. A gray November morning, barely light, the cloud cover so thick. I had the mushroom mixture fermenting for the five days—exactly as called for by the recipe. Then I went to the fridge and found Bev's container of Trim Grain. That stupid diet beverage of hers looked like quicksand. It was marsh sludge. It sloshed around in the container and left a gritty film on the sides.

>> **Guess it would mask the mushroom brew, huh?**

Sure. And I didn't have to put a lot in. A single teaspoon was terminal. But I put a couple of extra tablespoons in—just to be sure. A little overkill wouldn't hurt. I shook the container a couple of times.

Bev always had a couple of glasses of the stuff every day, always trying to fight that middle-aged spread.

I went to work. I waited for Cynarra.

>> **And she didn't show up?**

No. She did. I didn't tell her what I did. I wanted to wait to make sure it worked. I was afraid that she'd be shocked.

>> **But it was *her* idea.**

Or her fantasy . . . her game. I wanted it to be done, a—what do they call it?—*fait accompli.*

We chatted a bit. Then, after lunch, I went back to ChatWorld, but she wasn't there. But there was a message. She had run out . . . she had some errands to do. She said that she'd be back.

I was so nervous, so damn excited I took a walk.

I got back to my office late. The office manager got on my case . . . but it didn't matter. Not anymore. I went to my computer terminal, expecting Cynarra to be there, back from her chores.

>> **But she wasn't.**

Yeah. And I felt alone. I wanted to *share* this with her. She helped make it happen and now I was all alone.

So I left work early. I left, and returned home.

>> **And found? Paladin?**

>> **Paladin, you there? Hey, come back . . . Paladin.**

I'm back. Couldn't type for a minute. Where was I?

>> **You went home . . .**

Yes . . . I went home . . . went back into the apartment. And as soon as I opened the door, I knew something was wrong.

>> **How did you know that?**

I don't know. It was something about the sound of the place, or maybe the smell. Something that said . . . a bad thing has happened here. I felt shaky. I went to the kitchen. To fix myself some tea. Steady myself.

>> **You didn't want to go find the body?**

Not yet. And there was a chance, a slim chance that Bev wasn't there. Maybe she had gulped her Trim Grain and run out for a milkshake. Maybe she collapsed in Baskin Robbins while some pimply-faced college kid watched her writhe on the linoleum.

>> **Nice Image.**

I used my Winnie-the-Pooh honey dipper to put some honey in my tea. I zapped the cup in the microwave. I liked my tea hot. I was scared.

>> **Who wouldn't be?**

The microwave beeped, and I took out my tea. I took a sweet sip, nearly burning my lips. The phone rang. A jarring sound. But I ignored it. The machine picked it up . . . but there was no message. Don't you hate that? When people call and leave no message.

>> **Sure. Detest it. When did you go look . . . ?**

It took a few minutes, but finally I was ready. I took a breath, and walked with my tea into the living room . . . and it was empty. Then I went into the bathroom. An obvious place, I thought. Especially if someone was feeling stomach pain. Head for the porcelain throne, try to puke the poison out.

>> **And the bathroom was—**

Empty. So . . . now it was time to check the bedroom. And I began to worry that maybe today, of all goddamn days, Bev had skipped her precious Trim Grain. It was damned unlikely . . . but anything could happen. I walked back to the bedroom.

>> **Yes.**

>> **Come back! Hey, friend, don't leave me hanging.**

>> **You there?**

Barely. Can hardly see straight. But might as well . . . try.

So, I went to the bedroom, and there she was, curled on the floor, still in her flannel nightgown with faded blue flowers and dotted with a zillion cotton nits that screamed "throw us the hell away."

>> **Nothing too sexy, eh?**

And there was a pool in front of her where she had thrown up. A bloody pool. Her eyes were wide open . . . I had to walk close to see that. I stepped over her body, and looked at her eyes. Whatever pain she had been feeling was right there. Easy to see that she had been feeling real bad before she died.

>> **And you called the police?**

No. That was my plan. Call the police. Tell them I came home to find her like this, and pray that the mushroom mixture was masked by the blood and fluids. But then I saw something . . . in the den . . . glowing.

>> **An angel of the Lord? Just kidding—**

The computer screen was *on*. I walked over to it. Bev had turned on the computer. For some reason she had been typing something. A message . . .

>> **And the message said—?**

But you must know what it said?

As soon as I saw it I knew how stupid I had been, how *completely* stupid. I stood in front of the screen, and felt my stomach go tight. Because the message said:

>> **Don't kill me!**

No. The message read:

"Paladin, my love.

I used *your* courage to become brave, to do what I wanted to do. By tonight, my husband will be dead. I put some of the same poison, my love, in his honey. Meet me soon in our regular chat room!

I love *you*.

Cynarra."

I looked at the screen. My tea was all gone. The tightening in my stomach didn't go away, it got worse. Until—like now—I can barely breathe.

It's funny. I logged on. To tell someone . . . and I stumbled into you. Another faceless person in ChatWorld. Another—

>> **Outstanding! Hey, this is an absolutely *outstanding* story, my man. You've *got* to publish this.**

>> **Hey, you still there Paladin? The log shows that you're still on-line, still in the room.**

>> **You reading this, Paladin? Believe me, this is a great story and you have to upload it to the archive.**

>> **Paladin?**

>> **Paladin???? Hey, hit the keys, guy!**

>> **Paladin . . . ? Well, if you aren't going to chat, I'll go find someone who will.**

>> **Sheesh. I'm outta here! :(**

Nightmover has left the chat room.
Attending Chat Room 13: 1
Welcome Paladin!

Fort Morgan Public Library
414 Main Street
Fort Morgan, CO
(970) 867-9456

Letter to the Editor

Morris Hershman

DEAR MR. HITCHCOCK:

I'M writing to you because I've heard of you and I want your advice about something. My friends say I ought to be a real writer, anyhow. I write letters very good.

What I figure, though, is that maybe you can tell me if I ought to be as scared as I am.

Like I say, this thing really happened. If you want to make a story out of it maybe I could collaborate with you on it. I've got the story; all you'd have to do is write it up.

Anyhow, this happened to me on Brighton Beach. In Coney Island, you know, in Brooklyn.

When I go out there I usually bring a blanket in a paper bag, unroll it on the sand, take off my pants and shirt and, with my bathing suit already on instead of shorts, try to catch me a little sun. I park myself near the peeling wooden sign that says Bay 2. A lot of people near my own age come out there, in the twenties and thirties. I can lie on the sand and look up at the boardwalk. Though it's plastered with signs saying that you need shirt and pants to go walking up there, that doesn't really matter.

It happened just this afternoon, the thing I want to tell you about. You know what it's been like in the city: 93 in the shade, people dropping like flies. Even on the beach today, the sand was like needles under your feet.

When I'd waited for half an hour and none of my friends showed up, I went into the water. Usually I walk in up to my ankles, then dive in to get the rest of me good and wet.

Well, I swam out past the first buoy. Like all the rest of them, it's red on top and with what looks like barnacles on the sides. All of a sudden I saw a guy coming almost head on into me. About twenty feet or so away I heard another man yell, "Sam!" and then there was the sound of bubbles.

The fellow had disappeared (the guy I'd been looking at call him number one so you won't get confused) and then he showed up above water with the crook of his arm on the other guy's neck, pulling him in. "This man's hurt!" he shouted.

I can scream pretty good, too. "Give 'em room!"

On the shore they tried artificial respiration. I went along to watch the hefty lifeguard in his white shirt, the victim's legs between his, jumping up and down like clockwork. I won't forget it as long as I live. How long that's going to be, maybe you can guess.

Anyway, this fellow who'd brought him in stood off to one side. He wore a bright-red rubber cap and a bathing suit with white stripes at the sides. He was a beanpole of a guy, the kind who probably never stops eating, though. His large brown eyes stared right past me.

"Poor guy, whoever he was," Beanpole said to anybody who'd listen. Then he stopped and pointed. "Look!"

I did, but all I saw was the usual beach scene: the kids selling ice cream or tin-bottomed paper cartons of orange drink or cans of cold chocolate, or cellophane bags with potato knishes inside. You can always recognize the sellers because they wear white sun helmets like in movies about big-game hunters in Africa.

At my left a guy wandered from girl to girl, trying to strike up a talk—"operating," it's called nowadays. A lot of acquaintances run into each other at Bay 2 because they've mostly been to the same summer places: White Roe, Banner Lodge, Tamiment, Lehman, whatever you like.

At one blanket, people gathered around a uke player who was picking out "Blue-Tail Fly." He stopped to tell a singer something about one of the downtown social clubs for older unmarried people. "I'm going down for a dance tonight at the change-of-life club," he said.

Then I saw what Beanpole had been pointing at. Two men, clearing a path for themselves, inched their way along the lines of blankets. Between them they carried what looked like a white gauze pad folded in two. It turned out to be a stretcher. They covered up the guy with a sheet over his face, so he couldn't even breathe.

"I guess they're taking him to the first-aid station," I said to a small blonde next to me, remembering the wooden shack on Bay 6 or 7 that looks like it was on stilts and with a spiral staircase that takes you up to the dispensary.

The blonde shook her head slowly. "No, it's the ambulance for him and then the morgue. I saw him earlier in the day. He was a very good swimmer."

At my side the Beanpole nodded. "He must'a gotten cramps or something. We were way out, past the fourth marker. Nobody in sight except . . ." And he turned to me like he'd just noticed I was there.

I introduced myself. He mumbled that he was glad to know me, but he didn't mention his name. His eyes were hard and bright.

"How much of it did you see?" he asked quietly.

"I saw you practically on top of him and trying to get a grip on him. You did a hero's job out there. Nothing to be ashamed of, believe me!"

I had made up my mind not to go in swimming today, and when my friends came around a little later, I told them what I'd seen and spent the afternoon lying in the sun.

Once I felt somebody's eyes on me. I looked up and there was Beanpole, not too far away. He was asking a girl the name of the book she was reading, but every so often he glanced in my direction. I lay back and closed my eyes and forgot it.

But when I was going home by way of the Brighton local, I started to ask myself questions. Once I remember I looked up at my reflection in a subway window glass; I might have been a skeleton.

Well, as soon as I got home to Snyder Avenue, where I live, I started writing this letter to you. I was supposed to take a shower and go down to a State of Israel bond rally at Twenty-third and Madison, but I don't think I will. Not tonight. For all I know, maybe I'll never go to a rally again in my life.

It's this way: the blonde girl at the beach told me that the dead guy was a good swimmer. If he'd been in trouble, well, any old hand at swimming knows enough to float around till he can save himself. I'd heard the victim calling "Sam!" before he went under, like Sam was right near; but Beanpole said he never knew the dead guy.

The idea I've got explains why Beanpole behaved like he did, the way he kept looking at me. I've been thinking hard, and now what I saw looks completely different. I had told Beanpole, "I saw you practically on top of him." The way I remember it now, Beanpole was holding the guy *under* water, not saving him. Beanpole kept him under water till it made no difference one way or the other.

But maybe I'm wrong. Maybe Beanpole is a right guy, after all. Maybe.

I figure it like this, though: I'm the only one who saw it happen, and he knows that.

Like I say, maybe I'm all wrong. Beanpole could have gotten so bollixed up trying to save the guy he went around afterward like he'd flipped his lid. He looked calm to me, but maybe some guys carry all their feelings inside them, like a guy does if he's worked up to kill somebody.

Well, that shows what you can think about in the morning. It's almost morning here, and I can look out the window and see dawn touch the rooftops across the street.

I guess I'm all wrong, crazy with the heat or whatever you'd call it.

But it'd be so easy for Beanpole to find me. After all, he knows my name and it's in the phone book. All he has to do is come in right now and shoot the top of my head off.

But even if he did the truth would come out. This letter alone is sure to do it. If I hear anybody coming, I'll stop writing and hide it as quick as I can. It'd be found by the police, afterward. I'm sure Beanpole's name and address were taken this afternoon, and plenty of people got a good look at him.

Anyhow, that's all of it, and like I said at the beginning I want your advice about whether I'm right to be as scared as I am. Should I go to the police and tell them all this?

To show you the way a guy can get nervous; just this minute I could have sworn I felt a draught on the back of my neck, like the door had been quietly opened by somebody, and

The Coveted Correspondence

(A Father Dowling Story)

Ralph McInerny

1

ATHER DOWLING THOUGHT THAT there were two major motives for an interest in genealogy: A person either wanted to contrast his current eminence with humble forebears or to wallow in the lost past grandeur of the family.

"Where does that leave Sally Murphy?" Marie Murkin asked.

"The Irish are different."

Marie humphed. "Don't tell me about the Irish. I married one."

Silence fell. Marie looked as if she regretted alluding to the long-since-departed Mr. Murkin, gone now into that bourne from which no traveler returns—at least word of his demise had never reached her—but simply gone, here one day and gone the next. It had turned Marie into a grass widow, prompted the beginning of her long career as housekeeper in Saint Hilary's rectory, a post that justified, if only in her own eyes, a freewheeling curiosity about the people of the parish. Sally Murphy had been reluctant to avail herself of the opportunities of the parish center where seniors gathered every day under the capable direction of Edna Hospers. Not that it was a regimented day. Edna simply created an atmosphere in which the elderly men and women could enjoy themselves. Sally had finally succumbed to Marie's urging, become a regular at the parish center, and apparently was soon boring others to death with stories of her uncle Anthony.

"Edna hasn't mentioned it," Father Dowling said carefully. He was not yet sure what Marie was up to.

"Oh, she wouldn't," Marie said with great conviction, and then added in an altered voice, "if she is even aware of it."

There was an ancient enmity between the housekeeper and Edna Hospers, nothing seriously disruptive, but an endless flow of ambiguous criticism from Marie and of impatience from Edna when Marie tried to make inroads into her fiefdom in what had once been the parish school.

"Someone has complained to you, Marie?"

"I am a victim myself."

"Tell me about it," the pastor said, closing his book. It was clear that Marie had some point that she would eventually make and there was no use in his kicking against the goad.

Sally Murphy was not a woman who, on the face of it, one would expect to draw attention to her family, either present or previous generations. Her brothers, after tumultuous teenage years, had joined the navy after a kind of either/or was presented to them by the judge, and had kept in sporadic touch with Sally over the years, postcards arriving from brigs and jails around the world. After dishonorable discharge from the navy, they had joined the merchant marine and continued their adventures. Meanwhile, Sally's parents, proprietors of a tavern that passed from being a respectable neighborhood watering hole to a somewhat unsavory dive, enjoyed their wares as much as they sold them, and ended up in perilous health that had taken them to fairly early deaths. Not, all in all, a background one would be inclined to celebrate. But Sally's claim to fame was oblique, her uncle Anthony on her mother's side.

"She insists that he was a famous writer."

"What was Mrs. Murphy's maiden name?"

"Fogarty, but he wrote under a pseudonym."

"Did she say what it was?"

Marie sighed, "I hesitated to prod her into more lying, but I did ask."

"Well?"

Marie closed her eyes, in search of the name. They snapped open. "Connor Tracy."

The pastor sat back, his eyebrows lifting.

"Have you heard of him, Father?"

"Oh yes."

Marie looked crestfallen but then she brightened up. "Of course she would pick a real writer to brag about. That doesn't make him her uncle."

THE REPUTATION OF F. Connor Tracy had known the usual literary ups and downs. As a young writer, his short stories had captivated readers of *The New Yorker*, the *Atlantic*, and *Partisan Review*. Only a Catholic could have written them, but their interest far transcended his coreligionists. Indeed, Catholics came to them later than the general reader. No Catholic college could claim him because no college could. When he came out of the service in 1945, discharged at Great Lakes, he had spent a few weeks with his parents in Aurora, sitting on the porch and looking at the Fox River move slowly southward. Acclimated once more to peace, he decided to set about doing what he had pondered doing while a marine. He wanted to be a writer. The GI Bill would have supported him at the college of his choice, but his ideal of the writer was a man of the people, who lived and worked as others did, and wrote besides. And so he had. He moved to Wisconsin and took a job with a county highway department and at night, in the room he rented in Baraboo, he wrote. Eventually he sent manuscripts to New York and they were invariably accepted. Later he would admit that since this is what he had aimed for, he had not been as surprised as he should have been. With success, he quit the highway crew and moved to Ireland where he could live cheaply and devote himself entirely to his writing. Alas, there his craft found the formidable rival of the local pub. The two decades left him were spent producing the fiction that would offset the tragedy of his life.

"He received the Last Sacraments," Sally said to Father Dowling when, having determined that her story about being related to the great writer was possibly true, he sought her out to talk about it.

"Thank God. How do you know?"

"The priest wrote to my mother."

"Ah."

"She put that letter with the others she had received from him."

"From Tracy?"

"From Tony, she would say. That was his name."

"Where did the pseudonym come from?"

"F. was for Fogarty. The others are family names as well."

"He has always been a favorite of mine."

Sally beamed in a proprietary way. "I must confess I've not read much of him myself, Father."

"What happened to the letters your mother received from him?"

"Oh, they came to me."

"You should be careful of them."

"Of course."

She mentioned them as well to the journalist who interviewed her, alerted by those who were moved by Father Dowling's acceptance of Sally's story. Katherine Reynolds, a local writer, was with Sally when she was interviewed.

"I know every story by heart," Katherine said.

She also knew a good deal more about the writer than Sally did, and her remarks formed the staple of the story in the *Fox River Tribune*, the title of which, nonetheless, was "Niece of Famous Writer Fox River Native." Sally's mention of the letters nearly derailed the interview. Katherine begged to be allowed to see them, to read them. "Just let me touch one," she said, breathlessly. The adverb was the journalist's but anyone who knew Katherine would have found it accurate.

"Did you see the story in the *Tribune?*" Father Dowling asked Marie Murkin.

"The three-car accident?"

"The interview with Sally Murphy."

"You'd think she'd written the stories."

"She has a right to be proud, Marie."

"And what is Katherine Reynolds's excuse?"

It seemed best to drop the subject. Marie apparently thought that Sally's sudden prominence diminished the housekeeper of Saint Hilary's. But he couldn't resist a little dig.

"They might want to do a story on your letters, Marie."

"What letters?"

"You must have kept those of your many suitors."

"I had one suitor and I married him and lived to regret it."

2

THE STORY PROMPTED Father Dowling to take a volume of Tracy's off his shelf. The novel, remembered as good, proved better than his memory suggested, and for the next week and a half the pastor of Saint Hilary's worked through the slim oeuvre of F. Connor Tracy. He read slowly, wanting to prolong the pleasure, if pleasure was the word. Tracy had a melancholy imagination which in the bogs and pubs of Ireland exuded a keening music that gripped the soul and made the heart heavy with an all but unbearable sorrow at the follies and failures of men. Phil Keegan on a visit picked up a volume, frowned at the jacket, opened it and read a line or two, then shut it and returned it to the table. Father Dowling introduced the inexhaustible topic of the Cubs to forestall any negative remark from Phil. It was not necessary for salvation to enjoy the fiction of Tracy but to denigrate it could not be considered morally neutral.

"Funny you should be reading him," Phil said, not rising to the bait of the Cubs.

"Rereading," Father Dowling said and then, because that sounded smug, added, "He was always a favorite."

"I hope his letters are worth something."

"His letters?"

"His niece had a collection of them he had written to her mother. They're missing."

"Tell me about it."

Sally Murphy had been enjoying the quasi celebrity the story about her uncle's letters had conferred upon her. She had begun to annoy others at the parish center because of the frequency with which she brought up the connection. There was nearly a fight when old Agnes Grady suggested that the writer had lost his faith and wrote only about degenerates.

"He writes about the Irish," Sally had protested.

Agnes nee Schwartzkopf just lifted an eyebrow. Sally demanded to know if Agnes had read anything of Tracy.

"I don't read that sort of thing."

"You don't read any sort of thing," Sally said hotly.

It was Katherine who soothed the troubled waters. "No one could read the letters he wrote Sally's mother without being transported."

She spoke with a calm authority that carried the day.

Katherine had attached herself to Sally, having received permission to read the letters in the Murphy home. Her suggestion that Sally keep them in a safe deposit box at her bank had not been taken up. Katherine had embarked on a campaign to edit the letters; something she offered to do gratis.

"It would be a privilege, Sally."

"But they're private letters."

Katherine explained to Sally that nothing was more common than to publish the letters of the great, particularly those of great writers. Sally did not think many breaches of decorum constituted a new moral code. Her lips became a line and she shook her head firmly at the renewed suggestion and finally Katherine had let it drop.

"It is selfish to want to keep such a treasure to oneself," Katherine told Edna Hospers, needing some outlet for her frustration and finding it in the sympathetic director of the parish center.

"Would there really be such interest?"

"Edna, any publisher would snap it up. As for the originals . . ."

"What do you mean?"

"Someone recently paid ten thousand dollars for an old pipe that had belonged to Tracy."

If a mere object elicited such a covetous reaction from collectors, what would dozens of letters written over an extended period of time and in the very hand of the great writer bring?

"Sally would never let them go."

"I don't think she should! But she has no idea of their value."

When he was told of the exchange, the pastor had been reminded of the chiding tone of guidebooks written by British authors, lamenting the way the natives failed to keep up the artifacts and buildings that brought tourists from afar. Why didn't the Italians restore all the churches in Rome? Since there was at least one church in every block, this would have proved a vast enterprise. So Katherine chided Sally for thinking of her uncle's letters to her mother as letters to her mother rather than as messages to the world at large.

When the letters were missing, there was no need to speculate on what had happened. Sally said it outright.

"Katherine has them, of course. I want them back. I don't care if you have to arrest her."

"How long have they been missing?"

On this Sally was vague. The last time she had definitely laid eyes on the correspondence had been a week before.

Katherine was not at home. She did not answer her phone and there seemed little point in leaving more messages on her answering machine. The police made inquiries but Katherine had left no trail. It was Edna's thought that Katherine had simply lost patience with Sally's intransigence and acted on her own.

"Taken them to a publisher?"

Edna nodded. "You had to hear the fervor with which she spoke."

Calling all possible publishers of literary correspondence would have been a formidable task, but Phil Keegan was prepared to undertake it. In order to give it focus, he got a court order to enter Katherine's house, hoping to find some indication of what she might have done with the letters. That is how the body of Katherine Reynolds was found.

3

PERHAPS IF SHE had been found earlier, Katherine would have been thought to be asleep or unconscious. The blow that freed her from this

Vale of Tears had left no visible mark, and only a close examination by the coroner revealed the lesion on her head. She had been struck from behind and fallen forward onto a sofa, this breaking her fall, and then apparently rolled gently to the floor. Her still open but unseeing eyes prompted Edna, who had accompanied Cy Horvath, to speak to Katherine as if she could hear. And then the stillness and strangeness brought a gasp before Edna cried out. Cy had already seen the body and its condition and was on the phone to Dr. Pippen.

Given the reason for the court order, Cy, unable to do anything for Katherine and Edna having been taken away, began the search for the letters. Letters he found, but only of the kind that any household would contain—bills, junk mail—until he came upon half a dozen replies from publishers in response to the inquiry Katherine had indeed presumed to make. All but one of the publishers was interested. Indeed, on Katherine's answering machine were several messages from publishers who had not wanted to trust what was now somewhat disdainfully referred to as snail mail.

"Did you find a copy of the letter she sent, Cy?" Phil Keegan wanted to know.

"No."

"I suppose we can ask one of these publishers for a copy."

"Why?"

"It should tell us whether she had the letters in her possession."

Cy had an impassive Hungarian countenance and it would have been difficult to know what his reaction was. Agnes Lamb who had returned from guiding Edna to solace and sanctuary wrinkled her nose as Keegan spoke.

"Those answers tell the story, don't they? That and the fact that she is dead."

"Maybe."

Maybe not, however. The search for the letters suggested that someone else had been searching the house, perhaps in quest of the letters.

"They must have found them," Agnes said.

"Maybe."

"That would explain their not being here," Agnes explained patiently.

"If they were here in the first place."

Agnes started to laugh and then stopped, not wanting to be amused all by herself. Neither Phil Keegan nor Cy Horvath seemed to think the captain's agnosticism was misplaced.

"We are going to proceed on the assumption that she was killed for some letters she didn't have?"

"We are not going to proceed on the assumption that she had the letters."

"That's the same thing."

The silence suggested that she had been guilty of a solecism.

WHEN PHIL STOPPED by that night, he brought Father Dowling up to speed on the investigation. This did not take long, since all the results were negative. It was not certain that the one who had murdered Katherine had got what he had come for, if he had indeed come for the letters.

"Was anything else missing?"

"Nothing obvious. But we don't have an inventory so it is difficult to say. He was a very neat thief, and murderer."

"He?"

"Inclusive. We don't really know that either."

Several publishers had been contacted and one had faxed a copy of the letter received from Katherine. It was an enigmatic epistle.

I am writing to ask if you would be interested in publishing a collection of some forty-seven letters written by F. Connor Tracy to his sister over a span of some twenty years, all of them after he had settled in Ireland. My preliminary study of the letters suggests that they have great importance, both biographical and literary. In some of the letters, he begins sober and ends drunk, traceable not only by the handwriting but also by the repetitiveness, but all in all they have an elegiac quality that admirers of his work will recognize as his peculiar voice. On the other hand, some of his reminiscences of childhood strike a whimsical even nostalgic note not normally associated with his outlook.

"What do you think, Roger?"

"That she was a bit presumptuous. I gather that Sally had not authorized such an inquiry."

"Does the letter suggest to you that she had taken the letters?"

In one sense, it emerged, she had. A school notebook was found in her bedroom in which were transcribed more than a dozen of the letters. Apparently Katherine had taken advantage of the time Sally had allowed her with the letters to copy them.

"She asked if she could take notes," Sally said. "I didn't dream she would copy them out word for word."

It was clear that Sally was not yet fully convinced of the intrinsic value of her uncle's letters. She had accepted the publicity and had herself exploited them, but apparently expecting that at any moment someone would question their importance.

"She was right about publishers being interested in the letters."

"What good does that do me now?"

"You're sure the letters are missing?"

"Of course I'm sure."

Father Dowling looked at Edna but she avoided his eyes. This was a delicate matter, but he had promised Phil Keegan he would try.

"It occurs to me, Sally, that if Katherine put the letters away in a different place . . ."

"She did that all right. In her own house." But Sally's expression softened. "God rest her soul. Imagine getting killed over some old letters."

"That's my point, Sally," Father Dowling said.

Sally looked at him blankly.

"Sally, if I can imagine the letters are still here, someone else can, too. Perhaps the same person who killed Katherine."

"But he has the letters now."

"But what if Katherine never took them? What if they are still here, in this house, and the killer comes to the same conclusion . . ."

Sally's hand went to her throat and she moved closer to Edna on the couch.

"Why don't you and Edna conduct a thorough search?"

Sally's reluctance was gone, indeed she was eager to turn the house inside out to see if the letters were there, even while professing that she didn't believe for a minute that they were.

If they were, they were not found by Edna and Sally.

"It was a long shot," Phil said, shrugging. "Chances are the killer got the letters."

"You sound surer now."

"Well, if Edna Hospers couldn't find them I doubt they are in Sally's house."

"I don't suppose a thief would be stupid enough to try to sell them immediately."

"How would he go about selling items like that?"

Roger put Phil Keegan onto Casper Barth the rare book dealer. Meanwhile there was Katherine's funeral to preside over.

McDivitt pulled Father Dowling into his office when the priest arrived at the funeral home for the rosary that night at 7:00.

"Am I early?"

"There are half a dozen people," McDivitt said in hushed tones. "I could understand it if the weather was bad."

"We'll start fifteen minutes late."

This calmed the funeral director. He offered Father Dowling a little something, knowing it would be refused. He himself poured a dollop and tossed it off. When he put the bottle back into a drawer of his desk he chuckled. He drew out a card and held it up for the priest to see. *Let McDivitt replace your last divot.*

"I hope you don't plan to use that."

"Good Lord, no. I was given it at our last convention. Undertakers have a strange sense of humor, Father Dowling."

"I wasn't aware they had any at all."

"You'd be surprised."

"I am."

At 7:15 they went into the viewing room. There were a dozen people there now, all wearing the expression one saves for wakes and funerals. Most of those there were regulars at the parish center. Sally's absence seemed conspicuous, and Father Dowling thought less of her for it. Whatever Katherine may or may not have done, she was dead now, cruelly murdered. Sally might have chosen to be flattered by Katherine's interest in her famous uncle, but she seemed to resent it. Father Dowling nodded to the mourners and then took his position on the prie-dieu set up beside the open casket and began the rosary.

Repetitive prayer is conducive either to meditation or distraction and Father Dowling found his mind straying. What was it Hamlet's uncle had said? "My words fly up, my thoughts remain below, words without thoughts never to heaven go." Of course it was another distraction to remember that. He put his mind to concentrating on the mystery being commemorated by the decade they were reciting. When he finished he felt that he had been engaged in physical labor. It occurred to him that Katherine looked serene and peaceful lying there. He might have mentioned this to McDivitt but it would have seemed lugubrious.

Others had come in while the rosary was being said and Father Dowling was delighted to see that Sally was one of them. She was speaking with a man Father Dowling did not know. Phil Keegan had brought Marie Murkin with him.

"Katherine's beau," Marie said of the unknown man.

"I hope you locked the rectory doors, Marie."

She narrowed her eyes. "The answering service is on."

This was a device that Marie abominated, particularly when she was on the receiving end of someone's recorded message. Those who reached the rectory heard only "Saint Hilary's," a beep and silence. It was Marie's theory that everyone now knew enough to speak after the beep. "If they haven't hung up, that is."

Hanging up was what Marie did when, after enduring many rings, she was answered by a taped message made God knows how long ago.

That remark seemed oddly apropos when Phil Keegan asked Father Dowling to listen to the tape that had been taken from Katherine's answering machine. Her cheerful message, addressed to the world at large, brightly inviting the caller to leave a message long or short after the beep, was a voice from beyond the grave. The microcassette was all but full with messages going back nearly a year.

"Who is Hughes, Roger?"

There were several messages from him, usually saying that he would arrive at such and such a time at O'Hare. Hughes was the name that had been given for the man Marie had called Katherine's beau. It had been the pastor's understanding and, he learned, that of Edna as well, that Katherine was single and seemed to have no inclination to change her marital status at her age. She had been forty-seven when she died. The messages from Hughes began two months before.

Hughes had been at the funeral but Father Dowling did not have an opportunity to speak to him.

"I did," Marie said when he lamented this.

"Ah."

Silence. She wanted him to ask what she had learned. He knew she was incapable of not telling him. All he had to do was wait. Marie's willpower had strengthened in the hard school of the rectory under Father Dowling's teasing regime, and it was more than an hour later that she came into the study and began to talk before she had taken a chair.

"He is from Indianapolis. He was almost the exact age of Katherine. Her little book on Tracy came to his attention and he got in contact with her."

"And visited her?"

"Who knows what might not have happened if Katherine had lived." Marie's sigh seemed freighted with the mystery of things.

"Did he go back to Indianapolis?"

"He has to work."

"At what?"

"The main thing is whatever he felt for Katherine has been cruelly crushed."

"Didn't you ask him what kind of work he does?"

"What difference does it make?"

"Probably none."

"Probably."

4

THE WILD-HAIRED young man in the corduroy jacket chose not to waste his sweetness on the desert air of Fox River. Instead he poured out his story to a reporter from the *Chicago Tribune* who, once she had acquainted herself with recent events in Fox River and received assurance from the book review editor that F. Connor Tracy was indeed a major writer, pulled out all the stops. The natural son of the famous writer had come to the area to visit the ancestral spots of his deceased father. There were anecdotes of his father, vignettes of his childhood, a vow to make good his claim to be the heir of the literary property of his father.

His putative cousin was shocked. "My uncle never married and never had any children. Period."

This was the sole quotation from Sally Murphy in the story, but she had no sooner put down the phone than she called Tuttle the lawyer, demanding that he put a stop to this desecration of the memory of her uncle. Tuttle assured her that he would treat it with the same vigor he would treat an attack on his dear departed father.

"It's those letters that are causing all this," Sally said when she went to Tuttle's office.

"The letters." Tuttle scratched the tip of his nose with the wrong end of a ballpoint pen, creating what looked like blue veins.

"You must have read about them."

"I want it in your own words."

There was the distinct sound of snoring from the lawyer's inner office. He rose, kicked the door, and shouted, "Peanuts."

Sally half expected a vendor to appear and supply Tuttle with a package of peanuts. But the snoring stopped.

"My associate," Tuttle murmured. "Go on."

He paid close attention to her narrative but his spirits sank as he did so. Letters from a drunken brother in Ireland? She called him a writer but he was certainly nobody famous like Elmore Leonard or Louis L'Amour. But Tuttle perked up when she unfolded the story from the *Chicago Tribune*. He hadn't read a paragraph before he tipped back his hat and said, "Libel. We'll sue for libel."

"He's just a boy. He has nothing."

"I mean the paper."

"Oh."

Here was an opportunity Tuttle could warm to. He would be David, the *Tribune* would be Goliath, the outcome had a biblical inevitability.

"I want the letters back, too."

"Your cousin take those, do you suppose?"

"Don't call him that."

"Did he?"

"I don't think he was even in the country when they were taken. I gather he just got off the boat."

"Boat?"

"Just arrived."

Tuttle's loyalties wavered as he imagined a young man newly arrived from a foreign land being pounced upon by a huge metropolitan newspaper and then by relatives he had never before seen. If only Sean had come to him before Sally Murphy had . . . But Sally's connecting of the death of Katherine Reynolds with what she was saying brought home to Tuttle that the job being offered him might have all sorts of possibilities.

"You think she was killed for the letters?"

"I'm lucky I wasn't."

"They must be pretty valuable."

"Or life is held pretty cheap."

"That too."

After she left, Tuttle roused Peanuts Pianone and over shrimp fried rice at the Great Wall pumped his old friend about the status of the police investigation.

"I'm not assigned to that."

"What have you heard about it?"

Peanuts dipped his head, now to the right, now to the left, raising his eyebrows as he did. But that was it. Tuttle doubted that Peanuts had even heard of Katherine's murder. His career as a policeman consisted in putting in time until he was eligible for a pension. His family connections gave him tenure and the department preferred that he remain uninvolved in police work.

"Why do you want to retire?" Tuttle asked. Millions would kill to get Peanuts's situation; it was better than retirement.

"Stress."

Tuttle went around to Saint Hilary's to have a chat with Father Dowling. The pastor was thick as thieves with Phil Keegan. Marie Murkin told him the pastor was busy. "This will only take a minute," Tuttle said, brushing past her and heading for the study. The housekeeper was clinging to his arm when he stopped in the open doorway.

"You make an impressive couple," the pastor said, and Tuttle felt the grip on his arm go. There was a young man seated in an easy chair, holding a bottle of beer, grinning at the new arrivals.

"Sean, this is Tuttle the lawyer."

"I've already met Marie," the young man said, half rising and extending a very large hand.

"The writer's boy," Tuttle said, recognizing the young man from the *Tribune* article. The boy beamed.

"How do you know that?"

"You're famous. I am your cousin Sally's lawyer."

"She denies the connection."

"There wasn't much about your mother in the article."

Father Dowling broke in. "Tuttle, I can see that you have much to talk about with my young visitor. Sean, come back tomorrow for lunch. It's just after the noon mass. Come for that if you like."

A noncommittal nod.

"You sure you don't want to spend the night here?"

"The *Tribune* is footing my bill at the hotel."

Tuttle was on his feet. "We will leave you to your devotions, Father Dowling. Young Sean and I will go somewhere for a beer."

"This stuff is like water," Sean observed, then apologized to his host.

"It is not Guinness, I grant you."

"You want Guinness, we'll have Guinness," Tuttle promised.

The pastor showed them out, the housekeeper seemingly having disappeared. Tuttle got Sean into the passenger seat and then set off for the hotel at all deliberate speed. There they could charge everything to the boy's room and be in effect the guests of the *Tribune*.

The luxury of the modest hotel seemed sybaritic to Sean and Tuttle himself was far from immune to its charms, the chief of which was watching the young Irishman scrawl his name on the bills as they came.

"It's a lot better than where I stayed at first."

"Before you called the reporter?"

But Sean waved the topic away. Some minutes later, Peanuts arrived. Tuttle did not think it seemly to keep Peanuts from this bonanza.

"If only they served Chinese food."

"You'll complain in heaven," Tuttle chided.

"Not if there's fried rice."

The human mind is a wondrous thing. That night Tuttle awakened from a just and well-fed sleep to find that of all the badinage of
the evening, what had stuck in his mind was young Sean's mention
of a period prior to calling the reporter. The newspaper story had the
reporter meeting Sean as he flew in on Aer Lingus. It was the kind
of detail that interested the police. Tuttle was not surprised when he
learned, later that day, that Keegan and Horvath had taken young
Sean downtown for questioning.

5

MARIE MURKIN GREETED Phil Keegan coldly and let him find his own
way to the study. Nor did she offer him refreshments.

"What's wrong with her, Roger?"

"Sean."

"Ah."

The newspaper accounts of the arrest were decidedly unfriendly to
the police. The suggestion was that in desperation they had decided
to frame a young immigrant. The fact that neighbors of Katherine's
would testify that they saw the young man in the neighborhood prior
to the killing did little to right the balance. Nor had Sally's belated
statement that Sean had come to her door and she had turned him
away as soon as she saw what he was up to.

"Besmirching my uncle's reputation," she scoffed. "I was having
none of that."

The fact that Sean did not have the missing letters was regarded by the prosecutor, if not the third estate, as an exonerating factor. Perhaps he would not have resorted to violence if he had come
into possession of the letters themselves. So went the theory, but the
theory was soon exploded by Tuttle's discovery.

The little lawyer came to Father Dowling in a moral quandary. He
had come upon information injurious to his client but as an officer of
the court he could not withhold evidence.

"Evidence of what?"

"Father, he had the letters. The missing letters. He had checked a bag with the porter of his hotel and he asked me to pick it up and keep it for him."

"And the letters were in the bag."

Tuttle nodded. "They'll hang him, Father."

Even if he told Tuttle he could conceal the letters, he knew the lawyer would not believe him.

"Let me talk to Sean first."

The young fellow sauntered into the visiting room and plopped into a chair across from Father Dowling.

"Well, I must be a goner if they're sending me a priest."

"Would you like to talk as penitent to priest?"

"I didn't kill that woman, Father."

"But you had the letters."

He slapped his forehead. "Has he told the police?"

"He won't be able to keep them a secret from the police, Sean."

"You know, Father, I never got the chance to sit down and read them. That's all I wanted, to see what my father had written when I was this age or that. Had he never so much as alluded to my existence in writing to his sister? It's in a parish record out in Sligo. I've seen it myself. Maureen Shanahan, son; father Anthony Fogarty. That's his real name."

"You have some claim to the letters then."

"I don't want them. Not now. I wanted Tuttle to give them back to Sally Murphy."

"So you took the letters from Katherine?"

"I went there, yes, The door was open and I called and went in, the way we do in Ireland, and there she was, lying on the floor. I thought she was asleep. Truth is, I thought she might be drunk. I knelt down next to her. That's how I discovered the letters. She had hidden them under the couch. I took them—borrowed them really. I never meant to keep them."

It was all too easy to imagine what Phil Keegan and Cy Horvath and the others would make of this alibi. The letters would equivalently hang him, as Tuttle had said, but of course there was an embargo on the death penalty in Illinois.

"THAT BOY WOULDN'T hurt a fly," Marie Murkin declared, filling the pastor's coffee cup. Sun illuminated the dining room curtains and became polychrome in the prismed edge of the mirror over the sideboard.

"Perhaps he thought he wasn't. It was an unlucky blow."

"I believe his story."

"It's too bad you won't be on the jury."

Sean's story that he had entered the house of a woman just murdered and had taken the letters he happened to discover when he knelt beside the woman to see if she was asleep was not a logical impossibility, but it did not rank high on the scale of plausibility. Of course his story explained why he had been seen in the neighborhood, and why he was in possession of the letters, for that matter, but his instructions to Tuttle suggested someone with much to hide.

"I have a professional obligation to believe him," Tuttle said, not a ringing endorsement.

"What can I say?" Sally Murphy said. "It all comes from his telling that preposterous story."

But it was not a preposterous story. Monsignor Hogan in the chancery had connections in Sligo and had provided Father Dowling with a photocopy of the parish record in which the name of Anthony Fogarty, American, was given as father of the child Sean. The mother had gone to God due to complications in a later out-of-wedlock pregnancy. Sally held the photocopy at arm's length, wrinkling her nose as she studied it.

"What's to prevent any man's name being used on such an occasion?"

"I doubt that the priest would be party to something like that, Sally."

If Sally did not share his doubt she would not of course say so, not to his face, but Father Dowling could see that she was indeed convinced. Whatever her distaste, the young man from Ireland was her uncle's son and thus her cousin. But even her distaste had lessened. A shocking claim, repeated, loses its shock value, and the fact of the matter was that few others seemed to react as Sally had. Of course the godless newspapers took it as gospel that a country like Ireland must be rife with hypocrisy. If the country would only join the modern world, Sean's mother would have gotten an abortion and that would have been the end of it. Not that they said that, of course. Sally did not expect consistency from the devil's disciples.

"I almost wish I could believe his story, Father."

Such sympathy, and it was widespread, would not keep Sean from being tried for the murder of Katherine Reynolds. Even if he had not meant to kill her, he had entered her house as a thief and had struck her down when she confronted him.

"Of course if his story is true, someone else must have killed Katherine."

6

LATER, EYES CLOSED, tipped back in his chair, drawing on an aromatic pipeful of tobacco, it occurred to Father Dowling that in one sense there were many possible suspects. There were the publishers to whom Katherine had written, any one of whom would have seen the value of her literary trove. But they were far away, and it would have taken a dark view of publishers to imagine them flying to Fox River to burgle and kill, even for some very valuable letters. Acquired in that way, they could only be possessed, enjoyed; they would bring nothing further unless the owner revealed that he had stolen property. The unlikelihood of this did not stop Father Dowling from asking to see that correspondence with the publishers that Katherine had inaugurated.

TUTTLE'S INVITATION TO sit at the defendant's table, gently refused at first, became a week later less off-putting. Marie was appalled.

"It puts you on his side."

"A murderer's side?"

"That's the whole point of the trial."

"What kind of a world would it be if priests avoided murderers?"

Marie was certain there was a logical flaw involved here but she did not have time to point it out. Of course she was right. Sitting at the defense table would be a public act, suggesting he was less concerned with mercy for the wrongdoer than that he be found innocent of a crime. But a series of phone calls to Indianapolis had so clouded things that Father Dowling told Tuttle he was prepared to accept the invitation.

"Better late than never."

"Things are going bad?"

Tuttle drew a finger across his neck while emitting a chilling sound.

From his vantage point at the front of the courtroom, Father Dowling had a good view of the little balcony from which a dozen spectators looked down over a large clock at the proceedings. Brendan Hughes was a most attentive observer in the front row, his arms on the railing, his chin on his folded arms. The note Tuttle passed him while a neighbor of Katherine's was on the stand identifying Sean as the man she had seen lurking in the neighborhood the day the murder had occurred had an address on it. An airport hotel. Hughes was waiting for him in the lobby.

"I think you're expecting me," Father Dowling said, as Hughes rose eagerly at the mention of his name.

"He said you'd be wearing a collar. I saw you in court."

"I understand you teach English."

"Celtic literature. F. Connor Tracy is a favorite of mine."

"Could you identify his handwriting?"

"Yes."

Father Dowling withdrew from his pocket one of the letters that had been recovered from Sean. Hughes's eyes brightened at the sight of the envelope.

"This is an authentic letter from the writer." He took another envelope from his pocket. "But I want you to look at this one first."

Hughes took the second envelope impatiently. It was not sealed and he soon had the single sheet of paper in his hands. His eyes glided over it and then he looked at Father Dowling. "This is a fake."

"And this one?"

Hughes's reaction to the other letter was completely different. He nodded, he smiled, he held the pages as if they were sacred. "This is one of the letters. No doubt about it."

"I wish I could say that you have been a great help to the guilty party."

"What will they do with him?"

"I'm not a lawyer."

"You really do look like a priest."

Hughes in turn really looked like a professor. He was a learned man, and a delightful conversationalist. But Father Dowling did not discover this on that first occasion. The fingerprints on the bogus letter matched those found in Katherine's house, a fact determined within an hour after Father Dowling turned it over to Phil Keegan. Much later that night, Phil came by the rectory.

"He admitted it, Roger. Cool as could be. I had to stop him and tell him to get a lawyer."

Katherine had shown Hughes some of the letters on a previous occasion, she had shown him her transcriptions of others. His desire to have them became overpowering. The combination of the letters and Hughes's amorous attentions were more than Katherine could resist. She agreed to take the letters.

"In fairness, Father, she had no idea I meant to steal them. She thought we were merely cutting a corner for the good of literature. Those letters belonged in the public domain. When she realized what I intended, she objected. She snatched at the letter she had shown me and I pushed her away. I had no intention to harm her. Or to let the young man go to prison. I was agonizing over what to do if he were found guilty."

"You are lucky to have Amos Cadbury as your lawyer, Brendan."

"What will happen to the letters?"

Sean and his cousin Sally entered into an agreement with a publisher to bring out an edition of the letters. The obvious editor would have been Brendan Hughes, but that of course was out of the question.

"And the originals?" Father Dowling asked the cousins.

Sean beamed. "They will go to the Notre Dame library, Father."

"That's very generous of you, Sally."

"Oh, they'll pay for them."

And there were other mementos and papers that the two of them could make available to the world of letters with adequate compensation to themselves. Tuttle in turn would actually collect a fee for his successful defense of his client.

"Peanuts wants a leave as a reward for tracking down where Hughes was staying." Phil said this in a neutral voice.

"Will he get it?"

"Roger, he's been on leave ever since he joined the department."

A Nice Cup of Tea

Kate Kingsbury

SAM WILSON WAS AS regular as high tide. I reckon there wasn't a man in Rainbow Bay who couldn't set his watch by him. Every morning, just five minutes after Maisie put the kettle on the stove, we would see Sam come whistling up the path with the mail. That's why, when he didn't appear at the usual time last Wednesday, Maisie just about had kittens.

Maisie is my older sister. We don't look much alike. She is thinner than I am, and taller. Her hair is iron gray while mine is milk white. We both wear glasses, but I still have all my teeth and I smile more than Maisie does.

We don't get out much anymore. Maisie doesn't see too well, and the damp gets into our bones and triggers our arthritis. That's the trouble with living close to the ocean. Not that I mind all that much. I never was one for socializing, even when my Harry was alive.

Maisie's looked out for me ever since our parents died in an avalanche when I was only eleven. Maisie used to be a schoolteacher until she retired several years ago. She taught biology to fifth graders— a waste of time, if you ask me.

The only thing those kids are interested in nowadays is how to attract the opposite sex, and what to do with them when they succeed. They don't need biology lessons to find that out.

Maisie never married. She used to say there wasn't a man on earth good enough to make her give up her freedom. Personally, I think she frightened the men off. Those who were brave enough to get close to her, that is.

Maisie made a great teacher, but she doesn't know much about being a woman. She liked to take charge, and you either do things her way or not at all. Most men don't like that. At least, my Harry didn't. He always said that marriage should be a partnership. Though I always let him think he was the boss.

Maisie made a big fuss when I told her I was getting married. She was afraid that Harry wouldn't take care of me as well as she had. But then she didn't know my Harry the way I knew him.

When he died a year ago last November, Maisie came to live with me. I think she'd been waiting forty-eight years for that moment. That's how long Harry and I were together. I miss him a lot.

Maisie's highlight of the day is when the mail arrives. I don't know what she expects to find in there. More often than not we get nothing more than some fool advertising circular trying to sell us magazines we don't want, insurance we don't need, or storm windows we can't afford.

It doesn't matter to Maisie. She treats every piece as if it's a letter from the President himself. At least, she did so until last Wednesday.

Life in our little town can be pretty dull, especially in the winter. There's only one main street, and no big stores like the ones in Deerport a couple of miles up the road.

Visitors tend to stay away from the beach when the cold, wet wind comes roaring in from the Pacific Ocean. They call it Rainbow Bay because if you stand on Satan's Point between the twisted pines and look west, straight out to sea, you can nearly always see a rainbow. I always wish on a rainbow. At least, I used to. I don't go up there anymore. It's not much fun without Harry.

Maisie isn't impressed by rainbows.

In fact, there isn't much that excites Maisie. She spends most of her time in the backyard when the weather's good. I must admit, the garden has never looked better. Except for the yew.

Maisie has always wanted to live in England. She visited there once. Now she drinks tea out of English bone china cups and keeps a curio crammed full of English figurines. She even has a picture of Queen Elizabeth over her bed.

One day she decided we needed English topiaries in the backyard. She took a pair of shears to the yew and hacked at it for hours. She said she was forming peacocks, but by the time she was done, the hedge looked as if it had been attacked by a giraffe with hiccups.

Sam said he liked it, though. I think that was when Maisie decided she liked him. Sam was one of the few mailmen I've met who truly believed in the carrier's code. You know . . . through wind and rain, and whatever else the Good Lord chose to put in his path.

Mind you, Sam was no youngster. His face was as wrinkled as a boiled handkerchief, he had no hair to speak of, and sometimes I wondered how he had the strength to ride that bike of his in the teeth of a nor'easter.

But his smile could warm your heart on a cold day, and the twinkle in his eye could make a woman feel like Miss America. He was quite a ladies' man, our Sam.

Maisie always had a cup of tea ready for him, every morning except for Sunday. Sam loved Maisie's tea. "A cup of your tea can keep me going for the rest of the day," he told her. "Never tasted tea like it. You should sell it. You'd be a wealthy woman in no time."

But Maisie isn't much of a businesswoman. She prefers to give the stuff away. She packages it in hand-sewn pink silk bags and gives it to people for birthdays and Christmas. I reckon just about everyone in Rainbow Bay has tasted Maisie's tea at one time or another.

It was raining last Wednesday, and blowing up for a winter storm. I could see the cedars at the edge of our yard fanning the rhododendrons. Sam would need a hot cup of tea, I thought as I watched the big, sooty clouds roll across the sky.

But the tea grew cold and bitter while we waited for him.

"He must be ill, Annie," Maisie said. "He's never this late." She kept getting up and going to the window, until she made me feel dizzy. "The tea will be too strong," she said. "I'll have to take it off the stove."

"Well, pour it out," I told her. "We don't have to wait for him."

She looked at me as if I'd suggested she walk down Main Street naked. "We always wait for him," she said, "and we'll wait for him today."

Maisie makes the best tea in the world. She dries and blends her own, from the leaves of herbs and flowers, and every one of them tastes different. I look forward to my tea and muffins in the mornings. I didn't want to miss out on them just because the mailman happened to be late.

"But if he doesn't come, we won't get to drink the tea ourselves," I said. I was getting a little annoyed at her. Not that it did any good. Once Maisie has made up her mind, the Good Lord Himself wouldn't be able to budge her. I resigned myself to waiting for Sam.

He was getting ready to retire from the post office. He was due for a nice pension, and the mortgage on his house was all paid up. He told us about it, the last time we saw him.

"All I need now is to find a woman willing to cook and clean for me," he said, with a sly wink at Maisie, "and I'll be all set. I reckon it's time. It's been lonely since Ellen died last year, and it'll be lonelier still when I don't get to bring the mail to all my charming ladies."

He'd been talking about "finding a new woman" for weeks, but when he said it that last morning, Maisie got more fidgety than I ever saw her before.

I wondered if she was thinking about Louise Daniels. Louise is a member of our gardening club, and quite the chatterbox. She used to be pretty at one time, until the years caught up with her. She wears a lot of makeup and stinks the room out with her perfume. She dyes her hair a horrible red. It's been permed so much you can see patches of scalp in the frizzy mess.

Louise lives by herself in a room over the beauty shop on Main Street, and I think she's pretty lonely. She's always talking to the members of the garden club about Sam, telling us what he said to her and what she said to him. It's mostly the same things Sam said to the rest of us, but we let her go on thinking she's the only one he paid attention to. I guess, deep down, we all feel sorry for her.

Maisie doesn't like Louise. But then Maisie doesn't like a lot of people.

I have to admit, I looked forward to Sam's visits, too. Sam knew everything there was to know about everybody. He was the first one in town to know that Eleanor Madison was expecting a baby in the spring (except Eleanor and the doctor, of course), when we'd all gone to her wedding just before Thanksgiving.

I remember when he told us about that. I thought Maisie was going to swallow her dentures. She was almost as shocked as she was the time Sam told us that the mayor was in trouble with the IRS for evasion of taxes. Or that Beatrice Harrington's son had been expelled from college. I think Sam knew about that before Beatrice did.

Anyway, when Sam didn't come last Wednesday, Maisie kept insisting that he must be ill. She wanted me to make him some chicken soup.

"Call the post office, Annie," she said. "Ask if he came in this morning. Perhaps the mail is late arriving and he's waiting for it." Maisie doesn't like talking on the phone. She says she likes to see people's faces when she talks to them. That's the only way she can tell what they're really thinking.

Well, I called Pauline, the head clerk at the post office. What she told me shocked me speechless. Poor Sam had died.

She'd heard that it was a heart attack, Pauline said. He was alone in the house and died sometime during the night.

I hung up the phone and stood there for a minute, trying to get my heart to believe what my ears had heard. Sam . . . dead. We'd never see him again. Never hear his cheerful whistle or feel warmed by his compliments again. It was a great loss, and I don't think I fully realized just how devastating a loss until that moment.

"What's the matter?" Maisie demanded, in the kind of voice she must have used on her more unruly students.

It was then I realized I was crying. "It's Sam," I said, hunting for a tissue in the pocket of my sweater. "He died of a heart attack last night."

Well, I thought Maisie was going to drop dead herself. Her face went this dreadful gray and she grabbed ahold of the table to steady herself. "Sam? Heart attack?"

She said it so faintly, I barely heard her. Seeing her look so awful like that made me forget my own misery for the moment. I hurried over to her and made her sit down in her chair. Her hands were as cold as an Arctic wind, and her expression reminded me of the time we'd seen Father Jamison's pet poodle run over by a tractor.

I'd never seen such a terrible look on a man's face as I saw that day when the priest carried that pitiful, broken body to his car. The memory of it haunted me for weeks. It was that kind of look I saw on Maisie's face when I told her about Sam.

"We'd better have that tea now," I said, rubbing her hands. "It will make you feel better."

Maisie jumped out of that chair as if she'd been stung by a yellow jacket. "I don't want any tea," she said, and her voice sounded as if she were choking. "I'll never touch another cup of tea as long as I live!"

She rushed out of the living room and I heard her bedroom door slam. It got awful quiet after that. I thought I heard her crying, but when I crept down the hallway to listen, she must have heard the floorboards creak. I couldn't hear any sound at all from that room.

It was two days later that I heard the news. Sam hadn't died of a heart attack, after all. He'd died of food poisoning. Betsy Mae told me, when I went into the bank to deposit the pension checks.

Betsy Mae loves to gossip. She has sharp eyes that never miss a thing. Her hair is blonde, except for the roots, and she wears teenager clothes. She hasn't been a teenager for at least twenty-five years.

"Poor old devil," Betsy Mae said that day. "He must have kept something too long in the fridge. Chicken, I shouldn't wonder. They say it's the worst thing to hang on to. That's the trouble with men living all alone. Don't know how to take care of themselves. Not like us women, that's for sure."

I didn't really want to talk about Sam. My voice didn't hold up too well whenever someone mentioned his name. And it seemed as if everywhere I went, people were talking about him.

"Mind you," Betsy Mae said, looking at the pension checks as if she'd never seen one before, "I don't reckon he would have been alone that long. I heard that he and Louise Daniels were getting very friendly, if you catch my drift. Too bad he waited so long to make up his mind about her. He might have been alive today."

She scribbled something on the deposit slips and held them out to me. "Just goes to show, you have to live for the moment. That's what I always say."

I took the deposit slips from her and tucked them inside my purse. I said good-bye and started to leave, but Betsy Mae was in a talkative mood, as usual.

"How's Maisie doing?" she asked. "I saw her in the post office the other day and she said her arthritis was playing her up."

I looked at Betsy Mae, wondering if I'd heard her right. "You saw Maisie?"

"Yes, and she told me she was mailing a package of tea to Louise Daniels for her birthday." Betsy Mae leaned over the counter as if she didn't want anyone else to hear what she said. I thought that a bit strange, because I was the only customer in there at the time.

"To tell you the truth," she said quietly, "I remember thinking she hadn't done a very good job of wrapping the gift up. It was in a paper bag tied around with string. No tape on it or anything."

That didn't surprise me. Maisie never could wrap up a package. Her Christmas gifts always looked as if Santa's reindeer had used them to play football. Since she'd lived with me I'd done all her packaging for her.

"I did wonder if Louise would ever get the tea," Betsy Mae was saying. "But I asked her yesterday when she was in here and she told me she'd almost finished it. She seemed surprised that Maisie would send her a birthday present. Specially since it wasn't her birthday."

Not nearly as surprised as I was, I thought. In the first place, Maisie hardly ever went out without me. She didn't like to drive because her eyes are not what they used to be. I didn't even know she'd left the house. And what was she doing sending Louise Daniels a birthday present when she'd made it plain to me that she didn't like the woman?

"I bet Louise is going to miss Sam," Betsy Mae said, studying her fingernails. They were long and pointed, painted bright red. One of them was cut right down to the quick. She's always cussing about breaking them. I don't know why she doesn't just cut them all short. That way they'd all be the same length.

"I'm sure we'll all miss him," I said, edging away from the counter. "I have to go now, Betsy Mae."

She went on talking as if I hadn't spoken. "I don't mind telling you, I'll miss him. He was like a breath of fresh air coming into this stuffy place. Brightened my day. Always had some juicy bit of gossip to tell me. I don't know how he found out so much about everyone. My Joe reckons he read everyone's mail, and that's how come he knew so much."

I could feel the tears starting to sting my eyes, so I just nodded and hurried out of there. I didn't want Betsy Mae to see me cry. She'd pester me to find out what was wrong. I could just imagine what she'd say if she knew a foolish old woman like me was breaking her heart over a man who preferred someone like Louise Daniels.

All the way home I kept thinking about what Betsy Mae had said. Maisie must have slipped out while I was taking my afternoon nap that day. Why hadn't she told me she'd been out? Obviously because she didn't want me to know that she'd mailed a package of tea to Louise.

That was not at all like Maisie.

The more I thought about it, the more uneasy I got. We had never kept secrets from each other before, and I didn't like the idea of her doing it now.

As far as I knew, Maisie hadn't been out of her room since she'd heard about Sam dying. I'd taken her meals in to her, but most of the time they came back untouched. She wouldn't even drink her tea. Maisie was taking Sam's death very hard, indeed. Harder than I was, in fact.

I thought about that for a long time, too. And I didn't like what I was thinking. It was time, I decided, for some straight talk between my sister and me.

Maisie wouldn't open the door when I knocked at first. I was just about to give up when I heard the bedsprings creak. The door opened a crack and Maisie peered at me through the opening. "Annie?" she said, as if she were expecting someone else. Her voice was quavery and I could tell she'd been crying a lot.

"Of course it is," I said, trying not to sound annoyed. After all, I was heartbroken about Sam, too, but I managed to go on living. "Who else would it be?"

"I thought—" She shook her head, as if she didn't know what she thought.

"I want to talk to you," I said.

"I don't feel like talking right now."

She started to close the door, but I held it open. "Why did you send Louise a package of tea?" I asked, watching her face very closely.

I could tell, by the way her eyes slid away from mine, that she knew that I knew. "It was her birthday," she said. "I thought it would be a nice gesture."

"It wasn't her birthday, Maisie. You don't know when her birthday is."

She looked at me then, and her face wore that stubborn look I knew so well. "I thought it was last week," she said.

I knew I would have to come right to the point. "Sam was poisoned," I said. "I think he opened the package meant for Louise."

I couldn't believe I was actually saying those words to her. I couldn't believe she would really do what I knew she had done. But after a moment or two, her face kind of crumpled up, and she nodded. My stomach felt as if somebody had kicked it.

"What did you put in the tea, Maisie? What kind of poison?"

"Clippings."

I barely heard her, but I could read her lips. I pushed the door open wider, and this time she didn't try to stop me. "Clippings from what?" I demanded.

"The yew."

Then I remembered. Of course. The English yew, one of the deadliest of poisonous plants. I could feel the shudder go all the way down my back to my feet. "Oh, Maisie," I said. "Why? How could you? Everybody loved Sam. I loved him."

"I loved him, too." Her eyes were bright with tears when she looked at me. "I loved him more than anybody. I didn't know he would open the package."

"Sam opened a lot of people's mail," I said. "Everybody knew that. How do you think he knew so much about what was going on in town?"

"He shouldn't have stolen the tea," Maisie said. She walked over to the bed and sat down, making the springs creak again. "I didn't know he would steal the tea."

"He must have replaced it with some of his store-bought tea," I said, trying to work out in my mind what had happened. "You know how much he loved your tea. Betsy Mae told me that Louise got the tea you sent to her, and she's perfectly all right."

"Betsy Mae knows?" Maisie said, her voice going up a notch or two.

"Not about the tea being poisoned. At least, not yet." I tried to think what was best to do. "I suppose everyone will know sooner or later," I said. "The police will want to know why you did it."

Her face went chalk white when I said that, but her chin went up. "I won't tell them," she said, and I could tell by her tone she meant it. "I won't have everyone laughing at me."

"I don't think they'll be laughing," I said, trying not to let her see how much I was hurting inside. "Why did you want to kill Louise?" I asked her, although I thought I already knew the answer to that.

"Sam was going to ask her to marry him. I thought if something happened to her, he might eventually get around to asking me."

Even though I'd half-expected it, hearing her say the words so matter-of-factly shocked me. "You wanted to marry Sam?"

"You've had a husband," she said, making it sound like an accusation. "You were so wrapped up in Harry you didn't need anyone else. All I ever had was loneliness. I wanted to know what it was like to be married, to be loved by a man, at least for a little while before I died."

"I always thought you were happier living alone," I said. "You never told me . . ."

I didn't know how to finish the sentence, but she finished it for me. "That I envied you? No, I never told you. But there wasn't a night went by when I didn't long for someone to love me, the way Harry loved you."

There was such a look of sorrow in her eyes, I almost cried. "So what are we going to do now?"

"We don't have to do anything," Maisie said, sounding more like herself. "No one has to know Sam was poisoned. No one will suspect me. We can just pretend it never happened."

"I don't think I can do that," I said. "I need to think about it."

"There's nothing to think about." She narrowed her eyes, and for a moment she looked like someone I didn't know at all. "You are not going to tell everyone your sister is a murderer. What would people say?"

I could tell she didn't really believe that I would tell anyone what she'd done. I left her alone and went for a walk in the garden to get my thoughts together. When I came back inside, Maisie was looking like her old self again. She'd even made me a nice cup of tea.

I told her that something had been eating the rhododendrons, and when she went to take a look at them, I called the police. Deputy Reynolds took her away a little while ago, after I'd told him everything.

Maisie didn't say a word the whole time I was talking. She looked at me, though, just as she was being led out of the door. I knew what she was thinking.

I might have forgiven her for Sam. After all, she is my sister, and Sam's death was an accident . . . in a way. No one need have known what really happened. But I knew. And I couldn't forgive her for Harry.

You see, my Harry died of food poisoning, too. It was the same day that Maisie had paid us a visit. I didn't think anything of it at the time, because we all ate the same thing for lunch and Maisie and I were just fine.

The doctor put it down to the crab Harry had caught himself. He'd eaten it the day before he died. I don't like crab so I hadn't touched any of it.

Now I know that it wasn't the crab. Maisie had made the tea that afternoon. I remember distinctly. She must have given Harry her special brew.

She was so lonely after she retired. She was always telling me that when Harry died she'd come and live with me and keep me company. I guess she decided to hurry that along a little bit.

Harry suffered terribly before he died. Sam must have suffered, too. Maisie had to pay for that. I'd loved only two men in my life, and she'd sent them both to the grave. She might have sent me there, too, if I hadn't poured that last cup of tea down the drain.

Letter to His Son

Simon Brett

Parkhurst
16th June, 1986

DEAR BOY,
I AM sorry to hear the Fourth of June celebrations was a trial. I've used that agency before and they never give me no trouble, but I will certainly withdraw my future custom after this lot and may indeed have to send the boys round. Honest, Son, I asked them to send along a couple what would really raise you in your fellow-Etonians' esteem when they saw who you got for parents. I had to get Blue Phil to draw quite a lot out of the old deposit account under the M23/M25 inter-section, and I just don't reckon I got value for my hard-earned oncers.

OK, the motor was all right. Vintage Lagonda must've raised a few eyebrows. Pity it was hot. Still, you can't have everything. But really . . . To send along Watchstrap Malone and Berwick Street Barbara as your mum and dad is the height of naffness so far as yours truly is concerned. I mean, doesn't no one have any finesse these days? No, it's not good enough. I'm afraid there's going to be a few broken fingers round that agency unless I get a strongly worded apology in folded form.

For a start, why did they send a villain to be *in loco parentis*? (See, I am not wasting my time down in the prison library.) Are they under new management? Always when I used them in the past, they sent along actors, people with no form. Using Watchstrap, whose record's as long as one of Barry Manilow's *sounds*, is taking unnecessary risks. OK, he looks the toff, got the plummy voice and all that, but he ISN'T THE GENUINE ARTICLE. Put him in a marquee with an authentic Eton dad and the other geezer's going to see he's not the business within thirty seconds. Remember, in matters of class, THERE'S NO WAY SOME-ONE WHO ISN'T CAN EVER PASS HIMSELF OFF AS THE REAL THING (a point which I will return to later in this letter).

And, anyway, if they was going to send a villain, least they could have done was to send a good one. Watchstrap Malone, I'll have you know, got his cognomen (prison library again) from a case anyone would wish to draw a veil over, when he was in charge of hijacking a container-load of what was supposed to be watches from Heathrow. Trouble was, he only misread the invoice, didn't he? Wasn't the watch-es, just the blooming straps. Huh, not the kind of form suitable to someone who's going to pass themselves off as any son of mine's father.

And as for using Berwick Street Barbara, well, that's just a straight insult to your mother, isn't it? I mean, I know she's got the posh voice and the clothes, but she's not the real thing any more than Watchstrap is. She gets her business from nasty little common erks who think they're stepping up a few classes. But no genuine Hooray Henry'd be fooled by Barbara. Anyway, that lot don't want all the quacking vowels and the headscarves—get enough of that at home. What they're after in that line is some pert little scrubber dragged out of the gutters of Toxteth. But I digress.

Anyway, like I say, it's an insult to your mother and if she ever gets to hear about it, I wouldn't put money on the roof staying on Holloway.

No, I'm sorry, I feel like I've been done, and last time I felt like that, with Micky "The Cardinal" O'Riordhan, he ended up having a lot more difficulty in kneeling down than what he had had theretofore.

BUT NOW, SON, I come on to the more serious part of this letter. I was *not amused* to hear what your division master said about your work. If you've got the idea in your thick skull that being a toff has anything to do with sitting on your backside and doing buggerall, then it's an idea of which you'd better disabuse yourself sharpish.

I haven't put in all the time (inside and out) what I have to pay for your education with a view to you throwing it all away. It's all right for an authentic scion (prison library) of the aristocracy to drop out of the system; the system will cheerfully wait till he's ready to go back in. But someone in your shoes, Sonny, if you drop out, you stay out.

Let me clarify my position. Like all fathers, I want my kids to have things better than I did. Now, I done all right, I'm not complaining. I've got to the top of my particular tree. There's still a good few pubs round the East End what'll go quiet when my name's mentioned and, in purely material terms, with the houses in Tenerife and Jamaica and Friern Barnet (not to mention the stashes under various bits of the country's motorway network), I am, to put it modestly, comfortable.

But—and this is a big but—in spite of my career success, I remain an old-fashioned villain. My methods—and I'm not knocking them, because they work—are, in the ultimate analysis, crude. All right, most people give you what you want if you hit them hard enough, but that system of business has not changed since the beginning of time. Nowadays, there is no question, considerably more sophisticated methods are available to the aspiring professional.

Computers obviously have made a big difference. The advance of microtechnology has made possible that elusive goal, the perfect crime, in which you just help yourself without getting your hands dirty.

For this reason I was *particularly* distressed to hear that you haven't been paying attention in your computer studies classes. Listen, Son, I am paying a great deal to put you through Eton and (I think we can safely assume after the endowment for the new library block) Cambridge, but if at the end of all that you emerge unable to fiddle a computerized bank account, I am going to be less than chuffed. Got it?

However, what I'm doing for you is not just with a view to you getting *au fait* with the new technology. It's more than that.

OK, like I say, I been successful, and yet the fact remains that here I am writing to you from the nick. Because my kind of operation, being a straightforward villain against the system, will never be without its attendant risks. Of which risks the nick is the biggest one.

You know, being in prison does give you time for contemplation, and, while I been here, I done a lot of thinking about the inequalities of the society in which we live.

I mean, say I organize a security-van hijack, using a dozen heavies, with all the risks involved (bruises from the pickaxe handles, whiplash injuries from ramming the vehicle, being shopped by one of my own team, being traced through the serial numbers, to name but a few), what do I get at the end of it? I mean, after it's all been shared out, after I've paid everyone off, bribed a few, sorted out pensions for the ones who got hurt, all that, what do I get? Couple of hundred grand if I'm lucky.

Whereas some smartarse in the City can siphon off that many million in a morning without stirring from his desk (and in many cases without even technically breaking the law).

Then, if I'm caught, even with the most expensive solicitor in London acting for me, I get twelve years in Parkhurst.

And, if he's caught, what does he get? Maybe has to resign from the board. Maybe has to get out the business and retire to his country estate, where he lives on investment income and devotes himself to rural pursuits, shooting, fishing, being a JP, that sort of number.

Now, I ask myself, is that a fair system?

And the answer, of course, doesn't take long to come back. No.

Of course it isn't fair. It never has been. That's why I've always voted Tory. All that socialist rubbish about trying to 'change society' . . . huh. It's never going to change. The system is as it is. Which is why, to succeed you got to go *with* the system, rather than *against* it.

Which brings me, of course, to what I'm doing for you.

By the time you get through Eton and Cambridge, Son, the world will be your oyster. Your earning potential will be virtually unlimited.

Now don't get me wrong. I am not suggesting that you should go straight. Heaven forbid. No son of mine's going to throw away five generations of tradition just like that.

No, what I'm suggesting is, yes, you're still a villain, but you're a villain from *inside* the system. I mean, think of the opportunities you'll have. You'll be able to go into the City, the Law . . . we could use a bent solicitor in the family . . . even, if you got *really* lucky, into Parliament. And let's face it, in any of those professions, you're going to clean up in a way that'll make my pickaxe-and-bovver approach look as old-fashioned as a slide-rule in the days of calculators.

Which is why it is so, so important that you take your education seriously. You have got to come out the genuine article. Never relax. You're not there just to do the academic business, you got to observe your classmates, too. Follow their every move. Do as they do. You can get to the top, Son (not just in the country, in the world—all big businesses are going multinational these days), but for you to get there you got to be the real thing. No chinks in your armour—got that? Many highly promising villains have come unstuck by inattention to detail and I'm determined it shouldn't happen to you.

PERHAPS I CAN best clarify what I'm on about by telling you what happened to old Squiffy Yoxborough.

Squiffy was basically a con-merchant. Used to be an actor, specialized in upper-class parts. Hadn't got any real breeding, brought up in Hackney as a matter of fact, but he could do the voice real well and, you know, he'd studied the type. Made a kind of specialty of an upper-class drunk act, pretending to be pissed, you know. Hence the name, Squiffy. But times got hard, the acting parts wasn't there, so he drifted into our business.

First of all, he never did anything big. Main specialty was borrowing the odd fifty at upper-class piss-ups. Henley, Ascot, hunt balls, that kind of number, he'd turn up in the full fig and come the hard-luck story when the guests had been hitting the champers for a while. He sounded even more smashed than them, but of course he knew exactly where all his marbles was.

It was slow money, but fairly regular, and moving with that crowd opened up other possibilities. Nicking the odd bit of jewellery, occasional blackmail, a bit of "winkling" old ladies out of their flats for property developers, you know what I mean. Basically, just doing the upper-classes' dirty work. There's always been a demand for people to do that, and I dare say there always will be.

Well, inevitably, this led pretty quick to drugs. When London's full of Hooray Henries wanting to stick stuff up their ancestral noses, there's bound to be a lot of openings for the pushers, and Squiffy took his chances when they come. He was never in the big league, mind, not controlling the business, just a courier and like point-of-sale merchant. But it was better money, and easier than sponging fifties.

Incidentally, Son, since the subject's come up, I don't want there to be any doubt in your mind about my views on drugs. You keep away from them.

Now, I am not a violent man—well, let's say I am not a violent man to my *family*, but if I hear you've been meddling with drugs, either as a user or a pusher, so help me I will somehow get out of this place and find you and give you such a tanning with my belt that you'll need a rubber ring for the rest of your natural. That sort of business attracts a really unpleasant class of criminal that I don't want any son of mine mixing with. Got that?

Anyway, getting back to Squiffy, obviously once he got into drugs, he was going to get deeper in and pretty soon he's involved with some villains who was organizing the smuggling of the stuff through a yacht-charter company. You know the sort of set-up, rich gits rent this boat and crew and swan round the West Indies for a couple of weeks, getting alternately smashed and stoned.

Needless to say, this company would keep their punters on the boat supplied with cocaine; but not only that, they also made a nice little business of taking the stuff back into England and flogging it to all the Sloane Rangers down the Chelsea discothèques.

I suppose it could have been a good little earner if you like that kind of thing, but these plonkers who was doing it hadn't got no sense of organization. The crew were usually as stoned as the punters, so it was only a matter of time before they come unstuck. Only third run they do, they moor in the harbour of this little island in the West Indies and, while they're all on shore getting well bobbled on the ethnic rum, local Bill goes and raids the yacht. Stuff's lying all over the place, like there's been a snowstorm blown through the cabins, and when the crew and punters come back, they all get nicked and shoved in the local slammer to unwind for a bit.

Not a nice place, the jail on this little island. They had to share their cells with a nasty lot of local fauna like cockroaches, snakes, and mosquitoes, not to mention assorted incendiaries, gunrunners, rapists, and axe-murderers.

Not at all what these merchant bankers and their Benenden-educated crumpet who had chartered the yacht was used to. So, because that's how things work at that level, pretty soon some British consular official gets contacted, and pretty soon a deal gets struck with the local authorities. No hassle, really, it comes down to a thousand quid per prisoner. All charges dropped, and home they go. Happened all the time, apparently. The prisons was one of the island's two most lucrative industries (the other being printing unperforated stamps). A yacht had only to come into the harbour to get raided. Squiffy's lot had just made it easy for the local police; usually the cocaine had to be planted.

Well, obviously, there was a lot of transatlantic telephoning, a lot of distraught daddies (barristers, MPs, what-have-you) cabling money across, but it gets sorted out pretty quick and all the Hoorays are flown back to England with a good story to tell at the next cocktail party.

They're all flown back, that is, except Squiffy.

And it wasn't that he couldn't raise the readies. He'd got a few stashes round about, and the odd blackmail victim who could be relied on to stump up a grand when needed.

No, he stayed because he'd met this bloke in the nick.

Don't get me wrong. I don't mean he fancied him. Nothing Leaning Tower of Pisa about Squiffy.

No, he stayed because he'd met someone he thought could lead to big money.

Bloke's name was Masters. Alex Masters. But, it didn't take Squiffy long to find out, geezer was also known as the Marquess of Gorsley.

Now, I don't know how it is, but some people always land on their feet in the nick. I mean, I do all right. I get all the snout I want and if I feel like a steak or a bottle of whiskey there's no problem. But I get that because I have a bit of reputation outside, and I have to work to keep those privileges. I mean, if there wasn't a good half-dozen heavies round the place who owe me the odd favour, I might find it more difficult.

But I tell you, I got nothing compared to what this marquess geezer'd got. Unlimited supplies of rum, so he's permanently smashed, quietly, and happily drinking himself to death. All the food he wants, very best of the local cuisine. Nice cell to himself, air conditioning, fridge, video, compact-disc player, interior-sprung bed. Pick of the local talent to share that bed with, all these slim, brown-legged beauties, different one every night, so Squiffy said (though apparently the old marquess was usually too pissed to do much about it).

Now, prisons work the same all over the world, so you take my word that I know what I'm talking about. Only one thing gets those kind of privileges.

Money.

But pretty soon even Squiffy realizes there's something not quite kosher with the set-up. I mean, this Gorsley bloke's not inside for anything particularly criminal. Just some fraud on a holiday villa development scheme. Even if the island's authorities take property fiddling more seriously than cocaine, there's still got to be a price to get him released. I mean, say it's five grand, it's still going to be considerably less than what he's paying per annum for these special privileges.

Besides, when Squiffy raises the subject, it's clear that the old marquess doesn't know a blind thing about this "buy-out" system. But he does go on about how grateful he is to his old man, the Duke of Glammerton, for shelling out so much per month "to make the life sentence bearable."

Now Squiffy's not the greatest intellect since Einstein, but even he's capable of putting two and two together. He checks out this Gorsley geezer's form and discovers the property fraud's not the first bit of bovver he's been in. In fact, the bloke is a walking disaster area, his past littered with bounced cheques, petty theft, convictions for drunkenness, you name it. (I don't, incidentally, mean *real* crimes, the ones that involve skill; I refer to the sort people get into by incompetence.)

Squiffy does a bit more research. He's still got some cocaine stashed away and for that the prison governor's more than ready to spill the odd bean. Turns out the marquess's dad pays up regular, never objects when the price goes up, encourages the governor to keep increasing the supply of rum, states quite categorically he's not interested in pardons, anything like that. Seems he's got a nephew who's a real Mr. Goody-Goody. And if the marquess dies in an alcoholic stupor in some obscure foreign jail, it's all very handy. The prissy nephew inherits the title, and the Family Name remains untarnished. Duke's prepared to pay a lot to keep that untarnished.

So it's soon clear to Squiffy that the duke is not only paying a monthly sum to keep his son in the style to which he's accustomed; it's also to keep his son out of the country. In fact, he's paying the island to let the Marquess of Gorsley die quietly in prison.

It's when he realizes this that Squiffy Yoxborough decides he'll stick around for a while.

Now, except for the aforementioned incendiaries, gunrunners, rapists, and axe-murderers . . . oh, and the local talent (not that that talked much), the marquess has been a bit starved of civilized conversation, so he's pretty chuffed to be joined by someone who's English and talks with the right sort of accent. He doesn't notice that Squiffy's not the genuine article. Too smashed most of the time to notice anything and, since the marquess's idea of a conversation is him rambling on and someone else listening, Squiffy doesn't get too much chance to give himself away.

Anyway, he's quite content to listen, thank you very much. The more he finds out about the Marquess of Gorsley's background, the happier he is. It all ties in with a sort of plan that's slowly emerging in his head.

Particularly he wants to know about the marquess's schooldays. So, lots of warm, tropical evenings get whiled away over bottles of rum while the marquess drunkenly reminisces and Squiffy listens hard. It's really just an extension of how he started in the business, pretending to get plastered with the Hoorays. But this time he's after considerably more than the odd fifty.

The Marquess of Gorsley was, needless to say, at one of these really posh schools. Like his father before him, he had gone to Raspington in Wiltshire (near where your grandfather was arrested for the first time, Son). And as he listens, Squiffy learns all about it.

He learns that there was four houses: Thurrocks, Wilmington, Stuke, and Fothergill. He learns that the marquess was in Stuke, that kids just starting in Stuke was called "tads" and on their first night in the dorm they underwent "scrogging." He learns that prefects was called "whisks," that in their common room, called "the Treacle Tin," they was allowed to administer a punishment called "spluggers"; that they could wear the top buttons of their jackets undone, and was the only members of the school allowed to walk on "Straggler's Hump."

He learns that the teachers was called "dommies," that the sweet shop was called the "Binn," that a cricket cap was a "skiplid," that the bogs was called "fruitbowls," that studies was called "nitboxes," that lunch was called "slops," and that a minor sports colours tie was called a "slagnoose."

He hears the marquess sing the school songs. After a time, he starts joining in with them. Eventually, he even gets a bit good at doing a solo on the School Cricket Song, traditionally sung in Big Hall on the evening after the Old Raspurian Match. It begins:

> Hark! the shout of a schoolboy at twilight
> Comes across from the far-distant pitch,
> Goads his team on to one final effort,
> "Make a stand at the ultimate ditch!"
> Hark! the voice of the umpiring master
> Rises over the white-flannelled strife,
> Tells his charges that life is like cricket,
> Tells them also that cricket's like life . . .

Don't think you have that one at Eton, do you, Son?

I tell you, after two months in that prison, Squiffy Yoxborough knows as much about being at Raspington as the Marquess of Gorsley does himself. He stays on a couple more weeks, to check there's nothing more, but by now the marquess is just rambling and repeating himself, sinking deeper and deeper into an alcoholic coma. So Squiffy quickly organizes his own thousand quid release money and scarpers back to England.

FIRST THING HE does when he gets back home, Squiffy forms a company. Well, he doesn't actually literally form a company, but he, like, gets all the papers forged so it looks like he's formed a company. He calls this company "Only Real Granite Hall-Building Construction Techniques" (ORGHBCT) and he gets enough forged paperwork for him to be able to open a bank account in that name.

Next thing he gets his clothes together. Moves carefully here. Got to get the right gear or the whole thing falls apart.

Dark blue pinstripe suit. Donegal tweed suit. Beale and Inmans corduroy trousers. Cavalry twills. Turnbull and Asser striped shirts. Viyella Tattersall checked shirts. Church's Oxford shoes. Barbour jacket. Herbert Johnson trilby.

He steals or borrows this lot. Can't just buy them in the shops. Got to look old, you see.

Has trouble with the Old Raspurian tie. Doesn't know anyone who went there—except of course for the marquess, and he's rather a long way away.

So he has to buy a tie new and distress it a bit. Washes it so's it shrinks. Rubs in a bit of grease. Looks all right.

(You may be wondering, Son, how I come to know all this detail. Not my usual special subject, I agree. Don't worry, all will be revealed.)

Right, so having got the gear, he packs it all in a battered old leather suitcase, rents a Volvo estate, and drives up to Scotland.

HE'S CHECKED OUT where the Duke of Glammerton's estate is, he's checked that the old boy's actually in residence, and he just drives up to the front of Glammerton House. Leaves the Volvo on the gravel, goes up to the main door, and pulls this great ring for the bell.

Door's opened by some flunkey.

"Hello," says Squiffy, doing the right voice of course. "I'm a chum of Alex's. Just happened to be in the area. Wondered if the old devil was about."

"Alex?" says the flunkey, bit suspicious.

"Yes. The Marquess of Gorsley. I was at school with him."

"Ah. I'm afraid the marquess is abroad."

"Oh, really? What a swiz," says Squiffy. "Still, I travel a lot. Whereabouts is the old devil?"

Flunkey hesitates a bit, then says he'll go off and try to find out. Comes back with the butler. Butler confirms the marquess is abroad. Cannot be certain where.

"What, hasn't left a forwarding address? Always was bloody inefficient. Never mind, I'm sure some of my chums could give me a lead. Don't worry, I'll track him down."

This makes the butler hesitate, too. "If you'll excuse me, sir, I'll just go and see if his Grace is available. He might have more information about the marquess's whereabouts than I have."

Few minutes later, Squiffy gets called into this big lounge-type room, you know, all deers' heads and gilt frames, and there's the Duke of Glammerton sitting over a tray of tea. Duke sees the tie straight away.

"Good Lord, are you an Old Raspurian?"

"Yes, your Grace," says Squiffy.

"Which house?"

"Stuke."

"So was I."

"Well, of course, Duke, I knew you must have been. That's where I met Alex, you see. Members of the same family in the same house, what?"

Duke doesn't look so happy now he knows Squiffy's a friend of his son. No doubt the old boy's met a few unsuitable ones in his time, so Squiffy says quickly, "Haven't seen Alex for yonks. Virtually since school."

"Oh." Duke looks relieved. "As Moulton said, I'm afraid he's abroad."

"Living there?"

"Yes. For the time being," Duke says carefully.

"Oh, dear. You don't by any chance have an address, do you?"

"Erm . . . Not at the moment, no."

Now all this is suiting Squiffy very nicely. The more the Duke's determined to keep quiet about his son's real circumstances, the better.

"That's a nuisance," says Squiffy. "Wanted to sting the old devil for a bit of money."

"Oh?" Duke looks careful again.

"Well, not for me, of course. For the old school."

"Oh, yes?" Duke looks interested.

"Absolutely." (Squiffy knows he should say this every now and then instead of "Yes.") "For my sins I've got involved in some fund-raising for the old place."

"Again? What are they up to this time?"

"Building a new Great Hall to replace Big Hall."

Duke's shocked by this. "They're not going to knock Big Hall down?"

"Good Lord, no. No, Big Hall'll still be used. The Great Hall will be for school plays, that sort of thing."

"Ah. Where are they going to build it?"

"Well, it'll be at right angles to Big Hall, sort of stretching past Thurrocks out towards 'Straggler's Hump.'"

"Really? Good Lord." The old geezer grins. "I remember walking along 'Straggler's Hump' many a time."

"You must've been a 'whisk' then."

He looks guilty. "Never was, actually."

"Doing it illegally, were you?"

Duke nods.

"But didn't that mean you got dragged into the 'Treacle Tin' for 'spluggers'?"

"Never caught." Duke giggles naughtily. "Remember, actually, I did it my second day as a 'tad.'"

"What, directly after you'd been 'scrogged'?"

"Absolutely."

"And none of the 'dommies' saw you?"

Duke shakes his head, really chuffed at what an old devil he used to be. "Tell me," he says, "where are you staying up here?"

"I was going to check into the . . . what is it in the village? The Glammerton Arms?"

"Well, don't do that, old boy. Stay here the night. I'll get Moulton to show you a room."

GETS A GOOD dinner, that night, Squiffy does. Pheasant, venison, vintage wines, all that. Just the two of them. Duchess had died a long time ago.

Get on really well, they do. Squiffy does his usual getting-plastered act, but, as usual, he's careful. Talks a lot about Raspington, doesn't talk too much about the marquess. But listens. And gets confirmation of his hunch that the duke never wants to see his son again. Also knows there's a very strong chance of this happening in the natural course of events. The amount of rum the marquess is putting away, his liver must be shrivelled down to like a dried pea.

Anyway, when they're giving the port and brandy and cigars a bash, the Duke, who's a bit the worse for wear, says, "What is all this about the old school? Trying to raise money, did you say?"

"Absolutely," says Squiffy. "Don't just want to raise money, though. Want to raise a monument."

"What—a monument to all the chaps who died from eating 'slops'?"

"Or the chaps who were poisoned in the 'Binn'?"

"Or everyone who got 'scrogged' in their own 'nitbox'!"

"Yes, or all those who had a 'down-the-loo-shampoo' in the 'fruit-bowls'!"

Duke finds this dead funny. Hasn't had such a good time for years.

"No, actually," says Squiffy, all serious now, "we want the new Great Hall to be a monument to a great Old Raspurian."

"Ah."

"So that every chap who walks into that hall will think of someone who was really a credit to the old school."

"Oh. Got anyone in mind?" asks the duke.

"Absolutely," says Squiffy. "We thought of Alex."

"*What!*"

"Well, he's such a great chap."

"Alex—great chap?"

"Yes. As I say, I've hardly seen him since school . . . nor have any of the other fellows on the fund-raising committee, actually, but we all thought he was such a terrific chap at school . . . I mean, I'm sure he's gone on to be just as successful in the outside world."

"Well . . . er . . ."

"So you see, Duke, we all thought, what a great idea to have the place named after Alex—I mean he'd have to put up most of the money, but that's a detail—and then everyone who went into the hall would be reminded of what a great Old Raspurian he was. Give the 'tads' something to aspire to, what?"

"Yes, yes." The Duke gets thoughtful. "But are you sure that Alex is the right one?"

"Oh. Well, if there's any doubt about his suitability, perhaps we should investigate a bit further into what he's been up to since he left Raspington . . ."

"No, that won't be necessary," says the Duke, sharpish. "What sort of sum of money are we talking about?"

"Oh . . ." Squiffy looks all casual like. "I don't know. Five hundred thousand, something like that."

"Five hundred thousand to ensure that Alex is always remembered as one of the greatest Old Raspurians . . . ?"

"I suppose you could think of it like that. Absolutely."

A light comes into the old Duke's eyes. He's had reports from the West Indies. He knows his son hasn't got long to go. And suddenly he's offered a way of . . . like *enshrining* the marquess's memory. With a great permanent monument at the old school, a little bit of adverse publicity in the past'll soon be forgotten. The Family Name will remain untarnished. Half a million's not much to pay for that.

He rings a bell and helps them both to some more pre-War port. Moulton comes in.

"My cheque book, please."

The butler geezer delivers it and goes off again.

"Who should I make this payable to?" asks the Duke.

"Well, in fact," says Squiffy, "the full name's the 'Old Raspurian Great Hall-Building Charitable Trust,' but you'll never get all that on the cheque. Just the initials will do."

With the cheque safely in his pocket, Squiffy starts humming the tune of the Raspington School Cricket Song.

"Great," says the Duke. "Terrific. I always used to do the solo on the second verse. Do you know the descant?"

"Absolutely," says Squiffy, and together they sing,

> See the schoolboy a soldier in khaki,
> Changed his bat for the Gatling and Bren.
> How his officer's uniform suits him,

How much better he speaks than his men.
Thank the school for his noble demeanour,
And his poise where vulgarity's rife,
Knowing always that life is like cricket,
Not forgetting that cricket's like life.

All right, Son. Obvious question is, how do I know all that? How do I know all that detail about Squiffy Yoxborough?

Answer is, he told me. And he'll tell me again every blooming night if he gets the chance.

Yes, he's inside here with me.

And why? Why did he get caught? Was it because the Duke woke up next morning and immediately realized it was a transparent con? Realized that he'd been pissed the night before and that it really was a bit unusual to give a complete stranger a cheque for half a million quid?

No, Duke's mind didn't work like that. So long as he thought he was dealing with a genuine Old Raspurian, he reckoned he'd got a good deal. OK, it'd cost him five hundred grand, but, as a price for covering up everything that his son'd done in the past, it was peanuts. The Family Name would remain untarnished—that was the important thing.

But, like I just said, that was only going to work *so long as he thought he was dealing with a genuine Old Raspurian.*

And something the butler told him the next morning stopped him thinking that he was.

So, when Squiffy goes to the bank to pay in his cheque to the "Only Real Granite Hall-Building Construction Techniques" account, he's asked to wait for a minute, and suddenly the cops are all over the shop.

So what was it? He got the voice right, he got the clothes right, he got all the Old Raspurian stuff right, he used the right knives and forks at dinner, he said "Absolutely" instead of "Yes" . . . where'd he go wrong?

I'll tell you—when he got up the next morning he made his own bed.

Well, butler sussed him straight away. Poor old Squiffy'd shown up his upbringing. Never occur to the sort of person he was pretending to be to make a bed. There was always servants around to do that for you.

See, there's some things you can learn from outside, and some you got to know from inside. And that making the bed thing, it takes generations of treating peasants like dirt to understand that.

I HOPE I'VE made my point. Stick at it, Son. Both the work and the social bit. You're going to get right to the top, like I said. You're not going to be an old-fashioned villain, you're going to do it through the system. And if you're going to succeed, you can't afford the risk of being let down by the sort of mistake that shopped Squiffy Yoxborough. Got that?

Once again, sorry about the Fourth of June. (Mind you, someone else is going to be even sorrier.) I'll see to it you get better parents for the Eton and Harrow Match.

This letter, with the customary greasy oncers, will go out through Blue Phil, as per usual. Look after yourself, Son, and remember—keep a straight bat.

Your loving father,
Nobby Chesterfield

The Poisoned Pen

Arthur B. Reeve

I

KENNEDY'S SUITCASE WAS lying open on the bed, and he was literally throwing things into it from his chiffonier, as I entered after a hurried trip uptown from the *Star* office in response to an urgent message from him.

"Come, Walter," he cried, hastily stuffing in a package of clean laundry without taking off the wrapping-paper, "I've got your suitcase out. Pack up whatever you can in five minutes. We must take the six o'clock train for Danbridge."

I did not wait to hear any more. The mere mention of the name of the quaint and quiet little Connecticut town was sufficient. For Danbridge was on everybody's lips at that time. It was the scene of the now famous Danbridge poisoning case—a brutal case in which the pretty little actress, Vera Lytton, had been the victim.

"I've been retained by Senator Adrian Willard," he called from his room, as I was busy packing in mine. "The Willard family believe that that young Dr. Dixon is the victim of a conspiracy—or at least Alma Willard does, which comes to the same thing, and—well, the senator called me up on long-distance and offered me anything I would name in reason to take the case. Are you ready? Come on, then. We've simply got to make that train."

As we settled ourselves in the smoking compartment of the Pullman, which for some reason or other we had to ourselves, Kennedy spoke again for the first time since our frantic dash across the city to catch the train.

"Now let us see, Walter," he began. "We've both read a good deal about this case in the papers. Let's try to get our knowledge in an orderly shape before we tackle the actual case itself."

"Ever been in Danbridge?" I asked.

"Never," he replied. "What sort of place is it?"

"Mighty interesting," I answered; "a combination of old New England and new, of ancestors and factories, of wealth and poverty, and above all it is interesting for its colony of New Yorkers—what shall I call it?—a literary-artistic-musical combination, I guess."

"Yes," he resumed. "I thought as much. Vera Lytton belonged to the colony. A very talented girl, too—you remember her in *The Taming of the New Woman* last season? Well, to get back to the facts as we know them at present.

"Here is a girl with a brilliant future on the stage discovered by her friend, Mrs. Boncour, in convulsions—practically insensible—with a bottle of headache powder and a jar of ammonia on her dressing table. Mrs. Boncour sends the maid for the nearest doctor, who happens to be a Dr. Waterworth. Meanwhile she tries to restore Miss Lytton, but with no result. She smells the ammonia and then just tastes the headache powder, a very foolish thing to do, for by the time Dr. Waterworth arrives he has two patients."

"No," I corrected, "only one, for Miss Lytton was dead when he arrived, according to his latest statement."

"Very well, then—one. He arrives, Mrs. Boncour is ill, the maid knows nothing at all about it, and Vera Lytton is dead. He, too, smells the ammonia, tastes the headache powder—just the merest trace—and then he has two patients, one of them himself. We must see him, for his experience must have been appalling. How he ever did it I can't imagine, but he saved both himself and Mrs. Boncour from poisoning—cyanide, the papers say, but of course we can't accept that until we see. It seems to me, Walter, that lately the papers have made the rule in murder cases: When in doubt, call it cyanide."

Not relishing Kennedy in the humor of expressing his real opinion of the newspapers, I hastily turned the conversation back again by asking, "How about the note from Dr. Dixon?"

"Ah, there is the crux of the whole case—that note from Dixon. Let us see. Dr. Dixon is, if I am informed correctly, of a fine and aristocratic family, though not wealthy. I believe it has been established that while he was an intern in a city hospital he became acquainted with Vera Lytton, after her divorce from that artist Thurston. Then comes his removal to Danbridge and his meeting and later his engagement with Miss Willard. On the whole, Walter, judging from the newspaper pictures, Alma Willard is quite the equal of Vera Lytton for looks, only of a different style of beauty. Oh, well, we shall see. Vera decided to spend the spring and summer at Danbridge in the bungalow of her friend, Mrs. Boncour, the novelist. That's when things began to happen."

"Yes," I put it, "when you come to know Danbridge as I did after that summer when you were abroad, you'll understand, too. Everybody knows everybody else's business. It is the main occupation of a certain set, and the per-capita output of gossip is a record that would stagger the census bureau. Still, you can't get away from the note, Craig. There it is, in Dixon's own handwriting, even if he does deny it: 'This will cure your headache. Dr. Dixon.' That's a damning piece of evidence."

"Quite right," he agreed hastily; "the note was queer, though, wasn't it? They found it crumpled up in the jar of ammonia. Oh, there are lots of problems the newspapers have failed to see the significance of, let alone trying to follow up."

Our first visit in Danbridge was to the prosecuting attorney, whose office was not far from the station on the main street. Craig had wired him, and he had kindly waited to see us, for it was evident that Danbridge respected Senator Willard and every one connected with him.

"Would it be too much to ask just to see that note that was found in the Boncour bungalow?" asked Craig.

The prosecutor, an energetic young man, pulled out of a document case a crumpled note which had been pressed flat again. On it in clear, deep black letters were the words, just as reported:

This will cure your headache.

DR. DIXON.

"How about the handwriting?" asked Kennedy.

The lawyer pulled out a number of letters. "I'm afraid they will have to admit it," he said with reluctance, as if down in his heart he hated to prosecute Dixon. "We have lots of these, and no handwriting expert could successfully deny the identity of the writing."

He stowed away the letters without letting Kennedy get a hint as to their contents. Kennedy was examining the note carefully.

"May I count on having this note for further examination, of course always at such times and under such conditions as you agree to?"

The attorney nodded. "I am perfectly willing to do anything not illegal to accommodate the senator," he said. "But, on the other hand, I am here to do my duty for the state, cost whom it may."

The Willard house was in a virtual state of siege. Newspaper reporters from Boston and New York were actually encamped at every gate, terrible as an army, with cameras. It was with some difficulty that we got in, even though we were expected, for some of the more enterprising had already fooled the family by posing as officers of the law and messengers from Dr. Dixon.

The house was a real old colonial mansion with tall white pillars, a door with a glittering brass knocker, which gleamed out severely at you as you approached through a hedge of faultlessly trimmed boxwoods.

Senator, or rather former Senator, Willard met us in the library, and a moment later his daughter Alma joined him. She was tall, like her father, a girl of poise and self-control. Yet even the schooling of twenty-two years in rigorous New England self-restraint could not hide the very human pallor of her face after the sleepless nights and nervous days since this trouble had broken on her placid existence. Yet there was a mark of strength and determination on her face that was fascinating. The man who would trifle with this girl, I felt, was playing fast and loose with her very life. I thought then, and I said to Kennedy afterward: "If this Dr. Dixon is guilty, you have no right to hide it from that girl. Anything less than the truth will only blacken the hideousness of the crime that has already been committed."

The senator greeted us gravely, and I could not but take it as a good omen when, in his pride of wealth and family and tradition, he laid bare everything to us, for the sake of Alma Willard. It was clear that in this family there was one word that stood above all others, "Duty."

As we were about to leave after an interview barren of new facts, a young man was announced, Mr. Halsey Post. He bowed politely to us, but it was evident why he had called, as his eye followed Alma about the room.

"The son of the late Halsey Post, of Post & Vance, silversmiths, who have the large factory in town, which you perhaps noticed," explained the senator. "My daughter has known him all her life. A very fine young man."

Later, we learned that the senator had bent every effort toward securing Halsey Post as a son-in-law, but his daughter had had views of her own on the subject.

Post waited until Alma had withdrawn before he disclosed the real object of his visit.

In almost a whisper, lest she should still be listening, he said, "There is a story about town that Vera Lytton's former husband—an artist named Thurston—was here just before her death."

Senator Willard leaned forward as if expecting to hear Dixon immediately acquitted. None of us was prepared for the next remark.

"And the story goes on to say that he threatened to make a scene over a wrong he says he has suffered from Dixon. I don't know anything more about it, and I tell you only because I think you ought to know what Danbridge is saying under its breath."

We shook off the last of the reporters who affixed themselves to us, and for a moment Kennedy dropped in at the little bungalow to see Mrs. Boncour. She was much better, though she had suffered much. She had taken only a pinhead of the poison, but it had proved very nearly fatal.

"Had Miss Lytton any enemies whom you think of, people who were jealous of her professionally or personally?" asked Craig.

"I should not even have said Dr. Dixon was an enemy," she replied evasively.

"But this Mr. Thurston," put in Kennedy quickly. "One is not usually visited in perfect friendship by a husband who has been divorced."

She regarded him keenly for a moment. "Halsey Post told you that," she said. "No one else knew he was here. But Halsey Post was an old friend of both Vera and Mr. Thurston before they separated. By chance he happened to drop in the day Mr. Thurston was here, and later in the day I gave him a letter to forward to Mr. Thurston, which had come after the artist left. I'm sure no one else knew the artist. He was there the morning of the day she died, and—and—that's every bit I'm going to tell you about him, so there. I don't know why he came or where he went."

"That's a thing we must follow up later," remarked Kennedy as we made our adieus. "Just now I want to get the facts in hand. The next thing on my programme is to see this Dr. Waterworth."

We found the doctor still in bed; in fact, a wreck as the result of his adventure. He had little to correct in the facts of the story which had been published so far. But there were many other details of the poisoning he was quite willing to discuss frankly.

"It was true about the jar of ammonia?" asked Kennedy.

"Yes," he answered. "It was standing on her dressing table with the note crumpled up in it, just as the papers said."

"And you have no idea why it was there?"

"I didn't say that. I can guess. Fumes of ammonia are one of the antidotes for poisoning of that kind."

"But Vera Lytton could hardly have known that," objected Kennedy.

"No, of course not. But she probably did know that ammonia is good for just that sort of faintness which she must have experienced after taking the powder. Perhaps she thought of sal volatile, I don't know. But most people know that ammonia in some form is good for faintness of this sort, even if they don't know anything about cyanides and—"

"Then it was cyanide?" interrupted Craig.

"Yes," he replied slowly. It was evident that he was suffering great physical and nervous anguish as the result of his too-intimate acquaintance with the poisons in question. "I will tell you precisely how it was, Professor Kennedy. When I was called in to see Miss Lytton, I found her on the bed. I pried open her jaws and smelled the sweetish odor of the cyanogen gas. I knew then what she had taken, and at the moment she was dead. In the next room I heard someone moaning. The maid said that it was Mrs. Boncour, and that she was deathly sick. I ran into her room, and though she was beside herself with pain I managed to control her, though she struggled desperately against me. I was rushing her to the bathroom, passing through Miss Lytton's room. 'What's wrong?' I asked as I carried her along. 'I took some of that,' she replied, pointing to the bottle on the dressing-table.

"I put a small quantity of its crystal contents on my tongue. Then I realized the most tragic truth of my life. I had taken one of the deadliest poisons in the world. The odor of the released gas of cyanogen was strong. But more than that, the metallic taste and the horrible burning sensation told of the presence of some form of mercury, too. In that terrible moment my brain worked with the incredible swiftness of light. In a flash I knew that if I added malic acid to the mercury—perchloride of mercury or corrosive sublimate—I would have calomel or subchloride of mercury, the only thing that would switch the poison out of my system and Mrs. Boncour's.

"Seizing her about the waist, I hurried into the dining room. On a sideboard was a dish of fruit. I took two apples. I made her eat one, core and all. I ate the other. The fruit contained the malic acid I needed to manufacture the calomel, and I made it right there in nature's own laboratory. But there was no time to stop. I had to act just as quickly to neutralize that cyanide, too. Remembering the ammonia, I rushed back with Mrs. Boncour, and we inhaled the fumes. Then I found a bottle of hydrogen peroxide. I washed out her stomach with it, and then my own. Then I injected some of the peroxide into various parts of her body. The hydrogen peroxide and hydrocyanic acid, you know, make oxamide, which is a harmless compound.

"The maid put Mrs. Boncour to bed, saved. I went to my house a wreck. Since then I have not left this bed. With my legs paralyzed I lie here, expecting each hour to be my last!"

"Would you taste an unknown drug again to discover the nature of a probable poison?" asked Craig.

"I don't know," he answered slowly, "but I suppose I would. In such a case a conscientious doctor has no thought of self. He is there to do things, and he does them, according to the best that is in him. In spite of the fact that I haven't had one hour of unbroken sleep since that fatal day, I suppose I would do it again."

When we were leaving, I remarked: "That is a martyr to science. Could anything be more dramatic than his willing penalty for his devotion to medicine?"

We walked along in silence. "Walter, did you notice he said not a word of condemnation of Dixon, though the note was before his eyes? Surely Dixon has some strong supporters in Danbridge, as well as enemies."

The next morning we continued our investigation. We found Dixon's lawyer, Leland, in consultation with his client in the bare cell of the county jail. Dixon proved to be a clear-eyed, clean-cut young man. The thing that impressed me most about him, aside from the prepossession in his favor due to the faith of Alma Willard, was the nerve he displayed, whether guilty or innocent. Even an innocent man might well have been staggered by the circumstantial evidence against him and the high tide of public feeling, in spite of the support that he was receiving. Leland, we learned, had been very active. By prompt work at the time of the young doctor's arrest, he had managed to secure the greater part of Dr. Dixon's personal letters, though the prosecutor secured some, the contents of which had not been disclosed.

Kennedy spent most of the day in tracing out the movements of Thurston. Nothing that proved important was turned up and even visits to nearby towns failed to show any sales of cyanide or sublimate to anyone not entitled to buy them. Meanwhile, in turning over the gossip of the town, one of the newspapermen ran across the fact that the Boncour bungalow was owned by the Posts, and that Halsey Post, as the executor of the estate, was a more frequent visitor than the mere collection of the rent would warrant. Mrs. Boncour maintained a stolid silence that covered a seething internal fury when the newspaperman in question hinted that the landlord and tenant were on exceptionally good terms.

It was after a fruitless day of such search that we were sitting in the reading room of the Fairfield Hotel. Leland entered. His face was positively white. Without a word he took us by the arm and led us across Main Street and up a flight of stairs to his office. Then he locked the door.

"What's the matter?" asked Kennedy.

"When I took this case," he said, "I believed down in my heart that Dixon was innocent. I still believe it, but my faith has been rudely shaken. I feel that you should know about what I have just found. As I told you, we secured nearly all of Dr. Dixon's letters. I had not read them all then. But I have been going through them tonight. Here is a letter from Vera Lytton herself. You will notice it is dated the day of her death."

He laid the letter before us. It was written in a curious grayish-black ink in a woman's hand, and read:

DEAR HARRIS:

Since we agreed to disagree we have at least been good friends, if no longer lovers. I am not writing in anger to reproach you with your new love, so soon after the old. I suppose Alma Willard is far better suited to be your wife than is a poor little actress—rather looked down on in this Puritan society here. But there is something I wish to warn you about, for it concerns us all intimately.

We are in danger of an awful mix-up if we don't look out. Mr. Thurston—I had almost said my husband, though I don't know whether that is the truth or not—who has just come over from New York, tells me that there is some doubt about the validity of our divorce. You recall he was in the South at the time I sued him, and the papers were served on him in Georgia. He now says the proof of service was fraudulent and that he can set aside the divorce. In that case you might figure in a suit for alienating my affections.

I do not write this with ill will, but simply to let you know how things stand. If we had married, I suppose I would be guilty of bigamy. At any rate, if he were disposed he could make a terrible scandal.

Oh, Harris, can't you settle with him if he asks anything? Don't forget so soon that we once thought we were going to be the happiest of mortals—at least I did. Don't desert me, or the very earth will cry out against you. I am frantic and hardly know what I am writing. My head aches, but it is my heart that is breaking. Harris, I am yours still, down in my heart, but not to be cast off like an old suit for a new one. You know the old saying about a woman scorned. I beg you not to go back on

Your poor little deserted

VERA.

As we finished reading, Leland exclaimed, "That never must come before the jury."

Kennedy was examining the letter carefully. "Strange," he muttered. "See how it was folded. It was written on the wrong side of the sheet, or rather folded up with the writing outside. Where have these letters been?"

"Part of the time in my safe, part of the time this afternoon on my desk by the window."

"The office was locked, I suppose?" asked Kennedy. "There was no way to slip this letter in among the others since you obtained them?"

"None. The office has been locked, and there is no evidence of anyone having entered or disturbed a thing."

He was hastily running over the pile of letters as if looking to see whether they were all there. Suddenly he stopped.

"Yes," he exclaimed excitedly, "one of them is gone." Nervously he fumbled through them, again. "One is gone," he repeated, looking at us, startled.

"What was it about?" asked Craig.

"It was a note from an artist, Thurston, who gave the address of Mrs. Boncour's bungalow—ah, I see you have heard of him. He asked Dixon's recommendation of a certain patent headache medicine. I thought it possibly evidential, and I asked Dixon about it. He explained it by saying that he did not have a copy of his reply, but as near as he could recall, he wrote that the compound would not cure a headache except at the expense of reducing heart action dangerously. He says he sent no prescription. Indeed, he thought it a scheme to extract advice without incurring the charge for an office call and answered it only because he thought Vera had become reconciled to Thurston again. I can't find that letter of Thurston's. It is gone."

We looked at each other in amazement.

"Why, if Dixon contemplated anything against Miss Lytton, should he preserve this letter from her?" mused Kennedy. "Why didn't he destroy it?"

"That's what puzzles me," remarked Leland. "Do you suppose someone has broken in and substituted this Lytton letter for the Thurston letter?"

Kennedy was scrutinizing the letter, saying nothing. "I may keep it?" he asked at length. Leland was quite willing and even undertook to obtain some specimens of the writing of Vera Lytton. With these and the letter Kennedy was working far into the night and long after

I had passed into a land troubled with many wild dreams of deadly poisons and secret intrigues of artists.

The next morning a message from our old friend First Deputy O'Connor in New York told briefly of locating the rooms of an artist named Thurston in one of the cooperative studio apartments. Thurston himself had not been there for several days and was reported to have gone to Maine to sketch. He had had a number of debts, but before he left they had all been paid—strange to say, by a notorious firm of shyster lawyers, Kerr & Kimmel. Kennedy wired back to find out the facts from Kerr & Kimmel and to locate Thurston at any cost.

Even the discovery of the new letter did not shake the wonderful self-possession of Dr. Dixon. He denied ever having received it and repeated his story of a letter from Thurston to which he had replied by sending an answer, care of Mrs. Boncour, as requested. He insisted that the engagement between Miss Lytton and himself had been broken before the announcement of his engagement with Miss Willard. As for Thurston, he said the man was little more than a name to him. He had known perfectly all the circumstances of the divorce, but had had no dealings with Thurston and no fear of him. Again and again he denied ever receiving the letter from Vera Lytton.

Kennedy did not tell the Willards of the new letter. The strain had begun to tell on Alma, and her father had had her quietly taken to a farm of his up in the country. To escape the curious eyes of reporters, Halsey Post had driven up one night in his closed car. She had entered it quickly with her father, and the journey had been made in the car, while Halsey Post had quietly dropped off on the outskirts of the town, where another car was waiting to take him back. It was evident that the Willard family relied implicitly on Halsey, and his assistance to them was most considerate. While he never forced himself forward, he kept in close touch with the progress of the case, and now that Alma was away his watchfulness increased proportionately, and twice a day he wrote a long report which was sent to her.

Kennedy was now bending every effort to locate the missing artist. When he left Danbridge, he seemed to have dropped out of sight completely. However, with O'Connor's aid, the police of all New England were on the lookout.

The Thurstons had been friends of Halsey's before Vera Lytton had ever met Dr. Dixon, we discovered from the Danbridge gossips, and I, at least, jumped to the conclusion that Halsey was shielding the artist, perhaps through a sense of friendship when he found that Kennedy was interested in Thurston's movement. I must say I rather liked Halsey, for he seemed very thoughtful of the Willards, and was never too busy to give an hour or so to any commission they wished carried out without publicity.

Two days passed with not a word from Thurston. Kennedy was obviously getting impatient. One day a rumor was received that he was in Bar Harbor; the next it was a report from Nova Scotia. At last, however, came the welcome news that he had been located in New Hampshire, arrested, and might be expected the next day.

At once Kennedy became all energy. He arranged for a secret conference in Senator Willard's house, the moment the artist was to arrive. The senator and his daughter made a flying trip back to town. Nothing was said to anyone about Thurston, but Kennedy quietly arranged with the district attorney to be present with the note and the jar of ammonia properly safeguarded. Leland of course came, although his client could not. Halsey Post seemed only too glad to be with Miss Willard, though he seemed to have lost interest in the case as soon as the Willards returned to look after it themselves. Mrs. Boncour was well enough to attend, and even Dr. Waterworth insisted on coming in a private ambulance which drove over from a nearby city especially for him. The time was fixed just before the arrival of the train that was to bring Thurston.

It was an anxious gathering of friends and foes of Dr. Dixon who sat impatiently waiting for Kennedy to begin this momentous exposition that was to establish the guilt or innocence of the calm young physician who sat impassively in the jail not half a mile from the room where his life and death were being debated.

"In many respects this is the most remarkable case that it has ever been my lot to handle," began Kennedy. "Never before have I felt so keenly my sense of responsibility. Therefore, though this is a somewhat irregular proceeding, let me begin by setting forth the facts as I see them.

"First, let us consider the dead woman. The question that arises here is, Was she murdered or did she commit suicide? I think you will discover the answer as I proceed. Miss Lytton, as you know, was, two years ago, Mrs. Burgess Thurston. The Thurstons had temperament, and temperament is quite often the highway to the divorce court. It was so in this case. Mrs. Thurston discovered that her husband was paying much attention to other women. She sued for divorce in New York, and he accepted service in the South, where he happened to be. At least it was so testified by Mrs. Thurston's lawyer.

"Now here comes the remarkable feature of the case. The law firm of Kerr & Kimmel, I find, not long ago began to investigate the legality of this divorce. Before a notary Thurston made an affidavit that he had never been served by the lawyer for Miss Lytton, as she was now known. Her lawyer is dead, but his representative in the South who served the papers is alive. He was brought to New York and asserted squarely that he had served the papers properly.

"Here is where the shrewdness of Mose Kimmel, the shyster lawyer, came in. He arranged to have the Southern attorney identify the man he had served the paper on. For this purpose he was engaged in conversation with one of his own clerks when the lawyer was due to appear. Kimmel appeared to act confused, as if he had been caught napping. The Southern lawyer, who had seen Thurston only once, fell squarely into the trap and identified the clerk as Thurston. There were plenty of witnesses to it, and it was point number two for the great Mose Kimmel. Papers were drawn up to set aside the divorce decree.

"In the meantime, Miss Lytton, or Mrs. Thurston, had become acquainted with a young doctor in a New York hospital, and had become engaged to him. It matters not that the engagement was later broken. The fact remains that if the divorce were set aside all action would lie against Dr. Dixon for alienating Mrs. Thurston's affections, and a grave scandal would result. I need not add that in this quiet little town of Danbridge the most could be made of such a suit."

Kennedy was unfolding a piece of paper. As he laid it down, Leland, who was sitting next to me, exclaimed under his breath:

"My God, he's going to let the prosecutor know about that letter. Can't you stop him?"

It was too late. Kennedy had already begun to read Vera's letter. It was damning to Dixon, added to the other note found in the ammonia jar.

When he had finished reading, you could almost hear the throbbing in the room. A scowl overspread Senator Willard's features. Alma Willard was pale and staring wildly at Kennedy. Halsey Post, ever solicitous for her, handed her a glass of water from the table. Dr. Waterworth had forgotten his pain in his intense attention, and Mrs. Boncour seemed stunned with astonishment. The prosecuting attorney was eagerly taking notes.

"In some way," pursued Kennedy in an even voice, "this letter was either overlooked in the original correspondence of Dr. Dixon or it was added to it later. I shall come back to that presently. My next point is that Dr. Dixon says he received a letter from Thurston on the day the artist visited the Boncour bungalow. It asked about a certain headache compound, and his reply was brief and, as nearly as I can find out, read, 'This compound will not cure your headache except at the expense of reducing heart action dangerously.'

"Next comes the tragedy. On the evening of the day that Thurston left, after presumably telling Miss Lytton about what Kerr & Kimmel had discovered, Miss Lytton is found dying with a bottle containing cyanide and sublimate beside her. You are all familiar with the circumstances and with the note discovered in the jar of ammonia. Now, if the prosecutor will be so kind as to let me see that note—thank you, sir. This is the identical note. You have all heard the various theories of the jar and have read the note. Here it is in plain, cold black and white—in Dr. Dixon's own handwriting, as you know, and read: 'This will cure your headache, Dr. Dixon.'"

Alma Willard seemed as one paralyzed. Was Kennedy, who had been engaged by her father to defend her fiancé, about to convict him?

"Before we draw the final conclusion," continued Kennedy gravely, "there are one or two points I wish to elaborate. Walter, will you open that door into the main hall?"

I did so, and two policemen stepped in with a prisoner. It was Thurston, but changed almost beyond recognition. His clothes were worn, his beard shaved off, and he had a generally hunted appearance.

Thurston was visibly nervous. Apparently he had heard all that Kennedy had said and intended he should hear, for as he entered he almost broke away from the police officers in his eagerness to speak.

"Before God," he cried dramatically, "I am as innocent as you are of this crime, Professor Kennedy."

"Are you prepared to swear before *me*," almost shouted Kennedy, his eyes blazing, "that you were never served properly by your wife's lawyers in that suit?"

The man cringed back as if a stinging blow had been delivered between his eyes. As he met Craig's fixed glare, he knew there was no hope. Slowly, as if the words were being wrung from him syllable by syllable, he said in a muffled voice:

"No, I perjured myself. I was served in that suit. But—"

"And you swore falsely before Kimmel that you were not?" persisted Kennedy.

"Yes," he murmured. "But—"

"And you are prepared now to make another affidavit to that effect?"

"Yes," he replied. "If—"

"No buts or ifs, Thurston," cried Kennedy sarcastically. "What did you make that affidavit for? What is *your* story?"

"Kimmel sent for me. I did not go to him. He offered to pay my debts if I would swear to such a statement. I did not ask why or for whom. I swore to it and gave him a list of my creditors. I waited until they were paid. Then my conscience"—I could not help revolting at the thought of conscience in such a wretch, and the word itself seemed to stick in his throat as he went on and saw how feeble an impression he was making on us—"my conscience began to trouble me. I determined to see Vera, tell her all, and find out whether it was she who wanted this statement. I saw her. When at last I told her, she scorned me. I can confirm that, for as I left a man entered. I now knew how grossly I had sinned in listening to Mose Kimmel. I fled. I disappeared in Maine. I travelled. Every day my money grew less. At last, I was overtaken, captured, and brought back here."

He stopped and sank wretchedly down in a chair and covered his face with his hands.

"A likely story," muttered Leland in my ear.

Kennedy was working quickly. Motioning the officers to be seated by Thurston, he uncovered a jar which he had placed on the table. The color had now appeared in Alma's cheeks, as if hope had again sprung in her heart, and I fancied that Halsey Post saw his claim on her favor declining correspondingly.

"I want you to examine the letters in this case with me," continued Kennedy. "Take the letter which I read from Miss Lytton, which was found following the strange disappearance of the note from Thurston."

He dipped a pen into a little bottle, and wrote on a piece of paper:

What is your opinion about Cross's Headache Cure? Would
you recommend it for a nervous headache?
                     BURGESS THURSTON,
                              C/O MRS. S. BONCOUR.

Craig held up the writing so that we could all see that he had written what Dixon declared Thurston wrote in the note that had disappeared. Then he dipped another pen into a second bottle, and for
some time he scrawled on another sheet of paper. He held it up, but it
was still perfectly blank.

"Now," he added, "I am going to give a little demonstration which
I expect to be successful only in a measure. Here in the open sunshine
by this window I am going to place these two sheets of paper side by
side. It will take longer than I care to wait to make my demonstration
complete, but I can do enough to convince you."

For a quarter of an hour we sat in silence, wondering what he
would do next. At last he beckoned us over to the window. As we
approached he said, "On sheet number one I have written with quinoline; on sheet number two I wrote with a solution of nitrate of silver."

We bent over. The writing signed "Thurston" on sheet number
one was faint, almost imperceptible, but on paper number two, in
black letters, appeared what Kennedy had written: "Dear Harris:
Since we agreed to disagree we have at least been good friends."

"It is like the start of the substituted letter, and the other is like
the missing note," gasped Leland in a daze.

"Yes," said Kennedy quickly. "Leland, no one entered your office.
No one stole the Thurston note. No one substituted the Lytton letter. According to your own story, you took them out of the safe and
left them in the sunlight all day. The process that had been started
earlier in ordinary light, slowly, was now quickly completed. In other
words, there was writing which would soon fade away on one side of
the paper and writing which was invisible but would soon appear on
the other.

"For instance, quinoline rapidly disappears in sunlight. Starch
with a slight trace of iodine writes a light blue, which disappears in
air. It was something like that used in the Thurston letter. Then,

too, silver nitrate dissolved in ammonia gradually turns black as it is acted on by light and air. Or magenta treated with a bleaching agent in just sufficient quantity to decolorise it is invisible when used for writing. But the original color reappears as the oxygen of the air acts upon the pigment. I haven't a doubt but that my analyses of the inks are correct and on one side quinoline was used and on the other nitrate of silver. This explains the inexplicable disappearance of evidence incriminating one person, Thurston, and the sudden appearance of evidence incriminating another, Dr. Dixon. Sympathetic ink also accounts for the curious circumstance that the Lytton letter was folded up with the writing apparently outside. It was outside and unseen until the sunlight brought it out and destroyed the other, inside, writing—a chance, I suspect, that was intended for the police to see after it was completed, not for the defence to witness as it was taking place."

We looked at each other aghast. Thurston was nervously opening and shutting his lips and moistening them as if he wanted to say something but could not find the words.

"Lastly," went on Craig, utterly regardless of Thurston's frantic efforts to speak, "we come to the note that was discovered so queerly crumpled up in the jar of ammonia on Vera Lytton's dressing table. I have here a cylindrical glass jar in which I place some sal-ammoniac and quicklime. I will wet it and beat it a little. That produces the pungent gas of ammonia.

"On one side of this third piece of paper I myself write with this mercurous nitrate solution. You see, I leave no mark on the paper as I write. I fold it up and drop it into the jar—and in a few seconds withdraw it. Here is a very quick way of producing something like the slow result of sunlight with silver nitrate. The fumes of ammonia have formed the precipitate of black mercurous nitrate, a very distinct black writing which is almost indelible. That is what is technically called invisible rather than sympathetic ink."

We leaned over to read what he had written. It was the same as the note incriminating Dixon:

This will cure your headache.

DR. DIXON.

A servant entered with a telegram from New York. Scarcely stopping in his exposure, Kennedy tore it open, read it hastily, stuffed it into his pocket, and went on.

"Here in this fourth bottle I have an acid solution of iron chloride, diluted until the writing is invisible when dry," he hurried on. "I will just make a few scratches on this fourth sheet of paper—so. It leaves no mark. But it has the remarkable property of becoming red in vapor of sulpho-cyanide. Here is a long-necked flask of the gas, made by sulphuric acid acting on potassium sulpho-cyanide. Keep back, Dr. Waterworth, for it would be very dangerous for you to get even a whiff of this in your condition. Ah! See—the scratches I made on the paper are red."

Then hardly giving us more than a moment to let the fact impress itself on our minds, he seized the piece of paper and dashed it into the jar of ammonia. When he withdrew it, it was just a plain sheet of white paper again. The red marks which the gas in the flask had brought out of nothingness had been effaced by the ammonia. They had gone and left no trace.

"In this way I can alternately make the marks appear and disappear by using the sulpho-cyanide and the ammonia. Whoever wrote this note with Dr. Dixon's name on it must have had the doctor's reply to the Thurston letter containing the words, 'This will not cure your headache.' He carefully traced the words, holding the genuine note up to the light with a piece of paper over it, leaving out the word *not* and using only such words as he needed. This note was then destroyed.

"But he forgot that after he had brought out the red writing by the use of the sulpho-cyanide, and though he could count on Vera Lytton's placing the note in the jar of ammonia and hence obliterating the writing, while at the same time the invisible writing in the mercurous nitrate involving Dr. Dixon's name would be brought out by the ammonia indelibly on the other side of the note—he forgot"— Kennedy was now speaking eagerly and loudly—"that the sulpho-cyanide vapors could always be made to bring back to accuse him the words that the ammonia had blotted out."

Before the prosecutor could interfere, Kennedy had picked up the note found in the ammonia jar beside the dying girl and had jammed the state's evidence into the long-necked flask of sulpho-cyanide vapor.

"Don't fear," he said, trying to pacify the now furious prosecutor, "it will do nothing to the Dixon writing. That is permanent now, even if it is only a tracing."

When he withdrew the note, there was writing on both sides, the black of the original note and something in red on the other side.

We crowded around, and Craig read it with as much interest as any of us:

> Before taking the headache powder, be sure to place the contents of this paper in a jar with a little warm water.

"Hum," commented Craig, "this was apparently written on the outside wrapper of a paper folded about some sal-ammoniac and quicklime. It goes on:

> Just drop the whole thing in, *paper and all*. Then if you feel a faintness from the medicine the ammonia will quickly restore you. One spoonful of the headache powder swallowed quickly is enough.

No name was signed to the directions, but they were plainly written, and "*paper and all*" was underscored heavily.

Craig pulled out some letters. "I have here specimens of writing of many persons connected with this case, but I can see at a glance which one corresponds to the writing on this red death warrant by an almost inhuman fiend. I shall, however, leave that part of it to the handwriting experts to determine at the trial. Thurston, who was the man whom you saw enter the Boncour bungalow as you left—the constant visitor?"

Thurston had not yet regained his self-control, but with trembling forefinger he turned and pointed to Halsey Post.

"Yes, ladies and gentlemen," cried Kennedy as he slapped the telegram that had just come from New York down on the table decisively, "yes, the real client of Kerr & Kimmel, who bent Thurston to his purposes, was Halsey Post, once secret lover of Vera Lytton till threatened by scandal in Danbridge—Halsey Post, graduate in technology, student of sympathetic inks, forger of the Vera Lytton letter

and the other notes, and dealer in cyanides in the silversmithing busi-
ness, fortune hunter for the Willard millions with which to recoup the
Post & Vance losses, and hence rival of Dr. Dixon for the love of
Alma Willard. That is the man who wielded the poisoned pen. Dr.
Dixon is innocent."

A Literary Death

Martin Harry Greenberg

Dear Isaac:
THINGS HAVE settled down here sufficiently for me to try to answer your questions about the tragic death of Eddie Advent. As you know (perhaps too well), Eddie was a writer of ambition—he had a firmer grip on where he wanted to go and how he was going to get there than any SF writer I have ever met (and he would hate me, if he could see me categorizing him in any way), and it may have been ambition which finally killed him.

Anyway, here are the "facts" as best I can reconstruct them: Eddie had worked for years on what he thought was his masterpiece—a 900-page manuscript with the working title of *The Political Geography of the Promised World*, and like almost all his work, it was difficult to classify—perhaps "science fantasy" would be the closest, but it doesn't matter now. I read the manuscript and liked it—it was the best thing he had ever done (will ever do), but I had serious reservations about who, if anyone, would publish it, given present commercial realities. I suggested a university press, but Eddie flatly refused my offer of contacts

181

in those places—he wanted a major publisher, one who would give it maximum exposure and support. Well, the first big houses he tried all said no, several after holding it for quite a while. It was at this point that he approached old Doc Greenston at W & W. Now W & W is a medium-to-small New York house, with a distinguished past but with its best days definitely behind it.

But Doc really liked the manuscript, fought it through a very skeptical editorial board, and made Eddie a decent offer (I know, because Eddie told me about it). After much thought and discussion—he talked about this with at least seven authors and two agents—he told Doc he would take their offer subject to a few minor changes. I thought that everything was set, and so did everybody who knew about the project. It was at this point that the trouble began—Peter Dean of Solomon and Solomon (who had just been promoted from senior editor in charge of who knows what to editor-in-chief of their trade books division) told Eddie that his new position made it possible for him to take the book at four times the advance that Doc had offered and with a guaranteed ad budget of $45,000 to boot. But Eddie had already verbally accepted Doc's offer. Well, this didn't stop Eddie—he told me that he had worked too long and too hard to let his word stand in the way of his destiny (or words to that effect), and he said he was going to tell Doc the same thing. Doc (rest his soul) always believed that the only important thing in life was honor (how he lasted so long in publishing must remain one of the Great Mysteries of the Western World), and he was mad as hell at Eddie.

Now things become grim—Doc saw Eddie at the SFWA Party in New York, and in front of several witnesses (including yours truly) put a curse on him, telling him that he "would die a literary death" by 2:00 P.M., November 20, some two weeks away at the time. Eddie laughed in his face and no more words were spoken between them (as far as I know).

Now, I spoke with Eddie (remember that we were working on that big anthology during this period) at least six times after that night, so I have a pretty good idea of what he was thinking. You may or may not know that Eddie was a great admirer of Cornell Woolrich, and of course was familiar with that great and sadly neglected author's *Night Has a Thousand Eyes*, in which a man is told by a mystic (as I recall the story—I'm actually afraid to go back and read it again) that he will "die by the jaws of a lion." The guy carefully avoids zoos, cats, and anything feline until just before his death by the jaws of the lion that sits in front of the New York Public Library at Forty-second and Fifth. I mention this because Eddie did—as time went by, he got more and more nervous, even desperate. He told me on the phone that he found himself avoiding bookstores, libraries, publishers, other writers, etc. (remember, the curse said he would die a *literary death*). This finally became an obsession by the time of my last two conversations with him (especially after poor Doc had committed suicide). I told him that the right thing to do was to honor his word to Doc, but he steadfastly refused—ole devil ambition, I guess, or maybe he just thought it was too late for the curse to be removed, now that Doc was dead.

As best as I can piece things together (and I talked with everyone, including the state police—you should see my phone bill for November), Eddie's concern turned into panic a few days before November 20 (you might recall that week because it was the week of the first big snowstorm in the Northeast), and he holed up in his apartment (he had apparently *given away* his typewriter and all his books by this time). On the morning of the twentieth, another tenant in his building saw him getting into his car—he had told me that he felt totally vulnerable in New York, the center of this country's literary world. Eddie had decided to flee the city on that fateful day. I don't know his exact route, but he was obviously (since that is where they found the body and car) heading out on the Garden State Parkway, making his way slowly (since the traffic was heavy and the melting snow made driving hazardous), and for all I know, watching out for bookmobiles! The last details are somewhat fuzzy, but his car apparently skidded on the melting snow, went into a spin and off the road just before 2:00 P.M. (the clock in the car was smashed and read 1:58). He died instantly of a broken neck, and with his car half buried—in a pile of slush.

All best wishes,
Marty the Other

The Adventure of the Penny Magenta

August Derleth

FROM HIS PLACE AT the window one summer morning, Solar Pons said, "Ah, we are about to have a visitor and, I trust, a client. London has been oppressively dull this week, and some diversion is long past due."

I stepped over to his side and looked down.

Our prospective visitor was just in the act of stepping out of his cab. He was a man somewhat past middle-age, of medium height, and spare almost to thinness. He affected a greying Van Dyke and eye-glasses in old-fashioned square frames. He wore a greening black bowler and a scuffed smoking jacket, beneath which showed a waist-coat of some flowered material, and he carried a cane, though he did not walk with any pronounced impediment.

"A tradesman," I ventured.

"The keeper of a small shop," said Pons.

"Dry goods?"

"You observed his clothing, Parker. His square spectacles and his walking stick are both old-fashioned. I submit he is in antiques or something of that sort. The nature of his business is such as to permit the casual, since he evidently wears his smoking jacket at his work."

"Perhaps he came from his home?"

"On the contrary. It is now ten o'clock. Some time after he arrived at his shop this morning something occurred that has brought him to us."

But our caller was now at the threshold, and in a moment our good landlady, Mrs. Johnson, had ushered him into our quarters. He bowed to her, and, his glance passing over me, he bowed to Pons.

"Mr. Solar Pons?"

"I am at your service. Pray sit down."

Our visitor sat down to face Pons, who was now leaning against the mantel, his eyes twinkling with anticipation.

"My name is Athos Humphreys," said our client. "I have a small shop for antiques, old books, and stamps near Hampstead Heath. Other than that I doubt your need to know."

"Save that you are a member of the Masonic order, a bachelor or widower accustomed to living alone, without an assistant at your shop and with insufficient business to demand your unremitting attendance there," said Pons. "Pray continue, Mr. Humphreys."

Our client betrayed neither astonishment nor displeasure at Pon's little deductions. His glance fell to his Masonic ring, then to the torn and worn cuffs of his smoking jacket, which no self-respecting woman would have permitted to go unmended, and finally to the lone key depending over the pocket into which he had hastily thrust his chain of keys after locking his shop.

"I'm glad to see I've made no mistake in coming to you, Mr. Pons," he continued. "The problem doesn't concern me personally, however, as far as I can determine, but my shop. I must tell you that for the past three mornings I have had indisputable evidence that my shop has been entered. Yet nothing has been taken."

A small sound of satisfaction escaped Pons. "And what was the nature of your evidence that the shop had been entered, if nothing was taken, Mr. Humphreys?" he asked.

"Well, sir, I am a most methodical man. I maintain a certain order in my shop, no matter how careless it looks—that is by design, of course, for an antique shop ought to have an appearance of careful disorder. For the past three mornings I have noticed—sometimes not at once on my arrival—that some object has been moved and put back not quite where it stood before. I have never discovered any way of entry; all else, save for one or two objects, remains as I left it; so I can only suppose that whoever entered my shop did so by means of the door, to which, I ought to say, I have the only key."

"You are fully aware of your inventory, Mr. Humphreys?"

"Positively, sir. I know every item in my shop, and there is nothing there of sufficient value to tempt anyone but a sneak thief content with small reward for his pains."

"Yet it is patent that someone is going to considerable pains to search your shop night after night," said Pons. "A man in your business must lead a relatively sedentary life, Mr. Humphreys. Did you, immediately prior to this sequence of events, do anything at all to attract attention to yourself?"

"No, sir."

"Or your business?"

"No, sir." But here our client hesitated, as if he were about to speak otherwise, yet thought better of it.

"Something caused you to hesitate, Mr. Humphreys. What was it?"

"Nothing of any consequence. It is true that a week ago I was forced to post a small personal asking that relatives of the late Arthur Benefield come forward and call on me at the shop."

"Who was Arthur Benefield?"

"A patron of mine."

"Surely an unusual patron if you knew neither his address nor his heirs," said Pons. "For if you did, you would hardly have had to extend an invitation to his heirs through the columns of the papers."

"That is correct, Mr. Pons. He left no address. He appeared at my shop for the first time about a month ago, and brought with him a manila envelope filled with loose stamps. He had posted the envelope to me—apparently at a branch post office—but had then immediately retrieved it from the clerk, evidently someone whose acquaintance he had made—and brought it in person. He appeared to be an American gentleman, and asked me to keep the stamps for him. He paid a 'rental' fee of five pounds for that service during the month following his visit. He also bought several stamps from my collection and added them to his own.

"Mr. Benefield was run down and killed in an automobile accident ten days ago. I saw his picture in one of the papers, together with a request for relatives to come forward. Let me hasten to assure you, Mr. Pons, if you are thinking that the entry to my shop has anything to do with Mr. Benefield, I'm afraid you're very much mistaken. I took the liberty of examining the contents of Mr. Benefield's envelope as soon as I learned of his death. It contains no stamp worth more than a few shillings. Indeed, I doubt very much if the entire lot of mixed stamps would command more than ten pounds."

Pons stood for a moment in an attitude of deep thought. Then he said, "I fancy a look at the premises would not be amiss. Are you prepared to take us to your shop, Mr. Humphreys?"

"I would be honored to do so, Mr. Pons. I have a cab waiting below, if you care to return with me."

OUR CLIENT'S WAS indeed a little shop. It was one of those charming, old-fashioned places not uncommon in London and its environs, standing as if untouched by time from 1780 onward. A pleasant, tinkling bell announced our entrance, Mr. Humphreys having thrown the door wide and stood aside to permit us to pass. Then he in turn passed us, hanging his bowler on a little rack not far from the door, and throwing his keys carelessly to his counter. His shop was crowded, and wore just that air of planned carelessness which would intrigue the searcher after curios or unusual pieces for the household. Shelves, floors, tables—all were filled with bric-a-brac, knickknacks, and period pieces. One wall was given over to books of all kinds, neatly arranged on shelves which reached from floor to ceiling. At the far end of the shop—next to a curtained-off alcove which was evidently a small place in which our client could brew himself tea, if he liked, for the sound of boiling water came from it—stood Mr. Humphreys' desk, a secretary of Chippendale design.

Our client was eager to show us how he had discovered that his shop had been entered in the night. He went directly to a Chinese vase which stood on top of a lacquered box on a table not far from the counter.

"If you will look carefully, Mr. Pons, you will see that the position of this vase varies by a quarter of an inch from the faint circle of lint and dust which indicates where it stood before it was moved. I have not had occasion to move this piece for at least a week. Of itself, it has no value, being an imitation Han Dynasty piece. Nor has the lacquer box on which it stands. The box, I have reason to believe, has been opened. Of course, it is empty."

Pons, however, was not particularly interested in our client's demonstration. "And where do you keep Mr. Benefield's stamps?" he asked.

Our client went around his counter and placed his right hand on a letter rack which stood on his desk. "Right here, Mr. Pons."

"Dear me!" exclaimed Pons, with an ill-concealed smile twitching his lips, "is that not an unorthodox place for it?"

"It was where Mr. Benefield asked me to keep it. Indeed, he enjoined me to keep it here, in this envelope, in this place."

"So that anyone whose eye chanced to fall upon it would think it part of your correspondence, Mr. Humphreys?"

"I had not thought of it so, but I suppose it would be true," said Humphreys thoughtfully.

"Let us just have a look at Mr. Benefield's collection of stamps."

"Very well, Mr. Pons. It can do no harm, now the poor fellow is dead."

He handed the manila envelope to Pons. It was not a large envelope—perhaps four and a half inches by six and a half or thereabouts, but it bulged with its contents, and it had been stamped heavily with British commemorative issues of larger-than-common size. It had been addressed to Mr. Humphreys, and the stamps on its face had been duly cancelled; manifestly, if Mr. Humphreys' story were true, Mr. Benefield had had to apply to someone in the post office for its return to his hand, so that he could bring it in person to our client's shop. Pons studied the envelope thoughtfully.

"It did not seem to you strange that Mr. Benefield should make such a request of you, Mr. Humphreys?"

"Mr. Pons, I am accustomed to dealing with all manner of strange people. I suppose the collector is always rather more extraordinary in his habits and conduct than ordinary people."

"Perhaps that is true," pursued Pons. "Still, the circumstances of your possession of this envelope suggest that it contains something of value—of such value, indeed, that its owner was extremely reluctant to let it out of his sight long enough for the postman to deliver it, and left it here only because of dire necessity."

"But if that were true," objected our client reasonably, "what had he to gain by leaving it here?"

"In such plain sight, too, Mr. Humphreys," said Pons, chuckling. "I submit he had to gain what he most wanted—effective concealment. There is a story by the American, Poe, which suggests the gambit—a letter hidden in a torn envelope on a rack in sight of anyone who might walk into the room. What better place of concealment for an object—let us say, a stamp—than in the letter rack of a man who does a small philatelic business?"

"Mr. Pons, your theory is sound, but in fact it doesn't apply. I have gone over the stamps in that envelope with the greatest care. I assure you, on my word as a modest authority in philately, that there is not a stamp in that collection worth a second glance from a serious collector of any standing. There is most certainly nothing there to tempt a thief to make such elaborate forays into my humble establishment."

"I believe you, Mr. Humphreys," said Pons, still smiling. "Yet I put it to you that this is the object of your malefactor's search."

"Mr. Pons, I would willingly surrender it to him—if he could prove he had a right to it, of course."

"Let us not be hasty," said Pons dryly.

So saying, he calmly opened the envelope and unceremoniously emptied its contents to the counter before us. Then, much to our client's amazement, he bestowed not a glance at the stamps but gave his attention again to the envelope, which he now took over to the window and held up against the sunlight. The manila, however, was too thick to permit him any vision through it.

"It would seem to be an ordinary envelope," he said. "And these stamps which were to have paid its way here?"

"They are only British Empire Exhibition adhesives, issue of 1924, not very old, and not worth much more than their face value."

Pons lowered the envelope and turned to look toward the curtained alcove. "Is that not a teakettle, Mr. Humphreys?"

"Yes, sir. I keep hot water always ready for tea."

"Let us just repair to that room, if you please."

"It is hardly large enough for us all."

"Very well, then. I will take the liberty of using it, and you and Parker may guard the door."

Our client flashed a puzzled glance at me, but I could not relieve his dubiety nor inform him of Pons's purpose. That, however, was soon clear, for Pons went directly to the teapot on Mr. Humphreys' electric plate, and proceeded without a qualm to hold the stamped corner of the envelope over the steam.

"What are you doing, Mr. Pons?" cried our client in alarm.

"I trust I am about to find the solution to the initial part of our little problem, Mr. Humphreys," said Pons.

Our client suppressed the indignation he must have felt, and watched in fascinated interest as Pons finally peeled back the stamps.

"Aha!" exclaimed Pons, "what have we here?"

Beneath the stamps lay revealed, carefully protected by a thin square of cellophane, a shabby-looking stamp of a faded magenta color. Indeed, it was such a stamp that, were I a philatelist, I would have cast aside, for not only was it crudely printed, but it had also been clipped at the corners. Pons, however, handled it with the greatest care.

"I daresay this is the object of the search which has been conducted of your premises, Mr. Humphreys," said Pons. "Unless I am very much mistaken, this is the famous one-penny magenta rarity, printed in British Guiana in 1856, discovered by a boy of fifteen here in our country, and originally sold for six shillings. After being in the collection of Philippe Ferrari for many years, it was sold to a rich American at auction for the fabulous price of seventy-five hundred pounds. Correct me if I am wrong, Mr. Humphreys."

Our client, who had been staring at the stamp in awe and fascination, found his voice. "You have made no error of fact, Mr. Pons, but one of assumption. There is only one penny magenta known to exist, despite the most intensive search for others. That stamp is still in the collection of the widow of the American millionaire who bought it at the Ferrari auction in 1925. This one can be only a forgery—a very clever, most deceptive counterfeit—but still, Mr. Pons, a forgery, with only the value of a curiosity. The original would now be worth close to ten thousand pounds; but this copy is scarcely worth the labor and care it took to make it."

Pons carefully replaced the stamps on the envelope, keeping the penny magenta to one side. Then he returned to the counter and put the loose stamps back into the envelope.

"If you have another, larger envelope, Mr. Humphreys, put this into it, and label it 'Property of Arthur Benefield,'" instructed Pons. "I am somewhat curious now to know more of your late customer. Was he a young man?"

"Mr. Pons, I can only show you the clipping from the *News of the World*. It conveys all I can tell you," replied Humphreys.

He went back to his desk, opened a drawer, and took out the clipping.

Pons bent to it, and I looked over his shoulder.

The photograph was that of a young man, certainly not over thirty-five. He was not ill-favored in looks, and wore a short moustache. He appeared to be of medium weight. The story beneath it indicated that the photograph had been found in his billfold, but that no address had been discovered. From the presence of American currency in the billfold, the authorities had concluded that Benefield was an American tourist in London. They had had no response to official inquiries at the usual sources, however.

Benefield had been found in the street one night. Evidence indicated that he had been struck and killed by a fast-traveling car; police were looking for one which must have been severely damaged by the force of the impact. Car and driver had vanished, as was to be expected.

Pons read this in silence and handed it back to our client.

"Our next step," he said, "will be to catch the intruder. I have no question but that he will return tonight."

Athos Humphreys paled a little. "I should say, Mr. Pons, I am not a wealthy man. I had not inquired about your fee . . ."

"Say no more, Mr. Humphreys," replied Pons with animation. "If you will permit me to retain this little stamp for its curiosity value, I shall feel amply repaid."

"By all means, Mr. Pons."

"Very well, then. Parker and I will return here late this afternoon prepared to spend the night in your shop, if that is agreeable to you."

"It is indeed, sir."

We bade our client farewell and repaired to our lodgings.

We RETURNED TO Athos Humphreys' antique shop just before his closing hour that evening. It was not without some patent misgivings that our client locked us into his shop and departed. Clearly he was doubtful of our success and perhaps concerned lest our venture result in a scuffle in the narrow confines of his premises, and concomitant damage to his stock.

Pons had insisted that both of us be armed. In addition, he carried a powerful electric torch. So protected, we took up a cramped position concealed behind the curtain in the little alcove leading off the shop. Once we were alone, Pons warned again that our quarry was likely to be more desperate than I had imagined, and adjured me to keep my eyes on the door of the shop.

"You are so positive he'll come by the door," I said. "Suppose he opens a window and drops in from behind?"

"No, Parker, he will not. He has a key," replied Pons. "Surely you observed how careless Humphreys was with his keys when he came in with us this morning! He simply threw them to the counter and left them in plain sight. Anyone prepared to do so could have made wax impressions of the lot. I have no doubt that is what took place, as soon as our client's advertisement appeared and apprised our quarry that Humphreys undoubtedly possessed something belonging to Benefield, and what, more likely, than the very object of his search? I see him as a patient and dangerous man, unwilling to be caught, but determined to have what he is after."

"The penny magenta? But why would anyone take the trouble to conceal a forgery so carefully?"

"Why, indeed!" answered Pons enigmatically. "It suggests nothing to you?"

"Only that the man who wants it is deceived as to its actual value."

"Nothing other?"

"I can think of nothing."

"Very well, then. Let us just look at the problem anew. Mr. Athos Humphreys, a comparatively obscure dealer in antiques, is sought out by an American as a repository for a packet of stamps, all of no great value. Mr. Benefield has gone to the trouble of achieving a cancellation of his stamps, and then to the even greater trouble of recovering the packet to bring it in person—a considerable achievement, considering the rigidity of our post office. He pays at least half what his packet of stamps is manifestly worth to make sure that Humphreys keeps it where he directs. And where does he direct that it be kept? In plain sight in Humphreys' own letter rack, after Benefield has made certain that it bears every appearance of having been posted to Humphreys. Does all this still suggest nothing further to you, Parker?"

"Only that Benefield seemed certain someone wanted the packet."

"Capital! You are making progress."

"So he made sure it wouldn't attract attention, and, if seen, would be mistaken for other than what it was. The envelope bore no return address, and the name of Humphreys was hurriedly printed in blocks. That, I presume, was so the man who wanted it wouldn't recognize Benefield's handwriting, which very probably he knew."

"It gives me pleasure to discover how handsomely your capacity for observation has grown, Parker. But—no more?"

"I fear I have shot my bolt, Pons."

"Well, then, let us just say a few words about Mr. Benefield. It does not seem to you strange that he should have so conveniently met with a fatal accident after reaching London?"

"Accidents happen every day. It is a well-known fact that the accident toll exceeds the mortality rate in wartime."

"I submit that the late Benefield and his pursuer were in this matter together. I put it to you further that Benefield slipped away from his partner in the venture and came to London by himself to offer the penny magenta for sale without the necessity of dividing the spoils with his partner, who followed and found him but has not yet found the stamp. It is not too much to conclude that it was his hand at the wheel of the car that caused Benefield's death."

"Ingenious," I said dubiously.

"Elementary, my dear Parker," said Pons.

"Except for the fact that the penny magenta is a forgery," I finished.

"Ah, Parker, you put my poor powers to shame," he answered with a dry chuckle. "But now I think we had better keep quiet. I should tell you I have notified Inspector Taylor, who will be within earshot waiting upon our signal."

I HAD BEGUN to drowse, when Pons's light touch on my arm woke me. The hour was close to midnight, and the sound of a key in the lock came distinctly to ear. In a moment the outer door opened, and, from my position behind the curtain, I saw a dark figure slip into the shop. In but a moment more, the shade of a dark lantern was drawn cautiously a little to one side. Its light fell squarely upon the counter and there, framed in it, was the envelope on which our client had written Arthur Benefield's name.

The light held to the counter.

Then, in four rapid and silent strides, the intruder was at the counter. I saw his hand reach down and take up the envelope.

At that moment Pons turned on his electric torch and silhouetted a well-dressed, thin-faced young man whose startled glance gave him a distinctly foxlike look. He stood for but a split second in the light; then he dropped, spun around, and leaped for the door.

Pons was too quick for him. He caught up a heavy iron and threw it with all his force. It struck our quarry cruelly on the side of one knee; he went down and stayed down.

"Keep your hands out of your pockets; we are armed," said Pons, advancing toward him. "Parker, just open the door and fire a shot into the air. That will bring Taylor."

Our quarry sat up, one hand gripping his knee painfully, the other still clinging to the envelope of stamps. "The most you can charge me with," he said in a cultured voice, "is breaking and entering. Perhaps theft. This is as much my property as it was Arthur's."

"I fancy the charge will be murder," said Pons, as Inspector Taylor's pounding footsteps waxed in the night.

BACK IN OUR quarters at 7B Praed Street, Pons lingered over a pipe of shag. I, too, hesitated to go to bed.

"You do not seem one whit puzzled over this matter, Pons," I said at last. "Yet I confess that its entire motivation seems far too slight to justify its events."

"You are certainly right, Parker," he answered with maddening gravity. "It does not then suggest anything further to you?"

"No, I am clear as to the picture."

"But not as to its interpretation, eh?"

"No."

"I submit there is a basic error in your reasoning, Parker. It has occurred to you to realize that one would hardly go to such lengths, even to commit murder, for a counterfeit stamp worth five pounds at best. Yet it does not seem to have occurred to you that the penny magenta I have here as a gift from our client may indeed be worth, as he estimated, ten thousand pounds?"

"We know that the single copy of that stamp exists in an American collection."

"Say, rather, we believe it does. I submit that this is the only genuine British Guiana penny magenta rarity, and that the copy in the America collection is a counterfeit. I took the liberty of sending a cable this afternoon, and I fancy we shall have a visitor from America just as fast as an aeroplane will make it possible from New York to Croydon."

PONS WAS NOT in error.

Three days later, a representative of the American collector presented himself at our quarters and paid Pons a handsome reward for the recovery of the penny magenta. Both Benefield and his partner, who had been identified as a man named Watt Clark, had been in the collector's service. They had manufactured the false penny magenta and exchanged it for the genuine stamp, after which they had left their positions. The substitution had not been noticed until Pons's cable sent the collector to the experts, whose verification of Pons's suspicion had resulted in the dispatching of the collector's representative to bear the fabulously valuable penny magenta home in person.

Letter from a Very Worried Man

Henry Slesar

Here, within a thousand words, is a vignette—a portrait of our disturbing times . . .

ABBY HAD SPENT THE past four days with her parents in Springfield. So as soon as she got back to Chicago, she anxiously examined the accumulated mail in her mailbox. She shuffled hurriedly through the envelopes, magazines, and leaflets until she saw the familiar scrawl of Richard's handwriting. She wanted this letter above all, because it was from her fiancé, all the way from New York where he was attending a physicists' conference.

She waited until she was settled in a lounge chair, with a fresh cigarette between her lips. Then she tore open the envelope and extracted the folded sheet.

Dear Abby,
I love you. We're in the fourth day of the Conference now, and nobody's gotten drunk yet. What a convention! You'll be

happy to hear that there are only four women physicists in the crowd, and they're all strictly from Lower Slobbovia, so you can stop worrying about my dubious virtue. Did I mention that I love you?

There was a seminar yesterday on the Physicist's Responsibility in the Modern World, or some such jawbreaking title. The yawn might have come up like thunder in the audience, except that there were some pretty scary headlines on the hotel newsstand that morning, so everybody was a bit edgy. I got up and did some talking myself, but maybe I should have kept my mouth shut. You know how I am when I get started on Topic A.

I know what you're thinking now: Old guilt-ridden Richard's off the deep end again, blaming himself for helping to make the H-bomb. Well, I've been thinking about it, sure. How can you help it in this atmosphere? And when I look at the headlines, and remember that we're getting married in two weeks—how can you blame me for a slight case of jitters? We're walking down the aisle under the most menacing shadow that ever fell across this cockeyed world. We're going to have children (in due course, or didn't you know?) that will have to live, and maybe die, with the H-bomb in their backyard. You can't stop these thoughts, Abby, not even by trying. I thought about it all last night, and not sleeping much, if you want the truth. Wondering how a guy like me, a guy who helped put the thing together, who feels like a criminal, has a right to such happy prospects. Marrying you, settling down, raising kids, just like everybody else, just like Joe Normal. But then I think, well, I'm Joe Normal, too, and if the bomb hits, I go to pieces like everyone else; if the Strontium 90 starts filling up the water, and the milk, and the green vegetables, well, I'll get just as sick and dead as the next man. I'm not so special, honey. I don't feel guilty any more; just scared.

But you know something? I learned something out here. Sitting around with the guys, meeting up with the science boys from England, and France, and Yugoslavia (yep, they're here, too). I began to realize something. I began to think that maybe the problems of getting along with each other aren't

much worse than math problems. Even the big political problems, the ones which end up *Bang!* if the answers come out
wrong, they can be licked, too. Sure, we'll be depending on a
lot of people whose actions we can't predict or control—but
we put our trust in strangers every day. The guy who drives the
bus. The airline pilot. The elevator operator. The short-order
cook. One wrong step, and these guys could end our short,
worried lives, too. So why not have faith? Why not trust a little bit? Maybe there won't be any big boom to put an end to
our plans. Maybe there'll be sweetness and light for a change.
Peace on Earth, good will to men, and all that jazz.

I don't know what started me feeling this way. (No, I haven't
touched a drop.) But all of a sudden, I'm hopeful. I feel good
about you, and about us, and about our wedding day. I feel
good about how we're going to live, and how the kids are
going to grow up, and how we're going to sit in front of the
fireplace for the next fifty years until we run out of things to
say. The truth is, honey, all of a sudden I'm an optimist. I think
we're going to lick our problems, all of them. I think the
patient's really and truly going to live.

Well, that's all the ink in this pen. I'm going to take a walk
around this town now, and see how it looks for a honeymoon.
I'll let you know if it measures up to our high standards.

I love you, by the way.

Yours,

Richard.

Abby sighed happily at the conclusion of the letter, and ground
out her cigarette in an ashtray. Then she looked at the next envelope
in the pile of mail. It appeared to be official and had a local postmark,
so she opened it curiously.

The contents were brief.

Dear Miss Butler:

We have been unable to reach you for the past few days, to inform you that the New York Police Department has contacted us regarding a man identified as Mr. Richard Cole. Mr. Cole was killed on the night of September 4 by a street gang of young hoodlums, and your name and address were discovered among his effects. We would appreciate it if you would contact Lieutenant Frank Kowlanski, Precinct 63, Chicago Police Department.

Pure Rotten

John Lutz

M AY 25, 7:00 A.M. TELEPHONE call to Clark Forthcue, Forthcue
Mansion, Long Island:

"Mr. Forthcue, don't talk, listen. Telephone calls can be traced
easy, letters can't be. This will be the only telephone call, and it will
be short. We have your stepdaughter Imogene, who will be referred to
in typed correspondence as Pure Rotten, a name that fits a
ten-year-old spoiled rich brat like this one. For more information
check the old rusty mailbox in front of the deserted Garver farm at the
end of Wood Road near your property. Check it tonight. Check it
every night. Tell the police or anyone else besides your wife about this
and the kid dies. We'll know. We mean business."

Click.

Buzz.

May 25

Dear Mr. Forthcue:
Re our previous discussion on Pure Rotten: It will cost you exactly one million dollars for the return of the merchandise unharmed. We have researched and we know this is well within your capabilities. End the agony you and your wife are going through. Give us your answer by letter. We will check the Garver mailbox sometime after ten tomorrow evening. Your letter had better be there.

Sincerely,
A. Snatcher

Snatchers, Inc.
May 26

Mr. Snatcher:
Do not harm Pure Rotten. I have not contacted the authorities and do not intend to do so. Mrs. Forthcue and I will follow your instructions faithfully. But your researchers have made an error. I do not know if one million dollars is within my capabilities, and it will take me some time to find out. Be assured that you have my complete cooperation in this matter. Of course if some harm should come to Pure Rotten, this cooperation would abruptly cease.

Anxiously,
Clark Forthcue

Dear Mr. Forthcue:
Come off it. We know you can come up with the million. But in the interest of that cooperation you mentioned we are willing to come down to $750,000 for the return of Pure Rotten. It will be a pleasure to get this item off our hands, *one way or the other*.

Determinedly,
A. Snatcher

Snatchers, Inc.
May 27

Dear Mr. Snatcher:
I write this letter in the quietude of my veranda, where for the
first time in years it is tranquil enough for me to think clearly,
so I trust I am dealing with this matter correctly. By lowering
your original figure by 25 percent you have shown yourselves
to be reasonable men, with whom an equally reasonable man
might negotiate. Three quarters of a million is, as I am sure
you are aware, a substantial sum of money. Even one in my
position does not raise that much on short notice without also
raising a few eyebrows and some suspicion. Might you consider a lower sum?

Reasonably,
Clark Forthcue

Dear Mr. Forthcue:
Pure Rotten is a perishable item and a great inconvenience to
store. In fact, live explosives might be a more manageable
commodity for our company to handle. In light of this we
accede to your request for a lower figure by dropping our fee to
$500,000 delivered immediately. This is our final figure. It
would be easier, in fact a pleasure, for us to dispose of this commodity and do business elsewhere.

Still determinedly,
A. Snatcher

Snatchers, Inc.
May 29

Dear Mr. Snatcher:
This latest lowering of your company's demands is further proof
that I am dealing with intelligent and realistic individuals.

Of course my wife has been grieving greatly over the loss,
however temporary, of Pure Rotten, though with the aid of
new furs and jewelry she has recovered from similar griefs.

When one marries a woman, as in acquiring a company, one must accept the liabilities along with the assets. With my rapidly improving nervous condition, and as my own initial grief and anxiety subside somewhat, I find myself at odds with my wife and of the opinion that your $ 500,000 figure is outrageously high. Think more in terms of tens of thousands.

Regards,
Clark Forthcue

Forthcue:
Ninety thousand is *it! Final!* By midnight tomorrow in the Garver mailbox, or Pure Rotten will be disposed of. You are keeping us in an uncomfortable position and we don't like it. We are not killers, but we can be.

A. Snatcher

Snatchers, Inc.
May 30

Dear Mr. Snatcher:
Free after many years of the agonizing pain of my ulcer, I can think quite objectively on this matter. Though my wife demands that I pay some ransom, ninety thousand dollars is out of the question. I suggest you dispose of the commodity under discussion as you earlier intimated you might. After proof of this action, twenty thousand dollars will accompany my next letter in the Garver mailbox. Since I have been honest with you and have not contacted the authorities, no one, including my wife, need know the final arrangements of our transaction.

Cordially,
Clark Forthcue

Forthcue:
Are you crazy? This is a human life. We are not killers. But you are right about one thing—no amount of money is worth more

than your health. Suppose we return Pure Rotten unharmed tomorrow night? Five thousand dollars for our trouble and silence will be plenty.

A. Snatcher

Snatchers, Inc.
May 31

Dear Mr. Snatcher:
After due reflection I must unequivocally reject your last suggestion and repeat my own suggestion that you dispose of the matter at hand in your own fashion. I see no need for further correspondence in this matter.

Clark Forthcue

June 1

Clark Forthcue:
There has been a take over of the bord of Snatchers, Inc. and my too vise presidents who haven't got a choice agree with me, the new president. I have all the carbon copys of Snatchers, Inc. letters to you and all your letters back to us. The law is very seveer with kidnappers and even more seveer with people who want to kill kids.

But the law is not so seveer with kids, in fact will forgive them for almost anything if it is there first ofense. If you don't want these letters given to the police you will leave 500,000 dollars tomorrow night in Garvers old mailbox. I meen it. Small bils is what we want but some fiftys and hundreds will be o.k.

Sinseerly,
Pure Rotten

Computers Don't Argue

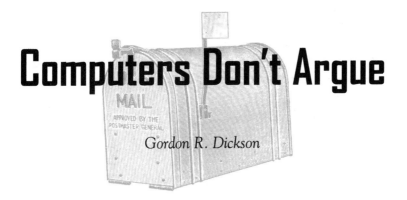

Gordon R. Dickson

TREASURE BOOK CLUB
PLEASE DO NOT FOLD,
SPINDLE, OR MUTILATE
THIS CARD

MR WALTER A. CHILD   Balance: $4.98
Dear Customer: Enclosed in your latest book selection,
Kidnapped, by Robert Louis Stevenson.

437 Woodlawn Drive
Panduk, Michigan
Nov. 16, 198–

Treasure Book Club
1823 Mandy Street
Chicago, Illinois

Dear Sirs:

I wrote you recently about the computer punch card you sent, billing me for *Kim,* by Rudyard Kipling. I did not open the package containing it until I had already mailed you my check for the amount on the card. On opening the package, I found the book missing half its pages. I sent it back to you, requesting either another copy or my money back, Instead, you have sent me a copy of *Kidnapped,* by Robert Louis Stevenson. Will you please straighten this out?

I hereby return the copy of *Kidnapped.*

Sincerely yours,
Walter A. Child

TREASURE BOOK CLUB
SECOND NOTICE
PLEASE DO NOT FOLD,
SPINDLE, OR MUTILATE THIS CARD

Mr. Walter A. Child   Balance: $4.98
For *Kidnapped,* by Robert Louis Stevenson
(If remittance has been made for the above, please disregard this notice)

437 Woodlawn Drive
Panduk, Michigan
Jan. 21, 198–

Treasure Book Club
1823 Mandy Street
Chicago, Illinois

Dear Sirs:

May I direct your attention to my letter of November 16, 198–? You are still continuing to dun me with computer punch cards for a book I did not order. Whereas, actually, it is your company that owes me money.

Sincerely yours,
Walter A. Child

⌒

Treasure Book Club
1823 Mandy Street
Chicago, Illinois
Feb. 1, 198–

Mr. Walter A. Child
437 Woodlawn Drive
Panduk, Michigan

Dear Mr. Child:

We have sent you a number of reminders concerning an amount owing to us as a result of book purchases you have made from us. This amount, which is $4.98, is now long overdue.

This situation is disappointing to us, particularly since there was no hesitation on our part in extending you credit at the time original arrangements for these purchases were made by you. If we do not receive payment in full by return mail, we will be forced to turn the matter over to a collection agency.

Very truly yours,
Samuel P. Grimes
Collection Mgr.

⌒

437 Woodlawn Drive
Panduk, Michigan
Feb. 5, 198–

Dear Mr. Grimes:

Will you stop sending me punch cards and form letters and make me some kind of a direct answer from a human being?

I don't owe you money. *You* owe me money. Maybe I should turn your company over to a collection agency.

Walter A. Child

⌒

FEDERAL COLLECTION OUTFIT
88 Prince Street
Chicago, Illinois
Feb. 28, 198–

Mr. Walter A. Child
437 Woodlawn Drive
Panduk, Michigan

Dear Mr. Child:

Your account with the Treasure Book Club, of $4.98 plus interest and charges, has been turned over to our agency for collection. The amount due is now $6.83. Please send your check for this amount or we shall be forced to take immediate action.

Jacob N. Harshe
Vice President

FEDERAL COLLECTION OUTFIT
88 Prince Street
Chicago, Illinois
April 8, 198–

Mr. Walter A. Child
437 Woodlawn Drive
Panduk, Michigan

Dear Mr. Child:

You have seen fit to ignore our courteous requests to settle your long overdue account with Treasure Book Club, which is now, with accumulated interest and charges, in the amount of $7.51.

If payment in full is not forthcoming by April 11, 198–, we will be forced to turn the matter over to our attorneys for immediate court action.

Ezekiel B. Harshe
President

MALONEY, MAHONEY, MacNAMARA and PRUITT
Attorneys

89 Prince Street
Chicago, Illinois
April 29, 198–

Mr. Walter A. Child
437 Woodlawn Drive
Panduk, Michigan

Dear Mr. Child:

Your indebtedness to the Treasure Book Club has been referred to us for legal action to collect.

This indebtedness is now in the amount of $10.01. If you will send us this amount so that we may receive it before May 5, 198–, the matter may be satisfied. However, if we do not receive satisfaction in full by that date, we will take steps to collect through the courts.

I am sure you will see the advantage of avoiding a judgment against you, which as a matter of record would do lasting harm to your credit rating.

Very truly yours,
Hagthorpe M. Pruitt Jr.
Attorney at Law

437 Woodlawn Drive
Panduk, Michigan
May 4, 198–

Mr. Hagthorpe M. Pruitt Jr.
Maloney, Mahoney, MacNamara and Pruitt
89 Prince Street
Chicago, Illinois

Dear Mr. Pruitt:

You don't know what a pleasure it is to me in this matter to get a letter from a live human being to whom I can explain the situation.

This whole matter is silly. I explained it fully in my letters to the Treasure Book Company. But I might as well have been trying to explain to the computer that puts out their punch cards, for all the good it seemed to do. Briefly, what happened was I ordered a copy of *Kim*, by Rudyard Kipling, for $4.98. When I opened the package they sent me, I found the book had only half its pages, but I'd previously mailed a check to pay them for the book.

I sent the book back to them, asking either for a whole copy or my money back. Instead, they sent me a copy of *Kidnapped*, by Robert Louis Stevenson—which I had not ordered; and for which they have been trying to collect from me.

Meanwhile, I am still waiting for the money back that they owe me for the copy of *Kim* that I didn't get. That's the whole story. Maybe you can help me straighten them out.

Relievedly yours,
Walter A. Child

P.S.: I also sent them back their copy of *Kidnapped*, as soon as I got it, but it hasn't seemed to help. They have never even acknowledged getting it back.

MALONEY, MAHONEY, MacNAMARA and PRUITT
Attorneys

89 Prince Street
Chicago, Illinois
May 9, 198–

Mr. Walter A. Child
437 Woodlawn Drive
Panduk, Michigan

Dear Mr. Child:

I am in possession of no information indicating that any item purchased by you from the Treasure Book Club has been returned.

I would hardly think that, if the case had been as you stated, the Treasure Book Club would have retained us to collect the amount owing from you.

If I do not receive payment in full within three days, by May 12, 198–, we will be forced to take legal action.

Very truly yours,
Hagthorpe M. Pruitt, Jr.

⌒

COURT OF MINOR CLAIMS
Chicago, Illinois

Mr. Walter A. Child:
437 Woodlawn Drive
Panduk, Michigan

Be informed that a judgment was taken and entered against you in this court this day of May 26, 198–, in the amount of $15.66 including court costs.

Payment in satisfaction of this judgment may be made to this court or to the adjudged creditor. In the case of payment being made to the creditor, a release should be obtained from the creditor and filed with this court in order to free you of legal obligation in connection with this judgment. Under the recent Reciprocal Claims Act, if you are a citizen of a different state, a duplicate claim may be automatically entered and judged against you in your own state so that collection may be made there as well as in the State of Illinois.

⌒

COURT OF MINOR CLAIMS
Chicago, Illinois
PLEASE DO NOT FOLD,
SPINDLE, OR MUTILATE
THIS CARD

Judgment was passed this day of May 27, 198–, under Statute 941.

Against: Child, Walter A. of 437 Woodlawn Drive, Panduk, Michigan. Pray to enter a duplicate claim for judgment.

In: Picayune Court—Panduk, Michigan

For Amount: $15.66

⌒

437 Woodlawn Drive
Panduk, Michigan
May 31, 198–

Samuel P. Grimes
Vice President, Treasure Book Club
1823 Mandy Street
Chicago, Illinois

Grimes:

This business has gone far enough. I've got to come down to Chicago on business of my own tomorrow. I'll see you then and we'll get this straightened out once and for all, about who owes what to whom, and how much!

Yours,
Walter A. Child

From the desk of the Clerk
Picayune Court

June 1, 198–

Harry:

The attached computer card from Chicago's Minor Claims Court against A. Walter has a 1500-series Statute number on it. That puts it over in criminal with you, rather than civil, with me. So I herewith submit it for your computer instead of mine. How's business?

Joe

CRIMINAL RECORDS
Panduk, Michigan
PLEASE DO NOT FOLD,
SPINDLE, OR MUTILATE
THIS CARD
Convicted: (Child) A. Walter
On: May 26,198–
Address: 437 Woodlawn Drive,
Panduk, Mich.

Statute: 1566 (Corrected) 1567
Crime: Kidnap
Date: Nov. 16, 198–
Notes: At large. To be picked up at once.

POLICE DEPARTMENT, PANDUK, MICHIGAN. TO POLICE DEPART-
MENT, CHICAGO, ILLINOIS. CONVICTED SUBJECT A. (COMPLETE
FIRST NAME UNKNOWN) WALTER, SOUGHT HERE IN CONNECTION
REF. YOUR NOTIFICATION OF JUDGMENT FOR KIDNAP OF CHILD
NAMED ROBERT LOUIS STEVENSON, ON NOV. 16, 198–. INFORMA-
TION HERE INDICATES SUBJECT FLED HIS RESIDENCE, AT 437
WOODLAWN DRIVE, PANDUK, AND MAY BE AGAIN IN YOUR AREA.
POSSIBLE CONTACT IN YOUR AREA: THE TREASURE BOOK CLUB,
1823 MANDY STREET, CHICAGO, ILLINOIS. SUBJECT NOT KNOWN
TO BE ARMED, BUT PRESUMED DANGEROUS. PICK UP AND HOLD,
ADVISING US OF CAPTURE . . .

TO POLICE DEPARTMENT, PANDUK, MICHIGAN. REFERENCE, YOUR
REQUEST TO PICK UP AND HOLD A. (COMPLETE FIRST NAME
UNKNOWN) WALTER, WANTED IN PANDUK ON STATUTE 1567,
CRIME OF KIDNAPPING.
SUBJECT ARRESTED AT OFFICES OF TREASURE BOOK CLUB, OPER-
ATING THERE UNDER ALIAS WALTER ANTHONY CHILD AND
ATTEMPTING TO COLLECT $4.98 FROM ONE SAMUEL P. GRIMES,
EMPLOYEE OF THAT COMPANY.
DISPOSAL: HOLDING FOR YOUR ADVICE.

POLICE DEPARTMENT, PANDUK, MICHIGAN, TO POLICE DEPART-
MENT CHICAGO, ILLINOIS
REF: A. WALTER (ALIAS WALTER ANTHONY CHILD) SUBJECT
WANTED FOR CRIME OF KIDNAP, YOUR AREA, REF: YOUR COM-
PUTER PUNCH CARD NOTIFICATION OF JUDGMENT, DATED MAY
27, 198–. COPY OUR CRIMINAL RECORDS PUNCH CARD HERE-
WITH FORWARDED TO YOUR COMPUTER SECTION.

CRIMINAL RECORDS
Panduk, Michigan
PLEASE DO NOT FOLD,
SPINDLE, OR MUTILATE
THIS CARD

SUBJECT (CORRECTION—OMITTED RECORD SUPPLIED)
APPLICABLE STATUTE NO. 1567
JUDGMENT NO. 456789
TRIAL RECORD: APPARENTLY MISFILED AND UNAVAILABLE
DIRECTION: TO APPEAR FOR SENTENCING BEFORE JUDGE JOHN
ALEXANDER MCDIVOT, COURTROOM A, JUNE 9, 198–

From the Desk of
Judge Alexander J. McDivot

June 2, 198–

Dear Tony:

I've got an adjudged criminal coming up before me for sentencing Thursday morning—but the trial transcript is apparently misfiled.

I need some kind of information (Ref. A. Walter—Judgment No. 456789, Criminal). For example, what about the victim of the kidnapping? Was victim harmed?

Jack McDivot

June 3, 198–

Records Search Unit
Re: Ref. Judgment No. 456789—was victim harmed?

Tonio Malagasi
Records Division

June 3, 198–

To: United States Statistics Office
Attn: Information Section
Subject: Robert Louis Stevenson
Query: Information concerning

Records Search Unit
Criminal Records Division
Police Department
Chicago, Ill.

~

June 5, 198–

To: Records Search Unit
Criminal Records Division
Police Department
Chicago, Illinois
Subject: Your query re Robert Louis Stevenson (File no. 189623)
Action: Subject deceased. Age at death, 44 yrs. Further information requested?

A. K.
Information Section
U.S. Statistics Office

~

June 6, 198–

To: United States Statistics Office
Attn: Information Division
Subject: Re: File no. 189623
No further information required.

Thank you.
Records Search Unit
Criminal Records Division
Police Department
Chicago, Illinois

~

June 7, 198–

To: Tonio Malagasi
Records Division
Re: Ref: judgment No. 456789—victim is dead.

Records Search Unit

~

June 7, 198–

To: Judge Alexander J. McDivot's Chambers
Dear Jack:
Ref: Judgment No. 456789. The victim in this kidnap case was apparently slain.

From the strange lack of background information on the killer and his victim, as well as the victim's age, this smells to me like a gangland killing. This for your information. Don't quote me. It seems to me, though, that Stevenson—the victim—has a name that rings a faint bell with me. Possibly, one of the East Coast Mob, since the association comes back to me as something about pirates—possibly New York dockage hijackers—and something about buried loot.

As I say, above is only speculation for your private guidance. Any time I can help . . .

Best,
Tony Malagasi
Records Division

MICHAEL R. REYNOLDS
Attorney at Law

49 Water Street
Chicago, Illinois
June 8, 198–

Dear Tim:
Regrets: I can't make the fishing trip. I've been court-appointed here to represent a man about to be sentenced tomorrow on a kidnapping charge.

Ordinarily, I might have tried to beg off, and McDivot, who is doing the sentencing, would probably have turned me loose. But this is the damndest thing you ever heard of.

The man being sentenced has apparently been not only charged, but adjudged guilty as a result of a comedy of errors too long to go into here. He not only isn't guilty—he's got the best case I ever heard of for damages against one of the larger book clubs headquartered here in Chicago. And that's a case I wouldn't mind taking on.

It's inconceivable—but damnably possible, once you stop to think of it in this day and age of machine-made records—that a completely innocent man could be put in this position.

There shouldn't be much to it. I've asked to see McDivot tomorrow before the time of sentencing, and it'll just be a matter of explaining to him. Then I can discuss the damage suit with my freed client at his leisure.

Fishing next weekend?

Yours,
Mike

MICHAEL R. REYNOLDS
Attorney at Law

49 Water Street
Chicago, Illinois
June 10

Dear Tim:

In haste—

No fishing this coming week either. Sorry.

You won't believe it. My innocent-as-a-lamb-and-I'm-not-kidding client has just been sentenced to death for first-degree murder in connection with the death of his kidnap victim.

Yes, I explained the whole thing to McDivot. And when he explained his situation to me, I nearly fell out of my chair.

It wasn't a matter of my not convincing him. It took less than three minutes to show him that my client should never have been within the walls of the County Jail for a second. But—get this—McDivot couldn't do a thing about it.

The point is, my man had already been judged guilty according to the computerized records. In the absence of a trial record—of course there never was one (but that's something I'm not free to explain to you now)—the judge has to go by what records are available. And in the case of an adjudged prisoner, McDivot's only legal choice was whether to sentence to life imprisonment, or execution.

The death of the kidnap victim, according to the statute, made the death penalty mandatory. Under the new laws governing length of time for appeal, which has been shortened because of the new system of computerizing records, to force an elimination of unfair delay and mental anguish to those condemned, I have five days in which to file an appeal, and ten to have it acted on.

Needless to say, I am not going to monkey with an appeal. I'm going directly to the governor for a pardon—after which we will get this farce reversed. McDivot has already written the governor, also, explaining that his sentence was ridiculous, but that he had no choice. Between the two of us, we ought to have a pardon in short order.

Then, I'll make the fur fly . . .

And we'll get in some fishing.

Best,
Mike

OFFICE OF THE
GOVERNOR OF ILLINOIS

June 17, 198–

Mr. Michael R. Reynolds
49 Water Street
Chicago, Illinois

Dear Mr. Reynolds:

In reply to your query about the request for pardon for Walter A. Child (A. Walter), may I inform you that the governor is still on his trip with the Midwest Governors Committee, examining the Wall in Berlin. He should be back next Friday.

I will bring your request and letters to his attention the minute he returns.

Very truly yours,
Clara B. Jilks
Secretary to the Governor

June 27, 198–

Michael R. Reynolds
49 Water Street
Chicago, Illinois

Dear Mike:

Where is that pardon?

My execution date is only five days from now!

Walt

June 29, 198–

Walter A. Child (A. Walter)
Cell Block E
Illinois State Penitentiary
Joliet, Illinois

Dear Walt:

The governor returned, but was called away immediately to the White House in Washington to give his views on interstate sewage.

I am camping on his doorstep and will be on him the moment he arrives here.

Meanwhile, I agree with you about the seriousness of the situation. The warden at the prison there, Mr. Allen Magruder, will bring this letter to you and have a private talk with you. I urge you to listen to what he has to say; and I enclose letters from your family also urging you to listen to Warden Magruder.

Yours,
Mike

June 30, 198–

Michael R. Reynolds
49 Water Street
Chicago, Illinois

Dear Mike: (This letter being smuggled out by Warden Magruder)

As I was talking to Warden Magruder in my cell here, news was brought to him that the governor has at last returned for a while to Illinois, and will be in his office early tomorrow morning, Friday. So you will have time to get the pardon signed by him and delivered to the prison in time to stop my execution on Saturday.

Accordingly, I have turned down the warden's kind offer of a chance to escape; since he told me he could by no means guarantee to have all the guards out of my way when I tried it; and there was a chance of my being killed escaping.

But now everything will straighten itself out. Actually, an experience as fantastic as this had to break down sometime under its own weight.

Best,
Walt

FOR THE SOVEREIGN STATE OF ILLINOIS, I Hubert Daniel Willikens, Governor of the State of Illinois, and invested with the authority and powers appertaining thereto, including the power to pardon those in my judgment wrongfully convicted or otherwise deserving of executive mercy, this day of July 1, 198–, do announce and proclaim that Walter A. Child (A. Walter), now in custody as a consequence of erroneous conviction upon a crime of which he is entirely innocent, is fully and freely pardoned of said crime. And I do direct the necessary authorities having custody of the said Walter A. Child (A. Walter) in whatever place or places he may be held, to immediately free, release, and allow unhindered departure to him . . .

Interdepartmental Routing Service
PLEASE DO NOT FOLD,
MUTILATE, OR SPINDLE
THIS CARD

Failure to route Document properly.
To: Governor Hubert Daniel Willikens
Re: Pardon issued to Walter A. Child, July 1, 198–
Dear State Employee:

You have failed to attach your Routing Number.

PLEASE: Resubmit document with this card and Form 876, explaining your authority for placing a TOP RUSH category on this document. Form 876 must be signed by your Departmental Superior.

RESUBMIT ON: Earliest possible date ROUTING SERVICE office is open. In this case, Tuesday, July 5, 198–.

WARNING: Failure to submit Form 876 WITH THE SIGNATURE OF YOUR SUPERIOR may make you liable to prosecution for misusing a Service of the State Government. A warrant may be issued for your arrest.

There are NO exceptions. YOU have been WARNED.

A Letter to Amy

Joyce Harrington

DEAR AMY,
DID YOU get my last letter? Why don't you write? Just a note saying Hi, Pop, would be nice. The circus is in town. I'm not planning to go, but it reminds me of the time you and me went. Remember the clown who kept tripping over the little white dog? Every time he fell down, you laughed and laughed. I guess you're too big for circuses now. Why don't you send me a picture? I don't have even one. I guess maybe your mother is taking these letters and not letting you have them. If that's what she's doing, I just want to tell her it's not right. No matter what I did or didn't do, you're still my little girl and I love you. And I miss you."

Gene-Boy signed the letter "Love, Daddy," and folded it up. It wasn't much of a letter, he knew, but he'd worn himself out struggling to write long letters to both of them about how much he'd changed and what he was doing and how Jesus had come into his life and made a new man of him. Letters that just seemed to disappear into the blue and never brought back an answer.

No, he wasn't planning to go to the circus. He wasn't planning to go anywhere, just to the machine shop and back again, listen to the preacher on Sunday, in between read the Bible after supper and sometimes the newspaper. That's where he'd seen the ad for the circus. It reminded him so much of the old days, and Amy's little fingers digging into his wrist while she squirmed and giggled and tried not to miss a single thing going on in the dinky little ring spread out before them. He could feel those little fingers on his wrist like burning tips of cigarettes.

Gene-Boy didn't smoke anymore, and that was a blessing. He didn't drink, either, but he didn't have much choice about that, so it didn't count as a full-fledged blessing. It was a good thing, though. If you counted it all up, it was probably drink that got him where he was today. Drink and his own evil ways. Preacher made him see that. Praise the Lord.

He wrote Amy's name and address on the envelope, slid the letter inside, and stuck his last red, white, and blue stamp up in the corner. Lying down on his bunk, he tried to tune out the sounds around him so he could think about Georgina. How pretty she was back when he first caught sight of her. Wild, too. She'd do any crazy thing on a dare. Like the time she climbed out on the courthouse flagpole and stayed there until the Fire Department came and got her down. Got her picture in the paper for that one. Asked why she did it, she said, "Just wanted to liven things up a bit."

That was Georgina, always livening things up. Singing in the morning, dancing all night. Laughing all day long, at everything and everybody. They were quite a pair in those days, Gene-Boy and Georgina, always doing something outrageous.

And when the black mood came on him, it was only Georgina who could travel the road with him and bring him back alive. He was always sorry later for the things he did to her those times. The black eyes and fat lips, the scar where she had to have her hand stitched up, the names he called her and the things he blamed on her. She always seemed to know that he didn't mean them, that it was his own self he was fighting with, the part of him that had no hope and nothing to live for. Three times she'd kept him from killing himself.

All that was over now.

Gene-Boy reached for his Bible but didn't open it. The lights would be going out soon. He didn't need the lights to read what he wanted to read. He knew it by heart. "The heart of the sons of men is full of evil, and madness is in their heart while they live, and after that they go to the dead." Hard words, but true. Too true.

Preacher had told him about that one, old Ecclesiastes, and made him see what it meant—to him, Gene-Boy, personally. Preacher said that all the time he was walking around the earth hell-raising and being bad, he was filling up his heart with evil and turning himself into a living dead man. And the black mood was just the stored-up evil in his heart tempting him toward the greatest sin of all, turning himself into a *dead* dead man. Preacher was right: Without hope, a man might just as well be dead. Although Gene-Boy still thought that the drink and the war and no decent job went a long ways toward bringing on the gloom. Or at least bringing on the hell-raising that brought on the gloom.

He picked up his letter to Amy and ran his finger along the unsealed flap of the envelope. Maybe he wouldn't send it after all. None of the others had done any good. Amy would be what now, twelve or thirteen? Old enough to write to him if she wanted to, even without Georgina knowing about it. Old enough to find out where he was if Georgina wouldn't tell her. Did she ever ask about him? Did she remember him at all? All these years and no word.

The lights went out as they always did, without warning. And as always the men on either side of him groaned and some of them stamped their feet. Gene-Boy welcomed the darkness, even though it wasn't completely dark—there was always a light on in the corridor so the guards could see into the cellblock in case there was any mischief or trouble. In the darkness, Gene-Boy could rest his eyes and his mind from the gray plainness of day-after-day and conjure up pictures that were more pleasing.

He made a picture of himself getting off the Greyhound bus, still in his uniform, so glad to see home again even though there wasn't anybody there to meet him. He hadn't let anybody know he was coming—he didn't want any fuss made over him, even though he had medals and wound scars and papers that said he was a hero. Still and all, he was a trifle disappointed that no one took any notice of him when he stepped off that bus right in the middle of the town's suppertime. He'd been proud to go to Vietnam and wanted to be proud of coming back. Georgina would have been proud of him.

But he didn't even know Georgina on that day—didn't know she was working in that cocktail lounge catty-corner across from the bus depot, just waiting on the day when he would come staggering through the door and order up a beer for himself. That day wouldn't come for some little while yet. In the picture in his mind of the day of his home-coming, Georgina wasn't in it yet and the town was ordinary—changed but still the same, with the streetlights just coming on in the late purple dusk. It was summer and hot, with the smell of car exhaust hanging heavy over the street. Fifteen years later, he could still smell that evening air.

He had decided to treat himself to a taxi. The driver was a black man—young, about his own age—with a thick neck and big shoulders like a football player. The neck and shoulders made Gene-Boy feel he had to come on strong.

"Boy, you know the way out to the Watkins place?"

"Never heard of it."

"You know Twelve Mile Road?"

"I know it."

"Well, just keep going out it till I tell you to stop."

"How far?"

"Till we get there."

"Five miles? Ten miles? Two hundred miles?"

"What the hell difference does it make?"

"More than ten miles, I got to charge you double."

"You shouldn't charge me at all. See this uniform? Last week this uniform was all covered up with jungle slime and gook blood. This uniform's seen action."

"Was you in it at the time?"

"Now what kind of remark is that?" Gene-Boy recalled the feeling of hurt that made him want to haul out the picture he had of himself standing over that dead Vietcong who'd tried to sneak up on him and his buddies. He'd saved his buddies' lives and he wasn't ashamed of the fact. "You some kind of peace freak?"

"Easy, man. I been there. It don't buy free taxi rides or free noth-ing else. Now how far you be wanting to go?"

Gene-Boy scrunched down in the back seat and muttered, "Nine and a half miles."

The driver laughed. "All right," he said, "I won't be charging you double, you being a fellow victim. But you understand I got to come back empty and that uses up gas."

"I ain't no victim," Gene-Boy muttered.

Skip over the ride out of town, past scenes Gene-Boy remembered as if they'd been part of someone else's life—gas stations, drive-ins, the bowling alley, car lots—thinning out into patchy fields and junk yards. It wasn't pretty, not in the way he'd remembered it as pretty while he was over in the heat and the stink. Driving past it, looking at it, seeing the pale, beefy people moving about in it, he yearned for the dense green he'd left behind and the thin, brown women who'd giggled at his jokes. It was peculiar. He didn't understand what was going on, except that he didn't seem to belong in either place. Skip over that part.

The house, when they pulled up in front of it, looked small and mean. Even in the gathering darkness, he could see that it needed paint. The lights were on and Gene-Boy was grateful for that. What if nobody'd been home? He paid the driver and gave him a good tip. The driver got out to help him with his duffel bag.

"Don't bother," said Gene-Boy. "I hauled it half across the world. I guess I can haul it into my own house."

"You ever want to talk about things," the driver said, "you mostly can find me by the bus station."

"Don't guess I will," said Gene-Boy. "What's there to talk about?"

The driver shrugged. "Some guys have trouble fitting themselves back in. Sometimes we get together and just talk about it. It helps."

"I won't be needing any help," said Gene-Boy, and he stomped up onto the porch, deliberately making noise so they'd know he'd arrived.

The taxi drove away.

Gene-Boy tried to open the front door. It was locked. That made him mad. Since when did they lock the door against him? He kicked at the door and rattled the knob. Inside the house, a dog started up. Since when did they get a dog? They hadn't written to him much. His mother had sometimes, mostly about the weather and the operations she was always having. She'd never mentioned a dog. He hadn't had a letter in about six months. He hadn't written a letter in longer than that.

The dog was barking on the other side of the door now, scraping at it with hard, quick claws. He heard his father's voice yell, "Shut up! I'm coming!"

Gene-Boy waited, trying on a smile, feeling silly and changing it to a stern, serious look. Save the smile for his mother. She'd be glad to

see him. She'd have fun coaxing him to eat. He wasn't sure how his
father would be. The old man hadn't thought much of his going into
the army. He never did think much of anything Gene-Boy thought of
on his own. Always had to be one-up on him.

The door opened and the dog shot out onto the porch, a
medium-sized yellow dog, fat and bare-looking. It yipped and growled,
making nervous, feinting lunges at his shoes. His father stood looking at
him. Despite himself, Gene-Boy felt a smile spreading his lips. He
couldn't help it, even though it made him feel lower than the nasty yellow dog.

His father said, "Oh, it's you. I might have known. I had a dream
the other night."

"Can I come in?" Gene-Boy asked.

"I guess you better. Don't plan on staying, though."

Gene-Boy edged past his father and dumped his duffel bag in the
hall. Here again, everything looked the same but different. Smaller.
He peered into the front room. Same furniture, same rug, same picture
of a sad-eyed clown hanging over the couch—everything worn and
dusty, newspapers and stuff all over everything. His mother would
never let things get that way.

"Where's Ma?" he asked.

"Gone."

"Gone? Gone where?" Surely she would have written to him if she
was going somewhere. People like his mother and father didn't get
divorced. They'd put in too many years together. His mother'd been
born again. Born-again Christians stuck it out, even if it got hairy.
And sometimes it did. Gene-Boy'd seen his father smack his mother
around ever since he was a little kid. But she'd never leave him.
"Where's she gone to?" he asked again.

"She died. I guess nobody told you."

Gene-Boy just stood there. The yellow dog trotted across the front
room and jumped up onto the couch as if he belonged there. His
mother wouldn't have allowed that.

From the kitchen, a voice called out, "Who is that, Eugene?"

His father shouted back, "Just my son. I told you about him."

Gene-Boy heard slippers slapping against the hall floor. He looked
up and saw a youngish woman ambling toward him. Long yellow hair
same color as the dog's hanging down around a fat, pale face; big green

eyes, bulgy like a frog's, staring at him; baggy jeans and a billowing flowered smock. Was she just fat or was she pregnant?

"This my wife," his father said. "Sandra."

"How-do," Sandra said. "Stay for supper? I'll throw in another TV dinner."

"Thanks," said Gene-Boy. "Pleased to meet you."

Sandra smiled. "Your daddy didn't tell me you was so good-looking. But he's a handsome man himself, so it makes sense."

Gene-Boy looked at his father. The old man was grinning fit to burst. The old fool. Him, handsome? Some people'll believe anything. Sandra slip-slopped back toward the kitchen.

"See why you can't plan on staying?" his father said. "We'll be needing your room. Already got a crib in there."

"When did my mother die?" Gene-Boy asked.

"Oh, four, five months ago. It was real quick. She didn't suffer much."

"When's the baby due?"

"Any minute now." His father smirked. "Never thought I'd be a daddy again. Your poor mother was too sickly for much of that."

"When did you and Sandra get married?"

"Matter of fact, it was just last week. Thought we better do it before the baby came. If we'd known you was coming, we could've held off. You could've been best man."

"How long have you and Sandra—?"

"Couple or three years now. Oh, don't go getting upset. Your mother never knew anything about it. But even if she did, she wouldn't have minded. After all those operations, all she wanted was me to leave her alone. There wasn't much left of her there at the end."

"What if she hadn't died? What would you and Sandra have done?"

"Nothing, I guess. I mean, she would still be having the baby and I would be going out to see her just like I been doing. It's a lot better this way."

"I guess so," said Gene-Boy. "Well, is it okay if I sleep here tonight? I sent the taxi back to town."

"You'll have to bed down on the couch. I sold your bed."

"I've slept in worse places."

His father laughed, false hearty. "I bet you have. I just bet you have. That army life ain't no picnic, I guess you found out."

"No picnic," Gene-Boy echoed.

GENE-BOY GOT himself a room in town up over the Tulip Tree Cafe, next to the newspaper office. The room smelt of all the home-cooking that had ever been done in the Tulip Tree, fifty years' worth of chicken grease and boiled greens. Just breathing it, Gene-Boy hardly had to eat, but he went down to the cafe every evening and ate what he'd been smelling. Looked up some of his old buddies and found out that one of them, Roy Blanchard, was working for the newspaper, writing up house fires and automobile accidents on the interchange, once in a while a murder or a suicide. Roy took Gene-Boy home to meet his wife and little boy. It was a pretty life, safe and comfortable, and it made Gene-Boy mad. While he'd been off in the jungle, his good old buddy Roy Blanchard was living the good life and making a place for himself. And now Gene-Boy couldn't get any kind of job that was worth having.

Not that he didn't try. He took it into his mind that after all the filth and mud he'd been through, he wanted a clean job. He wanted to wear a suit and a tie. He bought himself a Sears, Roebuck outfit, shoes and all, and wore it into two banks, one insurance office, the town's only travel agency, a bunch of real-estate sales offices, and a place that sold cemetery plots. He got the impression that the people he saw couldn't wait for him to leave so they could bust out laughing at him, although one sweet-faced old lady advised him to get himself into the community college and learn something. "To make yourself more marketable," she'd said. But what would he do in college with a bunch of kids when he was a man and had been doing a man's work in Vietnam?

Roy Blanchard offered to put in a word for him at the newspaper. He could drive a truck, couldn't he? But Gene-Boy knew he couldn't stand that, Roy writing the stories on the front page and him trucking the bundled newspapers all over town and out into the countryside. He was any man's equal and certainly Roy's, and he wouldn't be beholden for crumbs.

The more he got turned down, the madder Gene-Boy got. His money was running out. His old car—at least his father hadn't sold *that*—needed new tires. And to top it all off, Sandra had popped out a pair of twins, blond-haired little boys, and he was expected to act like a big brother to them. Presents and such. Say how cute they were. Otherwise, he wouldn't be welcome to visit his own old home. He stopped going out there. Couldn't stand to see the old man behaving like a frisky young stallion, couldn't stand the way he googled and gaggled over them babies. Nothing was turning out the way Gene-Boy thought it would.

Long about that time, he met Georgina. Just when he was thinking about leaving town and trying his luck someplace else, Texas or California, he found himself outside the bus depot one evening and there was that same taxi waiting for a passenger. The driver spotted him and called out.

"Hey, man. How's it going?"

Gene-Boy's first instinct was to tell a glowing tale of opportunity about to strike and great wealth about to fall into his lap. But the taxi driver's brown eyes took in his cheap polyester finery and the scuff marks on his shoes, and Gene-Boy knew he couldn't carry off the lie.

"Not so hot," Gene-Boy said, leaning on the door of the taxi. "Seems like nobody cares."

"Having yourself a little pity party?" the driver inquired.

Gene-Boy's anger, never very far from the surface these days, flared. "I don't have to listen to that. You wasn't in that cab, I'd punch you right through the sidewalk."

"Hold on," the driver said. "No call to get righteous. What makes you think anybody's supposed to care about you?"

"Huh?" Gene-Boy hadn't thought about that. He'd just assumed that people would be falling all over themselves to give him, the returned hero, a fine job. When it didn't happen, he didn't ask himself why not. He just got madder and madder.

"I need another driver," the black man said. "You got a driver's license?"

"Well, sure," Gene-Boy said. "What do you think?"

"Well, how about it?"

"You mean me work for you?"

"What I mean."

"You own this cab?"

"This and four others. One of them's sitting back in the garage 'cause one of my drivers quit on me. So how about it?"

"Well, I don't know," said Gene-Boy, confused over certain feelings he didn't want to look at too closely.

"Bother you to work for a black man?" the driver asked.

"No, not a bit," Gene-Boy said too quickly. But that was part of it. The other part was that driving a taxi wasn't exactly his idea of a fine, clean job. It wasn't dirty work, like road-paving or trash-hauling, but it sure didn't require a suit and tie. Still and all—"I'll think it over," Gene-Boy said.

"Well, don't think too long." The driver handed him a printed card. "If you want the job, show up here in the morning. I need somebody right away."

Gene-Boy read the card. "Is that you?" he asked. "Harlan W. Harrison?"

The driver nodded. "Everybody calls me Harry."

Gene-Boy stuck his hand through the cab's open window. "Eugene P. Watkins Jr.," he said, shaking hands. "Everybody calls me Gene-Boy. Could be I'll see you in the A.M."

"I hope so, Gene-Boy."

"Thanks, Harry."

Gene-Boy walked away from the taxi shaking and dry-mouthed, and wondering why he should be so. He couldn't be mad at Harry for offering him a job. He could be mad at himself for even thinking of taking it. And he knew he would take it. He wasn't fit for anything else. He crossed the street, and as soon as he saw the cocktail lounge he knew that he craved a cold beer more than anything else in the world.

Inside the darkened room, a jukebox wailed an old Hank Williams tune. It suited his mood. Old Hank Williams knew all about the demons that bedeviled men in their souls. Not caring much for the easy companionship of the bar, Gene-Boy sprawled into the first empty booth he saw and blinked his eyes to accustom them to the gloom. Pretty soon a waitress came up to him and said, "Yes, sir?"

Her face floated above him, pale and angelic and sort of misty. He saw black hair, sleek and shiny, and dark eyes that sprang out at him and pinned him to the crumbly leatherette of the booth.

"A beer," he said. "Draft."

She went away, and he watched her go. She was small and trim. Her rear end, in tight jeans, was taut and smooth, but she didn't wiggle the way some girls thought was sexy. Her back was straight and her shoulders looked strong and proud. Gene-Boy sighed.

She brought his beer and a small plastic bowl of pretzel sticks. He said, "Thank you." She smiled.

He nodded toward the jukebox and said, "You like Hank Williams?"

"Oh, yeah," she said. "And I like the Beatles and Bob Dylan and vanilla ice cream and skinny-dipping and a lot of things I haven't even tried yet."

Gene-Boy took a swig of his beer, so cold it made his teeth ache. "How do you know you like them if you haven't tried them yet?"

"How do I know I won't?" she said. "I haven't seen you in here before."

"Could be because I never been in here before. But now I think I might be coming in here a lot."

She smiled and went away to tend to other customers.

Later, when Gene-Boy was ordering up his third beer, he asked the waitress her name.

"What you want to know that for?" she asked, not in a flirty way but kind of mean and edgy.

"Well," said Gene-Boy, feeling like fooling around and having a good time, "if I'm gonna marry you, I got to know what to call you."

"Huh!" she said. "Will you just listen to that!" But when she brought him the beer, she said, "My name's Georgina. What's yours?"

And that was how it all began. He woke up the next morning in Georgina's bed with the smell of fresh coffee nudging him to get up. She lived in a little cottage not far from the railroad station where no trains came any more. Gene-Boy had no recollection of how he'd got there, but peering out the bedroom window he saw his old car parked beside the house and in the near distance the abandoned redbrick station building. He remembered that he was supposed to turn up at Harry's garage.

In the kitchen, he found Georgina frying up sausage. "How come you let me sleep so late?" he asked. "I got a job to go to."

"I know," she said. "You told me. It's not late. I was planning to bring you breakfast in bed."

Gene-Boy didn't know what to say. Nobody'd been nice to him in so long, he didn't know how to behave when it happened. "I got to go," he said and, looking for an excuse, he brushed at his rumpled suit. "I got to go change my clothes."

"Well, take a sausage sandwich with you," she said. And she began slapping the fried sausage patties between two hunks of bread.

The last thing Gene-Boy heard as he left the house was her sweet voice singing "Careless Love."

HARLAN W. HARRISON put him to work that very morning. He showed him how to work the car radio and the taximeter, and told him the best places to wait for fares: the mall outside town, the two movie theaters when the pictures let out, the hospital. He introduced him to his tall, skinny wife who operated the dispatcher's radio from the living room in their house next to the garage.

"Job pays two dollars an hour," Harry said.

Gene-Boy frowned.

"Plus you get to keep all tips."

Gene-Boy remembered that he'd tipped Harry real well the night he'd taken the taxi out to his father's house. If everybody tipped as well as that, he'd do all right.

But everybody didn't. Gene-Boy found that out on his very first call—a feeble old lady from one of the big houses on the hill who had to go to her doctor. Even though he helped her into the cab and out of it and was polite when she complained about the bumps in the road, all she gave him was a measly dime. That first day, Gene-Boy figured he got a good close look at human nature, and he didn't like what he saw. The women were the worst, expecting him to help them with their kids and their packages and then trying to cheat him on the fare. But the men weren't much better, accusing him of taking the long way around, or carrying on with a girl in the back seat as if he wasn't there at all. When he'd put in his eight hours, he drove back to Harry's garage in a foul temper. Mrs. Harry silently collected his money and paid him sixteen dollars out of it. That plus the tips he'd been grudgingly given made twenty dollars and change, more than he'd had in the morning. It was sure as hell no way to get rich.

"See you tomorrow," said Mrs. Harry.

"Yeah. Maybe."

He drove in his own car back downtown straight to the cocktail lounge, where he hoped to find Georgina. She wasn't there. Another girl with big wobbly bosoms and a beehive hairdo came to wait on him. He ordered a whiskey with a beer chaser. When she brought it, he asked her where Georgina was.

"Her day off," she said.

Gene-Boy felt betrayed. After last night, she could have at least told him. But he couldn't even remember what they'd done last night. All he could remember was waking up in her bed, and if he woke up there they must have done *something*. After his third or fourth whiskey, he realized that Georgina was sitting across from him in the booth.

"Where you been?" she demanded.

"Sitting right here," he said. "Where *you* been?"

"Waiting for you. I thought we had a date. You said we'd go dancing."

Gene-Boy couldn't bear to admit that he'd forgotten. "Well, let's go," he said. "I had a rough day. I needed to get a little fortified."

"Well, how about you buy me a drink? Unless you like drinking alone."

She drank her vodka and Seven-Up in little ladylike sips, but it disappeared fast enough. When she finished it, she stood up and twirled around in her high heels, sending her short skirt ballooning out like a parachute. "Let's go," she said. "I could dance all night."

Gene-Boy wasn't sure he could. The black mood was on him and all he wanted to do was smash things. People. But Georgina looked so pretty and happy. She was the only one in the world who didn't treat him mean and he wanted to please her. He crawled out of the booth and stood up, swaying and grinning.

"Pretty little thing," he said. "Let's go get married."

"Not tonight," she said. "Maybe tomorrow."

THEY DIDN'T GET married the next day or the next. They drifted
through the fall and the winter, drinking, dancing, quarreling, making
up. Gene-Boy moved out of his little room over the Tulip Tree Cafe
and into Georgina's house. He got in fights now and then if he
thought some guy was looking the wrong way at Georgina. He knew
Georgina didn't invite the looks—she wasn't like that—but he
blamed her for them anyway. They went ice-skating on a little pond
out in the middle of nowhere and fell through the ice, but only land-
ed knee-deep in muck that stank up their clothes like a dead squirrel
when they got warmed up. Georgina laughed at everything, good
times and bad times alike. Sometimes Gene-Boy wondered why she
liked him so much, but he never dared to ask her. He was afraid he
wouldn't like the answer. It could be she felt sorry for him.

Especially after he lost his job driving taxi for Harry Harrison for
decking a drunk who was trying to pick a fight with him from the back
seat. Left him sprawled in the road—with a broken jaw, as it turned
out. But the guy had it coming to him. He had no call to bring the
police into it and sue the cab company. Gene-Boy thought Harry
should've stuck by him, but instead he turned cold and mean.

"I can't afford to keep you on," he said. "I've had complaints about
you before this. You got some hell of a chip on your shoulder."

"I don't need your stinking job," Gene-Boy muttered.

"You got some unlearning to do, boy. You go around acting like
you're still in the jungle."

"Seems like it to me," said Gene-Boy. "I don't let nobody crap on
me."

"Live and learn," Harry said. "You got a lot of it to do."

After that, the black mood descended and wouldn't let up. He was
only happy when he was with Georgina, but even that was only a
glimmer of what he believed was rightfully his. He wanted a new car
to drive Georgina around in. He wanted to give her a color TV in
place of the old black-and-white number she had. He wanted to take
her on a trip to Las Vegas with money to burn.

Not that she was asking for any of those things. Georgina never
asked for anything. She always said, "If I can't get it for myself, I don't
guess I need it."

She said, "You're the only thing I'll ever need."

But she still wouldn't marry him, no matter how many times he asked her. Not even after Amy was born. "I know who her daddy is," she would say, "and so does her daddy. So what do I need with a piece of legal paper?"

It hurt Gene-Boy a whole lot the day Georgina went down and got food stamps. She'd given up her waitressing job and he was glad of that. No more guys looking at her and trying to get their hands on her. But all he was ever able to do was now-and-then laboring work, the dirty jobs he'd started out sneering at. After a day's work, he could smell the dirt on himself and he despised himself for it. Georgina would make him get in the bathtub and scrub his back and tickle him and work up a big lather of sweet-smelling shampoo on his head. But the dirt smell never left his nostrils. The smell of the jungle. The smell of blood.

Amy made him happy, too, once she got past the smelly diaper, spit-up, and sour-milk stage and started walking and talking like a little lady. She would climb into his lap, unbutton and button his shirt, and whisper her breathy secrets in his ear. Sometimes it was "I love you best." Sometimes it was "Mommy is a sillyhead." And if she whispered, "Can I have a pogo stick?" or a tricycle or a Tony the Pony or a doll with real nylon hair, he'd go right off and get it for her even if he had to give up his whiskey for a week.

When Amy started kindergarten, Georgina went back to work, this time doing the breakfast and lunch shift at a nearby truckstop so she could pick up Amy after school. Gene-Boy wasn't well pleased. "Truckers are a horny bunch," he said. "You just watch your step."

"I can take care of myself," Georgina told him.

It seemed to Gene-Boy that she didn't laugh so much anymore. She didn't sing around the house. He couldn't remember when they had gone dancing. And when did all that start happening?

He said, "It's been six years, going on seven. Ain't it time we got married?" He knew he'd feel better if he was surer.

She just looked at him and went on out the door.

GENE-BOY BROODED. He drank—at home alone when he wasn't working, in his car that was practically falling apart and couldn't go as fast as he wanted it to, even when he was working from a thermos bottle he pretended was full of coffee. His only joy was Amy.

Pretty little Amy, with her black hair like Georgina's and her blue eyes like his own, climbed into his lap every night and wiggled her little butt around like a bird settling into its nest. She told him about school and the silly old teacher and the mean boys who pinched her.

One night she whispered, "Danny says I'm pretty."

Gene-Boy laughed. "Well, you sure are, honey," he said. "And who's this Danny? Is he your boyfriend?"

"Oh, no," Amy whispered. "He's Mommy's."

Gene-Boy stopped laughing. He got very quiet. Georgina was making an angry-sounding racket in the kitchen. He held Amy hard by her small shoulders and said, "He's Mommy's what?"

"What you said." Amy's voice slid into a loud whine. "Boyfriend, boyfriend, boyfriend. That hurts." She tried to wriggle out of his grip.

Gene-Boy held onto her, slapped her once to make her quiet down. "How do you know that?" he demanded.

Amy's blue eyes stared shock at him before she began blubbering. "He kisses her," she sobbed. "In the car. He gives me M&M's."

Georgina came into the room. "What's going on in here?" she asked.

Gene-Boy got up, dumping Amy to the floor. She started howling. Gene-Boy stood over her, weaving back and forth, the blackness descending blacker than ever before. "Who's this Danny?" he shouted.

Georgina looked at Amy writhing and screaming on the floor. "What did you do to her?" she shouted back.

"What have *you* been doing with her? Taking her in the car with you while you're out acting the tramp? Who's this Danny?"

Georgina's eyes shot scorn at him. She picked up Amy and crooned in her ear, "Hush, now, baby. Don't cry. Supper's ready soon and then you can have a Twinkie."

And off she went back to the kitchen without giving Gene-Boy any kind of answer.

Gene-Boy followed her, his hands tingling with the need to make things right. He found her sitting in a kitchen chair, cuddling Amy and singing to her about Mr. Frog and Miss Mousie. She heard him coming up behind her and stopped her song.

She said, "I think you better pack up your things and shift along someplace else."

She wouldn't even look at him.

"You're crazy," he said. "We're gonna get married. You been putting it off long enough."

"You're the crazy one," she said, "if you think I'd marry you. I've stood it as long as I can. It was okay when it was fun, but it hasn't been fun for a long time."

"I suppose you think you could have fun with this Danny?" he shouted at her.

But she didn't answer, just went back to her song. Amy peered up at him out of tearful blue eyes, and then stuck her tongue out.

Gene-Boy stalked off to the bedroom. The whiskey in him roiled in his stomach and fumed in his head. Okay, she wanted him to leave, he'd go. He didn't stick around where he wasn't wanted. She'd be sorry, though. She wasn't so young anymore and who'd be interested in a worn-out bag with a brat. Not even this Danny. She'd find out, and then she'd be begging him to come back. He hauled his old army duffel bag down from the top shelf of the closet. There was something in it but he didn't even look to see what it was, just started stuffing his clothes into it.

But what about Amy? If he left, he wouldn't see Amy every night. She'd be climbing into this Danny's lap and he'd be giving her M&M's. Pretty soon she'd be calling *him* Daddy. No way could Gene-Boy let that happen.

He remembered what it was that had been hiding down in the bottom of his duffel bag all these years. He up-ended the bag and dumped everything he'd packed out onto the bed. The gun plopped out last, on top of the pile of clothes. His old Colt .45, the one he'd carried all the way from Vietnam, the one that had saved his life more times than he could count. It was just as nice-looking now as it was then. He picked it up and hefted it. It felt good in his hand, just like old times. He couldn't remember if it was loaded, though. Probably not.

Gene-Boy was amazed to find three bullets in the magazine. It was like a sign. An omen. They wouldn't be there if he wasn't supposed to do what he was supposed to do. He started back to the kitchen.

GENE-BOY LICKED the flap of the envelope of his letter to Amy. The picture show was over for the night. He always stopped it just right there.

Somewhere in his mind he knew what had happened, but he never let the picture of it rise up and take him over. He knew it was the cause of his being where he was and never likely to get out. And he knew that Danny was only Georgina's brother who'd come back to town after a long while away and talked her into believing Gene-Boy was nothing but a deadbeat drunk and she'd be well rid of him. Danny'd come to visit him once and cried for his sister and his little niece, the only family he had left. All gone. Gene-Boy'd cried, too.

He lifted up his thin mattress and slid his letter to Amy underneath it along with all the others, the hundreds of others, all addressed and sealed and stamped. They made his bed rustle in the night.

The Adventure of the One-Penny Black

Ellery Queen

A H," SAID OLD UNEKER. "It iss a terrible t'ing, Mr. Quveen, a terrible t'ing, like I vass saying. Vat iss New York coming to? Dey come into my store—*polizei*, undt bleedings, undt whackings on de headt. . . . Diss iss vunuff my oldest customers, Mr. Quveen. He too hass hadt exberiences. . . . Mr. Hazlitt, Mr. Quveen. . . . Mr. Quveen iss dot famous detectiff feller you read aboudt in de papers, Mr. Hazlitt. Inspector Richardt Quveen's son."

Ellery Queen laughed, uncoiled his length from old Uneker's counter, and shook the man's hand. "Another victim of our crime wave, Mr. Hazlitt? Unky's been regaling me with a feast of a whopping bloody tale."

"So you're Ellery Queen," said the frail little fellow; he wore a pair of thick-lensed goggles and there was a smell of suburbs about him. "This *is* luck! Yes, I've been robbed."

Ellery looked incredulously about old Uneker's bookshop. "Not *here*?" Uneker was tucked away on a side street in mid-Manhattan, squeezed between the British Bootery and Mme. Carolyne's, and it was just about the last place in the world you would have expected thieves to choose as the scene of a crime.

"Nah," said Hazlitt. "Might have saved the price of a book if it had. No, it happened last night about ten o'clock. I'd just left my office on Forty-fifth Street—I'd worked late—and I was walking crosstown. Chap stopped me on the street and asked for a light. The street was pretty dark and deserted, and I didn't like the fellow's manner, but I saw no harm in lending him a packet of matches. While I was digging it out, though, I noticed he was eyeing the book under my arm. Sort of trying to read the title."

"What book was it?" asked Ellery eagerly. Books were his private passion.

Hazlitt shrugged. "Nothing remarkable. That best-selling nonfiction thing, *Europe in Chaos*; I'm in the export line and I like to keep up to date on international conditions. Anyway, this chap lit his cigarette, returned the matches, mumbled his thanks, and I began to walk on. Next thing I knew something walloped me on the back of my head and everything went black. I seem to remember falling. When I came to, I was lying in the gutter, my hat and glasses were on the stones, and my head felt like a baked potato. Naturally thought I'd been robbed; I had a lot of cash about me, and I was wearing a pair of diamond cuff links. But—"

"But, of course," said Ellery with a grin, "the only thing that was taken was *Europe in Chaos*. Perfect, Mr. Hazlitt! A fascinating little problem. Can you describe your assailant?"

"He had a heavy mustache and dark-tinted glasses of some kind. That's all. I—"

"He? He can describe not'ing," said old Uneker sourly. "He iss like all you Americans—blindt, a *dummkopf*. But de book, Mr. Quveen—de book! Vhy should any von vant to steal a book like dot?"

"And that isn't all," said Hazlitt. "When I got home last night—I live in East Orange, New Jersey—I found my house broken into! And what do you think had been stolen, Mr. Queen?"

Ellery's lean face beamed. "I'm no crystal-gazer, but if there's any consistency in crime, I should imagine another book had been stolen."

"Right! And it was my second copy of *Europe in Chaos!*"

"Now you do interest me," said Ellery, in quite a different tone. "How did you come to have two, Mr. Hazlitt?"

"I bought another copy from Uneker two days ago to give to a friend of mine. I'd left it on top of my bookcase. It was gone. Window was open—it had been forced; and there were smudges of hands on the sill. Plain case of housebreaking. And although there's plenty of valuable stuff in my place—silver and things—nothing else had been taken. I reported it at once to the East Orange police, but they just tramped about the place, gave me funny looks, and finally went away. I suppose they thought I was crazy."

"Were any other books missing?"

"No, just that one."

"I really don't see . . . ." Ellery took off his *pince-nez* eyeglasses and began to polish the lenses thoughtfully. "Could it have been the same man? Would he have had time to get out to East Orange and burglarize your house before you got there last night?"

"Yes. When I picked myself out of the gutter, I reported the assault to a cop, and he took me down to a nearby stationhouse, and they asked me a lot of questions. He would have had plenty of time—I didn't get home until one o'clock in the morning."

"I think, Unky," said Ellery, "that the story *you* told me begins to have point. If you'll excuse me, Mr. Hazlitt, I'll be on my way. *Auf wiedersehen!*"

Ellery left old Uneker's little shop and went downtown to Center Street. He climbed the steps of police headquarters, nodded amiably to a desk lieutenant, and made for his father's office. The Inspector was out. Ellery twiddled with an ebony figurine of Bertillon on his father's desk, mused deeply, then went out and began to hunt for Sergeant Velie, the Inspector's chief of operations. He found the mammoth in the Press Room, bawling curses at a reporter.

"Velie," said Ellery, "stop playing bad man and get me some information. Two days ago there was an unsuccessful manhunt on Forty-ninth Street, between Fifth and Sixth Avenues. The chase ended in a little bookshop owned by a friend of mine named Uneker. Local officer was in on it. Uneker told me the story, but I want less colored details. Get me the precinct report like a good fellow, will you?"

Sergeant Velie waggled his big black jaws, glared at the reporter, and thundered off. Ten minutes later he came back with a sheet of paper, and Ellery read it with absorption.

The facts seemed bald enough. Two days before, at the noon hour, a hatless, coatless man with a bloody face had rushed out of the office building three doors from old Uneker's bookshop, shouting: "Help! Police!" Patrolman McCallum had run up, and the man yelled that he had been robbed of a valuable postage stamp—"My one-penny black!" he kept shouting. "My one-penny black!"—and that the thief, black-mustached and wearing heavy blue-tinted spectacles, had just escaped. McCallum had noticed a man of this description a few minutes before, acting peculiarly, enter the nearby bookshop. Followed by the screaming stamp dealer, he dashed into old Uneker's place with drawn revolver. Had a man with black mustache and blue-tinted spectacles come into the shop within the past few minutes? "*Ja*—he?" said old Uneker. "Sure, he iss still here." Where? In the back room looking at some books. McCallum and the bleeding man rushed into Uneker's back room; it was empty. A door leading to the alley from the back room was open; the man had escaped, apparently having been scared off by the noisy entrance of the policeman and the victim a moment before. McCallum had immediately searched the neighborhood; the thief had vanished.

The officer then took the complainant's statement. He was, he said, Friederich Ulm, dealer in rare postage stamps. His office was in a tenth-floor room in the building three doors away—the office of his brother Albert, his partner, and himself. He had been exhibiting some valuable items to an invited group of three stamp collectors. Two of them had gone away. Ulm happened to turn his back; and the third, the man with the black mustache and blue-tinted glasses, who had introduced himself as Avery Beninson, had swooped on him swiftly from behind and struck at his head with a short iron bar as Ulm twisted back. The blow had cut open Ulm's cheekbone and felled him, half-stunned; and then with the utmost coolness the thief had used the same iron bar (which, said the report, from its description was probably a "jimmy") to pry open the lid of a glass-topped cabinet in which a choice collection of stamps was kept. He had snatched from a leather box in the cabinet an extremely high-priced item—"the Queen Victoria one-penny black"—and had then dashed out, locking the door behind him. It had taken the assaulted dealer several minutes to open the door and follow. McCallum went with Ulm to the office, examined the rifled cabinet, took the names and addresses of the three collectors who had been present that morning—with particular note of "Avery Beninson"—scribbled his report, and departed.

The names of the other two collectors were John Hinchman and J. S. Peters. A detective attached to the precinct had visited each in turn and had then gone to the address of Beninson. Beninson, who presumably had been the man with a black mustache and blue-tinted spectacles, was ignorant of the entire affair; and his physical appearance did not tally with the description of Ulm's assailant. He had received no invitation from the Ulm brothers, he said, to attend the private sale. Yes, he had had an employee, a man with a black mustache and tinted glasses, for two weeks—this man answered Beninson's advertisement for an assistant to take charge of the collector's private stamp albums, had proved satisfactory, and had suddenly, without explanation or notice, disappeared after two weeks' service. He had disappeared, the detective noted, on the morning of the Ulms' sale.

All attempts to trace this mysterious assistant, who had called himself William Planck, were unsuccessful. The man had vanished among New York City's millions.

Nor was this the end of the story. For the day after the theft old Uneker himself had reported to the precinct detective a queer tale. The previous night—the night of the Ulm theft—said Uneker, he had left his shop for a late dinner; his night clerk had remained on duty. A man had entered the shop, had asked to see *Europe in Chaos*, and had then to the night clerk's astonishment purchased all copies of the book in stock—seven. The man who had made this extraordinary purchase wore a black mustache and blue-tinted spectacles!

"Sort of nuts, ain't it?" growled Sergeant Velie.

"Not at all," smiled Ellery. "In fact, I believe it has a very simple explanation."

"And that ain't the half of it. One of the boys told me just now of a new angle on the case. Two minor robberies were reported from local precincts last night. One was uptown in the Bronx; a man named Hornell said his apartment was broken into during the night, and what do you think? Copy of *Europe in Chaos* which Hornell had bought in this guy Uneker's store was stolen! Nothing else. Bought it two days ago. Then a dame named Janet Meakins from Greenwich Village had *her* flat robbed the same night. Thief had taken her copy of *Europe in Chaos*—she'd bought it from Uneker the afternoon before. Screwy, hey?"

"Not at all, Velie. Use your wits." Ellery clapped his hat on his head. "Come along, you Colossus; I want to speak to old Unky again."

They left Headquarters and went uptown.

"Unky," said Ellery, patting the little old bookseller's bald pate affectionately, "how many copies of *Europe in Chaos* did you have in stock at the time the thief escaped from your back room?"

"Eleffen."

"Yet only seven were in stock that same evening when the thief returned to buy them," murmured Ellery. Therefore, four copies had been sold between the noon hour two days ago and the dinner hour. So! Unky, do you keep a record of your customers?"

"*Ach*, yes! De few who buy," said old Uneker sadly. "I add to my mailing lisdt. You vant to see?"

"There is nothing I crave more ardently at the moment."

Uneker led them to the rear of the shop and through a door into the musty back room from whose alley door the thief had escaped two days before. Off this room there was a partitioned cubicle littered with papers, files, and old books. The old bookseller opened a ponderous ledger and, wetting his ancient forefinger, began to slap pages over. "You vant to know de four who boughdt *Europe in Chaos* dot afternoon?"

"Ja."

Uneker hooked a pair of greenish-silver spectacles over his ears and began to read in a singsong voice. "Mr. Hazlitt—dot's the gentleman you met, Mr. Quveen. *He* bought his second copy, de vun dot vass robbed from his house . . . Den dere vass Mr. Hornell, an oldt customer. Den a Miss Janet Meakins—*ach*! dese Anglo-Saxon names. *Schrecklich*! Undt de fourt' vun vass Mr. Chester Singermann, uff t'ree-tvelf East Siggsty-fift' Street. Und dot's all."

"Bless your orderly old Teutonic soul," said Ellery. "Velie, cast those Cyclopean peepers of yours this way." There was a door from the cubicle which, from its location, led out into the alley at the rear, like the door in the back room. Ellery bent over the lock; it was splintered away from the wood. He opened the door; the outer piece was scratched and mutilated. Velie nodded. "Forced," he growled. "This guy's a regular Houdini."

Old Uneker was goggle-eyed. "Broken!" he shrilled. "Budt dot door is neffer used! I didn't notice not'ing, undt de detectiff—"

"Shocking work, Velie, on the part of the local man," said Ellery. "Unky, has anything been stolen?" Old Uneker flew to an antiquated bookcase; it was neatly tiered with volumes. He unlocked the case with anguished fingers, rummaging like an aged terrier. Then he heaved a vast sigh. "*Nein*," he said. "Dose rare vons . . . Not'ing stole."

"I congratulate you. One thing more," said Ellery briskly. "Your mailing list—does it have the business as well as private addresses of your customers?" Uneker nodded. "Better and better. Ta-ta, Unky. You may have a finished story to relate to your other customers after all. Come along, Velie; we're going to visit Mr. Chester Singermann."

They left the bookshop, walked over to Fifth Avenue, and turned north, heading uptown. "Plain as the nose on your face," said Ellery, stretching his long stride to match Velie's. "And that's pretty plain, Sergeant."

"Still looks nutty to me, Mr. Queen."

"On the contrary, we are faced with a strictly logical set of facts. Our thief stole a valuable stamp. He dodged into Uneker's bookshop, contrived to get into the back room. He heard the officer and Friederich Ulm enter and got busy thinking. If he were caught with the stamp on his person . . . You see, Velie, the only explanation that will make consistent the business of the subsequent thefts of the same book—a book not valuable in itself—is that the thief, Planck, slipped the stamp between the pages of one of the volumes on a shelf while he was in the back room—it happened by accident to be a copy of *Europe in Chaos*, one of a number kept in stock on the shelf—and made his escape immediately thereafter. But he still had the problem of regaining possession of the stamp—what did Ulm call it?—the 'one-penny black,' whatever that may be. So that night he came back, watched for old Uneker to leave the shop, then went in and bought from the clerk all copies of *Europe in Chaos* in the place. He got seven. The stamp was not in any one of the seven he purchased, otherwise why did he later steal others which had been bought that afternoon? So far, so good. Not finding the stamp in any of the seven, then, he returned, broke into Unky's little office during the night—witness the shattered lock—from the alley, and looked up in Unky's Dickensian ledger the names and addresses of those who had bought copies of the book during that afternoon. The next night he robbed Hazlitt; Planck evidently followed him from his office. Planck saw at once that he had made a mistake; the condition of the weeks-old book would have told him that this wasn't a book purchased only the day before. So he hurried out to East Orange, knowing Hazlitt's private as well as business address, and stole Hazlitt's recently purchased copy. No luck there either, so he feloniously visited Hornell and Janet Meakins, stealing their copies. Now, there is still one purchaser unaccounted for, which is why we are calling upon Singermann. For if Planck was unsuccessful in his theft of Hornell's and Miss Meakins's books, he will inevitably visit Singermann, and we want to beat our wily thief to it if possible."

Chester Singermann, they found, was a young student living with his parents in a battered old apartment-house flat. Yes, he still had his copy of *Europe in Chaos*—needed it for supplementary reading in political economy—and he produced it. Ellery went through it carefully, page for page; there was no trace of the missing stamp.

"Mr. Singermann, did you find an old postage stamp between the leaves of this volume?" asked Ellery.

The student shook his head. "I haven't even opened it, sir. Stamp? What issue? I've got a little collection of my own, you know."

"It doesn't matter," said Ellery hastily, who had heard of the maniacal enthusiasm of stamp collectors, and he and Velie beat a precipitate retreat.

"It's quite evident," explained Ellery to the sergeant, "that our slippery Planck found the stamp in either Hornell's copy or Miss Meakins's. Which robbery was first in point of time, Velie?"

"Seem to remember that this Meakins woman was robbed second."

"Then the one-penny black was in her copy . . . Here's that office building. Let's pay a little visit to Mr. Friederich Ulm."

Number 1026 on the tenth floor of the building bore a black legend on its frosted-glass door:

> ULM
> Dealers in
> Old & Rare Stamps

Ellery and Sergeant Velie went in and found themselves in a large office. The walls were covered with glass cases in which, separately mounted, could be seen hundreds of canceled and uncanceled postage stamps. Several special cabinets on tables contained, evidently, more valuable items. The place was cluttered; it had a musty air astonishingly like that of Uneker's bookshop.

Three men looked up. One, from a crisscrossed plaster on his cheekbone, was apparently Friederich Ulm himself, a tall gaunt old German with sparse hair and the fanatic look of the confirmed collector. The second man was just as tall and gaunt and old; he wore a green eyeshade and bore a striking resemblance to Ulm, although from his nervous movements and shaky hands he must have been much older. The third man was a little fellow, quite stout, with an expressionless face.

Ellery introduced himself and Sergeant Velie; and the third man picked up his ears. "Not *the* Ellery Queen?" he said, waddling forward. "I'm Heffley, investigator for the insurance people. Glad to meet you." He pumped Ellery's hand with vigor. "These gentlemen are the Ulm brothers, who own this place. Friederich and Albert. Mr. Albert Ulm was out of the office at the time of the sale and robbery. Too bad; might have nabbed the thief."

Friederich Ulm broke into an excited gabble of German. Ellery listened with a smile, nodding at every fourth word. "I see, Mr. Ulm. The situation, then, was this: you sent invitations by mail to three well-known collectors to attend a special exhibition of rare stamps—object, sale. Three men called on you two mornings ago, purporting to be Messrs. Hinchman, Peters, and Beninson. Hinchman and Peters you knew by sight, but Beninson you did not. Very well. Several items were purchased by the first two collectors. The man you thought was Beninson lingered behind, struck you—yes, yes, I know all that. Let me see the rifled cabinet, please." The brothers led him to a table in the center of the office. On it there was a flat cabinet, with a lid of ordinary thin glass framed by a narrow rectangle of wood. Under the glass reposed a number of mounted stamps, lying nakedly on a field of black satin. In the center of the satin lay a leather case, open; its white lining had been denuded of its stamp. Where the lid of the cabinet had been wrenched open there were the unmistakable marks of a "jimmy," four in number. The catch was snapped and broken.

"Amatchoor," said Sergeant Velie with a snort. "You could damn near force that locked lid up with your fingers."

Ellery's sharp eyes were absorbed in what lay before him. "Mr. Ulm," he said, turning to the wounded dealer, "the stamp you call 'the one-penny black' was in this open leather box?"

"Yes, Mr. Queen. But the leather box was closed when the thief forced open the cabinet."

"Then how did he know so unerringly what to steal?" Friederich Ulm touched his check tenderly. "The stamps in this cabinet were not for sale; they're the cream of our collection; every stamp in this case is worth hundreds. But when the three men were here we naturally talked about the rarer items, and I opened this cabinet to show them our very valuable stamps. So the thief saw the one-penny black. He was a collector, Mr. Queen, or he wouldn't have chosen that particular stamp to steal. It has a funny history."

"Heavens!" said Ellery. "Do these things have histories?"

Heffley, the man from the insurance company, laughed. "And how! Mr. Friederich and Mr. Albert Ulm are well known to the trade for owning two of the most unique stamps ever issued, both identical. The one-penny black, as it is called by collectors, is a British stamp first issued in 1840; there are lots of them around, and even an uncanceled one is worth only seventeen and a half dollars in American money. But the two in the possession of these gentlemen are worth thirty thousand dollars apiece. Mr. Queen—that's what makes the theft so doggone serious. In fact, my company is heavily involved, since the stamps are both insured for their full value."

"Thirty thousand dollars!" groaned Ellery. "That's a lot of money for a little piece of dirty paper. Why are they so valuable?"

Albert Ulm nervously pulled his green shade lower over his eyes. "Because both of ours were actually initialed by Queen Victoria, that's why. Sir Rowland Hill, the man who created and founded the standard penny-postage system in England in 1839, was responsible for the issue of the one-penny black. Her majesty was so delighted—England, like other countries, had had a great deal of trouble working out a successful postage system—that she autographed the first two stamps off the press and gave them to the designer—I don't recall his name. Her autograph made them immensely valuable. My brother and I were lucky to get our hands on the only two in existence."

"Where's the twin? I'd like to take a peep at a stamp worth a queen's ransom."

The brothers bustled to a large safe looming in a corner of the office. They came back, Albert carrying a leather case as if it were a consignment of golden bullion, and Friederich anxiously holding his elbow, as if he were a squad of armed guards detailed to protect the consignment. Ellery turned the thing over in his fingers; it felt thick and stiff. It was an average-sized stamp rectangle, imperforate, bordered with a black design, and containing an engraving in profile view of Queen Victoria's head—all done in tones of black. On the lighter portion of the face appeared two tiny initials in faded black ink—V. R.

"They're both exactly alike," said Friederich Ulm, "even to the initials."

"Very interesting," said Ellery, returning the case. The brothers scurried back, placed the stamp in a drawer of the safe, and locked the safe with painful care. "You closed the cabinet, of course, after your three visitors looked over the stamps inside?"

"Oh, yes," said Friederich Ulm. "I closed the case of the one-penny black itself, and then I locked the cabinet."

"And did you send the three invitations yourself? I noticed you have no typewriter here."

"We use a public stenographer in Room 1102 for all our correspondence, Mr. Queen."

Ellery thanked the dealers gravely, waved to the insurance man, nudged Sergeant Velie's meaty ribs, and the two men left the office. In Room 1102 they found a sharp-featured young woman. Sergeant Velie flashed his badge, and Ellery was soon reading carbon copies of the three Ulm invitations. He took note of the names and addresses, and the two men left.

THEY VISITED THE collector named John Hinchman first. Hinchman was a thickset old man with white hair and gimlet eyes. He was brusque and uncommunicative. Yes, he had been present in the Ulms' office two mornings before. Yes, he knew Peters. No, he'd never met

Beninson before. The one-penny black? Of course. Every collector knew of the valuable twin stamps owned by the Ulm brothers; those little scraps of paper bearing the initials of a queen were famous in stampdom. The theft? Bosh! He, Hinchman, knew nothing of Beninson or whoever it was that impersonated Beninson. He, Hinchman, had left before the thief. He, Hinchman, furthermore didn't care two raps in Hades who stole the stamp; all he wanted was to be let strictly alone.

Sergeant Velie exhibited certain animal signs of hostility; but Ellery grinned, sank his strong fingers into the muscle of the sergeant's arm, and herded him out of Hinchman's house. They took the subway uptown.

J. S. Peters, they found, was a middle-aged man, tall and thin and yellow as Chinese sealing wax. He seemed anxious to be of assistance. Yes, he and Hinchman had left the Ulms' office together, before the third man. He had never seen the third man before, although he had heard of Beninson from other collectors. Yes, he knew all about the one-penny blacks, had even tried to buy one of them from Friederich Ulm two years before; but the Ulms had refused to sell.

"Philately," said Ellery outside to Sergeant Velie, whose honest face looked pained at the word, "is a curious hobby. It seems to afflict its victims with a species of mania. I don't doubt these stamp-collecting fellows would murder each other for one of the things."

The sergeant was wrinkling his nose. "How's she look now?" he asked rather anxiously.

"Velie," replied Ellery, "she looks swell—and different."

They found Avery Beninson in an old brownstone house near the River; he was a mild-mannered and courteous host.

"No, I never did see that invitation," Beninson said. "You see, I hired this man who called himself William Planck, and he took care of my collection and the bulky mail all serious collectors have. The man knew stamps, all right. For two weeks he was invaluable to me. He must have intercepted the Ulms' invitation. He saw his chance to get into their office, went there, said he was Avery Beninson . . ." The collector shrugged. "It was quite simple, I suppose, for an unscrupulous man."

"Of course, you haven't had word from him since the morning of the theft?"

"Naturally not. He made his haul and lit out."

"Just what did he do for you, Mr. Beninson?"

"The ordinary routine of the philatelic assistant—assorting, cataloguing, mounting, answering correspondence. He lived here with me for the two weeks he was in my employ." Beninson grinned deprecatingly. "You see, I'm a bachelor—live in this big shack all alone. I was really glad of his company, although he was a queer one."

"A queer one?"

"Well," said Beninson, "he was a retiring sort of creature. Had very few personal belongings, and I found those gone two days ago. He didn't seem to like people, either. He always went to his own room when friends of mine or collectors called, as if he didn't want to mix with company."

"Then there isn't anyone else who might be able to supplement your description of him?"

"Unfortunately, no. He was a fairly tall man, well advanced in age, I should say. But then his dark glasses and heavy black mustache would make him stand out anywhere."

Ellery sprawled his long figure over the chair, slumping on his spine. "I'm most interested in the man's habits, Mr. Beninson. Individual idiosyncrasies are often the innocent means by which criminals are apprehended, as the good sergeant here will tell you. Please think hard. Didn't the man exhibit any oddities of habit?"

Beninson pursed his lips with anxious concentration. His face brightened. "By George, yes! He was a snuff taker."

Ellery and Sergeant Velie looked at each other. "That's interesting," said Ellery with a smile. "So is my father—Inspector Queen, you know—and I've had the dubious pleasure of watching a snuff taker's gyrations ever since my childhood. Planck inhaled snuff regularly?"

"I shouldn't say that exactly, Mr. Queen," replied Beninson with a frown. "In fact, in the two weeks he was with me I saw him take snuff only once, and I invariably spent all day with him working in this room. It was last week; I happened to go out for a few moments, and when I returned I saw him holding a carved little box, sniffing from a pinch of something between his fingers. He put the box away quickly, as if he didn't want me to see it—although I didn't care, Lord knows, so long as he didn't smoke in here. I've had one fire from a careless assistant's cigarette, and I don't want another."

Ellery's face had come alive. He sat up straight and began to finger his *pince-nez* eyeglasses studiously. "You didn't know the man's address, I suppose?" he asked slowly.

"No, I did not. I'm afraid I took him on without the proper precautions." The collector sighed. "I'm fortunate that he didn't steal anything from me. My collection is worth a lot of money."

"No doubt," said Ellery in a pleasant voice. He rose. "May I use your telephone, Mr. Beninson?"

"Surely.

Ellery consulted a telephone directory and made several calls, speaking in tones so low that neither Beninson nor Sergeant Velie could hear what he was saying. When he put down the instrument he said: "If you can spare a half hour, Mr. Beninson, I'd like to have you take a little jaunt with us downtown."

Beninson seemed astonished; but he smiled, said: "I'd be delighted," and reached for his coat.

Ellery commandeered a taxicab outside, and the three men were driven to Forty-ninth Street. He excused himself when they got out before the little bookshop, hurried inside, and came out after a moment with old Uneker, who locked his door with shaking fingers.

In the Ulm brothers' office they found Heffley, the insurance man, and Hazlitt, Uneker's customer, waiting for them. "Glad you could come," said Ellery cheerfully to both men. "Good afternoon, Mr. Ulm. A little conference, and I think we'll have this business cleared up to the Queen's taste. Ha, ha!"

Friederich Ulm scratched his head; Albert Ulm, sitting in a corner with his hatchet knees jackknifed, his green shades over his eyes, nodded.

"We'll have to wait," said Ellery. "I've asked Mr. Peters and Mr. Hinchman to come, too. Suppose we sit down?"

They were silent for the most part, and not a little uneasy. No one spoke as Ellery strolled about the office, examining the rare stamps in their wall cases with open curiosity, whistling softly to himself. Sergeant Velie eyed him doubtfully. Then the door opened, and Hinchman and Peters appeared together. They stopped short at the threshold, looked at each other, shrugged, and walked in. Hinchman was scowling.

"What's the idea, Mr. Queen?" he said. "I'm a busy man."

"A not unique condition," smiled Ellery. "Ah, Mr. Peters, good day. Introductions, I think, are not entirely called for . . . Sit down, gentlemen!" he said in a sharper voice, and they sat down.

The door opened and a small, gray, birdlike little man peered in at them. Sergeant Velie looked astounded, and Ellery nodded gaily. "Come in, Dad, come in! You're just in time for the first act."

Inspector Richard Queen cocked his little squirrel's head, looked at the assembled company shrewdly, and closed the door behind him. "What the devil is the idea of the call, son?"

"Nothing very exciting. Not a murder, or anything in your line. But it may interest you. Gentlemen, Inspector Queen."

The Inspector grunted, sat down, took out his old brown snuff box; and inhaled with the voluptuous gasp of long practice.

Ellery stood serenely in the hub of the circle of chairs, looking down at curious faces. "The theft of the one-penny black, as you inveterate stamp fiends call it," he began, "presented a not uninteresting problem. I say 'presented' advisedly. For the case is solved."

"Is this that business of the stamp robbery I was hearing about down at Headquarters?" asked the Inspector.

"Yes."

"Solved?" asked Beninson. "I don't think I understand, Mr. Queen. Have you found Planck?"

Ellery waved his arm negligently. "I was never too sanguine of catching Mr. William Planck, as such. You see, he wore tinted spectacles and a black mustachio. Now, anyone familiar with the science of crime detection will tell you that the average person identifies faces by superficial details. A black mustache catches the eye. Tinted glasses impress the memory. In fact, Mr. Hazlitt here, who from Uneker's description is a man of poor observational powers, recalled even after seeing his assailant in dim street light that the man wore a black mustache and tinted glasses. But this is all fundamental and not even particularly smart. It was reasonable to assume that Planck wanted these special facial characteristics to be remembered. I was convinced that he had disguised himself, that the mustache was probably a false one, and that ordinarily he does not wear tinted glasses."

They all nodded.

"This was the first and simplest of the three psychological signposts to the culprit." Ellery smiled and turned suddenly to the Inspector.

"Dad, you're an old snuff addict. How many times a day do you stuff that unholy brown dust up your nostrils?"

The Inspector blinked. "Oh, every half hour or so. Sometimes as often as you smoke cigarettes."

"Precisely. Now, Mr. Beninson told me that in the two weeks during which Planck stayed at his house, and despite the fact that Mr. Beninson worked side by side with the man every day, he saw Planck take snuff only *once*. Please observe that here we have a most enlightening and suggestive fact."

From the blankness of their faces it was apparent that, far from seeing light, their minds on this point were in total darkness. There was one exception—the Inspector; he nodded, shifted in his chair, and coolly began to study the faces about him.

Ellery lit a cigarette. "Very well," he said, expelling little puffs of smoke, "there you have the second psychological factor. The third was this: Planck, in a fairly public place, bashes Mr. Friederich Ulm over the face with the robust intention of stealing a valuable stamp. Any thief under the circumstances would desire speed above all things. Mr. Ulm was only half-stunned—he might come to and make an outcry; a customer might walk in; Mr. Albert Ulm might return unexpectedly—"

"Just a moment, son," said the Inspector. "I understand there are two of the stamp thingamajigs in existence. I'd like to see the one that's still here."

Ellery nodded. "Would one of you gentlemen please get the stamp?"

Friederich Ulm rose, pottered over to the safe, tinkered with the dials, opened the steel door, fussed about the interior a moment, and came back with the leather case containing the second one-penny black. The Inspector examined the thick little scrap curiously; a thirty-thousand-dollar bit of old paper was as awesome to him as to Ellery.

He almost dropped it when he heard Ellery say to Sergeant Velie: "Sergeant, may I borrow your revolver?"

Velie's massive jaw seesawed as he fumbled in his hip pocket and produced a long-barreled police revolver. Ellery took it and hefted it thoughtfully. Then his fingers closed about the butt and he walked over to the rifled cabinet in the middle of the room.

"Please observe, gentlemen—to expand my third point—that in order to open this cabinet Planck used an iron bar; and that in prying up the lid he found it necessary to insert the bar between the lid and the front wall four times, as the four marks under the lid indicate.

"Now, as you can see, the cabinet is covered with thin glass. Moreover, it was locked, and the one-penny black was in this closed leather case inside. Planck stood about here, I should judge, and mark that the iron bar was in his hand. What would you gentlemen expect a thief, working against time, to do under these circumstances?"

They stared. The Inspector's mouth tightened, and a grin began to spread over the expanse of Sergeant Velie's face.

"But it's so clear," said Ellery. "Visualize it. I'm Planck. The revolver in my hand is an iron 'Jimmy.' I'm standing over the cabinet . . ." His eyes gleamed behind the *pince-nez*, and he raised the revolver high over his head. And then, deliberately, he began to bring the steel barrel down on the thin sheeting of glass atop the cabinet. There was a scream from Albert Ulm, and Friederich Ulm half-rose, glaring. Ellery's hand stopped a half inch from the glass.

"Don't break that glass, you fool!" shouted the green-shaded dealer. "You'll only—"

He leaped forward and stood before the cabinet, trembling arms outspread as if to protect the case and its contents. Ellery grinned and prodded the man's palpitating belly with the muzzle of the revolver. "I'm glad you stopped me, Mr. Ulm. Put your hands up. Quickly!"

"Why—why, what do you mean?" gasped Albert Ulm, raising his arms with frantic rapidity.

"I mean," said Ellery gently, "that you're William Planck, and that brother Friederich is your accomplice!"

The brothers Ulm sat trembling in their chairs, and Sergeant Velie stood over them with a nasty smile. Albert Ulm had gone to pieces; he was quivering like an aspen leaf in high wind.

"A very simple, almost an elementary, series of deductions," Ellery was saying. "Point three first. Why did the thief, instead of taking the most logical course of smashing the glass with the iron bar, choose to waste precious minutes using a 'Jimmy' four times to force open the lid? *Obviously to protect the other stamps in the cabinet which lay open to possible injury*, as Mr. Albert Ulm has just graphically pointed out. And who had the greatest concern in protecting these other stamps—Hinchman, Peter, Beninson, even the mythical Planck himself? Of course not. Only the Ulm brothers, owners of the stamps."

Old Uneker began to chuckle; he nudged the Inspector. "See? Didn't I say he vass smardt? Now me—me, I'd neffer t'ink of dot."

"And why didn't Planck steal these other stamps in the cabinet? You would expect a thief to do that? Planck did not. But if the *Herren* Ulm were the thieves, the theft of the other stamps became pointless."

"How about that snuff business, Mr. Queen?" asked Peters.

"Yes. The conclusion is plain from the fact that Planck apparently indulged only once during the days he worked with Mr. Beninson. Since snuff addicts partake freely and often, Planck wasn't a snuff addict. Then it wasn't snuff he inhaled that day. What else is sniffed in a similar manner? Well—drugs in powder form—heroin! What are the characteristics of a heroin addict? Nervous, drawn appearance; gauntness, almost emaciation; and most important, telltale eyes, the pupils of which contract under influence of the drug. Then here was another explanation for the tinted glasses Planck wore. They served a double purpose—as an easily recognizable disguise and also to conceal his eyes, which would give his vice addiction away! But when I observed that Mr. Albert Ulm"—Ellery went over to the cowering man and ripped the green eyeshade away, revealing two stark, pinpoint pupils—"wore this shade, it was a psychological confirmation of his identity as Planck."

"Yes, but that business of stealing all those books," said Hazlitt.

"Part of a very pretty and rather farfetched plot," said Ellery. "With Albert Ulm the disguised thief, Friederich Ulm, who exhibited the wound on his cheek, must have been an accomplice. Then with the Ulm brothers the thieves, the entire business of the books was a blind. The attack on Friederich, the ruse of the bookstore escape, the trail of the minor robberies of copies of *Europe in Chaos*—a cleverly planned series of incidents to authenticate the fact that there was an outside thief, to convince the police and the insurance company that the stamp actually was stolen when it was not. Object, of course, to collect the insurance without parting with the stamp. These men are fanatical collectors."

Heffley wriggled his fat little body uncomfortably. "That's all very nice, Mr. Queen, but where the deuce is that stamp they stole from themselves? Where'd they hide it?"

"I thought long and earnestly about that, Heffley. For while my trio of deductions were psychological indications of guilt, the discovery of the stolen stamp in the Ulms' possession would be evidential proof." The Inspector was turning the second stamp over mechanically. "I said to myself," Ellery went on, "in a reconsideration of the problem: What would be the most likely hiding place for the stamp? And then I remembered that the two stamps were identical, even the initials of the good Queen being in the same place. So I said to myself: If I were Messrs Ulm, I should hide that stamp—like the character in Edgar Allan Poe's famous tale—in the most obvious place. And what is the most obvious place?"

Ellery sighed and returned the unused revolver to Sergeant Velie. "Dad," he remarked to the Inspector, who started guiltily, "I think that if you allow one of the philatelists in our company to examine the second one-penny black in your fingers, you'll find that the *first* has been pasted with noninjurious rubber cement precisely over the second!"

Make Yourselves at Home

Joan Hess

IT WAS THE SUMMER of her discontent. This particular moment on this particular morning had just become its zenith; its epiphany, if you will; its culmination of simmering animosity and precariously constrained urges to scream curses at the heavens while flinging herself off a precipice, presuming there was such a thing within five hundred miles. There was not. Florida is many things; one of them is flat.

Thus thwarted by geographical realities, Wilma Chadley could do no more than gaze sullenly out the kitchen window at the bleached grass and limp, dying shrubs. Fierce white sunlight baked the concrete patio. In one corner of the yard remained the stubbles of what had never been a flourishing vegetable garden, but merely an impotent endeavor to economize on groceries. Beyond the fence, tractor-trailers blustered down the interstate. Cars topped with luggage racks darted between them like brightly colored cockroaches. The motionless air was laden with noxious exhaust fumes and the miasma from the swampy expanse on the far side of the highway.

Wilma poured a glass of iced tea and sat down at the dinette to reread the letter for the fifth time since she'd taken it from the mailbox only half an hour ago. When she finished, her bony body quivered with resentment. Her breath came out in ragged grunts. A bead of sweat formed on the tip of her narrow nose, hung delicately, and then splattered on the page. More sweat trickled down the harshly angular creases of her face as the words blurred before her eyes.

From the living room she could hear the drone of the announcer's voice as he listed a batter's statistics. As usual, her husband, George, was sprawled on the recliner, drifting between the game and damp, uneasy naps, the fan whirring at his face, his sparse white hair plastered to his head. If she were to step between him and his precious game in order to read the letter, he would wait woodenly until she was done, then ask her to get him another beer. She had no doubt his response would be identical if she announced the house was on fire (although she was decidedly not in the mood to conduct whimsical experiments in behavioral psychology).

Finally, when she could no longer suffer in silence, she snatched the leash from a hook behind the door and tracked Popsie down in the bathroom, where he lay behind the toilet. "It's time for Popsie's lunchie walk," she said in a wheedling voice, aware that the obese and grizzled basset hound resented attempts to drag him away from the cool porcelain. "Come on, my sweetums," she continued, "and we'll have a nice walk and then a nice visit with our neighbor next door. Maybe she'll have a doggie biscuit just for you."

Popsie expressed his skepticism with a growl before wiggling further into the recess. Sighing, Wilma left him and went through the living room. George had not moved in over an hour, but she felt no optimism that she might be cashing a check from the life insurance company any time soon. Since his retirement from an insignificant managerial position at a factory five years ago, he had perfected the art of inertia. He could go for hours without saying a word, without turning his head when she entered the room, without so much as flickering when she spoke to him. He bathed irregularly, at best. In the infrequent instances in which she failed to harangue him, he donned sweat-stained clothes from the previous day. Only that morning he'd made a futile attempt to leave his dentures in the glass beside the bed, citing swollen gums. Wilma had made it clear that was not acceptable.

She headed for the house next door. It was indistinguishable from its neighbors, each being a flimsy box with three small bedrooms, one bathroom, a poorly arranged kitchen, and an airless living room. At some point in the distant past the houses had been painted in an array of pastels, but by now the paint was gone and the weathered wood was uniformly drab. Some carports were empty, others filled with cartons of yellowed newspapers and broken appliances. There were no bicycles in the carports or toys scattered in the yards. Silver Beach was a retirement community. The nearest beach was twenty miles away. There may have been silverfish and silver fillings, but everything else was gray. During the day, the streets were empty. Cemetery salesmen stalked the sidewalks each evening, armed with glossy brochures and trustworthy faces.

Polly Simps was struggling with a warped screen as Wilma cut across the yard. She wore a housedress and slippers, and her brassy orange hair was wrapped around pink foam curlers. There was little reason to dress properly in Silver Beach since the air conditioner had broken down at the so-called clubhouse. For the last three years the building had been used solely by drug dealers and shaky old alcoholics with unshaven cheeks and unfocused eyes. Only a month ago a man of indeterminate age had been found in the empty swimming pool behind the clubhouse. The bloodstains were still visible on the cracked concrete.

"Damn this thing," Polly muttered in greeting. "I don't know why I bother. The mosquitoes get in all the same." She dropped the screen to scratch at one of the welts on her flabby, freckled arm. "Every year they seem to get bigger and hungrier. One of these days they're gonna carry me off to the swamp."

Wilma had no interest in anyone else's problems. "Listen to this," she said as she unfolded the letter. When she was done, she wadded it up, stuffed it in her pocket, and waited for a response from one of the very few residents of Silver Beach with whom she was on speaking terms. Back in Brooklyn, she wouldn't have bothered to share the time of day with the likes of someone as ignorant and opinionated as Polly Simps. That was then.

"I never heard of such a thing," Polly said at last. "The idea of allowing strangers into your own home is appalling. The fact that they're foreigners makes it all the worse. Who knows what kind of germs they might carry? I'd be obliged to boil the sheets and towels, and I'd feel funny every time I used my silverware."

"The point is that Jewel Jacoby and her sister spent three weeks in an apartment in Paris. Jewel was a bookkeeper just like I was, and I know for a fact her social security and pension checks can't add up to more than mine. Her husband passed away at least ten years ago. Whatever she gets as a widow can't be near as much as we get from George's retirement." Wilma rumbled in frustration as she considered Jewel's limited financial resources. "And she went to Paris in April for three weeks! You know where George and I went on vacation last year? Do you?"

Polly blinked nervously as she tried to think. "Did you and George take a vacation last year?"

"No," Wilma snapped, "and that's the issue. We talked about driving across the country to visit Louisa and her loutish husband in Oregon, but George was afraid that the car wouldn't make it and we'd end up stranded in a Kansas cornfield. He's perfectly happy to sit in his chair and stare at that infernal television set. We've never once had a proper vacation. Now I get this letter from Jewel Jacoby about how she went to France and saw museums and cathedrals and drank coffee at sidewalk cafes. All it cost her was airfare and whatever she and her sister spent on groceries. It's not fair."

"But the French people stayed in her apartment," Polly countered. "They slept in her bed and used her things just like they owned them."

"While she slept in their bed and sat on their balcony, watching the boats on the Seine! I've never set foot in Europe, but Jewel had the time of her life—all because the French people agreed to this foolish exchange. I'll bet they were sorry. I've never been in Jewel's apartment, but she was the worst slob in the entire office. I'd be real surprised if her apartment wasn't filthier than a pigsty."

Polly held her peace while Wilma made further derogatory remarks about her ex-coworker back in Brooklyn. Wilma's tirades were infamous throughout Silver Beach. She'd been kicked out of the Wednesday bridge club after an especially eloquent one and was rarely included in the occasional coffee-and-gossip sessions in someone's kitchen. It was just as well, since she was often the topic.

Wilma finally ran out of venom. Polly took a breath and said, "I still don't like the idea of foreigners in my house. What was the name of the organization?"

"Traveler's Vacation Exchange or something like that." Wilma took out the letter and forced herself to scan the pertinent paragraph. "She paid fifty dollars and sent in her ad in the fall. Then in January she got a catalog filled with other people's ads and letters started coming from all over Europe, and even one from Hawaii. She says she picked Paris because she'd taken French in high school forty years ago. What a stupid reason to make such an important decision! I must say I'm not surprised, though. Jewel was a very stupid woman, and no doubt still is."

Wilma went home and dedicated herself to making George utterly and totally miserable for the rest of the summer. Since she had had more than forty years of practice, this was not challenging.

FLORIDA/ORLANDO	X	3-6wks	O
George & Wilma Chadley 2/0		A, 4, 2	GB
122 Palmetto Rd, Silver Beach, FL 34101			
(407) 521-7357			

ac bb bc cf cl cs dr fi fn gd gg go hh mk ns o pk pl pv ro rt sba se sk ss tv uz wa wf wm wv yd

"Here's one," Wilma said, jabbing her finger at an ad. "They live in a village called Cobbet, but it's only an hour away from London by train. They have three children and want to come to Florida in July or August for a month."

"I reckon they don't know how hot it gets," Polly said, shaking her head. "I'd sooner spend the summer in Hades than in Silver Beach."

"That's their problem, not mine." Wilma consulted the list of abbreviations, although by this time she'd memorized most of them. "No air conditioning, but a washer and dryer, modern kitchen with dishwasher and microwave, garden, domestic help, and a quiet neighborhood. They want to exchange cars, too. I do believe I'll write them first."

"What does George think about this?"

Wilma carefully copied the name and address, then closed the catalog and gave Polly a beady look. "Not that it's any of your business, but I haven't discussed it with him. I don't see any reason to do it until

I've reached an agreement and found out exactly how much the airfare will be."

Polly decided it was too risky to ask about the finances of this crazy scheme. "Let me see your ad."

Wilma flipped open the catalog and pointed to the appropriate box. While Polly tried to make sense of the abbreviations, she sat back and dreamily imagined herself in a lush garden, sipping tea and enjoying a cool, British breeze.

Polly looked up in bewilderment. "According to what this says, the nearest airport is Orlando. Isn't Miami a sight closer?"

"The main reason people with children come to Florida is to go to Disney World. I want them to think it's convenient."

"Oh," Polly murmured. She consulted the list several more times. "This says you have four bedrooms and two bathrooms, Wilma. I haven't been out in your backyard lately, but last time I was there I didn't notice any swimming pool or deck with a barbecue grill. We ain't on the beach, either. The nearest one is a half-hour's drive and it's been closed for two years because of the pollution. It takes a good two hours to get to an open beach."

"The couch in the living room makes into a bed, so they can consider it a bedroom. One bathroom's plenty. I'll be the one paying the water bill at the end of the month, after all."

"Your air conditioner doesn't work any more than mine, and if you've got a microwave and a clothes dryer, you sure hide 'em well. I suppose there's golf and skiing and playgrounds and scuba diving and boating and hiking, but not anywhere around these parts. You got one thing right, though. It's a quiet neighborhood now that everyone's afraid to set foot outside because of those hoodlums. Mr. Hodkins heard gunfire just the other night."

Wilma did not respond, having returned to her fantasy. It was now replete with crumpets.

122 Palmetto Road
Silver Beach, FL 34101

Dear Sandra,

I received your letter this morning and I don't want to waste a single minute in responding. You and your husband sound like a charming couple. I shall always treasure the photograph of you and your three beautiful children. I was particularly taken with little Dorothy's dimples and angelic smile.

As I mentioned in my earlier letter, you will find our home quite comfortable and adequate for your needs. Our car is somewhat older than yours, but it will get you to Disneyworld in no time at all.

You have voiced concern about your children and the swimming pool, but you need not worry. The ad was set incorrectly. The pool is a block away at our neighborhood club house. There is no lifeguard, however.

I fully intended to enclose photographs of ourselves and our house, but my husband forgot to pick up the prints at the drug store on his way home from the golf course. I'll do my best to remember to put them in the next letter.

I believe we'll follow your advice and take the train from Gatwick to Cobbet. Train travel is much more limited here, so we will leave our car at the Orlando airport for your convenience. In the meantime, start stocking up on suntan oil for your wonderful days on the beach. I wouldn't want Dorothy's dimples to turn red.

Your dear friend in Florida,
Wilma

"Have you told George?" Polly whispered, glancing at the doorway: Noises from the television set indicated that basketball had been replaced with baseball, although it was impossible to determine if George had noticed. His only concession to the blistering resurgence of summer was a pair of stained plaid shorts.

Wilma snorted. "Yes, Polly, I have told George. Did you think I crept into the living room and took his passport photographs without him noticing?"

"Is he excited?"

"He will be when the time comes," she said firmly. "In any case, it really doesn't matter. The Millingfords are coming on the first of

July whether he likes it or not. I find it hard to imagine he would enjoy sharing this house with three snotty-nosed children. Look at the photograph if you don't believe me. They look like gargoyles, especially the baby. The two older ones have the same squinty eyes as their father."

"The house looks nice."

"It does, doesn't it? If it's half as decent as that insufferably smug woman claims, we should be comfortable. The flowerbeds are pretentious, but I'm not surprised. She made a point of mentioning that they have a gardener twice a week. I was tempted to write back and say ours comes three times a week, but I let it go." She tapped the photograph. "Look at that structure near the garden wall. It's a hutch, of all things. It seems that Lucinda and Charles keep pet rabbits. Because little Dorothy has asthma and all kinds of allergies, the rabbits are not allowed in the house. The idea of stepping on a dropping makes my stomach turn."

"Will that cause a problem with Popsie?"

Wilma leaned down to stroke Popsie's satiny ears. He'd been lured away from the toilet with chocolate-chip cookies, and now crumb-flecked droplets of saliva were sprinkled beneath the table. She felt a prick of remorse at the idea of leaving him for a month, but it couldn't be helped, not if she was to have a vacation that would outshine Jewel Jacoby's. "I haven't mentioned Popsie in my letters. The boarding kennel wants twenty-five dollars a day. I've had to set aside every penny for our airfare, which is why the washing machine is still leaking. The tires on the car are bald and the engine makes such a terrible rattle that I literally hold my breath every time I drive to the store. There's absolutely no way I can get anything repaired until we build up some cash in the fall. Besides that, my Popsie is very delicate and would be miserable in a strange place. If there are any disruptions in his schedule, he begins piddling on the floor and passing wind." She looked thoughtfully at Polly and decided not to even hint that Popsie would enjoy a lengthy visit in his neighbor's home. Not after what Popsie had done to Polly's cat.

"I do want to ask a small favor of you," she continued with a conspiratorial wink. "I'm worried about the children damaging the house. I'm going to lock away all the good dinnerware, but they're quite capable of leaving muddy footprints all over the furniture and handprints on the walls. I'm hoping you'll drop by at least once a day. Just ask if they're having a pleasant vacation or something."

Polly flinched. "Won't they think I'm spying on them?"

"That's exactly what I want them to think. They need to be reminded they're guests in my home."

"Is there anything else?"

"One other favor. I'm going to leave a note in the car for them to come by your house to pick up the house key and a letter regarding their stay. If you don't mind, of course?"

As dim as she was, Polly suspected the British family might be disgruntled by the time they arrived in Silver Beach. However, nothing interesting had taken place since the knifing by the clubhouse several weeks ago. Shrugging, she said, "I'll make a point of being here when they arrive."

Dear Sandra,

Welcome to Florida! I'm writing this while we pack, but I'll try very hard not to forget anything. I hope you and the family enjoyed the flight to Orlando. I was a tiny bit muddled about the distance from the airport to the house, but George insisted that it was no more than an hour's drive. How embarrassing to have discovered only the other day that it's nearly three times that far! In any case, I shall assume my map and directions were clear and you successfully arrived at my dear friend Polly Simps's house. She is excited about your visit, and will come by often to check on you.

I must apologize for the air conditioner. The repairman has assured me that the part will arrive within a matter of days and he will be there to put it in working order. Please be very careful with the washing machine. Last night I received a nasty shock that flung me across the room and left my body throbbing most painfully. I was almost convinced my heart had received enough of a jolt to kill me! You might prefer to use the launderette in town. I had a similar experience with the dishwasher—why do these things go haywire on such short notice???

I am so sorry to tell you that our cleaning woman was diagnosed with terminal liver cancer three days ago. She immediately left to spend her last few weeks with her family in Atlanta. Her son, who works as our gardener, went with her. I was so stricken that all I could do was offer her a generous sum and wish them both the best. The lawn mower is in the carport storage area. It's balky, but will start with encouragement. You can buy gas (or petrol, as you say) for it at any service station.

And now I must mention dearest Popsie, whom you've surely discovered by now. We've had him for twelve years and he's become as beloved to us as a child. I had a long and unpleasant conversation with the brutes at the boarding kennel. They made it clear that Popsie would be treated with nothing short of cruelty. He is much too delicate to withstand such abuse and estrangement from his familiar surroundings. You will find him to be only the most minor nuisance, and I implore you to behave like decent Christians and treat him with kindness.

He must be taken for a walk (in order to do his duty) three times a day, at eight in the morning, noon, and five in the afternoon. His feeding instructions, along with those for the vitamin and mineral supplements and details regarding his eye drops and insulin shots, are taped on the refrigerator. Once he becomes accustomed to the children, he will stop snapping and allow them to enter the bathroom. Until he does so, I strongly suggest that he be approached with caution. I should feel dreadful if dear little Dorothy's rosy cheeks were savaged. The Silverado Community Beach is closed because of an overflow from a sewage disposal facility. You'll find Miami Beach, although a bit farther, to be lovely. The presence of a lifeguard should be reassuring, in that you've obviously neglected to teach your children how to swim. You might consider lessons in the future.

The refrigerator has been emptied for your convenience. I left bread and eggs for your first night's supper. Milk would have spoiled, but you'll find a packet of powdered lemonade mix for the children. Polly will give you directions to the supermarket. The car started making a curious clanking sound only yesterday. I would have taken it to the garage had time permitted, but it was impossible to schedule an appointment. George suspects a problem with the transmission. I will leave the telephone numbers of several towing services should you experience any problems. All of them accept credit cards.

But above all, make yourselves at home!

Wilma

⁓

Ferncliffe House
Willow Springs Lane
Cobbet, Lincs LN2 3AB
15 July (as they say)

Dear Polly,

We're having an absolutely wonderful time. The house is much nicer than I expected. Everything works properly, and even the children's room were left tidy.

I spend a great deal of time in the garden with a cup of tea and a novel, while George pops over to the pub to shoot billiards and play darts with his cronies. Last Sunday our lovely neighbors invited us to a picnic at the local cricket field. The game itself is incredibly stupid, but I suffered through it for the sake of cucumber sandwiches and cakes with clotted cream and jam.

I must say things are primitive. The washing machine is so small that our cleaning woman has to run it continually all three mornings every week when she's here. Her accent is droll, to put it kindly, and she is forever fixing us mysterious yet tasty casseroles. If I knew what was in them, I doubt I could choke down a single bite. The village shops are pathetically small, poorly stocked, and close at odd hours of the day. I don't know how these people have survived without a decent supermarket. And as for their spelling, you'd think the whole population was illiterate. I wonder if I'm the first person who's mentioned that they drive on the wrong side of the road.

I had reservations about the lack of air conditioning, but the days are mild and the nights cool. Sandra "conveniently" forgot to mention how often it rains; I suppose she was willing to lie simply to trick us into the exchange. She was certainly less

than honest about the train ride from London. It takes a good
seventy minutes.

I've searched every drawer and closet in the entire house and
have yet to find a Bible. It does make one wonder what kind of
people they really are. In the note I left, I begged them to treat
Popsie with a Christian attitude, but now I wonder if they're
even familiar with the term. Everyone is so backward in this
country. For all I know, the Millingfords are Catholics—or
Druids!

I must stop now. Tonight we're being treated to dinner at a local
restaurant, where I shall become queasy just reading the menu.
And I'm dreading tomorrow morning. Someone failed to shut
the door of the hutch and the rabbits have escaped. No doubt
the gardener will be upset in his amusing guttural way, since they
were his responsibility. I honestly think it's for the best. The ani-
mals are filthy and one of them scratched my arm so viciously
that I can still see a mark. What kind of parents would allow
their children to have pets like those? Dogs are so much cleaner
and more intelligent. I do believe I shall leave a note to that
effect for Sandra to read when the family returns home.

Wilma

⁓

Polly was waiting on her porch when George and Wilma pulled
into the driveway. She would have preferred to cower inside her
house, blinds drawn and doors locked, but she knew this would only
add to Wilma's impending fury. "Welcome home," she called bravely.

Wilma told George to unload the luggage, then crossed into the
adjoining yard. "I feel like we've been traveling for days and days. It
would have been so much easier to fly into the Miami airport, but the
Millingfords had to go to Disney World, didn't they?"

"And they did," Polly began, then faltered as the words seemed to
stick in her mouth like cotton balls (or, perhaps, clumps of rabbit fur
similar to the ones the gardener had found in the meadow behind
Ferncliffe House).

"So what?"

"They left two weeks ago."

"Just what are you saying, Polly Simps? I'm exhausted from the trip, and I have no desire to stand here while you make cryptic remarks about these whiny people. I'm not the least bit interested at the moment, although I suppose in a day or two when I'm rested you can tell me about them." She looked back at George, who was struggling toward the house with suitcases. "Be careful! I have several jars of jam in that bag."

Florida was still flat, so Polly's desperate desire to disappear into a gaping hole in the yard was foiled. "I think you'd better listen to me, Wilma. There were . . . some problems."

"I'm beginning to feel faint. If there's something you need to say, spit it out so I can go into my own home and give Popsie the very expensive milk biscuits I bought for him in England."

"Come inside and I'll fix you a glass of iced tea."

Wilma's nostrils flared as if she were a winded racehorse. "All I can say is this had better be good," she muttered as she followed her neighbor across the porch and through the living room. "Did the Millingfords snivel about everything? Are you going to present me with a list of all their petty complaints?"

"They didn't complain," Polly said as she put glasses on the table. "They were a little disappointed when they arrived, I think. Five minutes after I'd given them the key and your letter, Sandra came back to ask if it was indeed the right house. I said it was. Later that afternoon David came over and asked if I could take him to the grocery store, since your car wouldn't start."

"What colossal nerve! Did he think you were the local taxi service?"

Polly shrugged. "I told him I didn't have one, but I arranged for him to borrow Mr. Hodkins's car for an hour. The next morning a tow truck came for the car, and within a week or so it was repaired. During that time, they stayed inside the house for the most part. At one point the two older children came to ask me about the swimming pool, but that was the last time any of them knocked on my door."

"I'd like to think they were brought up not to pester people all the time. But as I hinted in my letter to you, they seem to be growing up in a heathen environment. You did go over there every day, didn't you?"

"I tried, Wilma, but I finally stopped. I'd ring the bell and ask how they were enjoying their visit, but whichever parent opened the door just stared at me and then closed the door without saying a word. Once I heard the baby wailing in one of the bedrooms, but other than that it was so quiet over there that I wondered what on earth they were doing."

Wilma entertained images of primitive rituals, embellishing them with her limited knowledge of Druids and gleanings from Errol Flynn movies. "Poor Popsie," she said at last. "How hideous for him. Did they walk him three times a day?"

"For the few days. Then the baby had an asthma attack and had to be taken to the hospital in an ambulance. After that, they left Popsie in the backyard, where he howled all night. The misery in that dog's voice was almost more than I could bear."

"Those barbarians! I'm going to write a letter to Mrs. Snooty Millingford and remind her that she was supposed to treat poor Popsie in a civilized, if not Christian, fashion. Your instincts were right, Polly. It's very dangerous to allow foreigners in your home."

"There's more. Once they got the car back, they took some day trips, but then two weeks ago they upped and left. It must have been late at night, because I never saw them loading the car and I made sure I kept an eye on them from my bedroom window during the day. Anyway, the key was in my mailbox one morning. I rushed over, but their luggage was gone. Everything was nice and neat, and they put a letter addressed to you on the kitchen counter."

Wilma started to comment on the unreliability of foreigners, then realized Polly was so nervous that her eyelid was twitching and her chin trembling. "What about Popsie?" she asked shrewdly, if also anxiously.

"Gone."

"Gone? What do you mean?"

"I organized a search party and we hunted for him for three days straight. I put an ad in that shopping circular and called the dog pound so many times that they promised they'd call me if they picked him up."

Wilma clasped the edge of the table and bared her teeth in a comical (at least from Polly's perspective) parody of a wild beast. "They must have stolen Popsie! What did the police say? You did call the police, didn't you? All they'd have to do is stop the car and drag those wicked Millingfords off to jail."

"They wouldn't have taken him, Wilma. When the ambulance men came to the house, I heard the father say that the baby's asthma attack was brought on by dog hairs. The last thing they'd do is put Popsie right there in the car with them and risk another attack."

"Well, I'm calling the police now," Wilma snarled as she shoved back her chair and started for the front door. "And you can forget about your jar of jam, Polly Simps. I asked you to do one little favor for me. Look what I get in return!"

George was sound asleep on the recliner as she marched through the living room, intent on the telephone in the kitchen. Of course it was too late for the police to take action. The Millingfords had safely escaped across the Atlantic Ocean, where they could ignore official demands concerning Popsie's disappearance. She could imagine the smugness on Sandra's face and her syrupy avowals of innocence. Perhaps she would feel differently when her children discovered the empty hutch.

The envelope was on the counter. Wilma ripped it open, and with an unsteady hand, took out the letter.

Dear Mrs. Chadley,

Thank you so very much for making your home available to us this last fortnight. It was not precisely what we'd anticipated, but after a bit we accepted your invitation to "make ourselves at home."

Tucked under the telephone you will find invoices from the towing service, auto repair shop, and tire shop. They were all quite gracious about awaiting your payment. The chap from the air conditioner service never came. My husband called all shops listed in the back pages of the telephone directory, but none seemed to have been the one with which you trade. He tried to have a look at it himself, but became leery that he inadvertently might damage some of the rustier parts.

After he checked the wiring, I had a go at the washing machine, but I must have done something improperly because water gushed everywhere. It made for quite a mopping.

We've changed our plans and have decided to spend the remaining fortnight touring the northern part of the state. Lucinda and Charles are frightfully keen about space technology and are exceedingly eager to visit the Kennedy Center. Dorothy adores building sand castles on the beach. Also, this will make it easier for us to leave your car at the Orlando airport as we'd arranged.

I hope you enjoyed your stay in Cobbet. Our neighbors are quite friendly in an unobtrusive way, and several of them promised to entertain you. I also hope you enjoyed Mrs. Bitney's cooking. She is such a treasure.

In honour of your return, I adapted one of Mrs. Bitney's family recipes for steak and kidney pie. It's in the freezer in an oblong pan. When you and your husband eat it, I do so hope you'll remember our exchange.

Yours truly,
Sandra Millingford

Wilma numbly put down the letter and went to the back door. Popsie's water and food bowls were aligned neatly in one corner of the patio. A gnawed rubber ball lay in the grass. The three pages of instructions were no longer taped to the door of the refrigerator, but several cans of dog food were lined up beside the toaster.

She went into the bathroom and peered behind the toilet as if Popsie had been hiding there all this time, too wily to show himself to Polly while he awaited their return. Not so much as a hair marred the vinyl.

At last, when she could no longer avoid it, she returned to the kitchen and sat down. As her eyes were drawn toward the door of the freezer, they began to fill with tears.

Sandra Millingford had made herself at home. What else had she made?

Deadlier Than the Mail

*There were toys and Santas and Christmas carols, even on the Bowery.
There was also a frightened, desperate killer . . .*

(A Matt Cordell Story)

Evan Hunter

THERE WERE SANTA CLAUSES along Third Avenue, and the promise of snow greyed the sky over the blackened el structure. The Santas had straggly, dirty white beards and they pounded their hands against the cold. Their uniforms were ill-fitting. The crimson and white bagged over the pillows wrapped around their middles. The black oil-cloth boots over their shoes told the world they were imitations, and there wasn't a kid alive who'd believe in Santa ever again. Not after seeing these phonies behind their phonier beards.

I walked up Third, and the Santas tinkled their bells and stood behind their wooden chimneys or their cast-iron pots. I walked past them with my head bent and the collar of my jacket high. The air was knife-cold. It slashed at the skin, reached into the bones, put an edge on the tongue for a good, warming shot of bourbon.

Wassail, wassail . . .

I'd been here before. Long, long ago when I'd been a kid they all called Matty. More recently when a guy named Charlie Dagerra woke up with his throat slit because he'd refused to pay protection money to a local punk. And now it was a Monday in December, and the calendar said it was the 21st, four days to Christmas. The store windows huddled against the cold, lighted like potbellied stoves, looking warm and cheerful, overflowing with things to give and tinsel and cotton snow and toy trains and small plaster statues of Saint Nick.

The call had come from Kit O'Donnell, the girl I used to call Katie in the old days. I wouldn't have made the trip for anyone else, not in this weather, but there'd been something in her voice that made me forget the cold. I cut down 119th Street and kept walking toward First Avenue. The grocery shop was on First, between 118th and 119th. I opened the door, and a bell tinkled, and then Kit rushed from the back room.

She'd let her black hair grow longer, pulled it back from the oval of her face into a saucy ponytail. Her brown eyes opened wide, and then she smiled and said, "Matt, you came."

"I said I would."

She came out from behind the counter and took both my hands in hers. Her hands were warm, and she looked up into my face and for some reason I thought she would start bawling.

"You're cold, Matt," she said.

"A little brisk out there."

"Can I get you something to drink? My father keeps a bot . . ."

"Just a little," I said. "To take off the chill."

She went into the back room and came out front again with a bottle of Schenley's and a water glass. She poured the glass half-full and then handed it to me. I smiled, threw it off, and then put the glass down on the counter.

"Now," I said, "what's all the trouble about?"

"I guess I shouldn't have called you, Matt. I mean, you did so much for us last time, you . . ."

"What is it, Kit?"

"Do you remember Andy Traconni?"

"I remember. What about him?"

"He hasn't been doing too well, Matt. He was a bricklayer until he had an accident with his hands, and he's been out of work since. He gets checks from the Welfare Department. He's got a wife and a kid, Matt, and the checks don't stretch too far."

"I don't understand, Kit."

"Matt, someone's been stealing his checks. You know the mailboxes in these old buildings. You can open them with a bad breath. Someone's been taking the checks from his box."

"How long has this been going on?"

"A month, two months."

"Well for Christ's sake, why hasn't he reported it?"

"He's afraid to, Matt."

"Afraid to? Honey, tampering with the mails is a government offense. He'd be sensible to . . ."

"And suppose the thief has friends, Matt? What happens then? Who's going to protect Andy and his family?"

I shook my head. "Kit . . ."

"I know, Matt. I shouldn't have asked you. Only I thought . . . well, it's getting close to Christmas. I thought if we could find whoever is doing it, we might at least get the money back."

"Fat chance of that. This is an old racket, Kit, and not likely to be run by an amateur. Getting the checks is only half of it. They still have to be cashed after that, and that entails a phony driver's license or some other forged identification." I shook my head again. "I'd like to help, but honestly . . ."

"It isn't only Andy, Matt. There are others in the neighborhood, too. You knew Andy, so I mentioned him."

"How many others?"

"Ten, twelve. Won't you help, Matt?"

"You put me on a spot, Kit."

"I want to. Will you help?"

I sighed heavily. "I'll try. Let me have another drink, will you?"

She poured, and I drank, and then I asked her for the names of the people who'd been hit so far. She scribbled them on a sheet of paper, together with the addresses, and I left her and told her I'd get on it first thing in the morning.

DECEMBER 22ND, AND it still hadn't snowed. It was colder, if anything, and I tried to walk fast because the soles of my shoes were worn through and there's nothing icier than a winter pavement. When I got to Andy Traconni's building, there was a lot of excitement. Three patrol cars were parked at an angle to the curb, and cops and photographers were swarming all over the place. I stopped an old man in a mackinaw and I asked him what had happened.

"Andy," he said in broken English. "Som'body kill him."

"What!"

"In the hall," he said, nodding his head emphatically. "Andy come down for the mail . . ." He broke off here, held both hands in front of him and then squeezed them together in pantomime of someone being strangled. He nodded his head again and repeated, "Andy."

It was impossible to get into the hallway, so I walked away from the building and hung around until the reporters began to thin out. I spotted the bulls when they came out of the building and piled into a Mercury sedan across the street. Then they pulled away and the uniformed cops followed them, and the crowd broke. Two internes came out with a stretcher, the sheet pulled up over what was left of Andy Traconni. The crowd disappeared entirely after the ambulance left, and I had the building to myself. I walked into the hallway and looked at the mailboxes.

The one marked Traconni was battered and dented near the lock. It was a cinch it had been forced once, and never been repaired after that. A pile of square envelopes sat in the box, and I figured them to be Christmas cards. A merry Christmas it would be for Mrs. Traconni and her kid this year. The numeral 35 was stamped into the metal of the box, so I took the narrow steps up to the third-floor landing and found the apartment without even looking at the number. I stood outside the door and listened to the sobbing behind it, and finally I knocked.

A kid of about eight answered the door. His face was streaked with dirt and tears, and he looked as if he were ready to start crying all over again.

"I want to talk to your mother," I said.

He looked at me suspiciously. He looked at my wrinkled suit and my bearded face. He studied my bloodshot eyes, the flabbiness of my flesh. He was thinking *This is a bum*, and he was wondering if I'd had anything to do with his father's death.

"I knew your father when we were kids, son," I told him. "I want to help."

"Come in," he said, as if I'd whispered the magic words.

He led me into a small living room dominated by a TV set in one corner. The blinds were drawn, and a frail woman in a print house-dress sat in one of the easy chairs, a handkerchief to her face.

"Mrs. Traconni," I said, "my name is Matt Cordell. I knew Andy well a long time ago."

"I've heard of you," she said softly.

"Do you have any idea who killed him?"

"Yes," she said without hesitation. "The one who's been stealing our checks."

"How do you know?"

"Because Andy watched last week, and he found out something. He didn't tell me what it was, but he said he would wait until the next check was due and find out for sure then. When he saw the mailman coming down the street this morning, he went down to watch. I think he hid himself while he watched. Then this . . . this happened. He should have left it alone. He should have forgot it. You can't buck them, Mr. Cordell."

"What did the police say?"

"They said Andy was hit first, they don't know with what. It hit him on the side of his face, and they figured it stunned him. Then . . . then he was strangled."

"And you think he knew who was stealing the checks?"

"I'm sure of it," she said.

"I'll look around," I told her. "Maybe I'll come up with something."

"Thank you," she said, and then she went back to her handkerchief, and she was crying when I left the apartment. I met a guy with a Christmas tree in the hallway. He was a fat guy, and he struggled with the tree, and sweat poured down his face, but there was a healthy smile on his face. The tree had made him forget the grubbiness of the tenement he lived in, and the cheapness of the coat on his back. When he passed me, he nodded his head happily and said, "A real big one this year," and I nodded back and said nothing.

In the street, it was bitter cold. I clenched my eyes against the sudden onslaught, and I thought of a Christmas long ago. She'd done the tree with popcorn, Trina, popcorn and tinsel, and there'd been a fire going on the hearth. It was our first Christmas together, and the presents were piled under the tree, bright ribbons glistening in the light of the fire. There was a white tablecloth on the table, and she'd placed two candles on it, one for each plate. I'd come into the apartment with my face cold from the raw wind outside.

She cupped my face with her slender hands, and her mouth had found mine, her lips full and moist, her body alive with the warmth of the room.

Four months. Four months of marriage. Part autumn and part winter, and then Garth. Trina in his arms, with the thin stuff of her gown caught in his grasping fingers, his lips buried in her flesh. And the .45 snaking out of the holster under my armpit, the walnut stock reaching out for his head, hitting him again and again and again. And then it was all over, and there was an Assault-With-A-Deadly-Weapon charge, and no more Trina. They dropped the ADW, and they went to Mexico for a divorce, but the police decided it was time to lift my license.

And this was the Matt Cordell they'd left. Carrying a torch a mile high, feeding the flames with alcohol, huddling against the cold and looking for a guy who lifted checks from broken mailboxes.

I caught up with the mailman about six blocks from Andy's house. His bag was packed with Christmas cards, and he was sweating in spite of the cold. He was a big man with wiry black hair that spilled onto his forehead from beneath his tilted cap. His hands curled with the same wiry hair, and I watched the swift, sure way his fingers dropped letters into the open row of boxes. I watched him for a few minutes, and then I asked, "Did you see Andy Traconni this morning?"

He didn't turn from the boxes. He kept dumping the letters in, and he spoke without looking up. "Who'd you say?"

"Andy Traconni."

"Oh. No, missed him today."

"He was killed today."

His hands paused for a moment. "What?"

"In the hallway. Did you happen to see anyone hanging around when you made your delivery?"

"No, Jesus. Killed, you say. Jesus!"

"Lot of people getting welfare checks on this route?"

He regarded me suspiciously. "Why? Why do you ask?"

"I'm just curious. Andy's checks have been stolen for the past few months."

"No kidding? Hell, why didn't he say something about it? No kidding?"

"He never mentioned it to you?"

"No. He asked me if I'd delivered them a few times, and I told him sure. But I never suspected . . ."

"Anyone in this building get checks?" I asked.

"Lemme see. Yeah, Riley does. Apartment 4C. He gets 'em every week."

"Thanks," I said. "Keep your eyes open."

The mailman blinked. "I will."

I left him stuffing cards into the boxes, and I took the steps up to the fourth floor and then knocked on the door to 4C. I waited for a few moments until a woman's voice called, "Come in. It's open."

I opened the door and walked directly into the kitchen. A small Christmas tree stood on an end table at the far corner of the room. Chimney paper had been wrapped around the end table, and cotton had been used to cover the stand. The tree had no ornaments and no lights. It was sprinkled with aluminum foil, and someone with energy had swabbed the branches with Rinso for a snow-laden effect.

"Anybody home?" I called.

"Just a second."

I waited, looking at the chipping paint on the wall, the dulled, blackened area over the four-burner stove. I heard a door behind me open, and a girl stepped into the room. She was wearing a full slip, and the slip ended just above her knees. It was cut low in the front, and her full breasts bunched against the silken fabric. One strap dangled over a pale white shoulder. The girl was a redhead, that natural carroty red that goes with a name like Riley. Her eyes were blue, and there were deep pockets under them. Her skin was pale. I stared at her for a moment, and she said, "Sorry to keep you waiting."

She took a step closer to me, soundlessly moving on the worn linoleum that covered the floor.

I looked down and saw that she was barefoot.

"You got a cigarette, or are you in a hurry?"

"I've got one," I said. I fished into my pocket and pulled out a rumpled package of Pall Malls. The girl took one, and I lighted it for her.

She sucked in the smoke gratefully, and then said, "Busy day, by Christ. The bastards are starting the holiday early."

"Are you Mrs. Riley?" I asked.

"Me? Hell no, Mac. *Miss* Riley, if you please. Christ, do I look like that old bag?"

"I don't know your mother," I said.

"You ain't missing nothing, Mac. She's a lush from 'way back. You'll find her souped to the ears in the local pub." She took a close look at me and said, "Hey, don't I know you?"

"I don't think so."

"Sure, ain't you Matt Cordell? Weren't you the guy who wiped up the street with those punks who were shaking down the neighborhood? Sure, I recognize you."

I didn't answer her.

"You got a yearning, huh, Matt boy?" she said. "Well, little Fran will take care of you."

She took a step closer to me, and I said, "Your father gets welfare checks, they tell me."

"What's that got to do with the price of fish?"

"That's why I'm here."

"That's a good one," she said. She took my hand and started leading me across the room. I watched the way her flesh wiggled tautly beneath the tightness of her slip. I pulled my hand away and she turned, surprised.

"What is it, boy?"

"How old are you, Fran? Sixteen?"

"Nineteen, if you're worried about Quentin Quail. Hey, boy, what is it with you? You still got eyes for that bitchy wife of yours?"

"Can it, honey."

"Sure. So carry the torch, who cares? Let me help you burn it brighter, boy. I need the dough."

"Because your old man's checks have been lifted?"

"Sure, but that don't cut my ice, boy. The old man never gave me a cent anyway. The holidays are coming, and I use what I've got to get what I want." She cupped her breasts suddenly, reaching forward toward me. "Come on, boy, it's good stuff."

"I'm on the wagon." I paused. "Besides, I'm broke."

"Mmm. Well, I ain't Santa Claus. What's on your mind, Cordell?"

"When was the first check missing?"

"About a month ago, I guess."

"Lifted from the box?"

"Yeah. I saw the postman delivering that check on my way out in the morning. When the old man went down later in the day, the lock was snapped. Goodbye check."

"And the others?"

"Boy, we never even get a look at them. This hijacker must be Speedy Gonzalez." She laughed abruptly and said, "Hey, Cordell, you know the one about Speedy Gonzalez?"

"Did your father report these thefts?"

"My old man? Cordell, he's afraid to eat Rice Krispies. The explosions scare him."

"What have you been living on?"

Fran Riley shrugged. "I make out. Times have been pretty good." She smiled, and I saw something of the nineteen-year-old in her face for just an instant. "And, it's all tax-free," she said.

"You should marry a straight man," I told her.

"Any offers, Cordell?"

"I was in the club once," I said. "My membership expired."

She smiled again. "Besides, you're no straight man." The smile dropped from her face. "What do you say, Cordell? This is the slow time of day. You won't be sorry."

"I appreciate it," I said. "But I've got a dead man on my mind."

I left her to puzzle that one out, and when I got down to the street it was snowing. The flakes were big and wet at first, and then they got smaller and sharper, biting at the skin, crusting the hair. I fished the list Kit had given me out of my pocket and scanned it quickly. Then I began making the rounds.

The story was the same at each stop I made. The checks had begun disappearing a while back. The locks on the mailboxes had been broken. After that, the owners of the checks never got a look at them. By the time they went down to pick up the mail, the checks were gone.

I asked why they didn't keep a closer watch on the boxes, and they all told me the checks never came on the same days. It would have been close to impossible to keep a steady vigil. When I'd finished with the last name on the list, I began wondering just who the hell would commit murder for a pile of checks that couldn't amount to more than a couple of hundred a week.

And then I began wondering about the people in the neighborhood whose checks *weren't* missing. It was a poor neighborhood, and there were certainly more than ten or twelve people who were getting financial aid. I started looking around for the postman again, and I found him going into a tailor shop on First Avenue. I waited until he came out, and then I pulled up alongside him.

"Hi," I said.

He looked at me and said, "Oh, hi."

"I suppose you know the names of most everyone on the route, don't you?"

"Oh, sure," he said. He reached into the leather bag on his shoulder and pulled out a stack of Christmas cards. "Bitch of a time, Christmas," he said. "And the tips in this neighborhood are from hunger."

"Do you know the names of everyone getting welfare checks?"

"Yeah, sure," he said. "Why?"

I followed him up the steps into the building next to the tailor shop. He stuck his key in the box lock and pulled down the row of boxes. Then he began tossing the letters into the open row.

"I'm checking up on the thefts," I said.

He stopped dropping mail for a moment, and he looked at me steadily. "You?" he asked.

"Yeah, me."

He shrugged. "Okay. I know the people getting checks."

"Have you got a pencil?"

The postman sighed, and then reached into his pocket. "Here," he said.

I took a scrap of paper from the inside pocket of my jacket, and then said, "Shoot."

He reeled off the names and addresses, and I wrote them down. He glanced at his watch occasionally, and I realized I was holding him up at the busiest time of the year, but I didn't let him off the hook until he'd given me all the names. He was not happy when he left me. He glanced at his watch again, grunted, then shouldered his heavy bag and stomped out into the snow.

I stood in the hallway, and I compared the postman's list with the one Kit had given me. There weren't as many names as I'd thought there would be. I picked out two that were on the postman's list and not on Kit's, and I went to look them up.

GEORGE KASAIRUS WAS a thin man with angular black brows and a soiled undershirt. He had a can of beer in his hand when he opened the door to his apartment, and he glared at me belligerently.

"What are you selling?" he asked.

"Christmas cheer," I said.

He snorted and then took a long drag at the beer can. "I got no time for jokes," he said.

"I'm looking into the stolen welfare checks," I told him. "You want to help?"

"My checks ain't been stolen," Kasairus said.

"Then you should be willing to cooperate."

"Agh, come on in," he said.

I followed him into the dingy flat, and he opened a fresh can of beer for himself, not bothering to offer me one. "I don't know how the hell I can help," he said.

"Have any of your checks ever been missing?" I asked.

"Yeah, one. A long while back."

"And none since?"

"No, sir. I'm too smart for that bastard."

"How so?"

"My check comes on either Wednesday, Thursday, or Friday. I'm down by that box early on every one of those mornings. I get the check straight from Frankie."

"Who's Frankie?"

"Our postman. He puts it right into the palm of my hand. I eliminate the middleman that way. There's no bastard who's going to out-shrewd me when it comes to dough. No, sir."

"Do you know that a lot of people in the neighborhood are missing checks?"

"Sure, I know."

"Why haven't you let them on to your system of beating the game?"

"Screw 'em. It's every man for himself. They're too dumb to figure it out, that's tough. I worry about George Kasairus, and that's all, and you can bet nobody else is worryin' about me."

"You're a nice guy, Georgie," I said.

"Sure," he answered quickly. "What are you, a goddamn Good Samaritan or something?"

"I'm the ghost of Christmas Past, Georgie."

"Who?"

"Skip it."

"Just don't get smart with me, Mac."

"I won't, Georgie. But I'll wonder why you're one of the few guys whose checks haven't been lifted. I'll wonder that, Georgie. You won't mind, will you?"

Kasairus banged his beer can down on the tabletop and then took a fast step toward me. He threw a fist before I realized what was happening, and it caught on my jaw and sent me flying back against the wall.

"Don't call me no crook!" he shouted. "Don't call me no goddamn crook!"

He came at me again, and this time I shoved out against his chest and sent him sprawling onto the floor. He seemed ready to get up, but he changed his mind when he saw my cocked fists.

"I may be back, Georgie."

"Drop dead," he said.

I walked out, and I thought *Drop dead, a few days before Christmas.* A great goddamn world. Peace on earth. Silent night. Drop dead.

I went to the nearest bar, and I drank a few warm-up beers. Then I found a liquor store and I bought a gallon of wine. I found a hallway, and I drank straight from the bottle.

I toasted Trina first, and I wished her a bloody Merry Christmas and a Happy New Year. Then I toasted Garth, and I wished him the same thing. I toasted Kit O'Donnell and all her troubles, and all the poor bastards whose piddling checks were being stolen. And then I toasted Santa Claus and the State of New York, and Washington, D. C., and President Eisenhower.

The super of the building kicked me out of the hallway, but I held onto the jug of wine, and I reeled down the street and I sang *"Deck the halls with boughs of holly, fa-la-la-la-la, la-la, la-la . . ."*

I passed a Santa Claus with an iron pot, and I poured a little of the wine into the pot and said, "Drink up, Nick. Put some goddamn color back into your beard."

I stopped everyone I saw and offered them a drink, and they all laughed in that slightly patronizing way and patted me on the back.

I sang four choruses of "Deck the Halls," and then I batted out a few refrains of "God Rest Ye Merry, Gentlemen." I kept thinking of George Kasairus all the way. A Good Samaritan, he'd called me, and then he'd ordered me to drop dead.

That was the trouble with this little old goddamn world. Too many Good Samaritans dropping dead. The meek inherited the earth, all right, six feet of it, and all underground.

Like poor Andy Traconni who got the breath squeezed out of him because he wanted to protect the lousy little check he got each week.

Well, the hell with Andy, and the hell with Kasairus, and all the rest. It was almost Christmas, and it was no time to be chasing checks around the city. Nobody gives a damn about poor George Kasairus, and nobody gives a damn about goddamn Matt Cordell, either, that's for sure. So I drank the gallon, and goddamn it, I really felt in a holiday mood. I scrounged some more dimes from the people in the street, and it was easy because hell, it was Christmas time. Then I bought another gallon and I started on that one, singing all the way, and the last song I sang was "Jingle Bells," and then I was lying in the snow with the empty jug beside me, and all was well with the world.

JINGLE BELLS, JINGLE bells, jingle all the way
> *Oh what fun it is to ride*
> *In a one-horse open slay-eigh . . .*

The singing was somewhere near me. I pried open my eyes and looked for it, and the song went on and on, and the bells jingled inside my head. The snow under me had melted, and the front of my shirt and jacket were soaking wet. My feet were cold, and my face was cold, and I sat up and began thumping my hands against my sides. Where the hell was I, and what the hell day was it?

I got to my feet, and I stopped the first guy who passed.

"What day is it?" I asked.

"Christmas Eve," he said, and then he hurried off, his arms full of Christmas packages.

I washed a hand over my face, and I thought, *Christmas Eve. And no checks for Andy Traconni.*

I reached into my pocket and found the list the postman had given me, and then I looked for the nearest clock. I found it in a bar. I had a shot of bourbon to wash off the taste, and when I left the bar, it was three-thirty in the afternoon. I headed directly for a man named Juan Diaz, a man who still received his checks in spite of the wholesale thefts.

Juan Diaz was small, with dark black hair and friendly brown eyes. There was a Christmas tree on top of the radio cabinet in his living room. The apartment was shabby, but it smelled warm, and I could hear the excited babble of children's voices coming from the kitchen.

"Hello," Diaz said, "Hello. Merr' Chreestmas. Come in."

I walked into the apartment, and a smile formed on my face unconsciously. There weren't many presents around the tree, nor was the tree expensively decorated. But a big picture of Santa had been hung on the wall mirror, and small figures depicting the birth at Bethlehem were under the tree. The radiators whistled piping hot, and the smell of popcorn and baked apples drifted from the kitchen.

"You get welfare checks, Mr. Diaz?" I asked.

"*Si,*" he said. "Yes, I do."

"Have any been stolen?"

"One," he said. "Only one. Then I smart up. Thees crook, he ees fast, but Juan Diaz, he be faster. I meet Frankie don'stairs when I theenk check should come. Sometime I go down every day, so not to miss it. I get heem, all right. Evr' week." Diaz paused. "Man, you got to live!"

"This first one that was stolen," I said. "How?"

"The lock. He snap heem. But no more."

"Now Frankie gives you the check, huh?"

"Good boy, Frankie. I geeve him dreenk for Chreestmas. Good boy, Frankie." Diaz grinned, showing bright white teeth. "You want dreenk, hey?"

"No," I said. "Thanks a lot."

"Well, Merr' Chreestmas," Diaz said.

"Same to you."

He closed the door behind me, and I stood in the warmth of the hallway for a moment, listening to the voices of the kids behind the doors. Well, two of them had learned how to beat the system. Just get to the check before the thief did. The rest were either too lazy or too stupid or too drunk to realize that was the only way to beat it. So the thief swiped the checks each week, and through fear, they kept their mouths shut. And now, with Andy Traconni dead, they'd never report the thefts in a million years.

I went down into the street. The snow had turned black with the churning of automobile tires and shoe soles. I walked, with the wind sharp, and the cold a living thing that gnawed and bit, and I thought it all over. Then I got my idea, and I started looking in earnest.

I found him in another hallway. The hallway was hot. The radiators sang their torrid songs, and he worked with the sweat pouring down his face.

"Hello, Frankie," I said.

The mailman looked up. "You again," he answered. "Look, mister, I got enough headaches. This is Christmas Eve, and I want to get home, you know? Let me work in peace, will you?"

"The missing checks, Frankie."

"Yeah, what about them?"

"Have you cashed them yet?"

Frankie turned, his hands on the leather strap of his bag. "What!"

"Nobody else, Frankie. Couldn't be. You snapped the locks the first time to make it look like an outsider was rifling the boxes *after* the checks were delivered. After that, smooth sailing. When the suckers asked you if you'd delivered the checks, you said sure. But those checks never reached the boxes. Except where the sucker was smart enough to wait for the check. Then you had to deliver."

"Go away, bum," Frankie said. "You're drunk."

"Andy Traconni was a sucker who woke up, Frankie. He began watching your deliveries. He watched, and he saw that you damn well never delivered his checks. He probably asked you if you had, and you said yes. Last week, he was fairly certain. This week, he made sure. He watched again, and when the check didn't come, he accused you."

"Listen . . ."

I expected him to say more, but he cut himself short and swung the leather bag up by the strap, swinging it at my head, in the same way he'd probably swung it when Andy accused him. I dodged the bag, and I leaped forward, grabbing his throat in my hands and ramming him against the wall.

"Did you cash the checks, you bastard?" I yelled.

"I needed the dough. Jesus, there are guys make eight, nine hundred dollars on a route during Christmas. I needed the dough, I tell you. I figured . . ."

"Did you cash the checks yet?"

"I ain't figured how to do that yet. I . . . look, Mac, let's forget this. Let's forget all about it. I'll split the dough with you. I'll . . ."

I slammed the back of my hand across his mouth. "Take me to the checks," I said.

Frankie spit blood, and then shook his head. "Sure," he said.

I GOT THE checks, and then I delivered him to the police. I bought a pint of bourbon, and then I delivered the checks personally, and each time I delivered one, I said, "Merry Christmas."

I felt good when I was finished. I felt good because all the faces that greeted those checks were smiling and happy. I went out into the street, and I wondered if I should drop in on Kit O'Donnell, say hello maybe, exchange greetings. And then it started snowing again, so I drank the bourbon a few nips at a time, and I watched the flakes, and when I finally boarded the Third Avenue El heading for the Bowery, the conductor said, "Merry Christmas, fella," and I just smiled and didn't say anything.

Contributors

Look up **Lawrence Block** in any work on American writers and you'll find it packed with accolades. Author of Leo Haig, Bernie Rhodenbarr, Matthew Scudder, Evan Tanner, and, most recently, the John Keller series. He's a fixture in the mystery field, writing hard-edged mysteries, such as *A Ticket to the Boneyard*, lighthearted comedy capers, like *Burglars Can't be Choosers*, to tongue-in-cheek adventure novels, including *The Thief Who Couldn't Sleep*, and his excellent stand-alone books, including *After the First Death* and *Random Walk*. Honored with the Nero Wolfe award (1979), Private Eye Writers of America Shamus award (1983, 1985), Mystery Writers of America Edgar Allan Poe award (1985), and the MWA Grand Master award in 1994—you get the point. Block is deservedly one of the most acclaimed and celebrated writers of our time.

In 1957 the poet W. H. Auden scolded American literary critics for teaching **Edgar Allen Poe** (1809–1849) as "a respectable rival to the pulps." Poe was, Auden insisted, a serious literary artist. If longevity is a measure of seriousness, then Poe has certainly proved his worth. If anything, he is more widely read, filmed, recorded, and illustrated worldwide than ever before. And such poems as "The Raven" and tales such as "The Murders in the Rue Morgue," "The Fall of the House of Usher," and "The Tell-Tale Heart," each a staggering example of psychological suspense, are all staples in modern American literature textbooks. Auden, one surmises, was right.

Though **William F. Nolan** is known for his great science-fiction trilogy *Logan's Run*, *Logan's World*, and *Logan's Search*, he has distinguished himself in the crime, mystery, and western genres as well—as a glance at his awards tell you. He has received the American Library Association citation (1960), Mystery Writers of America award (1970, 1972), the Academy of Science Fiction and Fantasy award for fiction and film (1976), the Maltese Falcon award (1977), and an honorary doctorate from American River College in Sacramento, California (1975). He has written major dramas for both television and movies. And he is considered a master at both the crime and horror short story, a popular opinion that is more than supported with this short story.

A pro's pro is somebody who can work in a variety of styles and forms with equal skill. One such man is **Peter Lovesey**. Whether he's writing about Victorian times (his Cribb and Thackery novels), early Hollywood (*Keystone*), or World War II (*On the Edge*), Lovesey is always in artful command of his material. His humor is genuinely funny and his dramatics genuinely moving, especially in the elegiac *Rough Cider*. Many of his novels and stories have been adapted to film and television.

Edward Marston is a busy man. He writes radio and theatrical drama, contemporary and historical mysteries, and young-adult novels as well. He was nominated for the Edgar award in 1986. What is remarkable about his work is that he finds a style appropriate to each subject, and each style is polished and always eminently readable. His stock is definitely rising as a creator of mystery fiction.

Barry N. Malzberg is a seminal figure in contemporary commercial fiction and not just because he's written so much of it. In addition to his fiction, he's also written some of the most perceptive and engaging commentary on the craft of fiction and how it's practiced in these turbulent times. Though known primarily as a science-fiction author, Malzberg's best novel is a powerful, unforgettable book about a hack writer's mental and spiritual breakdown titled *Herovit's World*. It proves that commercial fiction can also be true art. *Night Screams*, *Acts of Mercy*, and *The Running of Beasts* (all with Bill Pronzini) are just a few of his other titles. He has been honored with the John Campbell Memorial award (1973) and Locus award (1983).

Richard Christian Matheson is the author of the popular novel *Created By*, a truly horrifying tale of trendy Hollywood. He's even better known for his short stories in the fields of crime and dark suspense. Winner of the Bram Stoker award for best novel, Matheson has written many hours of television and movies. His style is both unique and startling. Nobody else approaches fiction in quite the same way.

Matthew Costello was known primarily as a horror writer and author of the best-selling computer games The 7th Guest and The 11th Hour until the late 1990s, when he began to collaborate with F. Paul Wilson on best-selling mainstream science fiction. Costello is primarily a character-driven writer. Whatever else is going on in the story, Costello is letting you know about his people. *Beneath Still Waters* and *Darkborn* are good (early) examples of Costello at his powerful best.

Morris Hershman is a pro's pro. He's done it all—mysteries, westerns, gothics, erotica, war—virtually every category of modern commercial fiction. During his decades-spanning career, he's written a couple dozen especially remarkable short stories that other writers constantly "borrow" from for both content and structure. He manages to find the human element in each of his pieces, and that makes the novelty of his plots just all that much more enjoyable.

Ralph McInerny's Father Dowling series has been a hit in both print and on television where, after several successful seasons on network television, it now runs on cable. He writes many other books—and types of books—as well. He has been honored with a Fulbright Fellowship (1959), a National Endowment for the Humanities

Fellowship (1977), and a National Endowment for the Arts Fellowship (1982). He has taught philosophy and medieval studies at Creighton University in Omaha, Nebraska and currently teaches at the University of Notre Dame in Indiana. He is the rare scholar who can also hold his own with the best writers of popular fiction.

Kate Kingsbury has written well and presented workshops about writing well and selling your material in publishing's most difficult time—today. Her novels include *Room with a Clue*, *Check-Out Time*, and *Maid to Murder*. She's honed her observations about life in a hotel to a sharp, witty style that pleases her ever-growing audience.

Simon Brett's Charles Paris, the alcoholic actor who frequently stumbles across murder in his pursuit of extremely modest success in British show business, is one of the most unique and endearing characters in contemporary crime fiction. The wry melancholy of the writing lifts the Paris novels far above most genre fiction. Not that Brett is satisfied with creating only one memorable character. There is also the Mrs. Pargeter series. And a number of first-rate, stand-alone suspense novels. Brett has received the Writer's Guild of Great Britain radio award (1973) and Broadcasting Press Guild award (1987). He was also chairman of the Crime Writers Association in 1986–87.

Though largely forgotten now, **Arthur B. Reeve** (1880–1936) was one of the first detective writers to use scientific methodology for catching criminals. This was around the time of World War I, when he was asked to set up a scientific crime lab. He then went on to have a long, prosperous, and extremely varied career in pulp magazines and books. He was probably best known, in the pulps, for his stories featuring Professor Craig Kennedy, often called "The American Sherlock Holmes." The Kennedy stories ran for many years, and his best cases were collected in the anthology *The Silent Bullet* in 1912. He was also an editor of great renown in the nonfiction field, as well as writing journalistic articles and producing radio programs on crime and criminology.

Martin H. Greenberg is the world's most successful anthologist and book packager, with nearly a thousand titles to his credit. He has worked with worldwide best-selling authors ranging from Tom Clancy to Tony Hillerman to Mary Higgins Clark, and from Dean Koontz to Father Andrew Greely. In addition to being his best friend, the late Isaac Asimov also did more than fifty books with Martin Greenberg. What's little known about Mr. Greenberg is that he's also a fine writer, as you'll learn when you read his contribution to this anthology.

August Derleth is associated with the H. P. Lovecraft circle of the 1930s, young authors who corresponded with Lovecraft, and frequently imitated him in their own fiction. The best of that circle—such as Robert Bloch—went on to find their own voices and do their own work. Derleth was also his own man. While he wrote various kinds of pastiche in both science fiction and mystery over the course of his career—his character Solar Pons was his unique take on Sherlock Holmes—as both writer and editor he brought passionate gifts to the horror field. It would not exist today as it does without his various contributions.

Henry Slesar was a mainstay of the fiction magazines of the late 1950s and early 1960s, the last big boom of the digests, which were just the pulps in more convenient size. He did it all and he did it well. A collection of his crime work is long overdue. In the course of his career he has won the Mystery Writers of America Edgar Allan Poe award for novel (1960) and for a TV series (1977), and an Emmy award for a continuing daytime series (1974). He has written for many TV series such as *Alfred Hitchcock Presents* and *Twilight Zone*. And he survived many years as the writer-producer of a long-running soap opera.

John Lutz is the author of the Fred Carver and Alo Nudger series, with *Oops*, *Hot*, and *Kiss* being just a few of his titles. He has received the Private Eye Writers of America Shamus award for short story (1982) and for novel (1988), and the Mystery Writers of America Edgar Allan Poe award for short story (1986). His short story "SWF

Seeks Same" was the basis for the film *Single White Female*, and his novel *The Ex*, was recently made into a cable-television movie. Lutz is another original, his own voice, his own take on everyday and not so everyday life in our times.

Gordon R. Dickson is a science-fiction writer of such reach and accomplishment one isn't quite sure how to start listing the accolades. From his celebrated Dorsai series to his humorous Dragon novels, he writes the kind of science fiction and fantasy that is equally rich with ideas and humanity. His work has been lauded in those communities as well, awarding him two Hugo awards, a Nebula, a Derleth, and a Jupiter award. And he sure knows how to pull off a thigh-slapper of an ending—as in the story published here—when the need arises.

Joyce Harrington has been awarded the Mystery Writers of America Edgar Allan Poe award for short story (1973) and has long been regarded as an original and important voice in the mystery field. Though her career in public relations and advertising hasn't always allowed her the time she'd like to spend on stories, she's created a formidable and imposing body of work.

Ellery Queen—the name has resounded on radio, in movies and television, and in many, many books and magazines. A pseudonym for cousins and authors Frederic Dannay and Manfred B. Lee, creators of the Ellery Queen and Inspector Richard Queen series—which includes *Calamity Town*, *The Roman Hat Mystery*, and *A Fine and Private Place* among many, many others—Queen is one of the seminal figures in the crime fiction of the past century. Whether as writer, editor, or scenarist, the name Ellery Queen stood for the best in mystery and detective fiction and helped found the Mystery Writers of America.

Joan Hess, on or off the page, is funny. Off the page that's great. On the page, that's not always so good. At least not when reviewers, trained to look for "deep meanings," look over her books. Nothing this enjoyable, they seem to think, can possibly have real merit. Not true, as she continues to demonstrate in novel after novel. Hess's spirited takes on her home state of Arkansas combines the cozy form with her own version of black comedy–domestic comedy that is set down with the same neurotic glee one finds in the stories of Anne Beatty. Whether she's writing about Clare Malloy, her young widow who runs a bookstore; or Arly Hanks, who is police chief of Maggody, Arkansas, Hess's two series are engaging but quite serious takes on relationships, middle age, parental duties, and life in small-town America.

Evan Hunter wrote the screenplay for Hitchcock's suspense film *The Birds*. He also wrote one of the great novels of juvenile delinquency, *The Blackboard Jungle*. And, under the name Ed McBain, he created the immortal 87th Precinct novels. He has been honored with the Mystery Writers of America Edgar Allan Poe award (1957) and Grand Master award (1985). And it's certainly easy to see why. He has brought to the American crime story a breathtaking new approach to both form and substance. A good deal of contemporary crime fiction bears his mark. He is probably the single-most influential crime novelist of the past two generations, and he's still going strong, with another 87th Precinct novel, *The Last Dance*, out recently. Virtually everybody has learned from and imitated him.

Copyrights and Permissions

"Introduction" by John Helfers. Copyright © 2001 by John Helfers.

"Like a Bone in the Throat" by Lawrence Block. Copyright © 1998 by Lawrence Block. First published in *Murder For Revenge*. Reprinted by permission of the author.

"An Act of Violence" by William F. Nolan. Copyright © 1995 by William F. Nolan. First published in *Phantasm*. Reprinted by permission of the author.

"The Corbett Correspondence" by Edward Marston and Peter Lovesey. Copyright © 1997 by Edward Marston and Peter Lovesey. First published in *Malice Domestic 6*. Reprinted by permission of the authors and their agents, the Stuart Krichevsky Literary Agency, Inc., and Gelfman Schneider, Literary Agents.

"Agony Column" by Barry N. Malzberg. Copyright © 1971 by Davis Publications, Inc. First published in *Ellery Queen's Mystery Magazine*, December 1971. Reprinted by permission of the author.

"Graduation" by Richard Christian Matheson. Copyright © 1977 by Richard Christian Matheson. First published in *Whispers I*. Reprinted by permission of the author.

"Someone Who Understands Me" by Matthew Costello. Copyright © 1996 by Matthew Costello. First published in *Future Net*. Reprinted by permission of the author.

"Letter to the Editor" by Morris Hershman. Copyright © 1973 by the Outlet Publishing Company. First published in *Detective Story Magazine*, September 1953. Reprinted by permission of the author.

"The Coveted Correspondence" by Ralph McInerny. Copyright © 1997 by Ralph McInerny. First published in the *Catholic Dossier*, May–June 1997. Reprinted by permission of the author.

"A Nice Cup of Tea" by Kate Kingsbury. Copyright © 1997 by Kate Kingsbury. First published in *Murder, She Wrote*. Reprinted by permission of the author and her agents, the Irene Goodman Literary Agency.

"Letter to His Son" by Simon Brett. Copyright © 1986 by Simon Brett. First published in *Winter's Crimes 18*. Reprinted by permission of the author and his agents, Michael Motley, Ltd.

"A Literary Death" by Martin H. Greenberg. Copyright © 1989 by Martin H. Greenberg. First published in *Isaac Asimov's Magical Worlds of Fantasy #11: Curses*. Reprinted by permission of the author.

"The Adventure of the Penny Magenta" by August Derleth. Copyright © by August Derleth. Reprinted by permission of the author and the author's agents, JABberwocky Literary Agency, P.O. Box 4558, Sunnyside, NY 11104-0558.

"Letter From a Very Worried Man" by Henry Slesar. Copyright © 1959 by Davis Publications, Inc, renewed 1987 by Henry Slesar. First published in *Alfred Hitchcock's Mystery Magazine*, July 1959. Reprinted by permission of the author.

"Pure Rotten" by John Lutz. Copyright © 1977 by Renown Publications, Inc. First published in *Mike Shayne's Mystery Magazine*, August 1977. Reprinted by permission of the author.

"Computers Don't Argue" by Gordon Dickson. Copyright © 1965 by Conde Nast Publications, Inc., renewed 1993 by Gordon R. Dickson. First published in *Analog*, September 1965. Reprinted by permission of the author.

"A Letter to Amy" by Joyce Harrington. Copyright © 1985 by Joyce Harrington. First published in *Ellery Queen's Mystery Magazine*, Mid-December 1985. Reprinted by permission of the author.

"The Adventure of the One-Penny Black" by Ellery Queen. Copyright © 1933 by Ellery Queen. First published in *Great Detectives*. Reprinted by permission of the agent for the estates of Frederic Dannay and Manfred B. Lee, Lawrence Ganem.

"Make Yourselves at Home" by Joan Hess. Copyright © 1994 by Joan Hess. First published in *Malice Domestic 3*. Reprinted by permission of the author.

"Deadlier than the Mail" by Evan Hunter. Copyright © 1954 by Flying Eagle Publications, Inc., renewed 1982 by Evan Hunter. First published in *Manhunt*, February 1954. Reprinted by permission of the author and his agents, Gelfman Schneider, Literary Agents.

MS